EDIFICE OF LEARNING

EDIFICE OF LEARNING

A Fiction

Soma Dutta

KALPAZ

ISBN : 978-93-5128-019-4
Price : ₹ 475

First Published 2014

Published by

Kalpaz Publications
C-30, Satyawati Nagar,
Delhi-110052
Ph. : 9212142040
E-mail: kalpaz@hotmail.com

Laser Typesetting: Gyan Print
Printed at: G. Print Process, Delhi

Cataloging in Publication Data--DK
Courtesy: D.K. Agencies (P) Ltd. <docinfo@dkagencies.com>

Dutta, Soma, 1958-
Edifice of learning : a fiction / by Soma Dutta.
p. cm.
Novel.
ISBN 9789351280194

1. Students--Fiction. 2. Indic fiction (English). I. Title.

DDC 823.92 23

Contents

Acknowledgements

I express my heartfelt thanks to my husband Mr. Prasanta Kumar Dutta for his support and guidance in my endeavour to write this fiction. My family members, sons Seemanta and Deeganta, daughter-in-law Neha deserve my equal gratitude for their cooperation.

I whole-heartedly thank the honest and dedicated teachers whose contribution in preparing complete humanbeings is substantial.

I am indebted to my parents Lt. Santi Ranjan Basu and Smt. Uma Basu and I dedicate this book to them.

My special thanks are due to Mr. K.R.R. Nair who typed the whole book.

This book is a fiction. Any resemblance with any person in real life is unintentional and a coincidence. Liberties have been taken with location of cities, states etc.

I am indebted to Kalpaz Publications, Delhi for helping me to present this book to the readers.

Soma Dutta

Introduction

Edifice of Learning: is a fiction based on the manipulations and corruptions practised in the educational institutions, under the cover of brand names, reputations, so-called high standard and status. A stamp of a branded school or a tag today is a guaranteed talisman for a secured future and a matter of pride for the parents for whom getting admission to such schools for their ward is more difficult than landing up on the moon.

The future citizens grow up in the reputed educational institutions and become successful in life. But are they taught to be real human beings? There is a big question mark and the answer is uncertain. Whatever the young students observe around them, leave a deep impression in their mind and mould their character. The meanness, corruption, injustice, nepotism, favouritism, greed, lust and various other vices which are the characteristics of a modern society have not spared the educational institutions, leaving dire consequences of transforming the little angels into atrocious, unscrupulous, vindictive adults who care for nobody else but self. The proud parents, who once felt elated, being successful in procuring a place for their child in a reputed school, silently shed tears in Old Age Homes. The parents of adolescent girls spend sleepless nights, waiting for their daughters to return from discotheques. Boys and girls do not even hesitate to steal the hard-earned money of their parents to pay the bill for drugs or alcohol. And abortion? That has become a child's play! Under such circumstances if someone is honest to his or her profession, that person becomes a victim of mockery, criticism, politics etc., and has to suffer a lot in this modern society.

In this age of competition, climbing up the top most rung of the ladder is the goal of everyone. Even the educated people do not hesitate to compromise with their dignity in order to reach that height. Achieving success, walking along a straight path is nothing else but a wild imagination or a fantasy. Imparting values to the young generation is not the priority to the careerists but more important is banking on their results. Their success in NTSE, IIT-JEE, Board Exams, Olympiads etc. paves the way to success for the teaching community as they are able to attract more students in their commercial coaching centres.

Again, contacts play havoc in educational institutes where deserving candidates are deprived of whatever they deserve and undeserving people occupy the front seats. The game of money rules the fate of many. Greed, lust, jealousy, hatred play their role turning the edifice of learning into a living inferno.

In this novel, the characters are the replicas of real life characters although it is purely a fiction. If any character of this book has resemblance with any real life character, that is unintentional and a coincidence. Liberties have been taken with location of cities, states etc. The purpose of writing this book is to open the eyes of those involved in this noble profession.

The lessons imparted in the temples of learning have shattered the pipedreams of thousands of parents who had deep faith on these educational institutions. The young generations have the right to receive the right knowledge and wisdom to grow up into true human beings in a healthy and happy society. Is there anyone to present them with a conducive atmosphere where learning is a joy and growing up is a wonderful experience? Just as there is light at the end of a dark tunnel, there is hope for the student community because out of hundred, one different person is always there who fights against all odds and evils and brings positive changes, not caring for any personal benefit. Such type of a person, makes things happen. They are always the winners although evil seems to be powerful and victorious temporarily.

Edifice of learning teaches the lessons of life, bringing out the hidden factors which remain unknown to the society, into the broad daylight, exposing the bare reality. Only a person who has passion for teaching can transform the educational institutes which are the profit making business centres into real edifice of learning.

The novel has ten chapters and a conclusion. The characters speak about themselves, their feelings, their strength and weaknesses, their past and present, joy and sorrow, desire, lust, helplessness and emotions. This fiction deals with the bitter realities prevailing in the society.

Soma Dutta

26th January, Ghaziabad

1

A Fresh Start

As feared by Urja the previous night, the car got stuck up at the railway crossing. She could see the iron poles coming down with the cautioning siren, from a distance. Within no time there was a long queue of vehicles and as usual the riders of two-wheelers were impatiently crossing the lines–ducking through the closed heavy iron gates on both sides although the sound of the train's horn was coming nearer. The driver Chandu was wiping his sweat with a handkerchief and stealthily glancing at the big hoardings, one displaying the beautiful smile of the users of Tata Indicom mobiles and the other Sharukh Khan tightly clasping his heroine in a box-office hit film. There is one more hoarding, with the advertisement of Urja's present school, featuring the Director's younger son as an IITian (actually BHU-Ceramics) and an expert in Maths and Physics ensuring sure shot in IIT and other competitive examinations.

Within a gap of one minute two trains crossed each other and Urja heaved a sigh of relief as the gate opened. A competition started on who could cross the track first, even by jumping over the other vehicles if possible, with sound of shrill and screeching horns of various types, volley of abuses hurled by the driver of a jeep as the vehicle in front of it could not move due to some mechanical fault. A lorry, in its venture to overtake a bus obstructed the movement of other vehicles turning the place to a living inferno. The inhabitants of the make-shift houses on the right side were aloof from all these and carried on with their daily chores. On the left hand side the deity of Hanumanji in his grilled abode with a fixed donation box remained silent and unperturbed. The watermelon vendor had a brisk business.

Chandu proved to be an expert in crossing the lines and reaching the other side, with Urja on the back seat of the Wagon-R, overcoming all obstacles. Hardly proceeding forward a few yards, again they had to halt at the crossing of four lanes due to traffic red light. Urja started looking at her wrist watch, only two minutes were left. Before the light turned green some vehicles started crossing the road; Chandu also followed them. At any other time Urja would have shouted but looking at the wrist watch she kept quiet. The school gate would close sharp at 7.00 a.m. In front of the late comers being kept waiting outside the gate, it does'nt look nice for any Executive to enter when the gate is specially opened for her.

She reached school just in the nick of time. Because of the railway crossing only they had taken the decision ten years back not to construct their house in the so called posh area; children were too young, they had to attend school, swimming club, tuition classes etc. Thinking about their safety and also to stay near the school where she worked for long ten years, she had decided to build their house in the extremely opposite part of the city. Who had imagined that she would have to travel from one end to the other every day, twice, covering at least 10–12 kms., each time to and fro her newly joined school?

Veer Parsad had tried to discourage her in every possible way – reminding her of the distance, working atmosphere, standard of the school, etc., etc., etc. He had even said that the school belongs to a man who has engaged all his family members, giving them important positions although they do not have proper qualification, efficiency and experience. Outsiders will not get any importance there. They will be treated with ignominy. But Urja refused to listen to him. Why should she miss the opportunity to teach a lesson to Veer Parsad and his 'made for him only' wife Ranjita who continued to make her life a nightmare for a long time? After a prolonged dark period she is able to inhale fresh air again, able to laugh again with an open heart, able to dream again of a better life. A distance of 10-12 kms. or a closed railway gate is nothing compared to the torture she had suffered at the hands of Veer Parsad and Ranjita. It's better to be an important part of a small machine than an useless part of a big junkyard. She had been thrown away after over-use by the atrocious couple Veer Parsad and Ranjita.

Urja entered the school and the bell rang just as it used to ring with the arrival of Ranjita in her previous school. Veer Parsad usually came ten minutes late until and unless he had the intention of surprise checking. On such occasions some of the careless class teachers were sure to have a bad day, being called at his office later on and getting insulting rebukes for not taking the roll call properly or for not managing the lines on the way to the Assembly ground.

In this new school of course, there is no tension. The family members who are also the school executives, come late in a relaxed manner. So long there was nobody to check whether the teachers were reporting timely and going to their respective classroom to take the roll call. Now that responsibility has come on the shoulders of Urja. Teachers have lost their freedom to some extent and with a mixed feeling of respect, fear and dissatisfaction at the sudden loss of freedom, they have accepted her.

Only a tough person like Urja can accept the fact with a smiling face that the status of the school is far below than that of her previous school with a brand name. But this is a challenge to her and that's why she was appointed as the Vice Principal and H.O.D. English here inspite of there being so many family members working in the school. They have failed to enhance the reputation of the school, improving the quality because quantity is more important to them as quantity means money. The school runs in double shift with more than 5500 students and more than 2500 students in another newly opened branch in the Capital city. They run a music college also in the same campus where evening classes are held. In the locality around the school they have constructed hostels which look more like 3 star hotels and earn their second income by providing accommodation to the students.

Urja joined this school in the month of February when class XII students had already cleared their Pre-Board Examination. When their results of Board Exams were out, she was surprised to see not a single student got 90 per cent in English. Even the school topper with 95.4 per cent marks in aggregate got only 89 in English whereas in the previous school, Urja's student had scored 98 in Core English, which was the highest score in India. The Director and Principal of the school told her "We have great faith and trust on you. We know that with your expertise and guidance, you will be able to bring tremendous improvement in your department. Our teachers do not know how to guide the students, you train them, give them tips how to help the students in scoring more marks."

Urja assured them that she would do her best to bring improvement in result. But in the heart of her hearts she knew that it was almost impossible because she could study the situation prevailing in the school as well as the attitude of the teachers and the management including the family members. Each one in the family thinks "I am the Best." Each one expresses his or her opinion but nobody listens to or follows the suggestion or instruction of others, no matter whether that person is senior or junior. The teachers are utterly confused at the frequent changes of opinion and make full utilisation of this indisciplined and unsystematic situation. They know if they are not willing to obey the instructions of one Executive, they will get the consent of another Executive in their favour simply by flattering that person. No teacher has any positive attitude in this school. But are they to be blamed for this? In this 21st century teachers are getting Rs. 2000/-, 2500/-, 3000/- consolidated salary! No D.A., no P.F., no Medical reimbursement, H.R.A., L.T.C., L.L.T.C., or C.C.A., nothing! In a civilised country even a sweeper or a domestic help earns more than this. It's quite natural that such teachers will work mechanically with no mental involvement. Urja wonders what the children are learning from such teachers! In her previous school also she used to take interview of the probable teachers. There, until and unless the teachers could qualify in the interview, they never got appointment. But here a person who does not even know the spelling of tuition or can't say what is past perfect tense or the basics of their respective subject, are being recruited! The future of the students lies in their hands. The management purposely recruits such teachers so that they could be paid less and kept under control. The condition at the primary and pre-primary level is even worse. Tiny tots are growing up with a weak foundation because of incompetent teachers with inadequate knowledge. Ignorant parents have a craze for getting admission for their children in this school. It's a helpless situation because everybody can not get admission in a branded school.

Within a few months of her joining, once on PT meeting day, a lady met Urja in her chamber and asked –"Madam! So many activities are mentioned in the diary, are they being taught? I asked my daughter's class teacher, she said that nothing is taught; only the management people have mentioned all these things in the diary for creating a good image of the school." Urga glanced at the diary where atleast twenty SUPW Activities are mentioned including Drawing and Painting, Clay/Plasticine Modelling, Play in Sand-Pit, Splashing in the Kids Pool, Story Telling, Group Games, Collage/Cutting and Pasting, Origamy, Greeting Card Making, Recitation, Literary Activities, Fancy Dress, Paper Craft, Music, Dance, Memory Contest, Flower Decoration, Rangoli Making etc.

Urja thought how easy it was for the teacher to pass the buck on to the management but being an Executive she had to manage the situation. She said "All Activities are not compulsory for all students. As per their liking they are allotted some Activities and are guided by the teachers." But she knew that what that teacher had bluntly said is 100 per cent true.

It is said that 'Ignorance is bliss.' Those who are ignorant, they have nothing to worry. Nobody bothers about them. Those who are intelligent, who can read in between the lines, pose threat to others and as such are not liked by anyone. Urja could realise this very well at every juncture of her life.

On the very first day when she joined her present school, the Principal and the Director introduced her to other staff members. She noticed the dark shadow in the face of the daughter-in-law and daughter of the Director and a senior teacher of the English Department and immediately understood that her stay in this school would not be absolutely thorn-free. How does it matter? She has also become thick skinned, courtesy Veer Parsad and Ranjita.

* * * * * * * *

The evening is so pleasant today. After a shower in the late afternoon the temperature has reduced a lot and the cool moist breeze in the open roof is bringing a soothing complacence to the body and mind. So far the eyes travel in the south, there is a vast stretch of lush green field followed by a railway track with an unmanned railway crossing. In the twilight the birds are returning to their night shelters. The Gulmohar trees on both sides of the house are the abode of innumerable such birds. Urja had planted the trees in her own hands; now they are huge, spreading their branches on all sides. Urja came to the roof after a long time. Usually she spends the evening, writing the thesis for her Ph.D. and hardly finds any time to enjoy a cool breeze on the roof top. The enchanting smell of Jasmine on this wet evening is so intoxicating, it makes her forget the stress and strain she had undergone throughout the day.

On the Eastern side the concrete jungle has entirely engulfed the open space which used to be there five years back. The top floor of her previous school was clearly visible from the roof but now the co-operative flats have blocked the vision. Many changes took place during the last ten years, in the surroundings, in her life, in the family. Man proposes, God disposes but whatever He decides is good for all. At the age of fifty, looking back at life there is no regret. But, then why the desire for rolling back the wheels of time sometimes intensifies in her mind? Why life doesn't give one more chance to revise and do the necessary corrections to get if not full marks, at least 90%?

The shrill whistle of the goods train interrupted her thoughts. The rhythmic rattling sound of the wheels on the iron rail line broke the silence of the evening. Mr. Mukherjee, their neighbour was plucking lemons from his tree. He is a retired person and the first resident of this area. He had invested all his savings to construct the house and dreamt of living happily with his wife, two sons, daughters-in-law and grandchildren in that spacious and beautiful house. But something else was written in his fate. Neither the two daughters-in-law could adjust with each other nor could their mother-in-law adjust with them. The domesticity turned into rubbles being brittle due to the hollow relationship of the inmates, their self-interest, hostility, ego, impatience and intolerance. Mr.Mukherjee has disposed of the house to a Keralite gentleman for 17 lac Rupees. His sons have separated. Within a few days he will be shifting to West Bengal in his ancestral place.

In today's world everybody wants to have a special, unique identity of his own. The joint families are breaking up into smaller units and ultimately each individual is becoming a self-sufficient single unit like an island. Urja felt a suppressed pain for the helpless old man, placing herself in his position. With so much love and care the house was built up! Each brick, each nook and corner is so dear to the heart but it has to be left behind because the basic needs of life are so shameless, they don't allow human beings to be emotional or sentimental. One has to be practical for survival. This seventeen lac would help him and his sixty-five year old wife to survive, meeting up the expenses on food, clothes, and medicines. A man spends his whole life in taking care of his children, sacrificing many desires to fulfil their demands, only to find at the dusk of his life that he is alone like an island where a sailor may take rest for sometimes but no one would anchor forever.

Urja tries to make an assessment of her gain and loss in life. How many starry evenings, misty dawns, rainy afternoons, sunny winter morning she has sacrificed so long for her career and profession? How many marriages of cousins or nephews and nieces and other family functions couldn't she attend for her career? She could not even attend the first marriage anniversary of her son and daughter-in-law in Delhi. Those moments and occasions would not come back again; they are lost forever. The yearning for a better life, better opportunities where she could put her heart and soul together, made her blind and she missed the happiness which came in small proportions forgetting the fact that tiny droplets only make a big ocean. But after all for whom had she made all such sacrifices? Who will understand her?

Urja heard the telephone ringing downstairs. She had not taken the mobile to the roof as she wanted to feel the uninterrupted joy. At first she thought of not receiving the call but the next moment thought, it might be from one of her sons. The ringing stopped when she was halfway, coming down the staircase. She uses the staircase very cautiously as she has the bitter experience of slipping down and breaking her lumbar vertebrae region. She was confined to bed for one whole month and it was because of her husband's constant, untiring care, she could recover. She climbed down the remaining stairs in a relaxed manner and sat on the sofa. She was about to switch on the T.V.when the telephone started ringing again. She lifted up the receiver and said "Hello!"

"Hello! May I speak to Urja?"

Urja could not recognise the voice.

"Urja speaking. May I know who is on the line?"

"Urja, I'm Tulika. How are you?"

"Tulika, so nice to hear your voice after a long time. I'm absolutely fine. What about you?"

"I'm not fine. You know as my son was too young at that time when the new school started; I had to withdraw my resignation letter and stay back here after giving in writing that I've no complaint against Veer Parsad. I missed a good opportunity of joining the new school. Had I joined, I would have become the H.O.D. Social Science there. Now Veer Parsad and Ranjita are torturing me, knowing my weakness and helpless condition. They have given higher classes to the junior teachers whereas being a senior teacher I am taking the junior classes. As you all have left, now in every meeting I am his target."

Urja said – "Tulika, you are absolutely responsible for your miserable condition. When you knew that you won't be able to join the new school why did you put up your papers then? When your resignation was accepted here you should have joined there! There is no use of lamenting now."

Tulika said – "I wanted to see the end instead of quitting. I wanted to wait for the justice when Veer Parsad and Ranjita would be removed."

Urja heaved a sigh – "Justice delayed means justice denied. How long can one wait for justice, missing opportunities and spoiling the career?"

Tulika came to the point "Listen, I have decided to inform everything to the Education Management Society. I will report to Human Rights Commission also. But if I approach alone I may not get any justice. You also join with me. Together we can fight against them."

Urja laughed "Do you think I've not sought for justice from the Society? Veer Parsad has purchased them. It's very difficult to overcome the temptation of the shiny metals and the crispy notes. Why should they bother to listen to Urja or Tulika?"

Tulika insisted "If we jointly raise our voice, definitely they will listen. Single handed we can't do anything."

"And what accusation shall we bring against them? Exploitation? Availing our selfless service and then throwing us away? They will prove that we are not suitable for the responsibilities. Our own colleagues will write against us. Our complaints will be baseless."

Tulika -"We'll complain about the sexual harassment we had to face."

Urja- "How will you prove that? Don't you know what Ranjita had told me? Instead of feeling shame for her husband's debauchery she had accused me of seducing her husband! They will again prove that we are guilty and Veer Parsad is innocent."

Tulika tried to convince her – "Think over the matter Urja. Should we allow this dirty man and his wife to continue with their wickedness behind the mask of educationists?"

Urja – "Who are we to allow or reject them when the Society in Delhi is a mute, spineless witness of their evil deeds and those who have the power of judgment, have kept their lips tight because they are living on the bones thrown by Veer Parsad?"

Tulika still insisted that Urja must give a second thought over the matter and then after exchanging information about their respective family life, she concluded the conversation.

Urja's mood was absolutely spoilt. She was cherishing the rain-drenched cool evening with the fragrance of Jasmine in the air. Tulika spoilt her mood by mentioning the name of Veer Parsad and Ranjita. "Why should I join hands with anybody in punishing the wicked couple?" — thought Urja, "it's my battle which I'll fight alone. I know how to teach a lesson to Veer Parsad and Ranjita and their pet dogs. If we knock at the doors of law, we will be harassed in the court. In order to humiliate us they will ask all sorts of dirty questions. When

I suffered alone no one had taken my side; rather they felt a sadistic pleasure at my miserable condition. Why should I extend my support to them now?" Urja tried to put away her thoughts and concentrated in the fifth chapter of her thesis – 'Role of English Newspapers in the Independence Movement of India'............

Gagging of Press was a regular feature in British India resulting in sharp confrontation between the Press and the Government. During the first half of the 20th century Press was gagged several times when it was a crucial period in the Indian History at the dawn of Indian freedom. On the one hand it saw the climax of nationalist resistance of all shades, Congress Revolutionary, Socialist and even Communal; on the other hand, it coincided with the stiffest resistance of the Indian Press which reached its peak prior to Independence.

Their repressive policies during the Second World War led to the formation of All India Newspaper Editors Conference (AINEC) in 1940 and the evolution of a Voluntary Code for internal censorship for the Press gave a new twist to the development.

Inspite of the implementation of the repressive Press Laws the Press continued to defy the Government. The Government tried to suppress the Press with the help of Paper Control Order, Paper Economy Order, Newsprint Control Order and the arbitrary allotment of paper. Price page schedule was followed during the war period.

The Press fully cooperated with the freedom fighters and instigated the minds of the common people, promoted hostile activities against the Government and as such there were outbreaks of lawlessness. Press control was envisaged with the sensing of the growing influence of the Press by the British who felt the element of danger and collected objectionable articles. Press was highly defiant in U.P. inspite of the enactment of the newspaper (Incitement to Offences) Act VII of 1908. The local authorities were empowered by Minto & Morley to take severe action against the editor of any newspaper which was found to be publishing seditious and provocative matters. One Editorial in Swarajya (Allahabad) was written in the following manner:

"Brave men are not afraid of afflictions. They do not writhe (with agony) when dying on the scaffold. They are killed, they are trampled down, they are exiled. Oh ! what do they not accomplish who die for their country !"

The 'Englishman' and 'The Statesman' reacted violently at the transfer of capital. Mrs.Annie Besant who bought a daily paper in Madras and renamed it as New India, motivated the young generation, writing "Round this and the weekly Common Weal is destined to rage the battle for Home Rule." She also wrote "the chains of Press Acts here are inexpressibly galling but it is for India's sake and for her, even slavery is welcome. Better to be enthralled here, at the mercy of any ill-tempered official than to be in any other land."

The Madras Government suggested to the British authorities that she should be forced to leave India.

That the Press had massive potential power is clear from the statement of Barkat Ali which he gave to a Government Committee: "The passion for journalism had descended to the market; shopkeepers and the masses now read the newspapers. It is not merely the educated classes who read them. The man in the street has begun to read the newspapers."

The Govt. of India followed a repressive policy in the Punjab. The Bombay Chronicle had become very powerful in the hands of B.G. Horniman. Suspension order was issued by the Government against his papers. The Chronicle was resuscitated. The Young India which was being controlled by the Chronicle was removed to Ahmedabad and it became a strong tool for Satyagraha.

The Amrita Bazar Patrika (Calcutta) had given a tough fight to the Government ever since a security of Rs. 5000/- had been demanded from it in 1913, for its comments on the Jagat Shri Ashram Affairs under the Press Act 1910. Motilal Ghosh was successful in warding off the security forfeited by the Govt. of Bengal. He got the support of the Court and the case against him was dismissed when he was involved through his paper in the Barisal conspiracy case. The Amrita Bazar Patrika condemned the Press Act of 1910 as "a mere superfluity ushered into existence by a panicky government which read in the bomb its inevitable doom and was anxious to guillotine without the noise incidental to a regular trial. Certain newspapers which, in its opinion, openly encouraged violence of this kind."

Jawaharlal Nehru's Boycott of Simon Commission was given a widespread publicity by the Press. Mass demonstration and propaganda started and violent methods were adopted by the Govt. to stop this agitation. The unarmed demonstrators faced ruthless lathi-charge. The action of the authorities was condemned by public. The virulent Press Campaign was reported to the Govt. Again fresh restrictions were imposed on newspapers. The trial and execution of Bhaghat Singh and his associates including their hunger strike and the death of Jatin Das were highlighted in such a way by the Press that the general mob became violent with anger and the Govt. became more strict with the newspapers. The Revolutionary, Satyagraha Sangram, Hindustan Socialist Republican Association Manifesto, The Philosophy of Bomb etc. were considered provocative. Two out of seven ordinances promulgated by the Government of India were related to the Press.

The Congress Bulletins continued to be circulated which unnerved the Govt. On 17th June the Govt. of India sent a telegram to the Secretary of State for India, London to the effect: "Congress have as a counterblast to the Press Ordinance, for some time been issuing in many periodicals or daily bulletins or news sheets."

The Indian Press Ordinance which had been promulgated on April 27, 1930 and lapsed on October 26, 1930 was soon followed by the Press and unauthorised News Sheets and Newspaper Ordinance of Dec 23, 1930 which expired on June 22, 1931. Thereafter the most comprehensive Indian Press (Emergency Powers Act) came into operation from Oct 9, 1931.

Next came the Indian Press (Emergency Powers) Act of 1931, according to which when security was demanded by a District Magistrate his reasons were to be recorded in writing and no application could lie to the High Court against such orders. The deposited security was to be returned if within 3 months the local Government had not passed any order under section 4 of the Act.

The section covered such matters which incited or encouraged violence or even directly or indirectly expressed approval or administration of any such offence. According to this Act the Press or newspapers had the right to know their offence and to apply to the High Court. After becoming the Congress President, Nehru gave more stress to his idea of foreign propaganda. He talked of the Freedom of Press with the journalists and assured them of getting all cooperation from the foreign department of A.I.C.C. and the Civil Liberties Union which had 130 members in Calcutta and "heralded the end of an era of confrontation which lasted from 1930–35, but its scope was extremely limited."

The Press (Emergency Powers Act) of 1931 as amended by the Criminal Law Amendment Act 1932 and 1935 remained in force throughout the British rule in India. After Independence it was removed as recommended by the Press Laws Enquiry Committee. The Ordinance of 1931 was replaced by the Foreign Relations Act of 1932 which also remained in force throughout the British rule. The Indian States (Protection Act) continued till Independence.

The Nationalist Press and well established newspapers like Amrit Bazar Patrika in Bengal, The Tribune in Punjab and The Leader in U.P. didn't hesitate to criticise the Congress whenever its decision or policy went wrong. The Anglo Indian Press like the Statesman, The Times of India and the Madras Mail tried to strike a balance and were reluctant to criticise the Congress.

The 1941-42 were the years of total Control of Press and other Mass Media. Sayed Abdullah Brelni in his Presidential Address at the Newspaper Editor's Conference at Madras on 10th January, 1944 said – ".....the Press in India has never been free, but it has always been struggling to be free. The consultative machinery to the establishing of which Govt. were compelled to agree in 1940 as a result of the United Front presented by the Press, irrespective of political differences, offered an opportunity, such as the Press had never had, of carrying on that struggle with greater hope of success than ever before....." Ignoring the recommendations of the Provincial Advisory Committees, Pre-censorship orders were served on Hindustan Times, Sind Observer, Amrita Bazar Patrika and other newspapers.

The Press became explosive in 1945 following the Court-Martial of members of the Japanese sponsored I.N.A. Gandhiji's Private Secretary Pyarelal, the Editor of Harijan said, "the undertrial members of the I.N.A. who had fought the British in Burma for India's Independence were lionised by the public."

By the end of 1945, the Home Deptt. became more alert of the internal situation and decided to discontinue the 'Foreign Publicity.' On 1st January 1946, the necessary orders regarding this were issued. Despite the heavy odds against the Press, it could show the indomitable zeal and spirit of defiance and succeeded in keeping the foreign Government on their toes.

Writing upto this, Urja started feeling sleepy. She looked at the wall clock; it was only 8.30 p.m. Swapnil was out of station. In this big house she was alone. Urja went to the wash basin to sprinkle water in her face and eyes to get rid of sleep. She couldn't afford to sleep so early. She had to keep awake till she could complete the chapter. She prepared a cup of coffee and sat again with her papers. Those women who sacrificed their lives for the Independence of the country are her inspirations. They were hanged to death in the Viper Island of Andaman and their bodies were sent to the black water through a passage with sharp knives placed in a *zig zag* way. Before reaching the water the bodies were cut into pieces and then finally eaten up by the sharks in the sea. There was no scope for them to escape.

Urja tried to concentrate in her writing again. She was determined to prove herself and for that she was prepared to face any amount of hardship. It was a challenge. There was no one to favour her. Her completing M.Phil with 1st class inspite of Veer Parsad's objection and the obstacles created by him in various ways was a slap on his face. Her getting the post of Vice Principal and H.O.D. English was another slap on his face. Completing Ph.D. and achieving Doctorate will be the biggest slap on his face. Then there will be the last thing to do — that is to expose the hypocrite Veer Parsad before the world and shatter his image. Each second, each moment was so crucial, she couldn't afford to sleep. She had to reach the top and at the same time ruin Veer Parsad and Ranjita.

* * * * * * * *

"Madam, I will come late for a few days. I'm on fast due to Navratri. After performing pooja in the early morning I'll come." Savitri said in a pleading tone.

Urja said – "O.K. but do come, otherwise I'll have to face problem. By the way you can relax in the next week as I'll proceed on leave."

"No Madam, so long you are here I enjoy my work. If you are on leave, they will send me to work in their bungalows or hostels and that will be more hectic."

"Don't you get holidays?" Urja asked.

"Never, even on Sundays we have to come; otherwise they deduct from our salary." Savitri heaved a sigh.

"How much do you get?" Urja asked.

"Madam, this is my fifteenth year in the school. In the starting I used to get Rs. 300.00. Now I am getting Rs. 2200.00 consolidated – no D.A., no P.F., no holiday, - no work-no pay."

Urja didn't know what to say! She was dumbstruck at the exploitation of this poor helpless class IV staff. After coming to this block at the backside of the school, slowly she is able to know about these people. In the Administrative Block, where she used to sit earlier, there was no scope to know anything about them as these class IV staff are always on their toes but inspite of that, abuses are their only rewards. It was not possible for Urja to know about this middle aged woman from Bihar that she was abandoned by her husband who married another woman; her only issue expired in her womb and this single woman started her life struggle alone overcoming all hardships, silently suffering all sorts of injustice.

Opportunists capitalise on the helplessness of people and exactly the same thing is happening here. This has become the rule of the world. Urja can only feel bad but she can not bring any change.

Savitri came to this building along with Urja when she was shifted here from the Administrative Block as the Incharge of this Block. The Director had discussed the matter with her and taken her consent.

"Madam I think you will be the best person to control that block. It's at the backside and there is no body to monitor the building; students are becoming indisciplined day by day. If your office is shifted there I'm sure we will observe a remarkable improvement."

Urja could understand that behind this praise was his command. He had made up his mind to shift Urja to that block because she was the eye-sore of the daughter-in-law of the Director whose image was getting suppressed because of the strong personality of Urja.

The Director further said that "There is a big room with attached toilet. That room will be cleaned and your table and almirah will be shifted there." Urja nodded her head. The next morning she found her chair and table missing in her cabin. She could guess they were shifted to the new room. She went there but the room was locked. She came back again to the Administrative Block. By that time the Principal had arrived. With a stern face he glared at the empty chamber of Urja and asked her – "Who has shifted your table and chair?"

"I don't know Sir, " She said, "may be in my absence somebody shifted but that room is locked and I have no place to sit."

"Madam you'll sit in my room so long your room is not ready"- he said.

It was a very awkward situation for Urja. Nobody knew where was the key of Urja's new room. Under such circumstances she had no other option but to sit in The Principal's room.

He was furious at the decision of shifting Urja to that block because his tuning with Urja was very good and every now and then he needed the assistance of Urja. While Urja was sitting in his room, he came out and started shouting at each and everyone he found before him. He could not suppress his feelings and uttered un-parliamentary words against his eldest brother – the Director of the school. In extreme anger he said – "He is dominating everybody. What does he think of himself? He pretends to be pious by quoting Sanskrit shlokas from Ramayana and Mahabharat. I can understand the politics behind his hypocrisy." His voice was audible not only to everybody in the Administrative block but also to the teachers sitting in the staffroom.

Urja wondered why everytime it happens to her? Why she becomes the bone of contention?

The Principal came back to his room and told Urja – "Madam, you sit here without any hesitation or tension. My personal attendant Savitri will attend you and whenever your room is ready you will shift there. Savitri will be with you always. If you require I will send one typist also in your room. But I promise, within fifteen days I will bring you back to this block again." Saying this he went to take a class. Urja asked Savitri whether her room was ready. When she came to know that the room was cleaned, she told Savitri to carry her bag and immediately left The Principal's room.

The students of that block named after a famous scientist, were taken aback when they found Urja sitting in that room. It was like a prison without any window. The floor was spoilt by the painters who had dropped paint on it. Any person would feel depressed sitting there for even a minute.

Rumour started spreading like wildfire that Urja had been removed from the Administrative Block because Sarita demanded that and it is a well-known fact that Motilal dances at the tune of Sarita. People also started discussing that The Principal favours Urja and that's why he went against his elder brother and his family members in support of Urja. Urja knows how difficult and embarrassing such type of situations are ! What people were thinking was not at all true. It was a challenge which was thrown to her by the Director which she accepted and the Principal was annoyed because he was absolutely ignorant about the fact. Nobody had discussed with him the matter, neither the Director nor Sarita. He felt being belittled.

For a fortnight there was no communication between the two brothers although as a habit The Principal used to touch his elder brother's feet every morning. Then there started a competition between the two brothers how to please Urja and how to make her comfortable. A big window was constructed in her room. The flooring was replaced with white ceramic tyles. Painting was done on the walls, doors and window and glass was fixed on the entrance door. While the renovation was being done, for a whole week Urja sat in the room of the Principal which raised the blood pressure of the Director's daughter-in-law and daughter. They were furious because Urja's room appeared to be the best. Urja's position was also elevated and she heaved a sigh of relief, sitting in her new room, far away from these two replicas of Ranjita.

2

Veer Parsad–Behind the Mask

I, Veer Parsad witnessed the fifty-ninth autumn moon of my life yesterday. This is an occasion to relish success, otherwise where is the time to indulge myself into the luxury of looking back! I never celebrate but become nostalgic on this particular day, cherishing my success like the children enjoying each scoop of icecream. It's my standing order to Ranjita and Padma not to make the occasion public so that I can get the day absolutely as my own–my very personal day. Inspite of that, all staff members came to my chamber yesterday to wish me and to my surprise Ranjita was leading them. Now a days she is reluctant to follow my instructions and is taking decisions on her own. Perhaps she has lost all trust on me and is desperately trying to save the boat from sinking when the shore has come within our reach.

The table soon crowded with flowers, cards and mementoes but how many of them sincerely wished my long, happy and prosperous life, I really could not make out! My special women were also present among them; each one has contributed in a unique way in rejuvenating my life with the elixir of love, passion and sex. Each one tried to wipe off from my mind the inferiority complex of being one of the eight children of an agriculturist father and a simple, ordinary, home-maker mother, both illiterate, thumb-impressionists and unaware of the enlightened world of intellect.

My father had lost his parents in his childhood and was brought up by his uncle. He was not introduced to alphabets or numericals but it is only due to his hard work and perseverance, he could become the owner of five hundred acres of land before leaving the world at the ripe old age of ninety-three. Today, all his children and a large number of grandchildren are all well settled and are enjoying the return from those five –hundred acres as a bonus. No one can feel the drops of perspiration of my father which have mingled with the soil. He used to say–

"Land is our mother, land takes care of our each and every need and we must worship it." Being the son of such a father, I never felt any attraction towards land except after the death of my father when his property was divided among his children. Only at that time I could understand the value of land which I always used to ignore earlier.

I always thought of stepping out into the broader world where I could make a place for myself as if I had a connection with that world through my previous births. My childhood days now seem to be a dream to me, not a reality.

My parents' existence, understanding, concern and thoughts were confined within the boundaries of wheat fields, cattlesheds and the thatched kitchen of a joint family where meals were cooked in large vessels on charcoal fire. My dark complexioned mother with an oily face kept herself busy from dawn till mid-night in cleaning, cooking and thousand other household chores and even before surrendering herself before sleep at night, the only thought which occupied her mind was what meal to prepare for us the next day. Of course we never expected variety; thick chapattis with mixed vegetables, jaggery and milk was our daily diet with occasional changes. Jaggery was prepared at home and milk extracted from the buffaloes was sufficient to meet up the domestic need after supplying them to the dairies and sweet shops. Wheat and vegetables were available in abundance from our own farm.

May be ignorance is bliss and hence my mother was never discontented with her life. She preferred floating with the current and when my father decided to send me to the primary school of the village to learn the alphabets and basic Maths so that I could do the calculation and accounting work of our grocery shop and help my elders, she didn't react in any manner. Neither was there any ambitious dream in her eyes regarding my future, nor any expression of despair. The small village of Haryana was her heaven where she spent the whole of her life with her husband and other family members.

Sometimes I wonder whether my success could create any ripple in my mother's mind. Perhaps she doesn't have any idea about it as I always avoided bringing my parents to my bungalow which was allotted to me by the School Management Committee, along with the chauffeur-driven car, servants, cook, gardener etc. (certain things of course I manipulated and managed, out of the way). However my father sometimes used to twist his moustaches before the villagers when he told them "Veeru has become the Principal of the most reputed school in India." But I never took the risk of inviting or bringing them to the industrial township of Central India, where bit by bit, I have built up my empire. Perhaps, they got a hint of my new life when I visited my village, making out time from my official tour to Delhi. My hired air-conditioned cabs every time posed a contrast to the backdrop of my birthplace. My suited, booted appearance was too unfamiliar among my nearest and dearest ones clad in dhotis or plain saris. My parents left this world without having a glimpse of the dreamland where their Veeru dwells today.

After wishing me a long, successful life and many happy returns of the day, the staff went out and I indulged into reminiscence again. I like to exploit my root and childhood now, only as symbols of my virility and perseverance, only to show what a rough, long road I had to traverse before reaching this junction. Time to time when I share this with the staff in any meeting, I observe admiration and reverence in their eyes. When I explore the beautiful, sexy, sophisticated bodies and enjoy the scent of imported perfumes, submerging my sharp and sensitive nose into their bosom (one at a time of course), I forget my root, I forget the muddy village path, the winnowing of wheat, the cow-dung cakes on the broken compound wall, the churning of butter from milk, the oil lamps burning in the evening – creating huge shadows on the walls, the concert of crickets and frogs at the time of monsoon, the square mats of the village primary school where a boy of ten was receiving his first education of life. At those moments my cosy, comfortable rest room attached to my office room transforms into a Spa, where each time a beautiful woman provides me with the strength, freshness and energy to cope with everything and the essence of power, power and more power. Yes, the boy who was supposed to look after the accounts of a rural family business is today the head of the most prestigious institution, at whose dropping of hat, any lady is ready to pick it up. He is invited today as a Chief Guest at all important social function and is entrusted with the responsibility of inspecting all new schools of nearby places. Any businessman of the city and its surroundings is ready to sign a blank cheque for the admission of his child to the school. Any influential person whether a corporate chief or a minister is within his grip. The government may change but whoever comes to power is purchased in no time. But I know how many times the sun had been covered with dark clouds before reaching the zenith and how much struggle I had to do before attaining this stage where I can take account of the loss and profit of my life and feel that the scale is heavier on the side of profit. What I have gained is beyond my expectation and what I have lost is simply my character, my conscience and humanity. Just like the changing of skin of the reptiles I have made myself free from the burden of ethics which disturbs every successful man. Before the glitter and dazzling splendour of glamour, honour, prestige, position, money and power the loss is meagre and trivial.

I cannot go back today to that point from which I started, ignoring the status and importance with which, along with Ranjita, Ipsita and Amar, I have become habituated. Haven't I observed the twinkle of pride in Ranjita's eyes when the staff members arise in her presence to show their respect? And this they have been doing right from the beginning when I joined the school as the Principal. It's not because she was the Senior Mistress or now is the Vice

Principal, it's because she is my wife. Haven't I observed how obliged teachers felt to make some changes in the report cards to help my children securing better ranks? As a father I know their IQ level and merit; I know both of them have inherited the grey matter of Ranjita. But when I have the power to turn the wheel of fortune in their favour, why shouldn't I do it? I am not a fool; I don't want them to struggle like me. At this mid-noon I can think of a glamorous evening, not a misty morning.

The mist was there forty-six years back, when, at the age of ten, for the first time I was introduced to alphabets and numbers at the village primary school. Within a few days, Guruji could discover my intelligence and eagerness to learn and had he not discovered a genius in me, I would have learnt some new discoveries of Bio Technology today at some rural agricultural development programme and produced bumper crops in the land inherited from my father, which he had managed from his uncle who had brought him up as he had lost his father in his childhood.

Guruji took the initiative, discussed with my father and tried for my admission to the High School at the completion of my basic education at his village primary school. When I was denied direct admission in class five at all schools of Haryana at the age of ten, Guruji tried for my admission at a High School in Rajasthan, the neighbouring State and was successful. There was a river in between the two States which had to be crossed in order to reach the school. At the time of monsoon, there used to be waist deep water and Guruji used to take one of my class mates and me in his strong grip and lifting his dhoti crossed the river twice everyday. In this way we continued for a couple of months and then managed a transfer certificate from that school with the help of which I got admission at a school in Haryana near our village. That was indeed a turning point in my life.

In those days students were not so fortunate to get the exposure which they are getting now. But within the limited scope I always tried to remain focussed. One day, when I was at the matriculation level, my Language teacher praised me for a composition; most probably it was a précis writing or a paragraph. Born and brought up in a home where nobody knew any other language except our mother tongue, (that too not the refined version but only the colloquial language), I started floating on cloud nine when my style of writing in English was appreciated. I passed matriculation with 1st division and decided to go to the city for my Intermediate, which I did but had to apply a brake in my studies after that due to financial reason and take up a job at a Railway Station in a very insignificant place. Very few trains used to halt in that station and I had plenty of time to plan about my future. The fire remained unextinguished in my mind and after doing the job for a temporary period, I enrolled myself for graduation under Punjab University. A degree in English Honours and B.Ed from Punjab University enabled me to fetch the job of a teacher at a reputed school but I lost the hope of marrying Asha Yadav – my first love as she got married, persuaded by her parents when I was busy acquiring the degree of B.Ed. Today I have no regret for that and I congratulate myself for deciding my priority.

God has given me the strength and toughness of mind to sacrifice all beautiful and precious things of life to reach and remain in the position where I am. I don't hesitate to destroy the petals of a rose in order to extract the nectar. From one school to another – from the hustle-bustle of the capital to the cool, tranquillity of the snow-clad mountains – long fourteen years – the best part of my life. Ranjita came to my life, then Ipsita and Amar, one after another. They webbed a net of love, affection, warmth and dream around me, which lasted for a few years. The small staff quarter within the campus, the beautiful scenery all around, cloud floating over the mountains, my favourite places like the Kali Jhora, Ghoom, Teesta at monsoon time, the scent of wild roses on the roadside bushes, sunrise at Tiger Hills, excursion with students and adventures on the road will remain engraved in my mind for the rest of my life. Just as with each wave of the ocean, comes along a different sound, a new dimension which adds a new meaning to the surrounding, in the same way each memory of the days in the hills still creates a ripple in my mind. Dew drops couldn't have been more sparkling; the broad horizon couldn't have been more colourful than the thoughts, expressions and memories enriching the mind while capturing into the word web the captivating silhouettes of those fourteen years. I enjoyed each and every day, each and every moment of those long fourteen years with the students, colleagues, Ranjita and my children. Can I ever forget those adventurous trekking expeditions with the students and the feeling of being on the top of the world every time with Nature's bounty of the Himalayan wild flowers all around? The song of the hills "Kasto mazza hai lelaima, Ramailo o Kaali, Odhali" still reverberates, overflowing the valleys which I can hear from such a long distance. Can I ever forget that exciting bi-cycle race on the winding roads through the tea gardens with a group of students from Darjeeling to Siliguri and at a turning the falling of one of the riders into the deep gorge and ultimately he was rescued but there was no trace of the bi-cycle!

On another occasion I went on an outing with the senior boys in a jeep and we were supposed to come back by the evening. On our way back the tyres of the jeep got punctured for a couple of times and ultimately due to a major fault in the engine, we could not return to Darjeeling. We had to take a night-halt at a way-side rest house. Early in the morning there was a loud, unraptured knock at the door at which I shouted expressing my annoyance for disturbing my sleep but had to open the door because the knock didn't stop. To my great astonishment I found the Principal standing outside the door with a terrifying face and what followed after that it's better not to reminisce. In a dazed moment I was not even finding my trouser to put on over my brief.

Once, Ranjita was with me when we went to Bhutan by a matador. Those were the days and such was life with laughter, songs, thrill and adventure.

Then came greed, expectations, discontentment and the blind desire to rise at the top. My target was the Principal's chair and this desire was further aggravated by Ranjita who started her career at a nursery school after passing the Intermediate in a Metropolitan city and after marriage, joining the same school as a P.R.T. where I was teaching as a T.G.T. and later on promoted to P.G.T. She remained a Primary Teacher for fourteen years although she had added to her qualification the degrees of Graduation and Post Graduation. Lady luck has favoured me throughout my life and I got whatever I desired. I feel the same thrill to think even today, which I felt eleven years back when I got the appointment letter for the post of Principal of a school with a brand name which is not unknown to even a single person in the country; and why country alone, this brand name has gained popularity even outside the country. Today there are more than 170 schools belonging to the same brand in and outside the country.

I became the ruler from the ruled. Now there will be no more preparation of lessons, taking substitution classes, doing invigilation duties, no more waiting for an appointment with the Principal, no adjustments or compromise. I will instruct, others will obey without any question and this is the golden opportunity to give Ranjita freedom from her shackles of Primary teachership. After all, she is the Principal's wife. This is the opportunity to pave the way for her uphill journey.

Leaving behind the sleepy mountain and the enchanting landscapes and casting a last glance at the palatial quarter of the Principal comprising sixteen rooms with lawns, tennis court, swimming pool etc., I shifted to the plains of Central India amidst the industries, heat, dust, pollution and a tough life. For all these years I had to struggle hard to adapt manners, etiquettes and style forgetting my childhood habits. After all shifting from a charpoy to thickly mattressed spongy bed, from open field to the Commode, from – square mats and enamelled plates on the long verandah in front of the kitchen to the plates and glasses, fork and knife on the glass dinner table, from home-washed rough cotton shirts with faded and torn collars and ordinary trousers or dhotis to elegant suits – need practice. Yes, I had to undergo vigorous practice and self-training to secure a place of honour for myself in the civilized society of the modern world. I had to strive hard to polish my spoken English and I acknowledge Ranjita's contribution in this matter. Although she doesn't have the depth in this language, she deserves the credit of improving my rustic tone and pronunciation, adding sophistication to the same. I started reading the journals and magazines related to development in education in India and abroad to update my knowledge. While I was in the residential school I did my Master's degree in Social Science. Above all, I learnt how and where to bow my head and apply oil in whose feet to grab the opportunities.

As soon as I joined as the Principal I succeeded in winning the heart of the management and managed to elevate the position of Ranjita to the Senior Mistress of the Primary Wing. The staff members of course could not take it positively as she was a non B.Ed. and moreover there were many senior teachers who deserved the post. At that point, started my conflict with justice, humanity and conscience started. I told myself – "Veer Parsad, this is just the beginning. If you want to climb up the ladder and reach the top-most rung, then keep yourself in the water-tight compartment; take the lesson from Dale Carnegie, don't look back, live in the present. (Here I added, grab as much as you can today).

Ranjita also started feeling addicted to her newly achieved (or manipulated?) position and remained engrossed in it. A crack developed in our relationship. She decided not to interfere in my personal life but the condition was, I will support her blindly and lift her up to the highest position in the due course of time. She was never interested in sex right from the beginning of our marriage. In fact, after the birth of Ipsita and Amar, we hardly slept on the same bed. Till date she never insisted me for sex, nor cooperated with me in experiencing that satisfaction. She has a somewhat conservative attitude towards sex. When I started approaching the teachers, exploiting my power and position and their ambition and helplessness, Ranjita remained quiet. She had no objection in my seeking pleasure from extra marital relationships because by that time she had also tasted the nectar of success and started dreaming of reaching the zenith as my successor. Status, position, name, fame and money dominated our mind, totally wiping off love, passion, affection and romance, as if it was a contractual marriage.

We started experiencing the grudge and malice of our colleagues and even the parents. Notoriety doesn't take much time to spread and the weak points of my character were exposed before all. On the one hand management started pressurising me for joining another unit of the institution where there was no Principal for a considerable period of time and on the other hand, I started getting threatening for life from all corners. Ultimately I had to decide and on a hot summer day of May, with Ranjita, Ipsita and Amar, I arrived at this small industrial city, quite reluctantly, with a grim face because Ranjita had to lose her position of Senior Mistress and join as an ordinary trained graduate teacher. Uncertainty engulfed my mind as I knew how difficult it would be to recover the dice which had fallen into the mouth of the longest snake and finding a ladder for it again. But my opportunist mind and eagle's eyes soon realised there can't be a better place for us. I understood that it would not be difficult for me to control the staff because basically they were timid, nervous and peace loving. Majority of them had no ambition at all and remained in the same grade for more than a decade. My predecessor, who was famous for his sugar-coated smile had deprived them tactfully for such a long time but was able to win their heart. A few of them of course were ambitious and they all were senior to

Ranjita. My first goal was to make Ranjita – the Senior Mistress of the Middle Wing of the school. That post was adorned by a retired Head Mistress of another reputed school of the township. Rule can be made or changed as per one's own self interest and convenience when one is in power. I raised the point in the meeting of the governing body that a retired person should not be given any administrative position. I started inviting the members of the governing body over lunch or dinner frequently and Ranjita exhibited the best of her hospitality to win their heart. I started finding loopholes with the senior teachers and insulted them in every general meetings and sometimes even before the students. I did this to demoralise them but at the same time I promoted them all to show how considerate I am.

I placed the requirement for Senior Mistress before the management and showing the previous manipulated experience of Ranjita as the Senior Mistress of Primary Wing, I succeeded in securing the coveted post for her. I could hear people whispering about her getting a permanent grade and again the post of the Senior Mistress without doing B.Ed. which is compulsory now. I advised Ranjita to do B.Ed. and at this juncture Padma played a very important role. She also joined the B.Ed. classes after school with Ranjita and helped her with her notes etc. Otherwise it would not have been possible for Ranjita to complete the course.

Padmavati is very intelligent and although in the beginning she could not accept me as her boss, she didn't take much time to understand that she had no other way but to surrender. She was a petty typist at the time of my predecessor but today she enjoys almost the same status which Ranjita enjoys. They share a wonderful, unique relationship and are each other's substitute. I have fulfilled the sexual need of Padma which was never satisfied by her husband except for the initial couple of years after their marriage. They have a daughter who is standing at the threshold of youth, but Padma's sex hunger has not yet subsided. When she works at the computers in the evening, when there is no one else in the school except we two, I stand behind her and watch her cleavage and fleshy upper breasts which she keeps exposed deliberately, shaking vigorously with the movement of her fingers on the key-board, typing a confidential letter. Coming closer I feel her neck and watch the spring reaction in her. The letter remains half-typed and we play the role of primitive man and woman on the cot of my cosy rest room. She is my mare.

Sometimes we spend the whole night at school on pretext of work, without even a thread on our body. Neither Ranjita nor Padma's family members say anything against this because today, whatever status they are enjoying, it is only because of me. Ranjita is sitting on the chair of Vice Principal because of me. Padma's beautiful house 'Sai Ashirwad' could materialise only because of my philanthropy, not because of the blessings of the great Saibaba.

Padma knows about my polygamy; she is aware of my relationship with some teachers particularly those who are divorced or separated or spinsters. There are a few who do not enjoy sex with husband and my eagle eyes don't take much time to discover them. Most of them are playing the game of hide and seek and pretend to be happy and contented with their marital life but I know how deprived they are and how they satisfy their needs.

Padma just becomes absolutely silent when she can guess about my physical closeness with any other woman. Once in my presence she had pulled out somebody's Bindi from the wall of my rest room, just behind the cot and threw it into the waste-paper basket. On another occasion in order to avoid any disturbance, Bindiya had bolted the door of the reception from inside when we met in the evening, which was locked from outside by Padma while leaving for home. This reception is attached to my office and rest room and if somebody locks the reception door from outside, it can be bolted from inside also going there through my office. But who can do so until and unless I call somebody at odd hour without the knowledge of Padma? After enjoying a colourful evening, when Bindiya and I left the office, she forgot to unbolt the reception door from inside. I locked my office door from outside and unaware of the fact left for my home.

In the morning when the office peon unlocked the door of the Reception from outside it didn't open as it was bolted from inside and he was puzzled. He went to Padma's house to ask for the key of the door of my office which is facing the lounge and is next to the reception door, in order to enter and unbolt the reception door, going through my office, fearing the teachers would start coming and would have to wait outside for signing in the attendance register, which was kept in the reception. Although Padma had a duplicate key she sent the peon to my house to ask for the key. Silently she let me feel that she had understood everything but till date she didn't ask me why the reception door was locked from inside?

I have full confidence in my virility, my 6 ft. 5 inches tall, fatless figure and my numero uno position. Those who were ambitious and deserving are no more working in my institution. I have extracted as much as I could from them but not given them anything, not even any extra increment. On top of that I have ignored them to the possible extent to dishearten and demoralise them. Quite obviously, they left for better job and now some of them are holding the position of Principal or Vice Principal at various reputed institutions. I know how to keep the path clear for my wife but at the same time I give myself the credit for preparing so many Principals and Vice Principals. Is it called killing of two birds throwing a single stone?

I enjoy women but only their flesh, not their mind. Mind is very complicated and it is only the fools who go into the depth of it. I know they call me sadist, perverted, crooked but no one can ignore my invitation. Without having the slightest idea that its wings would be burnt, the moth rushes towards the glowing light of a candle. The thirsty ground receives the monsoon shower and allows the formation of muddy puddles on it. I don't love any one of these women although my intimacy with some is a matter of discussion among others. I have created the atmosphere of jealousy, hatred and mistrust among the teachers so that they can never rise against me unitedly. When I favour one particular teacher she becomes a victim of jealousy of others. As soon as I leave her high and dry, she joins one group of gossip mongers and criticises me and becomes jealous of my next victim. Those who come close to me can never reveal the truth in order to save their honour; but they suspect and hate each other. 'Divide and Rule' that is the best policy the British have taught us and in the matter of administration I am also following the same thing. I will continue to follow this so long these ambitious teachers surrender before me for fulfilling their dreams.

* * * * * * * *

Meanwhile Ranjita was promoted as Senior Mistress, Secondary Wing. One thing I observed after joining the school which I felt would go in my favour in the long run, that is-the contract between the two management i.e., the central and the local was a faulty one and the Principal, according to the contract was the most powerful person who could not be removed by either side single handed. Both the parties had to agree on this matter. I understood that it would be very wise on my part to always create a conflict or dispute between the two parties to be on the safe side. There was provision in the contract even for the local management to open a chain of schools without the consent of the Society in Delhi. I chalked out my plan and started proceeding according to my strategies. I extracted the maximum benefit from the Society in the capital including my foreign tours and then started poisoning the ears of the local management against it. I succeeded in convincing them and taking them into confidence. I totally stopped following the instructions of the central management and deliberately started a dispute with them and this I did with the full support of the local management. I was sure the institution will continue and the performance would improve rather than deteriorating because I am a hard taskmaster and I know how to extract the last drop from the staff. I made the local management understand that the Society in Delhi was not contributing in any way in the progress and development of the school and unnecessarily we had been giving them a share of the profit. The situation worsened to such an extent that the Society decided to withdraw the brand name and terminate the contract. The then Pro Vice Chairman from the local governing body agreed to that at my constant provocation and supply of crispy currency and terminated the contract. The Chairman of the Society Mr. Naresh Chandra issued a public notice in the local as well as National newspapers that our institution was no more under the aegis of the prestigious brand under which there are at present more than 170 schools in the country and abroad.

I was just waiting for this opportunity. Until and unless the school is separated from the Society, how will I make Ranjita my successor? The Committee members of the local management are too busy to think about the school. Most of them either retire within one or two years or get a transfer with promotion. They don't bother about the school administration. Moreover the extra income (unofficially) from the school keeps their pocket warm and their lips tight and insists them to sign blindly on the papers which I send them. Contact and money – these two things can play havoc anywhere, everywhere.

The Pro Vice Chairman of the school at that time who was about to retire, agreed to my decision and gave his consent in terminating the contract with the Society before its normal termination. He retired within a short time and got more from me than his company gave him as retiring benefit. For six months I was successful in keeping the staff members as well as the parents in darkness. Only Ranjita and Padma knew everything. Some of the senior members left one by one and became Principals of newly opened schools under the same brand name. Some even joined those schools, surrendering their seniority. It was a real threat but how does it matter? I was determined and desperate and this was the best opportunity to bring the school under my absolute control. Time was ripe to construct my empire with Ranjita as my successor and then Ipsita and Amar. I managed the new affiliation number from C.B.S.E. by showing the excellent performance of the school.

Things were not very easy; the parents came to know everything through the public notice issued in the newspapers and started agitation. After all they have taken admission for their children only because of the brand name and so long have paid through their nose, seeking a bright future for their children. They forced themselves into my office and when Padma resisted they hurled a volley of abuses at her. They demanded the brand name and refused to listen to any explanation regarding the matter. This happened during the Dussehra-Diwali break when most of the staff members were out of station. The school reopened on 1st November and on the very first day I called a general meeting in the evening. I announced the promotion of some staff members whom I felt were loyal to me along with one or two problematic ones but I didn't announce the promotion of Madhushree, my favourite English teacher and sweetheart. This I did in order to satisfy the ego of those teachers who were jealous of Madhushree. It is wiser to sacrifice one darling for getting the support of the majority.

I gave promotion to Urja – the fire brand English teacher who had the guts to refuse me with a slap on my left cheek. Nobody expected Urja to get promotion although there was full justification in what I did. Urja was senior to Madhushree and she won State and National level awards for her literary work, bringing laurels to the school and warmth to my wallet. As she competed on behalf of the school, along with her prize money, the organisers always gave me cash awards, I being the Principal of the school. I had kept her cornered for long five and a half years because she refused to respond to my call. When Madhushree joined as an *adhoc* teacher with the experience of teaching at a nursery school, I started giving her extra responsibilities like editing the school magazine, preparing my speeches, Press Releases etc., ignoring Urja and other senior English teachers in order to evoke jealousy in their mind against Madhushree. She enjoyed her importance and like a queen entered my chamber every now and then. So long she used to be in my chamber, I explored her tanned body, her exposed cleavage and the raised waves in her breasts with the dark brown teats. She is sexy and always made me amorous. On pretext of checking a Press Release or any article for the school magazine, prepared or edited by her, I used to call her every now and then in my office much to the raised eyebrows of others. Calling her by the side of my chair, I used to get lost in her.

In the name of checking the dummy of the magazine I used to call her every evening and drop her home at midnight. Her adventurous, sportsman husband was either too busy with his world tour by cycle or his exploration of the rain forests etc. and the children remained under the custody of the maid servant. Madhushree was like wine, always flowing down the brim; she raised the desire in me but never satisfied my hunger. I enjoyed gala evenings with her but she refused to sleep with me – a flirtatious coquette who stood naked before me but kept me waiting outside, prohibiting my entry. I could not hold my patience any longer – four years were more than enough but she was overconfident of retaining her position and winning my favour.

Madhushree's husband heard the rumour which was spreading very rapidly and became furious with me. He started using abusive words and threatened me over telephone. In the meantime Padma also started feeling insecure because of Madhushree and a blow hot-blow cold phase started between the two. Padma's background was in no way more impressive than that of mine and may be the toughest of struggle she had faced in life toughened her mind; she never hesitated to lock horns with anyone whom she felt a threatening to her existence. In such cases I always take the side of Padma; so when tension started brewing up between Padma and Madhushree, I started supporting the former because I was looking for an opportunity to get rid of Madhushree. Her time was up, she had to go. The end of any passion is hatred. We started hating each other and she lost all interest in work.

Blaming her for going slow and neglecting duties, I withdrew all responsibilities which once I had given her and involved Urja in all such work. Urja is the most efficient, systematic and talented lady I have met in my life. She is the heart-throbbing beauty also – my Helen of Troy. She carries an aura of English wherever she goes. I have come across so many women in my life but no one is like Urja. I can keep my life at stake for achieving her but she always maintains a distance. Looking at her, nobody would say that she is the mother of two grown up sons. When she invited me to attend her silver wedding anniversary, I could not help saying – "you look like a twenty-five year young, beautiful girl and you are celebrating twenty five years of your marriage."? I know she is a highly ambitious lady and I had to offer her the important responsibilities as baits. The dream of achieving this bewitching beauty remained in the core of my mind, nurtured by the slimy feeling of lust.

Madhushree could not get what she expected. A tigress, who once experiences the taste of blood, becomes ferocious when deprived of it. She joined hands with a group of teachers who had become rebellious and was supporting the Society and the Principal of the newly opened school with the same brand name under the Society. About eighty teachers applied for various posts at the new school. Those who had physical relationship with me but failed to get my favour in career development jointly gave written complaint of sexual harassment against me to the highest authority at the local level. I feel pity for these women. They just paved the way for some people to increase their bank balance with the fat packets I offered them. Only fools expect justice from corrupt people in power.

About nineteen teachers submitted resignation and joined the new school. Madhushree also left with them. Whatever I had promised to give her, I gave to Urja. I made her the Activity In charge, the Managing Editor of the school magazine and the H.O.D. of the English Department. But no one could have even an iota of the intention which I kept suppressed in my mind. I decided to exploit the talent, intelligence and qualities of Urja as there was doubt in getting her consent in sexual relationship.

This lady was highly ambitious right from the beginning and always remained focussed. I understood that bringing her to the limelight would enhance the position and status of the school at the time of crisis, or in the simple words would be publicity for the school. Ranjita however had a different opinion. She didn't want her own image to get suppressed before that of Urja. I know she suffers from inferiority complex and can't tolerate my admiration for the talents of any teacher. As she is unable to give me physical satisfaction, she has accepted my sexual relationship with other women but she becomes furious if I appreciate the qualities of any other woman. She hates Urja from the core of her heart and the burning jealousy remains unextinguished in her mind because she can sense my weakness for Urja (both for her beauty and qualities). When I brought Urja to the limelight, made her the Activity In charge, H.O.D. English, Managing Editor of the school magazine and started appreciating her quality of work, Ranjita started developing dark circles around her eyes very fast. Her cheeks became hollowed and she started aging. She suspected me, having an affair with Urja. Urja has the habit of using foreign perfumes. Whenever she came to my office room, she left a beautiful scent behind her; Ranjita started sniffing at my clothes when I returned home. She became a maniac and tried to find fault with Urja in each and every matter. Urja was a personification of sincerity. She could not tolerate any laxity in work among her colleagues and never hesitated to call a spade a spade. Moreover I had instructed her to be very firm and strict. Ranjita started exploiting the situation. She tactfully insisted the teachers to write complaint letters (with false accusations of course) against Urja that she was rubbing them on the wrong side. Ranjita knew that she being the Principal's wife most of them would follow her instructions in order to get her favour. Those who never had any chance of getting P.G.T., even some teachers who teach up to middle school level or Primary level – they all got P.G.T. at the recommendation of Ranjita, for pleasing her.

On the one hand Ranjita and on the other hand Padma convinced me that if we please the majority of the staff and get their support, it would be easy for us to fight against the Society at the capital and remain in position. Moreover, those who are efficient and talented should not be allowed to come to the forefront because Ranjita's image would be suppressed and in future the efficient teachers would draw the attention of the management and rise into power and position. There was a fear that they might rise into revolt and take the side of the Central Society.

I appreciated the shrewdness of both Ranjita and Padma and surrendered myself completely in the hands of these two women. As per their advice, I started recruiting new teachers, giving them high salary, evoking the jealousy of the old teachers. This is my policy of divide and rule. One by one my darling teachers left the school, cursing me for my cowardice and atrocity. But Urja didn't leave. She remained in spite of all humiliations and tortures inflicted on her.

In the meantime, pressurised by the parents, I applied for a stay order against the notice served by the Society and just in the nick of time, I managed it. It was the first step of victory against the Chairman. I started telling my staff members that the Chairman had terminated the contract and wished to withdraw the name and logo of the school because he had taken a huge amount from the promoter of the newly opened school. He disowned our school because in order to bring up the new school under the brand name he had to demolish our school and he knew that it would be possible if the lucrative brand was withdrawn. The parents would shift their children from our school to the new school because they had a fascination for the brand name. I don't know how far the teachers were convinced but at least they decided to wait and see till the end. Some of them expressed their doubt-why all of a sudden the Chairman was annoyed with me, because in the public notice issued by him in the leading newspapers he had mentioned that I was no more the Secretary of the Management Committee. I started confusing people by twisting facts and in every meeting explained things in such a way that facts would go above their heads. I also told them that I didn't agree to some proposals made by the Chairman as I am a man of principles. He had instructed me to follow certain books at various classes which were published by him. I refused to follow those books as they were full of mistakes. He also requested me for the admission of some students but they didn't qualify in the written examinations. He wanted to promote a Teacher-Incharge at the junior most level to the post of Vice Principal but how could I deprive the seniors and appoint a junior as the Vice Principal? That was my explanation before the staff. The fact was I wanted to preserve that coveted position for my wife – safe and secure.

I have only a few years to retire. Today the facilities which I have been enjoying will be withdrawn with my retirement. If I can place Ranjita on my chair then everything would go on smoothly for about one more decade. After that there are Amar and Ipsita to take over. At the same time I will also get the credit of opening a chain of schools, my empire will expand and flourish. We will be able to get rid of the brand of agriculturists and will come to be known as educationists. All these would be possible if the school is separated from the Society at Delhi. I will have absolute power in my hands and do as I wish and make people dance at my tune. The members of the local management are too busy with their work; they will not interfere in my business and if ever they do so, the amount in the already fat packets which they get every month will be doubled up.

When the staff members got the news of the stay order they distributed sweets and congratulated me. The music teacher who has been working since the first day of the school helped me with a spoonful of 'Rasmalai.' I suppressed my real feelings and told them to work sincerely as a team at the moment of crisis and not to pay heed to any rumour. I had already done the mental calculation that it would take at least three-four years to solve the problem and before that I will make Ranjita the Vice Principal. Society's permission was not required and once she becomes the Vice Principal, no one will be able to withdraw it. But in order to make her the Vice Principal I had to promote about thirty other teachers to various posts and give the post of Vice Principal to one more senior teacher who had been serving the institution from the very first day although he doesn't know anything about administration. I made him the H.O.D. of Language also although he was a teacher of Sanskrit and could not utter a single word in English. This of course I did at the instigation of Ranjita who had the intention of grabbing this honour, proving within due course of time that her counterpart was incompetent for holding the post of H.O.D. Language.

If there is only one example in the world of achieving stupendous success without doing any work, then the example of this Sanskrit teacher Ravishankar Shastri can be given. He has been relishing the cream both at school as well as in his personal life without any effort for preparing it. This is called sheer luck! But I needed him as a dice in my game and lady luck smiled behind the curtain. Ravi Shastri has two wives, who are again two sisters and total five children from both. Those who have been serving the institution right from the beginning have seen his first wife and two sons who are now in his ancestral village in M.P.

The second wife and three children (two daughters and a son) stay with him in the township near the school. Taking private tuitions is banned in our school but I failed in preventing him from doing so. Infact his income from private tuitions is more than his salary, otherwise bringing up five children and two wives in the 21st century is not a matter of joke. It is an open secret that he leaks examination papers, I mean question papers, taking money and gifts from children. Such a person, no doubt, is a precious asset in my mission, who will support me silently; after all he has to support his two families.

Those who had submitted their resignation letters were not happy when we managed the stay order. They had expected that I will be removed, the school will come under the aegis of the Society and they will stay back. But it's not so easy to remove Veer Parsad. I know from where I have come and where I have reached. Till there is the last drop of blood in my veins, I will protect and defend myself. One advantage was there – that is there were many students with VIP background. I started maintaining good rapport with those parents who were VIPs in some way or the other and took them into confidence. The M.Ps, M.L.As, Bureaucrats, Ministers, top bosses of the corporate world, Police Department etc. all became my friends. They felt obliged getting invitation as Chief Guests of various functions and Kingly treatment from us.

Those good for nothings, who had no chance of getting higher grade in their life, got promotion and I know they will remain my slave and work for me blindly. Urja was becoming very popular and because of her, Ranjita's image was getting suppressed. Ranjita's inferiority complex got aggravated day by day at Urja's success due to her hard work during the crisis period in a very systematic way which was working well. She is a very creative person and her writing style and skill had no match in the school. Whenever she prepared students for any literary activity, they came out with flying colours. She used to pen down dramas for the Annual Day and House Competitions or functions and direct them which were highly appreciated. Even I like her writing style very much. But Ranjita somehow could never appreciate that and always criticised her in a bitter way.

We got an invitation from a reputed school in Lucknow to participate in the National level music, dance and drama competition. The music and dance teachers were entrusted with the responsibilities of music and dance items and Urja was given the responsibility of selecting and preparing the drama team. She had also chosen a very good play with a nice theme and title – I Am A Girl. She gave me the script to read which was somewhat like this:

(Chorus) I have taken birth on this Earth, I have full right on the sky, the earth, all the seas and the whole Universe. I wish to bring them all under my control.

1st Character — Friends, you won't get anything except darkness. See observantly, the whole world is unhappy at your birth.

2nd Character — But what is this? Why is the sky turning black looking at you?

3rd Character — Why is the greenery fading away?

4th Character — Where are the waves of the sea?

5th Character — Hey Girl! Nothing will come to you. Your fist will remain empty (3 times)

1st Character — But my childhood? My laughter, my getting annoyed every now and then and being consoled by my mother? What about that? Girls, if it had been only me in your place (3 times)

2nd Scene

Mother — Oh God! These people are giving me a lot of trouble.

1st Character — But mother, I've to pay my school fees tomorrow.

2nd Character — Mummy, see the condition of my frock.

3rd Character — Daughter in law, I've no medicine left.

4th Character — Ma, I'll also go to school.

5th Character — Mummy, I'm hungry.

Mother — How will I take care of all? Earning member is one, but eight members are to be fed in the family. O God! in which hell have you sent me? Only you can help and guide me God!

1st Character But Ma, Lata of our neighbourhood is so happy. She gets whatever she wants.

2nd Character — She celebrates her birthday also. How happy she is, isn't she mother?

Mother — That's because she is the only daughter of her parents, but you are so many. Go, it's evening time, light the lamp in the courtyard before the Tulsi plant and give fodder to the cattle. Oh God! Give them wisdom.

Chorus — Give us wisdom (3 times)

3rd Scene

Chorus — Little friend is weeping sitting in the sun.

1st Character — I don't want any friend.

2nd Character — See, she is really weeping.

3rd Character — Nisha, why are you weeping? Has somebody said anything?

1st Character — No one loves me at home. Not only I, we all are facing the same predicament; either slog at home for the whole day or help father in the field. They neither let us study, nor show any love for us.

2nd Character — Why can't we go to school?

3rd Character — What do you know? How difficult it is for father to bring food for us! Sometimes mother goes to sleep without any food.

4th Character — Nisha, do you really want to study?

1st Character — Yes I do; but how does it matter? I know that's not possible. Mother will not send me to school (talking to herself) Copies, books, pencils – no, no, I'll never be able to study.

4th Character — Listen, we all will help you to study.

1st Character — How many girls can you help? There are so many like me suffering in the darkness of ignorance. Would you be able to uplift all?

Chorus — Yes; we will be able to uplift them all (3 times)

Song — We shall overcome……..

1st Character — Will you be able to show them the light of knowledge?

Chorus — Yes, we will show (3 times)

1st Character — Will you be able to free them from ignorance?

Chorus — Yes we will free them (3 times)

1st Character — Will you spread the flame of knowledge in all directions?

Chorus — Yes we will spread (3 times)

5th Character — We all are taking a resolution today that no one will remain illiterate. The suppressed flame of knowledge under the darkness of ignorance will come out with its luminosity.

Scene 4

1st Character — How nice I feel in this lonely room – so different from that overcrowded place. I feel as if I have become free from a curse. Only I will inherit the property of my father. Will you give me?

Chorus Standing

at the backside

of the stage — Yes we will give (3 times).

1st Character — Only I will get the love and attention of my parents.

Chorus — Yes, you will get (3 times).

1st Character — The whole world will sing my glory.

Chorus — Yes your glory.

1st Character — I am the queen of this world.

Chorus — Yes, you are the queen.

5th Character — You wanted everything for yourself. Won't you ask for a little love for us? Won't you ask for a little comfort for others?

2nd Character — Say something.

1st Character — What shall I say? If I had been the only one in place of all, I would have got all pleasure. I would have got everything. I would have been the winner.

Chorus while

Leaving the Stage — I would have been the winner (3 times)

Scene 5

Father-in-Law — Daughter-in-law, come here.

DIL — I'm coming father.

FIL — I think your father doesn't know the importance of keeping promises. I have brought up my son with proper education, not to give him away free of cost. Where is that promised 5 lac?

DIL — Father, from where will my poor father bring that huge amount? How will he arrange the money? He is jobless. I have four younger sisters. Moreover, I am also earning for this family.

FIL So what if you are earning? Do you expect me to forget the amount which your father had promised at the time of marriage? My son is a doctor. He can get even 10 lac if he wishes.

DIL — But father……

FIL — I don't want to hear anything. You just leave our house. I will arrange my son's marriage again with great pomp and show.

DIL — So long I am alive I will never allow that. I will take the help of law.

FIL — So you have decided to go to the Court and sling mud on us. If you don't survive then how will you go to the Court? Catch her, don't allow her to go (All will try to catch her).

DIL — Leave me, let me go, don't kill me – I want to live, I don't want to die, help me, please somebody save my life. Father, I won't tell any one, please forgive me; I don't want to die. Mother where are you? Where are you Mummy?

Scene 6 (Immediately taking place)

Same character — Men, have you made me Goddess in this way? Why can't you become God by passing the test of fire? Even Sita was not spared of this humiliation! Come, set yourself ablaze and feel the pain – burn that society in the same funeral pyre which burns helpless women. Fire, you spread your wings in all directions, burn down the rules of the society.

Chorus — Fire, you spread your wings (3 times).

Scene 7

1st Character — Should the illiterate remain confined to the darkness of ignorance?

2nd Character — Should we be deprived in future also?

3rd Character — Can we fulfil our aspirations in future?

4th Character — Will the society continue to burn helpless women?

5th Character — Should I continue to take birth in big families?

Chorus — No, no, no

1st Character — Hello friends! From the beginning to the end we have tried to solve the problems of the girl children and women by projecting all evils practised in the society before you. We are in search of that great saviour who can lead us to the path of light dispelling all darkness of ignorance.

Chorus — We are in search of that great saviour, who can lead us to light (3 times).

After reading the script I approved it. Urja took my permission to involve Mrs.Geetika Ghosh who had long experience in the field of drama; in fact she was a pioneer in staging English plays in the township. Mrs. Ghosh and Urja were progressing very well. Then all of a sudden, Ranjita took the script and made some unnecessary changes which were not at all relevant. Unnecessarily she corrected some words also which sounded horrible. Not only this she involved a

Hindi teacher and told him to direct the play. As he had no knowledge in English he directed the play in such a way that it got the shape of a Hindi street play and the aura of English was absolutely lost. Urja and Mrs.Ghosh had instructed the students who were enacting the play to wear black and white costumes. That Hindi teacher with the approval of Ranjita changed their costumes and told them to wear dark orange costumes and they were looking like monks. With the song 'We shall overcome' the children were asked to dance taking artificial weapons in their hands. On the whole it was horrible, also highly melodramatic and both Mrs. Ghosh and Urja were furious but they kept quiet because Ranjita was taking the leading role and they knew her nature very well. I tried to remain neutral. As it was expected the play could not fetch any prize. I got the feed-back from some of the students that people laughed to their hearts' content when the play was enacted. As Urja was the in charge the whole blame fell on her. Such type of incidents continued to happen and Urja was facing thousand and one problems because of Ranjita's bitchery. But she is a tough lady which made it possible for her to continue against all odds. She coordinated the Annual day function and compered the programme. The Governor of the State was the Chief Guest. The Governor's wife was highly pleased with the way Urja conducted the programme and sent her a letter of appreciation from the Governor's House. She also received a letter of appreciation from the Ex-President of India Dr. A.P.J. Abdul Kalam for a poem composed by her. Ranjita started nagging, instigating me to remove Urja from all her responsibilities. I also felt that time was ripe for clipping off her wings. She had been soaring too high. I had given enough time to her to take a decision in surrendering before me. Whatever I desire in life, I achieve by hook or by crook; only in the matter of achieving Urja, my desire remained unfulfilled. Madhushree had at least given me satisfaction to some extent. Urja by that time had already come to the notice of the management and other eminent personalities. "Either let me explore you or remain suppressed, subdued at the back stage" – I thought.

Removing Urja from her place was not so easy as everybody was aware of her efficiency and hard work. I had to find out some solid reasons, some excuses. Nothing could be said against her quality of work, her dedication and sincerity. Ranjita started provoking the teachers and students against her. Among the students were Amar and his friends. Ranjita handled the case very well, fully exploiting her position. She started collecting complaint letters against Urja accusing her of being short tempered, disrespectful, always showing her superiority etc. etc. It's very easy to ruin the career of an honest worker with the help and witness of ten other people if you are in power; but one should not be in a hurry. Everything takes its own time; so while I had the plan of removing Urja from her place as I had removed Madhushree earlier, I pretended to be her greatest well-wisher. I started praising her after every function co-ordinated by her and congratulated her with bouquets. I praised her in front of others to evoke jealousy in their mind, so that it becomes easy for Ranjita to turn them against her. Moreover when one falls from a great height, one is not able to stand up again due to multiple fractures and invalidity beyond treatment. I wanted to make Urja absolutely crippled so that she had to depend on me throughout her life and hence lifted her up to the zenith.

* * * * * * * *

The Delhi Society filed a case in the High Court against the stay order which was managed from the district court. Who wanted to be associated with the Society? I just wanted to retain the name and logo, pressurised by the parents of the students. I could also feel a suppressed dissatisfaction and agitation among the staff members although they were afraid to express. Many of them started looking for a job elsewhere. Time to time I assured them in the general meetings that things are going to turn in our favour, they need not worry; it is the duty of the teachers to teach and that of the students to study. The blank cheques which I had taken from the businessmen parents now came to use as I started purchasing the political leaders, ministers, police personnels, lawyers and other administrative authorities. The small bar at my official residence always remained open for them. The dais of our school was always adorned with the eminent politicians as special guests for all types of functions. Who will uproot me from here? I have established my empire and my progenies will rule here.

The High Court's order was not in our favour. We lost the case. The parents again started agitation. In the meantime somebody started circulating anonymous letters against me to the public but how could that person know about my plan until and unless he/she is very close to me? Nobody except Padma and Ranjita knew about it! The contents of the poison – pen letters were absolutely true including my clever plan of bringing everything in my grip, making my undeserving wife the Vice Principal, my relationship with teachers, the night party with wine and flesh held at the indoor swimming pool (organised by my sweet-heart Komolika–the sexy Chemistry teacher with whom my Chemistry works very well), Amar and Ipsita's poor performance in CBSE Exams, Amar's not getting admission in any reputed Engineering College, his failing in the 1st year at the Engineering College in Bangalore where ultimately he got admission (after I paid a huge donation) and losing NTSE scholarship which he had managed copying from his friends at the time of the Exam. Even my peeping through the empty classrooms above the swimming pool and watching the lady teachers and girls of higher classes in their swimming costumes was also mentioned in one of the letters. I lost my nights' sleep; was there anyone observing me closely? Who could write such letters to instigate the parents? It's still a mystery although I suspect Madhushree and a group who had left for the new school, working behind this and sometimes I suspect even Urja but without authentic proof I cannot charge them. The more the letters were circulated, the more the parents became impatient and started pressurising the local governing body of the school to compromise and settle the matter with the Society; at any cost they wanted the name and logo to be retained. The local management had tried several times to settle the matter with the Chairman but the conditions put forth by him was to dissolve the local governing body and to remove the Principal otherwise he would not budge an inch from his decision.

Challenging the order of the High court, a case was filed in the Supreme Court. The matter remained subjudice and the school continued to run well as usual. Provoking Urja to lose her temper and shout back at me, I got the opportunity to take back the important responsibilities from her and giving most of them to Ranjita, I gave a few to a House Warden Bindiya Bhalla. Her impotent husband supplies us with the alcoholic drinks required for hospitality and entertainment of VVIPs on monthly basis. I could not give time to Bindiya for a long period and due to my indifferent attitude she started mixing up with those teachers who had left the school. Bringing her back to the lime light I could pacify her and also maintain my domestic peace.

Ranjita is still unaware of the colourful relationship which I shared with Bindiya, otherwise a Tsunami would have taken place within the school premises. Bindiya is so poised, no one can have even an iota of her inner feelings. But what Urja did after this was also no less than a Tsunami. No other teacher ever dared, opening the mouth before me but she didn't even care to refine her language before expressing her mind. She had become so obsessed with her work, it was a great shock to her when Ranjita snatched away everything from her like a vulture. She cursed me, cursed my family, my children, spat on my face and I don't hesitate to say that for the first time in my life I was afraid, I felt something evil and harmful would occur in my life, would destroy everything I had built up so far and shatter my mental peace. I believe, curse which comes out of the core of a deprived heart comes true. May be because of that my son Amar was tortured by his senior students on his way and while coming back from the Engineering College and ultimately I had to send him to a far away place, managing admission after paying huge donation. May be because of the curse he lost NTSE scholarship, failing in his 1st year exam. May be because of the curse my daughter Ipsita could not qualify in the campus selection although all her classmates got good jobs.

But I will not give up so easily. I digested everything in a cool, composed manner as I did a few days earlier when Urja had slapped me in my office for misbehaving with her. I had suppressed a letter inviting her to attend a prize distribution ceremony in Delhi for receiving a prize from the Ex HRD Union Minister Shri Murali Manohar Joshi. She came to know about this from another teacher Neelima Pandey who was also invited and came to my office to verify. I thought before removing her from the position let me try for the last time. I pulled her near me, took her in my arms and tried to force my mouth on her lips with all my strength. She was not prepared for this, but she took just a few seconds to recover herself from the shock and gave me a tight slap on my left cheek. Pushing me back she shouted at me at the top of her voice, opened the door of my office room and slamming it with a bang she stepped out into the reception calling me "Bloody Fool, Bastard," loudly. That was enough for taking action against her. The people present in the reception enjoyed a matinee show free of cost. I was not ashamed because this was not a singular incident in my life. People saw her shouting and abusing the Principal but they didn't know the reason for her behaviour because that had taken place silently behind the closed doors.

I know from where I have come and how far I have reached. I have toiled hard, neglecting my family (of course people say that my whole family is always with me and each member is taken well care of because of my position). I know only how to achieve, not to lose. I have to win. So far, in my life, whenever I desired anything, I achieved it. I have no regret for playing the game of love with women. They never resisted, rather enjoyed my company. They cherished the importance of coming close to me. But whenever they were left high and dry, they reacted and criticised me, blamed me, called me characterless. But then, why did they respond to my call? Why couldn't they resist and protect themselves? I have no feelings for them. Women are playthings – I have played with them. But if they expect that I will give them everything that I have given to Ranjita, then it is their mistake. I don't love Ranjita, I love myself. I love my power, my position, my money, my name and fame. I am giving everything to Ranjita to enjoy everything for a longer period of time after my superannuation. I know how to keep the ball rolling in my court forever.

During this long period of dispute between the Society with the brand name and the local management, some teachers always supported me and Urja was one of them. Everywhere, she wrote in my favour and once I even got a long list of probable names for our institution written by her in case we had to surrender the name and logo. On the one hand I tried to make my staff members understand that Society was against us, they wanted to ruin us for bringing up their new school, on the other hand I never snapped the bond with Society. I tried to keep all doors open. I kept on sending them reports on the progress and achievement of the school although they didn't ask for any. I also came to know through reliable sources that majority of the members of the Society were against the Chairman and some of them challenged his selection for the second time. I remembered "Enemy's enemy is my friend."

A case had been filed by some members of the Society against the selection of Nareshchandra as the Chairman for the second time which was subjudice. I started communicating and negotiating with these members of the Society to win their confidence and favour. The appreciation letters written by them to me were published in the school magazine as a document; this idea of course was given by Urja when she was not aware of what was stored for her in future. I realised when there was so much demand for the brand name, it would be wiser on my part to try to get it back and bring the school again under the aegis of the Society as by that time I had already given that post of Vice Principal to Ranjita.

For the other things there was enough time but without the brand name and logo, parents would not have allowed me to exist. If the school is associated with the Society, it would be a matter of prestige for us to be the Principal and Vice Principal of the most prestigious school with a popular brand name.

I found, except the Chairman, all other members of the Society were in my favour. Among them were two very aged ladies and some new members with whom it didn't take much time to establish a cordial relationship. I understood that the Chairman alone would not be able to do any harm to me; in any case he was going to retire after two years. It will not be difficult for me to place Ranjita on my chair. After all I know the art of flattery, oiling, buttering and even boot-licking, in whichever way it may be expressed. At the same time I will keep the flow of money to different channels intact.

Now a days, I have been turning superstitious and have started following various rituals. Pressurised by Ranjita and Padma I also started a yagna at Skandhashram. Advised by a practitioner of Vastu Shastra, I changed my seating arrangement from South facing to North facing, much to the amusement of my staff members. I arranged a big fish aquarium in my room and brought some artefacts which are considered sacred and lucky. Is it a sign of losing faith in my own ability and strength? Whatever it is, I will not give up. I can see, my dream materialising before my eyes. The Principal's palatial quarter at the residential school in the hill station had occupied my mind, nurtured with great passion, which I visualise in my pensive mood time to time. My own quarter is coming up in the campus along with other staff quarters. This institution has become an inseparable part of my life. I will spend the rest of my life here, advising and guiding Ranjita as the Director after my tenure as the Principal is over. I have had enough enjoyment and satisfaction in my life regarding women and sex. Now I have to turn towards spiritualism. That is the only way to clean my image and also the dust which has accumulated in my relationship with my wife and children. Today, I am the most controversial and discussable personality in the township, a crispy topic among the ladies because of the grudge and malice of the exploited women whom I have left high and dry. Sometimes I feel like murdering them or burning their beautiful faces throwing acid with the help of hired killers. Because of them I will not be able to make myself free from the notoriety which is not leaving me inspite of my best efforts to improve my image by attending the Art of Living programmes and performing religious rituals. The stamp of notoriety and promiscuousness is more prominent than the red tilak adorning my forehead when I come out of the Hanuman temple or the red sacred thread tied up in my wrist and this prominence sometimes are reflected through the contemptuous expressions in the eyes of Ipsita and Amar or the fire in the eyes of Ranjita. No doubt, I am a good administrator, I know how to extract maximum from my employees by giving them minimum, I know how to trample them underfoot but I could not become a good husband and a good father. I have cheated everybody and even after crossing fifty-nine autumns, the taste of success is still bitter. I know it can never be sweet but I can't live without it. A winner will never quit and a quitter will never win.

Someone constantly started instigating the parents to try to remove me and agree to the dismissal of the local governing body so that the school can come under the aegis of the Society and retain its name and logo. Pressurised by them the local management, with the intervening of an arbitrator settled the matter and all disputes between the Society and the local management were amicably dissolved. The condition put forward by the Chairman was accepted by the local management and much to the joy of the staff and parents the school again came under the aegis of the Society. We started behaving in such a way as if there was no dispute between us. I started praising the Chairman and he started praising me in public but public remained unaware of the huge amount which went to the Chairman's account from my account. Only I know, from now onwards how many times I have to run to Delhi to satisfy the members of the Society to keep my position intact. My position has been saved for the time being just by the skin of my teeth, but anything might happen at any time. My dream of opening a chain of schools in the city and nearby areas remained a dream only and Ranjita's future also became uncertain. I curse myself for being intimate to women. I know, definitely the women who were once close to me have instigated people against me when they could not get justice from the local management after lodging written complaints against me.

I was proceeding very cautiously towards my goal in such a way that the stick would have remained intact even after killing the snake. The name and logo could have been retained even without coming under the Society. But why? Why should I miss the goal just for one foul? Are not the corporate heads enjoying a gala time with their P.A.s and Secretaries? The other day when Padma rang up the PRO of one of our local governing body members and asked him the name of his boss's wife, he laughed over the telephone and asked back – "Which wife? Gharwalee or Baharwalee" (the one at home or the one outside?) We show so much respect to these people, invite them as Chief Guests to distribute prizes to the children! Heaven starts falling on all only when the Principal Veer Parsad uses his tool! I have proof with how many women the widower Chairman Nareshchandra slept so far and who used to supply him with young, beautiful women!! That lady is the sister of our ex-incharge of the Primary wing, holding an important post at E.M.C. in Delhi. Even his own close relative, his brother-in-law has told me how he had been enjoying with women at his own residence when his wife was on her death-bed. This brother-in law's wife was at that time staying with them, taking care of the Chairman's wife – her sister-in-law. This man has not lost anything in his life. Nobody has pulled him out of his position – although his character is murky. Then why should I suffer? This constant tension, worries and stress have snatched my mental peace and are not letting me perform my work peacefully. Padma has brought a large aquarium in my office with eighteen colourful fishes to pacify my mind but every moment, I feel being chased by an unknown force; every moment I am afraid of losing everything which I have built up in these long ten years here. I have got entangled in the net which I have webbed myself.

When the school again came under the Society I started convincing the parents and teachers that it was I who negotiated with the Society at Delhi, convinced the Chairman and persuaded him to agree to take back our school under the Society. I started reading out the letters sent by the Chairman in the Morning Assembly to show how close I was to the Chairman and there was no dispute at all between us. But in fact silently I cursed those teachers who were in favour of the Society because I know that my position is not so secure now. If the Society which was formed with the local management and which had been functioning as an autonomous body is dissolved and everything is controlled by the Central administrative body, then where will I stand? I will lose my power and will have to follow the instructions of the Society for anything and everything. Moreover anytime the Society will be able to transfer me and bring a person of their choice in my place. The chair which I have kept reserved for Ranjita, guarding it myself, might be occupied by a migratory bird. But I will not give up so easily and so soon. Just like that, no one can uproot me and banish me from this place.

I started making a rapport with the Chairman and other members of the Society. Atleast twice a month I started going to the capital leaving everything under the care of Ranjita and in my absence, with absolute power she kept on torturing some rebellious teachers whom she suspected of spreading our notoriety to the public, including Urja to the possible extent. Being a psychopath Ranjita is noted for her habit of ill treating and torturing people and in this matter she can even surpass Hitler. This is called the penury of heart or darkness of mind which is caused by greed, abnormal, undeserving ambition, arrogance, inferiority complex and shameless display of power. Ranjita is a psychic no doubt and that's why she could never earn the respect of anyone. Teachers flatter her to extract something from her but in reality everybody hates her.

The major part of Activity was already withdrawn from Urja and given to my one time sweet heart Bindiya Bhalla. Our child who is growing up at her home is studying in the Primary wing. She was made the Cultural Activity Incharge and Urja was retained as Literary Activity Incharge just for name sake. Ranjita started snatching her responsibilities and doing those things herself. Actually she had nothing else to do. She could not understand administration at all and had I given her administrative work, I would have to part with Padma. I prefer doing administrative work with Padma as she can take care of my other needs also. Urja used to take interviews of the students and teachers at the time of admission or recruitment as the subject expert. Ranjita removed her from these two areas to show her power. Her own image was getting suppressed before Urja's magnetic personality in front of the parents, students and teachers. During the summer vacation a workshop for the H.O.Ds of English was organised in Delhi. Depriving Urja, Ranjita herself attended that workshop. Urja was completely cornered and we tried our best to curb her importance. She had started gaining too much popularity which was quite alarming for Ranjita. One thing I have learnt in my life which I always try to follow – that is – excellence should always be kept suppressed. Mediocrity should be encouraged because it can be kept under subjugation. Excellence of the subordinate is a threat to the existence of the ruler or the boss. Moreover I have given enough time to Urja to surrender before me and satisfy my hunger but she is adamant. How dare she could refuse me and that too with a slap?

There are two types of fools – one, who doesn't agree to the proposal of the boss and the other type of fools are those who get carried away by the promiscuousness of a casanova and fall in love with him only to be left high and dry. Urja belongs to the first group and there are many teachers who belong to the second group. Urja didn't care for the consequences of refusing me because she is a self-made lady, can proceed forward on her own, without my help. She started getting good offers from the reputed schools of various places, including some franchise schools under the same banner which we share. The Principal of the newly opened school with the same brand name and her promoter started alluring her with lucrative offers. The Chairman Naresh Chandra was also approached for her appointment. Even the posts of Principal and Vice Principal were also offered to her. But I knew her problems. She could not accept those offers as her husband and in-laws refused to let her go, leaving her home. It was a real handicapped situation for her and I realised how lucky Ranjita is to be the Principal's wife. Without making any sacrifice smoothly she will occupy my chair. She is shrewd enough to collect as many letters as she could in her favour from her followers and equal number of complaint letters, if not more against Urja and other teachers who left our school.

However Urja refused to give up. She never gave any scope to anyone to find out a loop-hole in her work. Whether it is teaching, class management, maintaining discipline among the students, organising any literary programme, editing school magazine or adding to her qualification – everything she did with complete devotion and dedication.

But Madhushree was completely shattered. She didn't possess the strength of mind like Urja. She had made the mistake of trusting me, not understanding the difference between love and love making. First she had to leave the school; then she left the township. I also came to know that she was planning to go to Bangalore but finally she decided to stay back. Through Bindiya I sent words and tried to bring all those teachers back to my school as there was a rumour in the air that they were not happy in the new school. One of the reasons to withdraw the responsibilities from Urja was to create a hope in the mind of Madhushree. It was a bait to bring her back so that I could prove that she was not happy at her new school with the same brand name. Moreover I was yet to explore her internally and so far kept myself satisfied with her outward beauty. Neither Madhushree nor any other teacher came back. Shamelessness is only for those who try to retain the chair but ego is the ornament of ordinary mass and because of their super ego, they refused to come back to this institution.

With raised walls here and there in between the relationships, days rolled on. There was a compromise between the Society in Delhi and the local management as a result of which the school could retain its name and logo. I agreed to accept the text books published by the Chairman. The local management agreed to the terms and conditions put forward by him. I personally went to Delhi to invite him as the Chief Guest of the Annual Function of the Pre-Primary Wing. I gave him a VIP treatment, arranged his and the whole team's stay at the best Hotel nearby. We paid a bill of Rs. 15,000.00 only for the flowers and bouquets arranged for them in two days. Although the Chairman came at my invitation, he accepted the invitation of my counterpart at the new school to grace their cultural function also. Nobody in my school could guess what agreement took place behind the closed doors. On the stage, in his historical speech the Chairman declared the amicable solution of the problems which existed between two parties amidst the loud applause of the parents and teachers.

The next day was the day of my extreme humiliation I ever met in my life. I had to accompany the Chairman to the other school with the same brand name with my wife and the other Vice Principal, uninvited. I can swear in the name of God that only Veer Parsad can perform such a shameless act. The Chairman praised the Principal of that school like anything for her efficiency in the tremendous progress and development of the school and asked everybody to give her a standing ovation. Ranjita and I could not avoid doing that and at that moment I felt had there been any method of becoming invisible or going inside the Earth we would have done that. I, Veer Parsad and Ranjita, my foolish, vainglorious wife had to stand up and clap our hands in honour of one of our greatest enemies on the Earth.

Within three months of this great drama, the Chairman resigned after playing his great role and managing two crores – each from the sponsors of the newly opened schools as well as me. He could feel that his end was coming nearer and it was impossible for him to win the case which was pending at the Supreme Court. Very timely he stepped down after filling his belly, leaving no space even for a belch. Now I have to win the heart of the new Chairman. Of course, most of the members of the Society are very old and some again are ladies. They have dedicated their lives for the sake of education. It's easy to manage them, particularly the lady members by shedding crocodile tears. Already I find them very sympathetic and affectionate towards me. By hook or by crook I have to retain my position and save that of Ranjita.

Ranjita and Padma's fasting and prayers, my connections and the strength of money will definitely improve the situation in my favour. Curses of my victims will not be able to harm me in any way. Neither their complaint letters, nor their anonymous letters could shake my position. I have purchased everybody but enemies should never be considered weak. It's always unpredictable from which direction the attack will come! In fact now-a-days I don't trust any one except Ranjita and Padma.

What a unique way Urja had chosen to voice her protest! She was expressing her mind on the pages of her Teaching Diary without any fear and whatever she had been writing was absolutely true. She is a born poetess and in a poetic way she had been mocking at me, reading which I felt amused but Ranjita boiled with rage. I had invited Urja to taste my virility as I give this offer to all women. But due to restrictions imposed on me by the local management, regarding my interaction or meeting with the lady teachers, during office hours I stopped meeting the lady teachers alone. Whenever any lady teacher came to my chamber, either Ranjita or Padma used to be present there. Urja very ironically criticised the situation and wrote:

"What a wonderful way of exhibiting virility of the superman who is now hiding behind his 'Remote Control" and his 'Head' Mistress ! Doesn't he deserve a standing ovation? Definitely, he deserves the Best Wrestler's Award which must comprise a dozen colourful petticoats and a box full of bangles." Any other Principal would have fired her but I had to digest because I had done injustice to her in spite of her selfless service. in spite of all injustice done to her, still she had been writing my speeches, preparing "From the Principal's Desk" for the school magazine, my Annual Day Report etc. On the one hand she had been working for me as a part of her duty; on the other hand she had been constantly voicing her protest both verbally as well as through her writings. Each time the Teaching Diary came first to Ranjita and then to me for our signature, Urja taught us a lesson. The Poem which she had composed on us was titled:

THE MUCH REPEATED STORY OF THE INNOCENT PLAY BOY

It's not his fault, he is innocent

He just likes to play with dolls, live dolls I mean

of flesh and blood, beauty and brain

He just wants to have his way.

If he finds a pretty doll, he must possess it.

It has to smile at his tickling

It has to cry at his pinching
But it is not his fault, he is innocent
He will play with the doll so long he wishes,
Keep it nearest his heart, give it all happiness of the world,
show the world how much he cares for it,
Evoking jealousy in the minds of others for it.
And then, one fine morning lose all attraction for it.
Then he will find fault with it and make it inactive,
blame it, humiliate it, torture it and go for another.
Repetition of the same story makes everything clear
But is it his fault? No he is innocent!
He is as innocent as a chubby cheeked baby
Licking a pink lollipop
He needs two 'veils' to protect himself as one is not enough.
Time to time, he feels suffocated under the veils
And comes out in the open air
To take breath and just can't resist himself
If hc finds a bcautiful doll nearer.
It's the fault of the doll, why is she so pretty?
She was destined to suffer.
His two protective 'veils' watch him playing with the dolls
Silently, but ring the warning bell timely
And caution him to come under their covertures
What an obedient, innocent child is he
to carry out their order!
As soon as the game is over
The doll has no right to remain alive
Its time is up, it must turn into a puppet
The chubby – cheeked however has 'veils' to hide
After all, it's not his fault, he is too innocent.

He is the only innocent one in the world,
He and his two sacred 'veils'!
The 'once pretty' dolls are wicked,
Dishonest, liars, characterless, opportunists and what not?
They are spoiling the baby again and again,
Robbing him of his virginity and innocence!
The chubby cheeked enjoys his life under the 'veils'
Well protected with luxury and comfort.
Under the same roof, the dolls play their roles as puppets
Staring at each other with hatred and doubt.
That's what the innocent child desires
let his dolls fight amongst themselves
let them sling mud at each other
He will carry on with his innocence.
Dolls, neither hatred towards each other
Nor shedding tears will ever bring you justice
That is not the way to deal with enemies.
Pick up your whip and lash him with all your might.
With repeated blows, strip the imp of a child
Off his fake innocence
Expose his real self before the world
Tear off the dark 'veils' into pieces
Don't just let the much repeated show go on.

Had she composed the poem on any other person, I would have enjoyed and appreciated but I know the innocent child is I, myself and my two protective veils are Ranjita and Padma. The pretty dolls of course are the beautiful ladies who were my victims.

I can understand Urja's grudge and malice. She really worked hard for so many years. She did the work of ten teachers at the same time and all of a sudden, ignoring her, I withdrew everything from her and made her useless. She came back to her original position where she was five years back – cornered, side-tracked, ignored. I couldn't help; I have given her more than enough time to change her decision and agree to my proposal but she refused to budge an inch from her decision. Bindiya had to wait for a long time. Before Madhushree came, it was Bindiya, who had made my life colourful. I had to do some justice to her. I had to take care of Ranjita's image also which was being totally suppressed by Urja. The Vice Principal and future Principal of the school had to rule with full authority, without her image getting suppressed before anyone. Above all I had to take care of my own life. I have crossed fifty – nine autumns through the ups and downs, sunshine and dark clouds. Now, no more looking back, only smooth sailing on calm water amidst cool breeze.

Urja's profile was becoming too high, there was no match to her, not only in this institution but also in the whole township. She bagged so many State and National level awards and received letter of appreciation from eminent personalities including the President of India and Queen of Britain. She was adding to her qualification also. Ranjita can never stand before her; and I, as the Principal never won any award! This thought never came to my mind but Padma and Ranjita opened my eyes. What a blunder I did by praising and encouraging Urja for winning awards and prizes! I should have clipped her wings long back but now she started crossing my height and growing like an oak. The only way left was to demoralise her; humiliate her so that losing enthusiasm and interest she would keep herself aloof from everything.

No one remembers a dead tree; so long there are fruits and flowers adorning the green, leafy branches, birds come there twittering and twitching, people halt for a while to appreciate its beauty and rest under its cool shade but the lifeless log of wood with its withered branches are of no use except as firewood turning them into ashes or waiting for the sharp sedentary teeth of a saw to fall into large chunks. With that thought in mind and at the instigation of Ranjita and Padma I removed all responsibilities from Urja and kept her cornered.

With borrowed words and expressions from her, I had already carved a niche in the intellectual society. Now I thought to win some State and National level awards to establish my fame. This was not at all a difficult task for me. The DEO is absolutely under my control. I need not compete for anything, my position is an advantage. Others will work like slaves for me and I will eat the fruit; of course a large share had to be given to my better half – Ranjita whose brain is always filled with cow-dung along with all the scums of the Earth.

I made Science Olympiad, Mathematics Olympiad, Physics Olympiad, Chemistry Olympiad, Astronomy Olympiad, Biology Olympiad etc. compulsory in the school. The teachers worked hard in preparing the students and collecting the money for entry fee. They conducted the tests spoiling their holidays. As a large sum of money was collected and sent to these Olympiad Foundations they awarded me with The 'Best Principal' Award for four consecutive years.

I nominated myself for the CBSE Teacher of the year 2005 award and bagged that too bribing the concerned authority at the State level for forwarding my application. So far I have kept it a secret from all teachers about the procedure of applying for any State, National or CBSE Award. These are to be won by the Principal and the Vice Principal and nobody else.

When I got the CBSE Award, my staff members demanded lunch. Some teachers who were regularised and confirmed wanted to contribute. I grabbed the opportunity and had to spend very little (that too from the school fund). Ranjita, with a silly smile welcomed the teachers. Amidst dead silence, they gulped down the food. As expected Urja was not present in the party.

I know the Principals of other schools in the township criticise me out of jealousy. They take great pleasure in discussing my negative side. What else can they do? They can never be equal to me. But they don't hesitate to emulate our institution, our system. Will they ever make their pay scale at par with my school? Never; and there lies my strength. Striking the faces of my employees with shoes of silver I have purchased them. I know they will never go anywhere else until and unless there is any case of transfer of anybody's spouse. Most of the employees are spineless except a few like Urja or Madhushree, who ignoring the comfort and security of a cocooned shelter here, ventured to jump into an unfamiliar land and ultimately emerged winners.

My next two targets are to become a National Awardee and the Director of the school; then I will try for Padmashree. Why should I bother for anyone? Time to time I will give them a good dose so that the standard of my school is maintained and academic results remain excellent. Both Ranjita and I had to carve a niche in the intellectual world and for that who could have been better than Urja? We exploited her to the greatest extent. I didn't hesitate to indulge myself into plagiarism. Stealing her ideas, her language, her expression I impressed the intellectual society. The school magazine was her brain child. She devoted her time, energy, everything for it. At the final stage of its composition she used to go to the Printing Press at least for ten days after attending school for the whole day and worked with the printers till midnight and sometimes even beyond that. When the whole township was tranquilised under the quilt of sleep, she used to come back home, absolutely exhausted and hit the bed without taking any food. This magazine became the main source of publicity both for the institution as well as myself. It reached the hands of the eminent personalities both within the country as well as abroad. People were impressed to read 'From the Principal's Desk' and formed a very high impression of me but not a single soul is aware of the fact that each and every word was penned down by Urja. She left the school two years back but still her article on Human Rights was published in the magazine in the name of Ranjita with her photograph. Coming back to the main issue, as an amateur allows the fish to play in water, slowly releasing the fishing cord (line) after hooking it and before pulling it up on the ground, causing its death, I also had allowed Urja to compose the magazine with full liberty as the Managing Editor. It became her passion, she was absolutely obsessed with it and then I applied my vital weapon. In August 2006, when due to the singular effort of Urja, the school magazine got a concrete shape, I, like a perfect Satan, removed her name as the Managing Editor and included Ranjita's name in her place. Ranjita, the stupid, greedy woman, who had not even scribbled a single letter, who had not done any coordination work became the Managing Editor of the magazine because she is my wife. Only the people of the township will know this but what about people outside the State and the country? They will appreciate Ranjita and boost up her foolish pride. Actually we didn't need Urja anymore. She had streamlined everything and made everything easy for us. Following her footsteps we can manage and take credit. I enjoy when she reacts. She abused me and physically assaulted Ranjita as she had become mad with anger at the unparliamentary words uttered by Ranjita and also at her constant provocation. Within a fortnight I called a general meeting and officially declared that Urja is being relieved of all her extra duties and responsibilities with immediate effect. Bindiya Bhalla was given charge of Activity and Neelima Pandey, who had been trying for a long time to grab a chair in the front row was made a House Warden. She managed it by writing four pages report against Urja which has been carefully preserved by Ranjita.

I came to know that Urja was applying at various schools for administrative posts. She has that quality but I know her problems. She would not leave her home and go somewhere else and in the township there was no scope, no vacancy for administrative post in any school. We were enjoying her suffocated condition, her yearnings, her sufferings each and every moment. The face which always used to shine was overcast with cloud. The person who always used to be in the forefront at any event, any function was left behind. This is the result of refusing Veer Parsad.

Urja never neglected her duty as a teacher. Students can make out very easily who are sincere teachers, who really bother for them and who are least concerned. Urja could win the heart of the students because of her genuine concern for them. They all supported her and even now through Orkut and Facebook they express their love and respect for Urja and hatred for Ranjita and myself.

Within a month Urja got the post of Vice Principal and H.O.D. English in a CBSE, English medium school with a strength of more than 6000 students. It was another slap on my cheek because I never expected that this door of opportunity will open before Urja and that too in a school which was rapidly spreading its name in the State and earning reputation. Even we, sometimes invite the Governing Body members of that school as Chief Guest for various functions.

Urja put up her papers and started counting her days. She kept herself absolutely aloof from everything and prepared herself to snap all bonds with the past. Her new employers belong to the businessmen cum educationist class. They have long experience in the field of education and are associated with various schools. They started their own school in a humble way but today, after fifteen years there are five schools under their banner in and outside the township two Engineering Colleges and coaching classes at various places. They are doing a flourishing business, opening a chain of schools which was once my dream. Had the school not come under the Society, I could have become successful in my venture but now I have to save my chair and that of Ranjita first.

I knew it would be impossible for me to prevent Urja from joining that school. But the very thought that my prized possession would be the asset of somebody else started pricking my mind. Urja was after all an experienced, knowledgeable and skilled teacher with a good reputation. Her joining any other school in the same township in a better position definitely was my defeat. I wanted her to continue in my school and suffer. My perverted soul would have relished her choking, suffocating condition. But just as the vultures can see any deadbody from a great height, the owners of that school could sense that Urja was not happy in our school and hence trapped her by alluring her with an attractive bait i.e, the position of Vice Principal and H.O.D. English.

That afternoon all three of us – Ranjita, Padma and myself sat in my chamber and had a long discussion. Ranjita was of course happy; after all the thorn was going to be removed from her path. She had no regret but Padma pretended to be worried and gloomy. She is cleverer than Ranjita. Of course she could sense the consequences also. I instructed them not to misbehave with Urja any more and to be polite in their dealings with her.

Urja's elder son's marriage was fixed. She applied for leave and then just three days before the marriage, her father, who had come to attend the function, got a cerebral attack. He was admitted to the hospital and was kept in the intensive care unit as his condition was serious. Leaving him in the hospital and arranging attendants for him Urja had to go to Delhi and then to Rajasthan where the marriage took place. When she came back with her son and daughter-in-law I was the first to call and congratulate her. I also enquired about the health of her father. Her son's reception was on the next day and purposely I scheduled teachers' interview on that day. Neither I attended the reception function, nor allowed my office staff to do so. My informer and cousin of Padma, who was present there enlightened us with his first-hand experience of the function and about the invitees who attended the programme.

Just one month after this Urja's father-in-law expired in Kolkata. I got an opportunity to show my generosity again. Along with Ranjita, Padma and

Ravi Shastri, I paid a courtesy visit to her house, expressing my condolence. Urja's ailing father was also present in the house who mistook us for her new employers. Condolence meeting was also held in the Assembly at school. But nothing could prevent Urja from her joining another school, leaving behind the salt and peppery memories.

It was a tough time for the English department when Urja left. Ranjita lacked in experience but tried to dominate. Most of the teachers had done M.A. in English after doing B.Sc. or B.Com. Some of them were not even from reputed Colleges or Universities. Their lack of knowledge on the one hand and Ranjita's wrong instructions on the other hand created a volatile situation and children were the worst sufferers. Every now and then Urja's reference was given both by the students as well as the parents. Even people started saying that what Urja used to do single-handed, all other English teachers together could not do that.

Naresh Chandra resigned within two months of his giving back the name and logo to the school. The very thought of two crores which I had to bribe him still pricks my mind but when the ground starts shaking under the feet, no alternative is left but to take preventive measures which sometimes surpasses the means. My skin was saved but what about Ranjita? Will she survive? Ranjita of course has collected letters from the staff members in her support. At right time these will be used but still everything is unpredictable. My dream of carrying on with a hierarchy was shattered. I don't know what will happen after my superannuation! But I have the will power and I know the tricks of winning the hearts of influential people to get their favour. I have spent more than a decade in this school. I don't wish to snap my bonds so easily. The Principal of the new school under the same brand name, who once had worked under me gave me a leg-break by grabbing the position of the Director of three such schools; although I am senior to her in all respects the Society didn't consider me to hold that post. This is my defeat but I have to ignore certain things.

On 15th April 2007 we shifted to our official quarter within the school campus. Staff members were invited to attend the pooja followed by lunch. Ranjita took great pride in showing the house to the staff. I could observe expression of tension in the faces of those staff members who were allotted quarters within the school premises. The very thought of the Principal and his wife being their neighbour snatched away sleep from their eyes; the greenery and peaceful ambience of the campus was vitiated with an evil shadow cast upon it. From the very first day I could sense hostility, dissatisfaction, fear and tension around me but why should I care? In the evening cocktail party was arranged at the expense of school where all VIPs of the city and the State were invited. The party continued till midnight and my subordinate cum neighbours once again were made accustomed to my power.

Life is going on in the same stereotype, monotonous manner. In absence of some of my darling, sweethearts, the school has lost half of its charm and glamour. Another new problem has cropped up. One of the schools in the township has tied up with a coaching centre preparing students for competitive examinations. For the last two-three years all the meritorious students of the school were taking T.C. after class X and joining that school with the hope of cracking IIT and other important competitive examinations. Those who were nurtured and groomed in my school didn't hesitate to join that school for their self interest. I just wonder how any school could take such a daring decision to allow the students to join the classes for competitive examinations neglecting the course for CBSE. The school authority is interested only in business; their intention is to draw the attention of the parents of the meritorious students of our school and also the other reputed schools of the township. Of course we are getting good students with 85 per cent and above in class X Board Exam for class XI but our own students are leaving the school and going somewhere else – that is really painful. But then, this seed of selfishness was sowed by me. I can't expect to reap something else.

The most disheartening fact we are facing whenever we conduct any written test or personal interview is the poor quality of teachers particularly language teachers. Their degree certificates pose a horrifying feature making bare the reality that degrees are not given because of knowledge or real education. They are given just for mugging up something at the time of exam and vomiting them on paper to get some marks. From where will I get teachers like Urja, Madhushree, Mrs. Sita Krishnan? The reason may be the bright students aim at becoming doctor, engineer, or think of taking up any other glamorous profession but never think of becoming a teacher. It is only when they find all other doors closed, they knock at the door of any school to try their luck as a teacher. Teaching is the least in the priority list of any person in the 21st century. Nowadays parents dream big dreams about their children. Ask a child of class two or three – he knows about N.T.S.E. or KVPY ! He knows how many lacs packages are offered by the multinational I.T. Companies. Why should anybody opt for the profession of a teacher? Science or Mathematics teachers can earn some extra money by running coaching or tuition classes but language teachers don't even have that opportunity. Parents are ready to pay a substantial amount of their hard earned money for Science or Maths tuition but for English or any other language? Never. One day will come when a single language teacher will not be available in any school and my experience tells me that day is not far away.

The interference of the Society is also troubling us. I was proceeding very tactfully and was almost successful in killing the snake without breaking the stick. I could have managed the brand name and logo without coming under the aegis of the Society and that would have given me absolute power and freedom but those anonymous letters against me provoking the parents and hurting the ego of the local management stopped me from reaching my goal. Not only the letter, copies of stay order of the district court, revealing the fact of snapping all bonds with the Society were also circulated. I had no other way but to beg for retaining my position before the Society members touching their feet. Except the old lady members, all others become impatient if their monthly fat packets do not reach timely. The money which I extract from the owners of the private schools under C.B.S.E. whenever I visit them as a member of the inspection committee for affiliation, goes to their pocket. Thank God! I need not pay anything to the local shop owners for any expensive purchase as their wards are mostly our students and they are obliged to pay my bills.

My relationship with my counterpart in the other school with the same brand name can never be cordial; it will always remain strained. Whenever we meet in any seminar or function, we behave like strangers. It is so awkward but can't be helped. This lady had ignited the spark of unrest in the school which took the form of conflagration in no time. She managed so many teachers whom I had groomed. With my invested capital, now she is making profit.

Naresh Chandra's futile effort to unite us will never be possible. The owners of the franchise schools are also unhappy with him as they don't have the power to recruit any teacher or administrator of their choice. Everything is controlled by the Society. They have invested huge amount but do not have any power. When some of them tried to absorb Urja, offering her high posts, I brought the matter to the notice of the members of the Society. I told them that my school is one of the best Schools of the Country, producing excellent results year after year due to my leadership and the teamwork of teachers. The Society is opening up new schools, that is appreciable but why should my teachers be shifted? It resulted into applying through proper channel and bringing of no objection certificates at the time of facing the interviews. Who will dare ask for a no-objection-certificate from me? Should I not make his/her life a hell? The long road I traversed had always been uneven, rough. I don't want to forget anything. Whenever I think about my hardships and struggles, I get redoubled strength to continue with my effort and proceed further towards my goal. I have achieved much in life. But I don't want to halt; I have to keep going because even a frog kicks on the face of a dead elephant. I will stop only at the drop of the final curtain.

Urja has challenged me. She will expose me and my wife before the world. Let her try. Even if people know about my treachery, my atrociousness, they will come to me for favour. If anybody needs job that person will try to please me by lying on the ground and licking my boots. If somebody wants the admission of his child, he will be ready to do anything, including offering me blank cheques. What will Urja get by exposing me? Nothing. People will just laugh at her foolishness, her impractical, immature behaviour. She has challenged me that she will prove that "Pen is mightier than sword." Who is using sword? She, most probably does not know that money and position are mightier than even pen. I have accepted her challenge. Let us see who can have the last laugh ?

3

Ranjita's Reminiscence

My dream palace took a shape before my eyes – bit by bit. It has to outshine the Principal's house in the hills which taught me to dream about my own house – officially earned. Veer Parsad has wiped off all colours from my life but has compensated everything in a different way; otherwise that Ranjita, who spent eighteen years of her life as a Primary Teacher is now the Vice Principal of the most reputed school, getting four promotions within a span of ten years! Waoh! Sometimes I just can't believe at my own success. When we attended the Golden Jubilee Celebrations of my parents in Mumbai how proud and elated I was feeling amidst my siblings and relatives. Getting the attention and respect from all corners add glow to the face but why can't I get rid of the dark circles around my eyes? And why inspite of getting everything as per my wish, I am constantly feeling the thorn-pricks in my mind? Why is there a void, a craving for happiness in my mind? I have got a slap at the most precious and coveted area of my life that is my femininity. Veer Parsad has insulted my femininity by seeking from other women the pleasure and satisfaction which I failed to give him. He has given me everything I wanted, money, coveted position, greatest importance, everything but somehow I could not keep pace with his vulgarity and perversion in the matter of sex. He wants to do it sometimes on the dinner table, sometimes in front of the mirror, sometimes even under the shower.

Till the birth of Amar, we met once a month but with age, the more I started losing interest in sex, the more he started getting the urge. Ignoring the comfort and peace of the cosy home, he became attracted towards the outside world–glamorous women, their beauty, sensuality, appeal….. every time new and different from ordinary, familiar Ranjita whose sagging breasts and layers of tyre-like flab around the waist above the flat buttocks could not attract Veer Parsad anymore.

People live in present. How easily today becomes yesterday and a heavenly pleasure of this moment is stored into the treasure trove of memory to be taken out occasionally to cherish the beauty of it. My initial years of married life with

Veer Parsad, shifting from a metro city to the mystic tranquillity of the hills and tea gardens, sharing the warmth under the same quilt in the small cottage type staff quarter, going on excursions with students, pleasure ride by toy train, rendezvous at Kali Jhora, endless, meaningless chit – chats, birth of Ipsita and Amar within a gap of two years –all seem to be incidents of our past life. We used to sit hours together with our babies, watching their each and every movement, amused at their toothless smile and worried by their cries. Their growing up, admission to school, infant stage to childhood to adolescence covered the best part of our life. Simultaneously our teaching job, Veer's House Master ship, Principal's occasional scoldings – all these went on as usual. Our world was limited but there was joy, hope, light and love within that limit. A visit to Bhutan or Gangtok (one of our colleagues used to call it Gun – Thok) was a bonus like the topping of a cherry on a piece of cake.

One thing I had noticed right from the beginning of our married life, that is, Veer Parsad is very ambitious unlike his other family members. In fact it is his persistent effort in any work which has elevated his position to the zenith and like a pin attached to a magnet I have also been lifted up along with him. I have played my role in adding fuel to the fire of ambition in his mind. The thought of overcoming the sentiments of mediocrity obsessed my mind and in this game of climbing up the ladder, the delicate strings which had so long maintained the synergy of our relationship, were pulled apart. Veer Parsad and I remained husband and wife in the eyes of the society but the relationship had lost its charm and was transformed to only a habit of staying together.

Veer Parsad started applying at different schools for the post of Principal and ultimately became successful. When he informed me, a Kaleidoscope of thoughts quickly flashed through my mind and Ranjita died on that very day.

Next three months were spent on packing and planning for the future and attending farewell parties. The thought of leaving the hills made my mind heavier but I didn't allow tears to swell up in my eyes. The Tibetan carpet presented by our colleagues still adorns our drawing room floor and reminds us of the hills.

I had to sit back at home for a few months after shifting to the new place. There was no vacancy at that moment but I was sure Veer Parsad would find out a way. We tried our best to please the Pro-Vice Chairman of the school. Then came the Annual Day of the school and taking advantage of his position Veer Parsad gave me the responsibility of compering the programme although I was not associated to the school directly. Our long stay at the residential missionary school had improved my pronunciation and diction although Veer could not overcome his North Indian style. I compered the programme and I think, it went off well although the staff members and parents passed comments and giggled behind my back. Veer had taught me not to react at any situation, so, I ignored their comments and gestures. When time came for filling up the annual requisition of staff, Veer Parsad felt the need of a Senior Mistress for the Primary

Wing. He started inviting the Pro-Vice Chairman quite often over dinner. The Pro-Vice Chairman smiled and said "Why do you need to appoint a Senior Mistress from outside? you have one at home, shift her to school." The pegs of golden liquid with occasional falling down of my pallu, revealing the cleavage of my padded breasts worked well. There is one advantage with old people; they get the pleasure of feeling soft boobs simply touching the spongy pads.

In 1995, in the month of April, I stepped into the school premises as the Senior Mistress of the Primary Wing, much to the chagrin of the senior teachers. From that day Veer Parsad became 'Sir' to me and till date I call him 'Sir' only. Life was not very smooth. Veer Parsad's increasing greed led him to the path of corruption. People were hostile and never tried to hide their feelings. Parents were dissatisfied, teachers were dissatisfied, complaint against Veer Parsad reached the Society at Delhi and his transfer order came as a bolt from the blue. He was not willing to accept this transfer and somehow managed a whole year. But situation worsened and one fine morning he was severely beaten up by the parents. They demanded his immediate transfer and he had no other way but to accept. I had to lose my post of Senior Mistress and joined the new school as a T.G.T., teaching History at the middle school level. The then Acting Principal who had a chronic throat problem had to step down to the position of Vice Principal.

I still remember the hot summer day of May when we reached this steel city with Ipsita and Amar. As the Principal's quarter was not vacant because the founder Principal of the school had gone to the Middle East on deputation without surrendering his quarter, we were given a temporary accommodation in a small quarter. Turnwise our lunch and dinner were arranged by the teachers staying in the same sector. The present H.O.D. Science was staying just opposite to our quarter and she used to prepare varieties of dishes with fish for us everyday which Veer Parsad relished with his daily quota of whisky. She could make a place for herself in our mind and we decided to lift her up from the position of PRT.

A chaotic condition was prevailing in the institution. Senior persons were continuing on the same posts for more than a decade. The previous Principal had deprived the staff of their dues with a sugar coated smile and earned popularity. The Acting Principal was a simple lady, a spinster with chronic problem in her vocal chord. There was no feeling of dedication among the staff. Indiscipline was clearly visible everywhere; gossipping and whispering, leg pulling of each other, laxity in work etc., were the hall marks of the school. Veer Parsad called a general meeting and addressed the teachers. He said that he was against any lobbying and dirty politics and he expected team work and cooperation from all.

Veer Parsad has the capacity to talk for hours together and to preach all those things which he never practises. He also knows how to terrorise people by insulting them publicly in the general meetings. Out of fear, in order to protect their prestige and honour nobody ever dared opening his or her mouth before him although inwardly everybody suffered and disagreed to him. The only exception is Urja who never hesitated to call a 'spade', a spade. Veer Parsad's dominating character and magnetic personality helped him to secure his position as the Principal and as soon as he was successful in consolidating his position at the completion of one year, he elevated my position from T.G.T. (History) to the Senior Mistress of the Middle Wing. Whisperings and mud slingings started but nothing could take a violent shape as it had taken at our previous school. Two other ladies were also given the posts of Senior Mistress Pre-Primary Wing and Senior Mistress Primary Wing respectively. Urja was appointed as a T.G.T. English. Who had imagined that one day she would turn out to be a conflagration?

Veer Parsad met with an accident within a few months of his joining as the Principal. He was driving himself and going to the house of Reema Jha, the A.V. Hall In charge, the then heartthrob of Veer. The official car was damaged but Veer luckily was saved with only some minor injuries. A crispy story started spreading from mouth to mouth and reached even our previous school. Veer was not ashamed but he never thought of my prestige; how difficult it became for me to show my face to others! I never guessed what was in store for me while my fate smiled twisting her lips.

Veer's unusual attraction towards Urja could not escape my eyes. She became the sand grain of my eyes right from day one. I started thinking day and night how to harass this bewitching beauty. In all workplaces there are some people who instead of doing their work, just try to flatter and please the boss and the best way to do that is to complain about a person who is not liked by the boss. This institution is also not an exception. A group of teachers became my followers or in plain and simple words my 'chamchas' and didn't leave any stone unturned to create problems for Urja. They turn wise made complaints against her son who had taken admission in class VIII. No mother can tolerate any complaint or false report against her son and she also lost her mental peace. In the half-yearly examination, Urja's son could not do well as following my instructions; teachers had given him very poor marks. She was humiliated in the meeting by Veer Parsad and accused of favouring her own section and also for the poor performance of her son. This was surprising to me but hardly did I know about Veer's approach and dirty proposal to Urja and her firm rejection. Moreover Veer was compelled to divert his attention to the sex-bomb Madhushree, rejected by Urja. Urja reacted very sharply in the meeting and refused to accept the false charges against her. My ego was satisfied at her humiliation and I felt elated at the enmity which started between Veer Parsad and Urja. Next day when all teachers submitted their Teaching Diaries with monthly lesson plan, my eyes got fixed at one page of Urja's diary. She had expressed her protest in a unique way by composing a poem in her diary which I copied in my personal diary. Even after so many years I turn the pages of my diary to read her poem:

Divine Inspiration

I had kept myself aloof from the world
I was surrounded by a dark shadow
Deep frustrations and depressions had
Numbed my feelings
My wounded soul wanted to break open the window.
Piercing the blanket of darkness came a bright ray
Which rebuked at me and said –
"Leave aside all tensions, all botheration
For the future and past
Don't murder your today for the sake of Tomorrow or yesterday.
Burn yourself like me, spread your fragrance and reflect your flame,
Smile, be happy and gay."
I stood up, leaving aside all despair
Life seemed to be meaningful to me
I remembered the missions for which I had been sent.
I have to fulfil it, however difficult it might be
Nothing can prevent me from proceeding forward.
I am above all criticisms and appreciations
No barriers can obstruct my way
I care neither for rewards, nor deprivations.
Not realising the value of diamond
People are attracted by the glitter of ordinary glass
God is the supreme judge of the world
To me only Heavenly Judgement is precious.

Most probably Urja could feel that the intimacy between Veer Parsad and Madhushree was the cause of her harassment and humiliation at the workplace and I could feel that the water would flow down the river a long way. The spark in Urja would definitely take the shape of conflagration one day and burn everything with a blaze. However, I tried to gain something from the situation and if stealing the expression of any other person from his or her literary creation is called plagiarism, exactly that's what I did the next day.

In absence of Veer, I was asked to hand over the report cards of the students of each class who had secured the 1st position in the Annual Examination, on the stage in the Morning Assembly. After presenting the children with their report cards, I addressed the gathering in the Assembly and stealing the idea from Urja's poem, I preached my words of wisdom – "Work hard selflessly, burn yourself, spread your fragrance and reflect your flame." From the stage I could see the fire in the eyes of Urja, as she heard her own words in my mouth. How easy it is to provoke the sincere fools and also to take credit at their cost! It's a game played everywhere and why should an educational institution be an exception? That was just the beginning of my game and I made Urja realise that time and again what a veteran player I am !

The Madhushree episode continued for long three years although occasionally he used to try new faces. I learnt how to ignore people and face any awkward situation with normal expression in my face. My target was the Vice Principal's chair and within two years of our joining the school, the Vice Principal was sent to a new school under the Society, in collaboration to a Cement Company as the Principal, at the recommendation of Veer Parsad although she was not willing to shift to the interior, 40 Kms. from the capital.

Even after becoming the Principal, Veer Parsad sometimes could not overcome his rural, rustic nature; particularly, whenever he was angry he used to forget his position and status. Several times he raised his hands on me in front of the class IV staff of the school who were appointed as our domestic help also. Turnwise they used to work in our bungalow. Our children grew up amidst our quarrels, sometimes exchange of heated words and arguments, sometimes shattered silence. I could have left Veer Parsad and stayed with my parents together with my children but I preferred dragging on with him somehow, otherwise there was no chance of getting this unique identity of the Vice Principal.

No one, neither my parents and relatives, nor my colleagues ever came to know about my pain, sufferings and humiliation, although rumours continued to spread through the brazen mouthed support staff.

Now after occupying the chair, I can understand why is it necessary to show power and terrorise people. These are required to keep them under subjugation. Veer Parsad was doing exactly that and he tried to show that if required he didn't spare me even. Manipulation and exploitation are nothing else but exhibiting authority to keep everybody under control. Veer Parsad started behaving in such a way with the experienced teachers that one after another they started leaving the school, getting better position elsewhere. He was, actually clearing the field for me to score the significant goal. But in the matter of sex he was least bothered to consider my dignity and prestige and shamelessly continued with Madhushree, Padma, Kanchan, Reema, Aarti, Kajol, Komolika, Neelima, Bindiya etc. etc. etc. myriad, innumerable women. Those who kept their mouth shut are today enjoying respectable position and those who reacted or refused, either had to leave the school or are suffering unbearable humiliation and pain. Sometimes he used to cross limit and acted desperately, not understanding where to draw a line. The Spinster Physical Education teacher Ritu Devi raised an alarm when Veer reached her house at 10.00 p.m. with greed in his eyes and dirt in his mind. Her neighbour, the dance teacher came to her rescue and Veer had to come back home, unsuccessful in satisfying his lust. Ritu was given shelter that night by Lalita, the dance teacher and next morning her father came, getting a call from Lalita and took her back to Indore.

Veer's next target was Moumita, the Biology teacher whose husband was in Hyderabad for completing a course he had been undergoing at that time. She had taken leave due to sickness; her daughter had come to school. Veer took the opportunity and driving the school car, went to her house during the school hours. What happened after that is still a mystery but that Biology teacher narrated the story (fact) of Veer's coming to her house in absence of her husband to the people of the township in the pandal of Durga Puja (to be on the safeside, pretending to be innocent) and this crispy story became a source of entertainment for sometime till Veer's next venture.

The Madhushree episode was a regular one of course, which continued atleast for three years and Padma is still batting, not out, but I am handicapped in this matter because like Veer, I also depend upon Padma almost in any and every matter. I don't hesitate to say that I have soft corner for both Padma and Moumita inspite of knowing Veer's weakness for them. These two ladies are loyal to me and at every step I get their help and cooperation

The cold war between Madhushree and Padma was not unknown to anyone. Whenever Padma found any threat to her existence, she followed the Chanakya Neeti of trampling the enemy under shoes and totally destroying it.

Madhushree refused to attend the Golden Jubilee Celebrations of the oldest school under the Society and Urja was sent in her place. Amar had also accompanied the team and after coming back he gave an assertive report about Urja. Lalita, the dance teacher who was also one of the escort teachers reported to me that as instructed by Veer Parsad, Urja attended a seminar on inclusivity which was attended by Veer also and he offered Urja a lift in his car which she politely refused.

Madhushree started feeling insecure and lost all interest in work. She was the class teacher of Amar when he was in class X. She made a serious mistake in filling up the form containing name and other details of the examinees of CBSE

Class X and forgot to take the signature of Amar before he left for Inter School Tennis tournament in Rajasthan. Veer Parsad was furious with her. He had got what he wanted from Madhushree, now she could no more attract him. Her drawbacks seemed to be more prominent to him rather than her talents.

Urja got the Divine Justice she had been seeking for. She was awarded the 1st prize at the State level Essay Writing Competition on Petroleum Conservation. Veer got an opportunity to withdraw the responsibilities from Madhushree and give them to Urja. Three years back he had done the same thing by depriving Mrs. Sita Raman and her assistant Bindiya Bhalla, giving everything to Madhushree.

Bindiya had become busy with her newly born son. People say this son was gifted to her by Veer Parsad. The situation was quite alarming for me. Urja also got felicitation from the Rotary club on Teachers' Day as the 'Best Teacher.' She could produce excellent results in CBSE Board Examination also. Everybody started praising her for her hard work and quality of work. Veer had to give her promotion and the position of Activity Incharge, H.O.D. English and the Managing Editor of the School magazine. Madhushree was asked to assist her which perhaps she didn't like. I was trying to know the real intention of Veer behind his generosity towards Urja. It was difficult for me to swallow or digest that simply because of Urja's talents she was given so much importance. I tried to convince Veer that it would not be wise on his part to ignore Madhushree totally. I was feeling threatened because I know my husband better than anybody else. He was attracted towards Urja in the same way as a moth is attracted towards a burning candle. I could visualise this fire will not only destroy him but ruin our home, our children, our career everything. Veer's passion for Urja was uncontrollable. The more he faced rejection the more his lust increased. He wished to get her company everyday, everytime on pretext of work. Urja, the ambitious fire brand English teacher started floating on cloud nine, cherishing the jealousy of her competitors. She started working in such a way, as if the school belongs to her and would not run without her. Veer Parsad started praising her in the meetings, in the Assembly in front of the faculty, in front of the students. Everywhere only one name 'Urja' reverberated. Even my image got suppressed because of Urja. Veer started discussing important issues regarding the school directly with Urja. She could not realise what was the real intention of Veer.

Madhushree and a number of teachers wrote complaint letters to the local management bringing charges of sexual harassment against Veer. They also submitted resignation letters and joined hands with the Chairman and the promoters of the new school under the same brand name. Veer Parsad called Madhushree into his chamber and tried to convince her not to leave the school. He also told her "You carry on with your work. You will be given back everything. I didn't want to give any responsibility to Urja but she has proved herself. That's why I had to give her some important responsibilities. Within a year I will give you P.G.T. also. You are not able to imagine to what extent I can lift you up. "But no amount of allurement could hold her back and she left the school without caring for her career. Before going she didn't forget to tell Urja whatever Veer Parsad had told her."

The English department was in a turmoil as Mrs.Sita Raman had also left. Another senior teacher was given administrative post in the Primary Section and was shifted there. I myself had no background in English although in order to be eligible for teaching Senior Secondary classes I managed the Masters Degree in English from the State University with the help of a Professor whose financial condition improved after I started attending his tuition classes. I managed the notes prepared by a junior teacher Jolly when she had done M.A. in English. This degree was required to enable me to teach classes XI and XII and three years experience of teaching Senior Secondary classes is a criterion for becoming Vice Principal. The subject which I used to teach i.e., History was there upto class X in our school. That's why it became absolutely necessary for me to do M.A. in English for teaching in classes XI and XII which is compulsory at the Senior Secondary level. Padma also joined M.A. classes with me and I got a lot of help from her. At that time Urja alone managed the situation and improved the status and standard of English of our school by her individual performance as well as by improving the English of the students. Her students made record in scoring 95 and 98 in Core English in XII Board Exam which is also a record for the school till date.

I could sense Urja's ignoring attitude towards me or maybe it was my inferiority complex. Whatever it is, I could not tolerate Veer Parsad's praise for Urja. Not understanding Veer Parsad's intention Urja used to like him and respect him but I could feel her hatred towards me. Under such circumstances I had no other way but to take the help of Padma.

Padmavati has struggled a lot in her life. She is loyal to me inspite of her physical relationship with Veer Parsad. Veer and Padma are inseparable. She starts her day wishing Veer early in the morning over telephone and before going to bed at night, if for any reason she is not able to talk to Veer, she spends sleepless night. She remains with Veer like his shadow and brings him to the right track when he walks a few steps with any woman on a wrong track. Her duty is to inform me about the intimacy of any woman with Veer and to make her life a hell. That's why I like her so much. I have allowed Veer Parsad to get his sexual satisfaction from Padma as I am unable to give him what he wants. Padma knows that in order to retain her position she has to listen to me and follow my instructions blindly.

For three and a half years Urja had her way. She made Veer Parsad dance to her tune. On 2nd October we celebrated Gandhi Jayanti and Inter School English Debate. Urja, being the H.O.D. was the coordinator of the programme.

Earlier Mrs. Sita Raman used to do it but Veer Parsad had never shown her honour by allowing her to sit next to him and the Chief Guest at the time of any programme. In our school, the House Wardens or the programme coordinators are supposed to sit with the Principal and the Chief Guest at the time of the respective programme which they coordinate. No one ever thought of giving that much honour to Mrs. Sita Raman and I didn't encourage it as I was cherishing this idea of becoming the H.O.D. of Language in mind, to cut a figure in the intellectual world and impress the elite society. Also it would have paved the way for me to become the Principal. I was irritated like anything when I found Urja sitting next to Veer Parsad and watching the programme. Veer must have told her otherwise how will she have that much audacity? After the programme, when the Chief Guest was taken to Veer's room for refreshment, Urja was supervising outside the room. Veer sent the Senior Mistress Middle Wing Mrs. Uma Banerjee to call Urja and ordered the Refreshment In charge to bring her refreshment also. My blood boiled with rage but I could not do anything in front of the Chief Guest and the Judges for the debate. Veer was showing so much concern for Urja that the guests also became interested to know about her and her platter was full to create a unique identity for her by which the guests were much impressed. My image was absolutely suppressed and Urja was shining with pride and glory.

In the evening Veer Parsad was going out somewhere, driving the car himself. Ipsita asked him where he was going, to which he replied, "That's none of your business." I kept quiet because I was familiar with the situation. It was not difficult for me to understand where he was going but I had the fear that he would be publicly insulted as I knew the nature and character of Urja; she would never give in to the weakness and dirty desires of Veer Parsad. She only wanted to climb up the topmost rung of the ladder, capitalising on her efficiency, hardwork and talent.

Veer Parsad didn't even look at my face while going out. At about eleven p.m., he rang me and told me to have my dinner as he would take his dinner outside. He jokingly told me, "I'm with my girlfriend." I said – "Nice, carry on." I don't know when Veer Parsad came back that night because I went to my room and locked the door. Next morning Veer woke up with great difficulty and after getting ready when we were about to enter the car, the driver pointed out at a remarkable scratch mark and dent on the front left side of the car. Veer Parsad felt uneasy and could not say anything. I remembered the accident which had happened in the past when Veer visited Reema Jha's house in absence of her husband. I was scared of visualising the casting of an evil shadow on my life. But I had to give time to Veer because who knows him better than me? He doesn't take much time to lose interest in any woman. Those are temporary phases but I am permanent. I knew he will come back to me. The end of any passion is hatred and it would not be different in the case of Urja, particularly when she was not interested.

When the school was passing through a period of crisis, there was fear at every moment of losing our position. The parents, time to time, created problem. A parents association was formed who met and discussed about their action plan. Padma started getting threatening calls because people knew that she was close to Veer Parsad. I had tension regarding the safety of Amar and Ipsita. Veer doesn't smoke. But he takes one or two pegs in the evening before dinner regularly, which, somehow I don't like. I tried my best to persuade him to abandon this habit but failed. Whenever I insisted he used to be very much annoyed with me. Once I picked up the glass and bottle and locked the door of the small built-in bar on the wall. Next evening he didn't come home from the school and even Padma could not tell me where he was. I tried to contact him over his mobile and asked him where he was to which he replied – "Mein Jahannum Me Hun, Tujhe Keya?" (I am in the Hell, what's your problem?). I told him I was on fast due to Karwa Chauth. Until and unless he comes back I won't be able to take any food. He told me not to wait for me. I told Veer that Amar and Ipsita would also not have their dinner if he doesn't come home. He became furious and uttered abusive words. What was so attractive that could hold him back from his wife who was on fast for his welfare and the children who refused to take food in absence of their father? Even after knowing that children would not take food, he came home at ten o'clock. After taking our dinner when we were about to take rest for the night, he got a call in his mobile and in a tensed voice said, "Mr. Gupta doesn't stay here." I could understand that he was managing the situation; the person on the other side of the line was not asking for any Mr. Gupta but Veer Parsad himself and if I am not wrong Veer Parsad had spent his evening with that person. It may be Maumita or Komolika or Aarti or Sunita ! Why did he try to hide it from me?

I lost my mental peace absolutely. Not because Veer was flirting with the lady teachers but because he was giving so much importance to Urja. She became the most popular person in the school. Ignoring me, teachers and students started consulting her in each and every matter. She was preparing the duty roster for any function. She conducted the written examinations for the interviewees and also interviewed them as subject expert. At the time of Staff selection Veer Parsad started having lunch with her at the break along with the External Head Interviewer. This lunch was arranged by Bindiya Bhalla – the Home Science teacher and she started spreading rumour about Urja. Her husband was a regular supplier of whisky for the distinguished guests of the Principal and she was the ex-girl friend of Veer Parsad. It was quite obvious that she would be jealous of Urja.

There was one more reason for giving so much importance to Urja. She used to write everything on behalf of Veer. All his speeches, reports etc. sent to various places, "From the Principal's Desk" in the school magazine, his Annual Day Report everything was written by Urja. Not only that, Urja also prepared the speeches to be delivered by the Chief Guest and other guests for any function. They just read out the papers prepared by Urja in praise of the school and Veer Parsad, making him popular. With borrowed words of Urja, Veer Parsad carved a niche in the intellectual world. Everybody praised him for his strong English and writing style but no one came to know that it was Urja who deserved the whole credit.

Padma started playing her role again as she had played earlier. She started harassing Urja in every possible way. She instructed the typists not to type the Press Releases or other write-ups of Urja timely. She misplaced important files and documents which were related to Urja's work. She started giving false reports about Urja to Veer Parsad and provoked others to do so. I also did the same. On the one hand Padma, one the other hand I myself carried on with the dirty game against Urja. I am the Principal's wife. Does any one have the guts to oppose me? On my face no one has the right to say any thing and I care a fig for the comments passed about me in my absence or behind me. I created problems and unamicable situations between Urja and some of her colleagues and collected complaint letters against her. She started feeling insecured. The first step of winning a battle against an enemy is to shake his or her confidence. Due to constant mental torture and disturbance Urja started losing her confidence. It was time for Veer Parsad also to play a different tune and clip the wings of Urja because ultimately he realised that giving too much importance to Urja will result in digging the grave for his wife Ranjita. Ranjita had to establish the fact that she was indispensable otherwise there was no justification in her becoming the Vice Principal and then the Principal. Urja was gaining popularity and the fragrance of her fame and talent was spreading far and wide. She had to be undermined, belittled in order to bring Ranjita to the forefront. Inspite of being the Principal's wife and the Senior Mistress, Secondary Wing, Ranjita still could not create a ripple in the steel township; everywhere there was gossiping only about her rude behaviour, incorrect English, manipulation and cunningness whereas Urja could carve a niche proving her talent in the literary field, in her excellent coordination of all cultural functions, her teaching etc. My grudge against her was she was destroying my image unknowingly and Veer Parsad's grudge against her was she dared to refuse him.

In 2003 the Hon'ble Governor of the State was the Chief Guest for our Foundation Day. Urja conducted the function and compered the cultural programme. It was highly appreciated by all. Veer Parsad wanted to present an album to the Governor and his wife. He called Urja and asked her to prepare it with nice caption for each photograph. When she completed it, Veer Parsad was highly impressed by the artistic sense of Urja. She had composed a poem and included it at the end in the name of the Principal and staff. She showed it to Veer Parsad in the evening and left it with him. Padma was asked to keep it in her almirah. After two days before presenting the album to the Hon'ble Governor,

Veer Parsad brought it home to show me. "This album will be presented to the Governor. Have a look at it whenever you are free." Next morning he went to school and it being a holiday I was at home. I opened the album and turning a few pages, was shocked to find ink smudges at various places on the typed captions. Not only that, wrong captions were pasted at various places. This was an opportunity to harass Urja. Veer Parsad came home at 2 p.m. When people are tired and hungry, fire can be added to the fuel in their mind by saying something unpleasant. Knowing that very well, I drew his attention as soon as he removed his shoes. "Have you seen the album properly?" - I asked. "Why; what happened to it?" "It is in a horrible state," I exclaimed. "What nonsense are you talking about? Do you know it has been prepared by Urja? Can't you see anything good in her? You always try to find fault with her." I opened the pages of the album and drew his attention towards it. Then he flared up and hurled abuses at Urja. I laughed inwardly at my first victory against Urja and silently congratulated Padma for spoiling the album. The memory of getting a slap from Veer Parsad a few months back when I said something against Urja was still fresh in my mind.

Veer Parsad could not enjoy his afternoon nap and went to school at 3 p.m. again calling Padma from her home. Both of them tried to contact Urja frantically but there was no response at the repeated ring of her telephone, confirming the fact that she was not at home. Padma, ultimately had to type the captions again and they spent the whole evening in rearranging the album. Padma is an expert in damaging the image of others while enhancing that of her own but she always got my support in this matter because she helped in removing the thorns from my path while doing that for herself. We have that understanding. Without joining hands it is not possible for us to be successful in our mission.

Veer Parsad will never know that the album prepared so painstakingly by Urja was actually spoilt by Padma. Till date he is under the impression that it was Urja who had spoilt the album although she is innocent. It was her creation, her art, why should anybody ruin one's own creation?

November 2003 was an eventful time for both Urja and me. Hornby ELT Seminar was held at Chennai and New Delhi, organised by British Council. Veer Parsad wanted both of us to attend the seminar. I wanted to go to Chennai because my brother was staying there. Urja preferred going to Delhi because her children were staying there. As a coincidence Veer Parsad also went to Delhi at the same time to attend another programme and the fire started burning in my heart fuelled by colourful imagination.

I could not benefit much from the seminar but Urja was much benefited by it. She became a member of ELTecs, developed a permanent friendship with the Course Director Stella Smyth and created a ripple in the field of International literary world also. The more she excelled the more I started getting nightmare. She came to the notice of the Board of Governors, became popular with the students, teachers and parents because of her caring, helpful nature and also her talents. In my life she is nothing else but weed and weed should be uprooted before it can grow.

The school was running well without any interference from the Society. Veer Parsad had managed a stay order against the termination order challenging which, a case was filed in the High Court. This time was ripe for elevating me to the position of Vice Principal: Once my position gets consolidated it will not be possible for the Society to remove me if at all it is associated with the school in future.

In April 2004 Veer Parsad promoted me to the position of Vice Principal. My long cherished dream came true. But in order to get the support of the majority we had to please them. Those who never expected higher grade were given so. Mr. Ravi Shastri, who used to conduct the Morning Assembly in absence of Veer Parsad was also given promotion and made the Vice Principal. Urja congratulated me and I suppressed my smile at her ignorance. She couldn't understand what was lying in store for her in the near future.

Veer Parsad announced that he would delegate most of his responsibilities on the academic side to me and the upkeep of the school will be taken care of by Mr.Shastri. This was my opportunity to snatch everything from Urja in the name of seniority and keep her cornered again. I utilised my absolute authority to humiliate Urja at various situations. I called my favourite teachers and instructed them not to follow her instructions in the matter of Activity.

In order to please me and to get my favour they agreed without any hesitation. The first incident happened when the P.E. teacher brought to my notice the duty roster for the school and House Appointees for supervision after Assembly and after school at 1 p.m. This duty roster was prepared by Urja and followed by the Prefectorial body members. Without consulting with Urja I prepared a new duty roster with my signature as the Vice Principal and instructed the P.E.teacher to circulate it to the Appointees. The same was circulated to the House Wardens and it was a humiliation for Urja when the students asked her which duty roster they should follow!

The second thing I did was whenever departmental meetings were conducted by Urja, all of a sudden I used to enter and interfere in her work purposely. Whatever she said I used to contradict that, puzzling the teachers and disturbing and humiliating Urja a lot. This I did with the intention of curbing the importance of Urja and shattering her mental peace because one thing was clear to me that she was highly ambitious. Ruining her confidence was absolutely necessary to make her unpopular and to make my position consolidated.

In the beginning of 2005 my fate looked at me with a smiling face. At the end of 2004, along with Urja two other teachers Neelima Pandey and Sudipa Sarkar had participated in the Essay Writing Competition conducted by Avantika. Like every year, that year also Urja got the prize and Merit Certificate and it was given to her in the Morning Assembly by Veer Parsad. Neelima and Sudipa started burning with jealousy. They discussed amongst themselves and directly spoke to the Director of Avantika from whom they came to know that invitation letters had been sent to the school in the name of Urja and Neelima to attend a cultural programme and prize distribution ceremony to receive their prizes from Ex HRD Minister Shri Murli Manohar Joshi as both of them qualified – Urja in the category of English and Neelima in Hindi. Veer Parsad had kept the letters suppressed because he did not want them to come to the limelight. Sudipa however had not got anything but she started spreading the rumour that the Activity Incharge Urja had not sent her essay to Avantika whereas the fact is that Urja had not only sent Sudipa's essay but also paid her entry fee which has not been returned by Sudipa till date. I know this woman, Sudipa-Sarkar is a Bengali medium pass-out and used to teach music and dance in another school of the township but as it is difficult to get English teachers, she had to be recruited as a teacher of English. She is a typical manipulative woman who can indulge into village-type politics quite often but I need the help of such type of woman in order to fulfil my desire. I wanted to get rid of Urja by hook or by crook. Thorns are to be picked up by thorns only. The whole problem had cropped up because Avantika had made a mistake in sending the prize of Urja when Veer Parsad had written a letter to them that the teachers would not be able to go to Delhi to receive the prizes. Poor Urja, she was ignorant of the whole thing. Neelima Pandey and Sudipa Sarkar met the Principal and told him that they had spoken to the Director of Avantika and came to know that Neelima also won a prize and was invited to Delhi and Sudipa's essay was not sent. This of course was utter lie. Veer Parsad became furious and shouted at them. When Neelima failed in convincing Veer Parsad she instigated Urja and told her that every year Urja got the prize for essay writing but Veer Parsad suppressed her invitation letters and deprived her of receiving the prizes from the eminent personalities.

Veer Parsad found himself in a very embarrassing position and tried to put the blame on Urja. Provoked by Neelima when she asked Veer Parsad very politely whether they can just see that invitation letter once, he made meaningful gestures at her and said – "Come, sit on my lap, I'll show you the letter." She turned red in humiliation and was about to go out of the room when Veer Parsad shouted at her and said-"You are depriving others of what they deserve. Since responsibilities have been given to you, you are trying to manipulate everything in your favour." That was enough to add fuel to the fire. Honest people, when falsely accused, lose their temperament very soon and same was the case with Urja. When her honesty was at stake she could not hold her patience and shouted back at Veer Parsad in his office, hurling abuses at him. Already she was overburdened with work and the constant mental torture and humiliation which she had to face created a pressure on her nerve, hence, the outburst was natural and expected. We were just waiting for this moment. In order to remove her from her position and responsibilities with false accusations, some excuses were required and what could have been a greater offence than shouting at and abusing the Principal? People could not know what had happened in Veer Parsad's office but everybody saw Urja coming out of his office with her face red in anger, shouting and abusing Veer Parsad.

Our next opportunity came when Urja applied for leave for going to Chennai for the Viva Voce of her M.Phil. Veer Parsad refused to sanction her leave as he didn't want her to add any more qualification to improve her C.V. Veer Parsad told her not to go as Blessing Ceremony was scheduled at that time, but Urja could not change her programme as without attaining Viva Voce her M.Phil. Exam would have remained incomplete. She arranged everything for the Blessing Ceremony and left for Chennai. When she came back I started ignoring her openly and showed my authority. I had decided to compel her to leave the school.

Before the beginning of the new session, a meeting of the Executive Committee was held which was attended by Ravi Shastri, Uma Banerjee, Padma and myself. After discussing various issues, Veer Parsad started discussing about Urja. Everything was discussed and decided upon between us at home of course.

Veer Parsad, in the meeting said – "No one is indispensable. Mrs.Urja Sen has started thinking that without her the school would not function properly. She has been showing airs quite often, so much so that she didn't hesitate to shout at the Principal. She is showing her superiority to all. In the ministry reshuffling takes place time to time, so we have also decided to reshuffle responsibilities and duties. We will divide Activity into two parts – Literary side will be supervised by Urja and Cultural side by Bindiya Bhalla. What do you think?"

Padma and I had given him this idea because we knew that practically there was nothing to do in literary activities except conducting Inter-school English Debate once a year; and Bindiya Bhalla was already a House Warden, so it will not be possible for her to manage Activity and naturally the most important areas will come under my control. I will keep everything in my grip and for name sake Bindiya Bhalla will be made Cultural Activity In charge. As soon as Veer made the proposal, Padma and I agreed to that. Ravi Shastri and Uma Banerjee had to nod their head supporting the proposal like puppets. With great difficulty I had to suppress my joy; just imagined the face of Urja, her reactions at this important announcement. In the evening I went to the Sai Baba Temple with Padma and offered flowers, coconut, sweets and incense sticks.

On 31st March the General Meeting was called and it was officially declared by Veer Parsad. He had of course called Urja and Bindiya Bhalla separately and informed them. Veer Parsad kept the suspense till the end and post facto made the announcement when everybody thought that the meeting had been adjourned. There was pin-drop silence in the M.P. Hall. I was trying to see the reaction of Urja but she remained normal till the end. Later on I came to know that after going home she rang up Padma and Veer Parsad separately and thanked them for ruining her career.

Urja didn't turn up for the next two days. I called Komolika and asked her to call Urja as it was already scheduled that she would come to the house of Komolika on the next Saturday. Komolika rang her up and she behaved in a normal way and told her that she would come to her house as scheduled. When she came to her house with her husband, both Komolika and her husband tried in various ways to know her mind, her reactions but she remained cool.

Urja came to school the next day but started ignoring me totally. She stopped wishing me and never stood up although others did so whenever I entered the Staff Room. Sometimes I found myself in embarrassing situation in front of the students or staff or both because of Urja's deliberate disrespect and casual attitude towards me.

It was a 'news' full of 'mirch-masala' in the township that Urja was removed from her powerful position. When a flower starts spreading fragrance, bees, butterflies, birds etc. are attracted towards it. Likewise Urja had achieved a unique distinction because of her talents and achievements. She started getting good offers and I was thinking how to get rid of her totally. But Veer Parsad didn't want her to go. Right from the beginning he had weakness on Urja and he tried to discourage her from joining any other school. It would be his defeat in that case. I had a plan of snatching the editorship of the magazine also from her.

In 2005 we took another attempt by provoking Urja. Continuously for ten days she went to the Printing Press, far away from the township and worked till midnight. She was extremely tired both physically and mentally because during day time she had to attend classes and perform her other duties also. I signalled Veer Parsad, considering the time to be ripe. We decided to accuse her of not accepting the articles of any other teacher for the magazine. I knew she would flare up because earlier she had collected the articles written by teachers for the magazine but Veer Parsad rejected all.

While checking the final dummy of the magazine one day, Veer Parsad told Urja – "How come only Urja's article is there in the magazine?" She said "Because others have not contributed." He said – "Others have not contributed or you are not accepting anybody's write-up?" She said – "Sir, when I collected articles from the teachers, you told me not to accept even a single one because the school magazine is only for the students and now you are blaming me for not accepting any teacher's article?" Veer Parsad shouted at her and said – "Don't pretend to be innocent. You think only about yourself and not about anybody else." His voice could be heard from outside but Urja could not be dominated so easily. She also shouted back – "You are so mean, we can't even imagine. You have exploited me to the greatest extent and now you want to snatch everything from me to give the credit to your wife. Do you think I am not able to understand anything? I just hate you." She slammed the door with all her might coming out of Veer Parsad's chamber. Then she came straight to the staff-room and asked the teachers – "You tell me, who among you submitted your article for the school magazine which I have not accepted? " She repeatedly asked the question but everybody was silent. I went to the staff room and asked the teachers to close all windows and told Urja, "Don't wash your dirty linens in the public." Actually I was afraid of getting exposed before the public with my own dirty linens and Urja was spreading them before others. I called her into my room where Padma was also present and at my indication she bolted the door. We tried to make Urja understand that no amount of tears, anger, protest or anything will be able to soften our mind. It would be better for her to accept our decision and cooperate with us. Urja said – "I am ready to leave the school but I will not accept any nonsense. I promise, I will expose each one of you either before leaving or later on but I will not spare you."

Urja remained absent for two days. Ravi Shastri was sent to her home to bring the dummy of the magazine which she refused to hand over to him expressing her fear that her name will be deleted and my name will be included instead. Ravi Shastri came back with empty hand, he was asked to give in writing that he was not handed over the dummy of the magazine. The magazine was scheduled to be released on 20th August but Veer Parsad deliberately took time in approving the dummy and gave his green signal in the second week of August. Earlier Urja used to prepare the duty roster for any function; that year I prepared the duty roster for Foundation Day and wrote Urja's name in releasing the magazine. The Chief Guest was the Chief Minister and Urja was supposed to hand over the first copy of the magazine to him. I knew very well that the magazine will not be delivered within that time but this was an opportunity to show my generosity and concern for Urja before the public and also to put the blame on her for not being able to release the magazine on the scheduled day. When the invitation cards and programme brochures were prepared 'Releasing of Magazine' was not mentioned in either of them as it always used to be because we knew very well that magazine could not be released. We didn't expect Urja to be so clever so as to ask Bindiya Bhalla to give her a copy of the invitation card and the programme brochure to verify whether it was mentioned or not. Later on when Veer Parsad accused her of not being able to get the magazine printed on time she asked him "Why 'Releasing of Magazine' was not mentioned in the invitation card and the programme brochure which were printed at least one week before the programme? How did you know that Magazine will not be released on that day? Not only that, I asked the Printers about the delay in printing of the magazine but they said that they have sent 200 copies for Release, three days before the function." All her logic and reasoning were however trampled under feet as Veer Parsad had been sitting on the Principal's chair from where, if anybody says that the Sun rises in the North, people will accept that. Moreover some teachers were happy to see Urja suffering, they were elated to find her losing her position. Ordinary people particularly women who can never rise beyond a certain limit get sadistic pleasure in observing the humiliation and pain of any talented and deserving person. This world is full of bitches like Ranjita and Padma and our edifice of learning is not an exception.

Urja was the incharge of prize distribution in the Assembly also. Whenever any teacher or student or a team is awarded with any prize for any competition outside the school, the same prize is given in the Assembly by the Principal as a special honour. Urja single-handed used to manage that – noting down the name, class, section, details of the prize, arranging the prizes according to sequence, informing the students, requesting the Principal to spare his time for handing over the prizes etc. Veer Parsad started harassing her in that matter also. He never used to tell her in advance when he will be available for prize distribution but always at the last moment, just one minute before the Assembly started, told her to arrange everything. Once she asked Padma whether Sir will be able to give the prizes the next day. Padma, as usual reported the matter in a distorted way while warming the bed of Veer Parsad. Next day he called Urja and asked – "Are you trying to find out the movement of the Principal?" Actually Veer was afraid of Urja. He could sense that Urja was intelligent enough to read between the lines.

Veer had already done a blunder by giving a copy of the stay order of the District Court to Urja, asking her to translate it into English. The Stay Order clearly says that the contract between the Society in Delhi and the local Promoter of the school, which is a reputed organisation not only in the State but also in India, was terminated by the Pro Vice Chairman of the local body (Ba, Ba, Black Sheep) which could not have been possible without the help and support of Veer Parsad. He had not thought of the future of 5000 students but made crafty calculations for our future. Urja came to know the truth from the Stay Order.

For the whole year, Veer Parsad and I, with the help of Padma and a few other manipulative teachers continued to make the life of Urja a Hell. As Head of the English Department Urja used to chair the Departmental meetings and discuss various points with the teachers. Taking advantage of my position as the Vice Principal I started joining the meeting as per my whims and fancies and contradicted everything she told the teachers, belittling and ignoring her to the possible extent. When she prepared the reports of the departmental meetings and submitted to the Principal, I copied the same in my handwriting and signed as the H.O.D. These were preserved for future to impress the members of the Society. I instructed the teachers of the English Department not to listen to her or to follow her instructions. In spite of all these, in the CBSE Board

Examination 2006, maximum distinctions were from Urja's class and one of her students in the Commerce section scored 98 out of 100 in Core English which was the highest score in India that year in Core English.

The preparation of magazine was going on in full swing during the summer vacation, under the supervision of Urja. Like every year, that year also she prepared the magazine from A–Z, including Veer Parsad's speech. When the final dummy was given to Veer Parsad for checking, he wrote my name as the Managing Editor, cutting Urja's name. Urja tried to convince him saying-"Sir, I've done the work of Managing Editor. I've coordinated with English, Hindi, Sanskrit, Art, Physical Education, Examination Departments, Pre-Primary, Primary, Middle, Secondary and Senior Secondary Sections, Typists, Printers etc. Madam has not done anything! (How foolish of her; she didn't know that Principal's wife need not do anything for getting any credit. Teachers should feel obliged to do something for the Principal's wife). If you want to include her name please give her a better position, make her the Chief Editor; why are you bringing her down to my level?"

Veer Parsad refused to listen to her and I thought if I miss this opportunity to get rid of her for good, I may never get the chance for the second time. It's now or never. I was sitting on her left side. I started poking her with the sharp nails of my fingers constantly and told her "You have deprived others of getting a chance to work for the magazine. You are standing like a wall before others not letting them come up. You are not the only person who can do all these things; there are other teachers also who are talented and willing to work but because of you no one is getting a chance."

She said "I've never asked for anything. Five years back all these responsibilities were given to me by the Principal. At that time no one was interested. Single handed I did everything and so far I have never neglected my duty. Rather I have neglected my family, my children, my health and this is the reward I'm getting today."

I said "You have not even submitted your pass certificate of M.A. English degree and you claim to be the H.O.D.?

She said "Then on what basis I got the job in this school?" I told her "you are a liar, you are bitch. You have seduced the Principal and managed all these important responsibilities. You wear transparent clothes and move about in the school; you can move around naked also." While saying all these I was constantly pricking her with my nails trying to provoke her. I knew she would flare up and exactly she did. Ravi Shastri and Neelima Pandey were also present in the room as we needed some witnesses. In self defence, Urja grabbed my hands and pushed me back. I had kept my 'pallu' lose and it fell down from my shoulder exposing my sagging breasts through my loose blouse. I was practically standing there in my blouse only as the sari came off my body and was lying on the floor. In that condition I told Urja – "You are shameless; you wanted to enjoy a peg with the Principal and went to his hotel." She became furious and tried to shut my mouth. My gold chain got entangled in her finger and it also came off. By the meantime Veer Parsad had called Padma through the intercom and she also came in. There were three witnesses in our favour. Urja became hysteric and started shouting :"How dare you call me bitch! You belong to the family of bitch. You have grabbed this position by sleeping with many people. It is in your blood. Your husband is a characterless, dirty rapist. Ask him with how many women he has slept? Ask him with what intention he had come to my house on 2nd October 2002 in absence of my husband? It is his forefather's good fortune that I didn't use my shoes on his face on that day. You bloody, whore, you have no control on your husband; that's why he runs after women like a mad dog."

Veer Parsad continued to instigate her by saying "shout, shout, let the whole school hear your voice." Urja hurled a volley of abuses at him and went out of his room crying and telling everybody on her way "See, that bloody man has got his work done by me and now is giving the credit to his bitchy wife." But who will listen to her? Who has the guts to oppose Veer Parsad and me?

When all this was happening, Urja's husband was waiting outside who had come to pick her from school. She was practically not in her sense and we were hundred per cent successful.

I told Veer Parsad that she should be sacked. Next day she sent her leave application along with the medical certificate applying for leave for a week as she had been diagnosed by the doctor to be suffering from Depressive Psychosis. Although she was on leave, the One Act Play written and directed by her was staged at a House function and was highly appreciated. Sitting in the front row we were watching it and each and every scene, each and every dialogue and action seemed to be whipping us pointing out at our atrocities. Or was it our guilty conscience?

Urja joined after a week. We studied her for a few days and then Veer Parsad called a General Meeting. Officially she was relieved of all her responsibilities except teaching English in classes XI and XII. Neelima Pandey, who was one of the witnesses of the got-up incident was made the House Warden of Ganges House. She had written four pages Report against Urja at our instructions. What else could she have done? Being a House Warden and sitting in the front row was her long cherished dream and for achieving that she could come down to any extent. After all one has to look at her background. A few years back she used to live in a servant quarter of a club, her father-in-law being a waiter of that club. Naturally this position of House Warden was beyond her imagination.

Amidst pin-drop silence the announcement was made. Urja was cool; she didn't react at all. May be she had decided to leave. In the month of November she put up her paper and as per rules gave a notice of three months. That was the happiest day of my life. I couldn't tolerate Urja moving around the school because I know Veer Parsad's intense, magnetic attraction towards her. She had never given up before his immoral, unethical desires; moreover she had refused to write a book in the name of Veer Parsad when he got an offer from a publisher. Because of this reason Veer Parsad ultimately listened to me and went against Urja, otherwise the picture would have been different. There was, of course every possibility of changing mind or decision on Veer's side. So it had become absolutely necessary that Urja should leave. Earlier too, I was always successful in removing the thorn from my way. The month of November was eventful indeed. One of our senior faculty members in the department of English expired which was really shocking but I could not resist my happiness at Urja's resignation and celebrated the occasion by dancing on the stage before the whole school on Children's Day.

Urja remained totally aloof from all events and functions of the school. May be she was preparing herself for the final day when she would step out of her familiar boundaries forever. Although she had not disclosed the fact, we came to know that she got the post of Vice Principal and H.O.D. (English) in another reputed, C.B.S.E. affiliated school within the township.

Veer Parsad told me – "She deserves the post, do you realise that? This is her achievement as she is not so lucky like you. Without my help you have no position." His words sprinkled salt in my wound but there was nothing to say. I had to digest his words.

Veer Parsad had instructed Padma and me to behave very nicely with Urja for the last few days. We all including Veer visited her house to show how sad we were at the demise of her father-in-law. We also, met her ailing father, confined to the bed due to cerebral attack and spent some time there. We saw the album of her son's marriage photographs and minutely watched the teachers who had attended the function. These teachers deserved a piece of our mind which they got in the due course. How dare they attended her function when they knew very well that we would not like that?

On Sports Day, the familiar voice of Urja compering the programme could not be heard. She preferred to sit at one end of the ground, reading a book. People were stunned to see her peaceful stature. Then came the Annual Day. I assigned her duty in Refreshment. She didn't even turn up to the Refreshment Room but throughout the programme sat quietly in the staffroom and left before the function came to an end.

On the Annual Day of the Primary Wing she entered from one gate, signed the Register and left through the front gate. We watched everything but didn't have the face to tell her anything. For a long period of time she had done so much for the school, so much publicity for Veer Parsad and we compelled her to leave the school. I have no regret for that but Veer Parsad was feeling bad.

On 14th February, in the farewell meeting of Urja, Veer Parsad told her in presence of everybody " I told you in the morning and again I am telling you, still there is time, you review your decision and continue with your service here.

I don't want you to go elsewhere". But like everyone else he also knew very well that Urja will not stay back. She would never, in her life work under us. She would rather sit back at home than accepting us as her boss. I care a fig for her feelings. I care a fig for the feelings and thoughts of any one in this world. I have power in my hands. I'll make full utilisation of that.

From the next day I started giving stress on the completion of the construction of the Principal's Residence within the school premises. It is my dream house which I had been cherishing since our stay in Darjeeling. After Veer Parsad's term, I will be his successor. I still have a decade to go; by that time Amar and Ipsita will be able to manage the steering.

14th April, Bengali New Years Day was an auspicious day. On that day we decided to perform puja and enter our newly constructed quarter within the school campus. With this target in mind, day and night I started supervising the construction work and in front of my eyes my dream gradually turned into reality.

That day came to my life with all satisfaction of fulfilment which brings tears in my eyes. Whatever Veer desired in his life, he got and being his wife, I too relished his success as my own. But in spite of everything, the taste of success was not all sweet; there was some bitterness mixed in it, I don't know why! Or, may be I know but always pretend to be not knowing. When everybody left after enjoying the lunch and appreciating the house, I moved around the house, entered from one room to another, from the roof top to the ground and the bare walls seemed to be mocking and laughing at me. Is it my home? - simply the marble floor, the modular kitchen, five spacious bed rooms, a large hall, balconies, terrace – simply the concrete cage where my soul is being trapped, where every moment I feel like a fish out of water, gasping for breath trying to catch hold of the trivial most object to save myself from drowning into the bottomless pit of darkness. If this is my home, then where is that trust, that faith, love, respect and concern for each other which makes a house – a home? Veer Parsad and I have been exposed before everybody in a shameless, naked way. Our children have gone out of control, particularly Amar. The tune which was alive twenty five years back, when with innocent hope and joy I had started my life with Veer Parsad, could not be traced any more. Veer Parsad has damaged the strings and distorted the tune, cheating and betraying me again and again. He has robbed me of my honour each time he slept with a woman, each time people started whispering about him, each time he gave an explanation before the staff members although they didn't ask for any and each time I had to say in a loud voice "I don't believe that my husband can do that. It is a conspiracy against him. Out of jealousy some people are spreading rumour against him." But who knows the truth better than me? Veer Parsad is a crooked, cunning, characterless person who loves only himself and no one else. He is least bothered about the feelings of others. If somebody can accept him as he is, that person will have no problem but if ever anyone dares pointing out his faults or mistakes, that person will have to wash hands with peace for ever because Veer will not take rest before finishing him off totally.

Students chat amongst themselves being members of Orkut and Facebook where they have created a profile of Veer Parsad defaming him to the possible extent. The nickname given to him has similarity with Dawd Ibrahim but his notoriety is even worse than that of the latter. In a helpless manner Veer Parsad pleaded the students in the Assembly to make that profile bogus and delete it but will they? Because of his dirty character we had to suffer so much otherwise no one would have shown any dissatisfaction or raised any objection in my elevation as the Vice Principal or in future as the Principal. We had our dreams, our visions and we planned according to that. Things were going on smoothly as per our plan but Veer Parsad spoilt everything. Students are leaving the hostel and availing P.G. accommodation because they don't want to stay within the same premises with us. Each year hundreds of meritorious students are leaving the school and joining some other institution in the same township.

Urja is no more with us but time to time I get her news through my personal gazetteers. She has consolidated her position in her new school and is the right hand of the Principal. Her school topped AISSCE 2007 immediately after her joining; the beginning was good and she was taken as lucky and auspicious for the school. For the first time they beat us in Inter School Quiz and Hindi Debate organised by us and proudly lifted up the trophies. Veer Parsad was furious and glared at me with fire in his eyes. They knocked us down by forming the Sahodaya Complex and making Veer Parsad the Vice President along with his greatest rival – the Principal of our rival school under the same banner, while their own Principal was declared the President. It was Urja who nominated the posts and I am 100% sure the idea came from her fertile brain. She didn't miss the opportunity to show her power and pinched the ego of Veer Parsad, curbing his importance. Veer Parsad hates being No. 2, who else knows that better than Urja?

Urja didn't forget to send us the new school magazine prepared by her. I felt a pin prick in my heart to see her name as the Chief Editor. Her talents, her achievements reflected throughout the magazine. The fact can not be denied – she possesses that dominating personality which suppresses all others, even her seniors.

Let her stay with her dominating personality in her new school with her new employers – I am relieved. Before me lies a thorn less path which I have to traverse before reaching my destination. Veer Parsad quite often tells us one thing whenever he comes back from any school inspection, appointed by CBSE i.e., about the excellent infrastructure of the upcoming schools. In the near future these schools will be our great competitors. Urja has gone to one of these schools with a long experience of working in our school and she is definitely sharing her experience with the management of her new school. She is aware of some of the secret policies of the school also. There is a rumour that a parallel chain of schools under the same brand name will be opened all over the country and some in the State also. There is always a fear of being uprooted, I mean, shifted to any other unit. There is no other alternative but to surrender at the hands of fate or destiny. Throughout our lives we never accepted defeat in any situation. We always fought back fiercely whenever we faced any challenge. The coming back of the school under the aegis of the Society is already a defeat of Veer Parsad but so long our position is retained here, this defeat can not knock us out of the arena. In this last game Veer Parsad moved a few dice like a novice, out of his weakness towards women. But every cloud has a silver lining and through the apparent darkness sometimes a sparkle of light illuminates the surroundings. Two old ladies, who are the members of the Society, are in our favour. Padma and I didn't leave any tactics unattempted to please these two gullible ladies. Most probably the talebearers who poisoned the ears of the Chairman, thought it futile to approach these two ladies. So, it didn't take much time for us to make a place in their heart. So long they remain members of the Society they will keep on extending their support to us.

Like the birth certificates which we managed bearing false age, we managed false experience certificates also. Nothing is impossible in the modern times when money speaks and works for you. Moreover if you belong to special category by virtue of your birth you need not worry about anything. Today backward classes are ruling everywhere. One big reality of life is that you have to be bold and shameless if you want to proceed in life. When you are on the stage and the light is focussed right on you, it would be foolishness on your part to hide your face behind a veil. Urja has exposed us before the Society – so what? We have to play our part smartly. Both of us are attending the 'Art of Living' classes for mental peace and satisfaction. We have to achieve maximum from this life as we will never get a second chance. Ignoring the grudge, malice, curse of people we have to move forward. It's a 'Do or Die' situation. All beauty and tenderness with which we had started our life in the small two-room quarter of the residential school in the hills, where foggy, misty mornings started with stirring of spoon in steaming tea-cups, where clouds floated over the tiled roofs, wild roses greeted us at every nook and corner of the roads, Kanchenjhangha sparkled like a crown of silver, Teesta flowed down the mountain with torrents in monsoon, the fresh aroma of tea gardens stimulated the senses, where being together was the happiest feeling in life, have fizzled out in the thin air like bubbles, replacing them with the hell fire of greed, lust, discontentment, corruption and disease gnawing the mind and heart, leaving them hollow. In this eventual transformation our children lost their childhood and missed all those things which children of their age enjoy. They know their father is characterless, their mother is jealous and crafty, their family is the most talked–about and they are caught in a spider's web from which there is no freedom. They know they will never get the love of people, only hatred, only envy.

Bit by bit we have accumulated, constructed and now relishing that. But if at one stroke everything tumbles down like a structure of cards, I will not be able to tolerate that.

* * * * * * * *

Lolita Banerjee's niece, our ex-student and class mate of Ipsita became pregnant in the very first year of her college and was compelled to marry her professor, the father of her child, drawing a line in her studies and career. Sometimes I become worried about Ipsita. She is far away from us and her father's blood is flowing in her veins. She has grown up witnessing the scums of the society in and around the home and school. She has seen humiliations which I had to suffer on account of Veer Parsad. Last time when she came home from her residential college during the festival break I noticed a remarkable change in her dressing style. Never before I found her in such revealing clothes. There was a change in her attitude also. She remained quiet at home, not conversing with us much but for hours together, she kept on chatting with her boyfriends. This I checked, when she was in the toilet by ringing back at the numbers from the list of miss calls. When I asked her with whom she kept on talking day and night she replied – "I am grown up enough and I should have my privacy." Amar had gone out of control even when he was with us. In the Assembly his father delivered long lectures to the students asking them not to organise any farewell party outside the school for the outgoing batch of class XII. But at home we could not prevent our son from attending one such party at a happening restaurant where he along with his friends participated in Paper dance, where a boy and a girl as a partner dance on a piece of paper and after each round folds the paper until it becomes so small that practically it is not possible to stand on that paper without embracing each other. The girls press their pointed breasts in the chest of the partner and in the dim light of the dancing floor they explore each other, making full use of their cutaneous sense. Amar had to face the grudge of his friends who were compelled to stand in the prayer ground and listen to the lecture of Veer Parsad, discouraging them to attend such parties. Amar is also pursuing his Engineering degree from a college in Bangalore. He could not retain his N.T.S.E. Scholarship as he failed in the first year. Veer Parsad, the toughest person I have come across in my life becomes weak before his children and can not take any severe step against them. One more rumour had rocked the township that is the first rank holder in IIT had become drug addicted after going to Bombay. He was a jewel of our school and we were shocked to receive the news. Some people who never contribute anything substantial for the society do not miss a single opportunity to express their critical comments in any situation. They started blaming the school for imparting wrong education and no moral values to the students. In a way it is true. Although in front of others I always defend my husband but as a Principal of the school and as a father what instances has he left before the students and his own children which they could have emulated? Nothing. I can feel the pain of my children when their friends and classmates discuss about Veer Parsad in a negative way.

Veer Parsad has one more year to serve. We have accumulated enough to start a school of our own. But there we have to start from the scratch. During our stay here for more than a decade, the school has grown from strength to strength. It's my long cherished dream to succeed Veer Parsad and rule from his chair. So long the school was free from the control of the Society there was no problem; I could smoothly climb the steps. But the final step remained out of bound as the school has come under the aegis of the Society again. Everything is uncertain now; only time will tell us.

Our mechanical life has separated us from our roots. My old parents at Mumbai, brother in U.S.A., Veer's brothers and sisters at various places, childhood memories – everything is becoming faint. The lust for power has covered everything with a layer of dust. Once in a while in a nostalgic moment the desire to go back to those innocent childhood days strongly surfaces the mind. But at this juncture there is no question of turning back. I have to proceed forward suppressing all my wishes and not allowing my heart to be tender. There is no time to waste now with any silly thought. Ranjita you can't afford to be weak, you have to reach the peak. Your target is only the fish eye – neither left nor right, neither up nor down, only march forward towards your goal.....

A very interesting thing happened yesterday. It was the third day of the Annual Examination and the subject for class VIII was Mathematics. As usual the exams started at 7.30 a.m. After taking a round around the whole school, I was sitting in my room enjoying my first cup of tea at school – the second in the day. Hardly after half an hour one teacher brought a boy to my room. He was found to be copying from a guide book. When asked why he had done so, he kept himself rigid for a long time and after being persuaded, started weeping and finally said – "Madam, I am passing through a sad phase of life. I feel so lonely and cannot concentrate in my studies. My parents have separated. My father left the house leaving us alone. My mother always cries, there is no peace at home. Under such circumstances I could not prepare for the exam."

As per rules he was given zero in that particular paper. But I felt sorry for him. Sending him back I discussed the matter with the class teacher and instructed her to call the mother of the child. As per my instructions the class teacher informed his mother to meet me the next day at 10.00 a.m.

I was baffled to see the stylish lady in my chamber who filled the air with the scent of strong, enchanting foreign perfume. She didn't appear to be lonely or sad at all. I shared with her whatever her son told us the previous day and then it was her turn to be wonderstruck. I came to know from her that there was absolutely no problem between the husband and the wife. There was perfect harmony at home and it was a close knit family. She gave me the mobile number of her husband and told me that if I wish I could speak to him or call him to my office at any time. She apologised on behalf of her son and was ready to accept any action taken by the school. How desperate the young generation has become today!

In the evening I narrated everything to Veer Parsad while three of us – Veer, Padma and myself were discussing about the inner side of the back cover of the magazine. Usually that space is preserved for N.T.S.E. Scholarship holders and IIT qualifiers. As the number of IIT qualifiers was less, Veer suggested that those who qualified during the last three years should be included. Among them were some students who passed class X Board Exam from our school but went to Kota and other places for taking preparation for IIT and other competitive Exams along with plus two course. They didn't have any contact with us for two years but Veer Parsad said – "Who is going to verify whether they are our students or not? We have to project a large number of qualifiers before the public." As usual – mendacious but privileged; nobody will ever dare pointing out the unfair means Veer Parsad always tries to adopt. But how easy it was for us to award a big zero to that boy for adopting unfair means in the exam!

In the evening we were to attend the 'Annaprasan' (Rice-eating ceremony of Aarti's son. Veer Parsad had already decided not to go. He told me to attend the function and to tell them that he had to attend an important meeting with the members of the Education Management Society. Neither I could ask him the reason for not going, nor could he give me any explanation because the truth was crystal clear to both of us. I don't know whether any other women in the world had ever faced a similar situation! Aarti had become pregnant before her second marriage and Veer Parsad was a regular visitor to her house where she used to stay alone.

Aarti is a dance teacher at the primary wing, a specialist in Kathak. Her first marriage was a negotiated one which could not last for a long time. Aarti's family was cheated by the groom's parents who projected their son to be earning in lakhs abroad. The marriage was done in a hurry. The initial days were colourful, no doubt but it didn't take much time for the colours to become fade. He was actually doing a contractual job of an electrician in Dubai and as soon as the contract ended, he came back to the country, jobless. Whatever he had earned vanished in a jiffy paying the bills for alcohol and other addictions. Aarti, at that time was desperately in need of a job. She joined our school on adhoc and took up some dance tuitions. Her parents advised divorce but her husband created a scene at the court. Kneeling down on the floor he touched the feet of Aarti with both hands and pleaded mawkishly- "Please, give me a second chance, don't break the relationship." Aarti's heart melted and she came back to her in-law's house – much to the annoyance of her parents. Then started a long chapter of torture, deprivation and humiliation. Whatever little she earned had to be handed over to her mother-in-law and husband. Her attractive looks caused her sorrow as her husband suspected her to be having affairs with other men folk. He took the extreme steps of beating her mercilessly and when the situation became unbearable she was compelled to take a rented house near the school.

Veer Parsad's eagle eyes could capture her at this juncture of her life and he started calling her every now and then to his office – during school hours, after school in the evening, on holidays. This spicy news didn't take much time to spread. Aarti was helpless; she had to take help of Veer Parsad who arranged bank loan for her. Telephone was installed at her house just within a day at the initiative of Veer. She wanted divorce and this time her husband could not change her mind. She had stopped giving money to them. Aarti's mother-in-law had no other way but to take up assignments as domestic help or in plain and simple word – maid – servant. She satisfied her malice by informing people about Veer Parsad's affair with her daughter-in-law, about his visit to Aarti's house at odd hours.

When Aarti's house was ready, we missed Veer Parsad at home every evening. An anonymous letter was circulated in the township at that time indicating at the illegal relationship of Veer Parsad with the divorced or unmarried teachers. Aarti had conceived by that time, which her family members didn't know. But her relationship with Veer Parsad was not unknown to anyone. With the initiative of her elder sister and brother-in-law, Aarti got married for the second time with a gentleman whose wife had left the house leaving her ten year old daughter with her husband. We attended her marriage in the middle of May and got the news of her being pregnant within a month. She gave birth to a fully matured baby boy on 31st December. Only the inquisitive Nosy Parkers started whispering and expressing their doubts how could a baby, born within seven months of marriage, look so developed and healthy?

I had to attend the rice-eating ceremony of Aarti's son without Veer Parsad. How could he be present in his own son's important social ceremony and function as an invited guest?

Difficult and challenging situations in life have made me tough and stoic. Nothing can shake the ground under my feet. The more I face critical situation, the more I pretend to be confident. This edifice of learning has imparted the most meaningful and difficult lessons to me and prepared me for the long journey to achieve my goal.

I have noticed this fighting spree in some of the students also. At this moment the face of Manisha an ex-student, who was in Urja's class, is knocking the doors of my memory. The terrible news of her accident reached us through telephone. She was going to Maharashtra by car and on the way when their Summo stopped at a railway crossing, a speeding truck hit the Summo from behind and all passengers of the Summo were more or less injured. Manisha's right leg was broken into several pieces and her heel was crushed into particles. She lost her consciousness and when she gained it, she found herself on the hospital bed and her body from the waist to the toe absolutely paralysed. In the beginning a deep feeling of depression and frustration engulfed her. But gradually she could overcome that. After three months when she came to school with the help of a walker, her classmates extended their helping hands. Urja arranged her seating in the first bench and instructed all students to help her as and when required. She used to encourage her a lot and never left her behind when the senior school was taken for a picnic. The fighting spirit of the girl enabled her to stand on her feet again and not only that she could make up the loss in her studies and came up with flying colours in the Model Exams for class XII. Due to Padma's carelessness she had to suffer a lot inspite of her good results.

As per CBSE rules 75 per cent attendance is required in order to appear for the Board Examinations. Earlier there were many instances of manipulations where students having short attendance were given the required attendance by the school to avoid any problem related to their candidature for Board Exams. This girl had submitted her leave application along with all medical certificates and her leave was granted by me. When it was submitted to the Principal's office, Padma misplaced it and later on when the Examineration In charge, who wrote a letter to the CBSE informing about the short attendance on medical ground, asked for a copy to attach with the application, Padma put the blame on Urja and said that she had not submitted it to the office. Dire false statement! But as per our verbal contract we were not to go against each other and even knowing the truth, I had to support Padma. Urja's position was down before Manisha and her parents as they were asked to go to Ajmer – the regional headquarter and take permission for appearing in the Exam from the regional officer. The poor girl who had not recovered from her disability completely was panick-stricken and the parents were absolutely baffled. Denied any type of help or cooperation from the school, ultimately they went to Ajmer and settled the matter.

Padma's daughter was also in the same section. We used to get all feedback from her. It was not unknown to us that Urja was becoming very popular to the students of her section. They shared their personal problems with her. The Cultural Secretary was somewhat outspoken and as per my instructions her badge was taken off and she was removed from her duty. Urja was sympathetic towards the girl and counselled and motivated her to prove herself in the ensuing Board Examination. Her counselling acted as a tonic and she could overcome her depression and produced excellent results in class XII Board Examination. Much was expected from Padma's daughter but she disheartened us when the results were out. Her name was not there in the list of top ten. Those who topped in the Commerce section were not informed that they were to come on the Annual Day and receive their prizes. They missed the opportunity to receive their prizes and certificates from the Chief Guest, the Governor of the State. But the parents didn't accept it easily. They came in a group and complained against Padma. She tried to put the blame on the class teacher again. But the matter was no more a secret that Padma purposely didn't inform the parents of the toppers because her daughter could not get a single prize.

The atmosphere in and around the school has vitiated so much that how long we will be able to continue here–is unpredictable. Although both of us – Veer and myself are tough and have the stamina and courage to fight against all obstacles, still at one point we would like to have profound peace. All struggles should stop once for all and we must be able to put our heart and soul together in our own venture. This is our plan for the future but before that I must occupy the Principal's chair and nowhere else but here. In that room where Veer Parsad has been ruling for more than a decade, only I have the right to rule. My hurt and enraged ego due to the debauchery and lust of Veer Parsad will be tamed and contented only then, otherwise my toleration, adjustment, compromise, sufferings–everything will go waste. I believe in utilitarian philosophy and know that all human action is governed by self-interest, and 'cash' which are the basis of all human relationships. I have got this life on lease and as soon as the period of lease is over I have to quit. I am not a fool to miss any opportunity of reaching the peak. For that I can come down to any extent and be as evil as it is possible.

It is only because of Veer Parsad's dirty habit and sexual desire that things have become so complicated for us. Padma and I never let him spend even a minute alone with any lady in his office. Urja had mocked at us by using the term coverture. Yes! We are the covertures of Veer Parsad and Veer Parsad's each and every movement is in our knowledge. We are trying to save the boat from both sides from being capsized.

4

Urja's Soliloquy

As usual, the meeting started one hour late. This was expected because Veer Parsad likes to keep people waiting. Visitors waiting at the reception outside his office is a familiar scene. I have seen people waiting for him since morning having a tiffin break before getting entry to his room in the afternoon although, for the whole time he had been sitting comfortably in his A.C. room doing simply nothing, but giving the impression to the visitors of being awfully busy. He tries to show his importance by keeping visitors waiting.

The conference room was full but unlike other occasions there was an abominable lull. I occupied a seat in the second row next to Bindiya Bhalla though she pointed out a chair in the first row. Surprisingly for the first time, Ranjita called me and asked me to sit in the first row. There was deadly silence in the conference hall except the ticking of the wall clock, keeping pace with the heart-beat of the members present. Many of the senior teachers were absent or rather they were not called purposely. The puppets were called to witness the greatness of Mr. Veer Parsad and his equally great wife Madam Ranjita – how generous they were to arrange a farewell of their greatest enemy Urja, who had physically assaulted Ranjita and called Veer Parsad 'the son of a bitch.'

He had shown his sense of duty, responsibility and concern a few days back also when he came to my house with his wife Ranjita, his 'kept' Padma and his 'pet donkey' Ravi Shastri to express his profound grief at the death of my nonagenarian father-in-law and also to meet my father who was confined to bed due to cerebral attack. My father of course, could not understand that he is the Principal of the school which I decided to leave and took him to be the Principal of the new school which I was supposed to join. Veer Parsad was clever enough to understand that and tactfully managed the situation. I had to suppress my laughter with great difficulty.

Breaking the silence Veer Parsad entered the Conference Hall from his chamber, adjacent to it, in his typical manner and everybody stood up making an irritating sound in their blow-plast chairs. Bindiya was signalled and she started in her nasal tone "Change is an inseparable part of life and Madam Urja has opted for a change. We all have assembled here to bid her farewell. I request our Principal Sir to present her with a memento." In a robotic manner he presented me with a memento. Bindiya continued "If anyone is interested to speak on the occasion he/she is most welcome." But everybody seemed to have become absolutely dumb. Then she said " I request Madam Urja to share her feelings with us." I was waiting for this moment.

"Good evening everybody." I started. "It's a very emotional, sentimental moment and at this moment I have been asked to share my thoughts, my feelings with you. I would like to tell you a story; the story of my school days."

Veer Parsad anticipated danger and said – "What's the use of telling a story? You can say something very briefly."

"I will take just five minutes Sir."

"O.K. as you wish."

I started again – "Count down has stopped. The time has come to say goodbye. Is it so easy? I have worked in this institution for ten long years; each and every nook and corner is so familiar to me; in fact, there is so much to say, I don't know where to start, how much to say and where to stop. I am standing at the threshold and at this point, if I look back, it was 30th March, 1997 when I first joined this institution. It was the last day of the session and Sir had asked me to attend the general meeting which is held every year before the new session commences. I came to school and met Sir. He briefed me about my duty and told me to meet the time table In charge Madam Daisy. She is the first person whom I met in this school and I will never forget the help which I got from her. She advised me to go to the library to issue the required text and reference books. There I met the librarian Shiny and here I would like to say, since day one till date, she helped me a lot. She is very efficient in her profession; you approach her for any book, she will tell you on which shelf you will find it. She helped me a lot when I did my M.Phil and as I started doing my Ph.D she helped me in every possible way.

On the very first day, after issuing the books when I came back and was standing outside the staff room, waiting for the meeting to start, Lolita Banerjee came out of the staffroom and told me — "Why are you standing here? Come and join us." That was the beginning. I started sitting next to her and for the last ten years we had been sitting side by side, sharing our tiffin, joy and sorrow. Here I would like to mention – that table and the place are very lucky; whoever sits there, gets administrative posts for example I can take the names like Kaveri and Uma and I wish in the near future we will get some more good news.

A very sweet natured teacher Rajlaxmi also sits there. She was the first class teacher of my son when he joined this school in class VIII and Meenakshi Roy was his class teacher for three years – X, XI and XII. My son is fond of her but I have a complaint against her – she told my son to grow long hair after completing school and because of that I am facing a great problem today." Here I was interrupted by Veer Parsad as he could not understand the joke – his intelligence is limited to crooked and cunning things only but he lacks the wit which is so essential to add spice to life.

However, I proceeded, "Then, I would like to mention the name of Suman Ahuja, one of the senior teachers who had taught me how to do invigilation duty in public examinations. (I know both husband and wife's blood pressure would rise up at the mention of her name) I am grateful to each one of you in some way or the other but if I start saying about each one of you, one evening will not be enough. So I have to fast forward and present before you that day in 2002, when it was the farewell of Mrs. Sita Raman and Mrs. Renu Agrawal. Since morning, many of us had been thinking who will be conducting the programme because earlier Mrs. Raman used to conduct all programmes as the Activity in charge and also as the H.O.D. of English. We all came in the evening. I was sitting somewhere in the M.P. Hall. Just one minute before the programme, Sir called me and asked me to do the compering. I was not at all prepared. I asked Padma to give me a glass of water and then coming to the Multipurpose Hall, somehow conducted the programme. When it was over, Sir called me again, congratulated me and said — "Until and unless, I push you into the water, you will never learn swimming." Since then, on several occasions he pushed me into water and maybe because of that, today, I am a very good swimmer. If somebody pushes me into the middle of an ocean, I will be able to swim and reach the shore. Sir entrusted me with many responsibilities and I became obsessed with work. Work became a passion to me and I forgot everything else. My family got neglected. I had to come to school on holidays, sometimes even on Sundays. For five years I didn't get summer vacation and Dussehra – Diwali break. My children left Bhilai for higher studies and went to Delhi. Their absence was compensated by the school magazine 'Deep Vision' which was my third child, my baby daughter. But unfortunately, for some reason I had to part with my lovely daughter. (Here I controlled myself from saying that it is because of the greed of a vulture Ranjita and her stupid followers, I had to part with my lovely creation; what was the quality of the magazine five years back? The cheaters will now follow my footsteps and take all credit; projecting themselves before the elite world.)

The last five years had been very eventful and we all have witnessed many undesirable as well as desirable happenings. In the month of August 2006, a general meeting was called and Sir made an announcement that I was relieved of all my extra duties and responsibilities. I still remember he had made a comment that day. With quotation marks I would like to say what he had said – "I know when to pull out whom." On 15th November 2006, I submitted my resignation letter and as a reason I mentioned that in pursuit of Ph.D. I had to devote more time in my studies, that's why it would not be possible for me to continue with my job. I also remember what Sir said that day. Again within quotation marks I am saying "Do you think, I will believe that Urja will sit back at home? She is not that type of a lady. I know where you are going and for which post and I knew it before you were informed by your interviewers."

I promised him that I will tell him where I was going before I leave. Although he knows very well where I am going, today in the presence of everybody I have to keep my words – Yes, I will be joining another reputed C.B.S.E. affiliated Public School of the city tomorrow as the Vice Principal and H.O.D. of English. (I mentioned the name of the school). I think Sir should feel proud of me because had he not pushed me into the water, I would have never learnt swimming. If he is the Guru, I am his Chela." Veer Parsad made a silly comment – "She is my Cheli, not Chela" and the puppets laughed as if he has made a very amusing remark. I restrained myself from saying that "Look here, I have achieved that, which Ranjita has manipulated. It is my sheer hard work and dedication towards my service that I could get the position of Vice Principal and H.O.D. English in a reputed school of the State. If Urja is thrown away by some unworthy people she knows how to make a place for herself amongst the worthy."

I came to the vital point of my story of 'My School Days' - "I'm happy to see that my absence will not create any void because whatever I have done single – handed for a long time are now being done by Madam Ranjita with the assistance of various teachers. I wish them all success in their work (In fact it's my pleasure to see the greedy vultures licking the leftovers from my rejected plate. I have my platter full, let me enjoy it.)

Now it's time to say thank you to all. I whole-heartedly thank the Principal Sir for whatever he has given me and also for teaching me swimming. I am thankful to all my colleagues particularly the teachers of my English Department for their love, help and cooperation (not to mention the name of those who wrote complaint letters and reports against me in order to ruin my career and improve their own.)

I still love this school from my heart and this school will always remain in my memories forever. No one is perfect; even I am not perfect. Knowingly or unknowingly, I have made many mistakes but I will never say 'sorry' because love means not ever having to say you're sorry and I love this school, I love you all. Thank you and good bye till we meet again and wish you all a very happy Valentines Day." The puppets clapped their hands. Veer Parsad said – "So, that was her account of ten years in a nutshell, I know she will not stop here. Today she is going as the Vice Principal and very soon she will be the Principal also." Then he turned towards Ranjita and asked her if she was willing to say anything. Ranjita was waiting for this opportunity. Immediately she stood up and started,

"Ladies and Gentlemen, Madam Urja has forgotten one thing that when she joined this school she had only four years experience of working as a PRT and I was already the Senior Mistress. Today she is the Vice Principal and she has started thinking that she is equal to me. Attitude and approach of a person is very important in life. Anyway, I wish her good luck." The puppets again clapped but if they had a little bit of thinking power then they would have understood that Ranjita was boiling with rage and jealousy and whatever she said was absolutely irrelevant and balderdash.

Already she had exposed herself several times and on the evening of 14th February she made herself more prominent, revealing her dark side. I never forgot that I was a PRT (Primary Teacher) at my previous school. I never forgot that I had only four years experience when I joined this School and it was a real challenge to me when I was asked to teach English in class XI. I did my best to do justice to my students, my profession and my school. I proved myself bit by bit, day by day and today what I am is by the grace of God and my hard work. I neither have anyone to favour me nor could I flatter anyone to climb up the ladder.

I remember, on the same day when I joined the school, Ranjita's name was announced as the Senior Mistress – Middle Wing, depriving other deserving persons. Kaveri remarked on the occasion: "Superseding all efficient and senior teachers of the school, Veer Parsad has made his wife Ranjita the Senior Mistress who had fourteen years experience of working as a Primary Teacher only and who didn't have the degree of B.Ed., which is a must for school teachers. What is her contribution in the development of the school? Zero. We have been working since day one in this school but his wife is the only deserving candidate !"

I could have given a proper reply to Ranjita's statement and taught her a lesson in front of all but I kept my lips tight and all these thoughts remained in my mind. I could have asked why all these responsibilities were given to me knowing that I was junior and she was senior? When I streamlined everything and it became easy for her to follow the rules and methods prepared and started by me, then all of a sudden they realised that I was junior? Wonderful ! Is there any doubt that the quality of work improved in leaps and bounds with my effort? As if that was not enough, in order to sprinkle salt on the wound, Veer Parsad started, " I've nothing to say against the efficiency and quality of work of Madam Urja. She is no doubt very hard working but she should have taken care of her T and T. Only because of these two Ts situations didn't go in her favour. By the way how many of you know the meaning of T and T?" Some of the stupid arse-licking puppets raised their hands; the sensible ones remained silent. Tea and snacks had been served which I found difficult to push down my throat. Veer Parsad said – "Those who don't know keep on guessing." (Showing T and T is the monopoly of Mr. Veer Parsad only; only he can hit the ceiling) After a pause he said "The door of this school will always remain open for you. If you feel you are not happy in the new environment, you can always come back. I am hundred percent sure that you will not be able to adjust in your new school because it is their family business. The family members will dominate there and you will not get any importance." (As if I am going there to get importance) He looked at the puppets and said – "We are not enemies of Urja. In fact today in the morning also I told her to review her decision and now in front of everybody I am saying she is most welcome if she wants to come back." Who knows better than me that had I given in to his tricks how much torture and humiliation I had to suffer later on? I will never, never, never come back so long Veer Parsad and Ranjita rule the school.

Some teachers were asked to sing songs; they tried but the songs seemed to be out of tune. The meeting was concluded. Many members congratulated me. Ranjita and her 'chamchis' left in a hurry. For the last time I came out of the Conference Hall.

I was asked to collect my Release Order from Veer Parsad. For the last time I entered the room. The Release Order was kept ready on his table but he took time to sign it. With his X-Ray eyes he started ogling me and using one of his Ts(tongue) said "You are leaving today. Incidentally it is Valentines Day and a lot of memories are coming back to my mind. This is not the end of everything. Your memories will linger in my mind always" – he started making dirty indications and at that moment I felt like picking up the paper weight from his table and hitting him with it right on his forehead but couldn't do that. Because of this bastard and his bitch wife I had to snap all bonds with the most prestigious school in the country. I had to count numbers backward because till then he didn't clear my dues and the Release Order although I had submitted the clearance certificate well in advance.

I received my Release Order and came out. Leaving behind a part of my heart I stepped out and the wheels of our red Maruti rolled out of gate no.1 into the broad road reminding me of the bitter truth that I am no more a part of this school. Because of the arriviste, amorous, characterless Veer Parsad, his barmy, empty headed wife Ranjita and his kept Padma I lost association with my beloved school which was not just a workplace but a temple to me; where each day added a golden frame to the freeze shots of experience, where I witnessed children growing up into adolescence, where our joys and sorrows, hopes and frustrations mingled and flowed in one common stream. I lost association (on paper of course) with the institution which I still love from the core of my heart and will continue to do so for the rest of my life. I left my most precious treasure in the hands of the vultures.

In order to achieve something in life one has to part with certain other precious things. It's a turning point of my life, a new challenge which I had to accept. I have no regret to take up my new assignment; rather I feel happy and proud because I know the difference between achievement and manipulation.

I have earned, I have achieved the position of Vice Principal and H.O.D. English which Ranjita has manipulated. To cut a long story short they have created their fate, their destiny in their own hands, strangling to death the potential of deserving and efficient persons. Nobody could do anything against them and here I had been dreaming of heavenly justice! It has been truly said God helps those who help themselves. Veer Parsad and Ranjita have helped themselves to such an extent that God has no other option but to help them survive and not only to survive but also to survive 100 per cent as per their wish, in their own style.

But one thing I am not able to understand – Why I met Veer Parsad and Ranjita? Was it destined by God? If so why? It's really beyond my comprehension! I turn the pages in reverse order quite often in search of an answer but till date I am not able to find it !

* * * * * * * *

I love loneliness or rather I have a passion for it. I am obsessed with each and every moment of solitude when I speak to myself. I can see my true self, keeping aside the mask which I am compelled to wear in a company. In the presence of others one has to smile even with hatred in mind, one has to compliment such persons who may be called hippopotamus or buffalo in secrecy. In my solitude I can laugh to my heart's content at myself as well as at others; I can cry, complain to God and ask him to punish my exploiters. A very innocent, ordinary, simple girl stands face to face, outshining the glamorous, intellectual, so called successful lady and ask her "Are you happy?" It's not so easy to satisfy her curiosity although apparently I am happy. All ingredients of happiness are with me – degrees and qualifications, a coveted job, a husband who can evoke jealousy in many a heart, two precious gems – my children, own house, car, material prosperity, talent, name and fame and above all bewitching beauty which is desirable to all women. in spite of all these am I happy? A very difficult question indeed. Happiness depends on one's self; one who is a keen obsever, who reacts at any and every wrong thing, who can't relax until and unless things are right, cannot be happy. In order to be happy one has to look at things through a colour-glass and ignore any such details which might prick the conscience. If such type of questions as to why my middle aged widow aunt has to wear a white sari and can not eat non-vegetarian food although she prepares fish or chicken for lunch or dinner for the whole family, why the domestic help Dulpo – a girl of twelve can not join our evening game of hide and seek and help mother instead – trouble the mind from childhood, how can one feel happy? Such type of questions never leave you alone if you keep on seeking the answers. The little girl grows up with thousands of questions in mind.

From her childhood the girl could feel that she was different from other girls of her age – both in appearance as well as nature. She became a victim of mockery and teasing of others.

Before I could understand what it means to step into youth, I got married. I was still in my teens and was in the second year of my graduation course. My father was constantly worried about me because of my beauty. On my way to school and college, many street Romeos used to follow me; love letters were thrown into the roof of our house attached to stones wrapped in paper, causing high B.P. of my father. He started searching for a suitable groom and was successful within no time. Swapnil is the cousin of my father's friend (younger than him of course). A Mechanical Engineer by profession, he was working at a Public Sector company at that time and was posted at Durgapur in West Bengal. We met for the first time on 25th January 1978 at our residence in Marlin Park, on a candle-lit evening as severe power cuts used to take place in those days.

We started life together on 27th April 1978. I got compliments for my beauty from everyone who attended the marriage and reception functions. My sensitive mind didn't fail to observe the jealous attitude and gesture of my aunt – in – law (Husband's Mausi), M.Sc. 1st class and Ph.D., Ex H.O.D., Chemistry, Jadavpur University, who on the pretext of preparing me for the reception party, dabbed extra face-powder on my face and applied thick eyeliner around my eyes in such a way that I was looking older than my actual age. Her constantly looking_at her own face in the mirror revealed her insecurity and cautioned me. But one good thing she had done, that is, observing my mother-in-law's benevolence in distributing the sarees (which I received as gifts) to anyone and everyone, she kept them in my almirah and locked it. Because of her smart action at least I was left with a few.

In those days, every moment my husband and I felt intoxicated, engrossed in each other, ignoring the frowning and retorted remarks of people around us. Remaining awake till dawn, then getting up late in the morning, never-ending meaningless conversations, honeymoon in Darjeeling and extending the pleasure trip which resulted in cancellation of reservation and then returning in unreserved compartment, compelling others to keep their eyes closed - days just passed away in a jiffy. My husband had to join his office in Durgapur and I stayed back with my in-laws in Calcutta, attending college and preparing for my B.A. Part I examination. He used to come in every weekend and go back on Monday mornings. The whole week's separation was compensated by two nights.

One thing I can never forget in my life that is the encouragement I got from my husband to continue with my studies. There are instances when I fell sick just before my exams and he used to read the books loudly and just by listening to him, I appeared in the exams and did well. But he could not stay with me constantly and in his absence I faced a lot of problems. My mother-in-law didn't want me to continue with my studies and tried her best to resist. She even commented when I topped my college in B.A.Part I and at the same time my brother-in-law could not get honours in B.Sc. Part II, "Examiners are partial towards the female candidates." Isn't she a female?

Anyway, at the completion of one year, just fifteen days before my B.A. Part II exam, my elder son came on my lap with a bundle of joy. I never sang any lullaby to make him fall asleep; he fell asleep listening to the critical appreciation of Robert Browning's poems or an account of plot and characterisation in Shakespeare's dramas. I came out with flying colours in B.A. with Honours in English and took admission for M.A. in English at Calcutta University. By that time Swapnil was transferred to the beautiful port town of Haldia. He was allotted a two bedroom quarter in the township situated on the banks of the river Haldi. I used to spend one fortnight in Haldia and the other in Calcutta, attending my classes.

The long, dark corridors of Asutosh Building of Calcutta University, the serious lectures of the highly knowledgeable professors, short breaks at Coffee House, venturing through the footpaths of College Street, in search of second-hand books at a cheaper rate on the one hand and strolling by the river side pushing the pram of my son or holding his hand as he toddled, enjoying the evening tea with my husband and guests, attending office parties, trying various recipes with fresh Hilsas caught from the Haldi river, teaching alphabets and nursery rhymes to my son – amidst all these my son started growing up and my mental growth, awareness about my surroundings and maturity went on simultaneously.

I crossed the threshold of teenage and stepped into youth with my eyes wide open and mind ever receptive. I started becoming more familiar with the known world and observed many things which had escaped my eyes earlier. The possessiveness of my mother-in-law, her irritation at the continuation of my studies, my father-in-law's blind support extended to my MIL, neighbours' instigations adding fuel to the fire, husband's untiring hard work in spite of dirty office politics, extra-marital relationship of some of his colleagues and their wives, longing for me in the greedy eyes of some of his colleagues, constant advice of my parents to try to adjust with everything and make my husband and child happy – all these enriched me with experience and wisdom.

I got my results of M.A. but was afraid to apply for a job. I had no self-confidence and tried to console myself thinking I have to take care of my husband and child. I was an excellent homemaker. Whoever visited our house used to praise me for my housekeeping, the interior decoration, the recipes I prepared and the overall aura of happiness which prevailed in my home. It was a great moment when I mustered enough courage to join a group of ladies to start a pre-school in the township; we were both the organisers as well as teachers. I never felt the want of anything and thought life would go on like that forever. In 1984 two remarkable things happened which brought a change in life – one is the changing of job of my husband and shifting to Central India and the other is the birth of my younger son, just after a few days of the assassination of Mrs. Indira Gandhi. On 16th November, when I was taken to O.T., my doctor said

"A second Indira is going to take birth soon," knowing my desire for a girl child. When the baby was shown to me, I sobbed for not delivering a girl child and the doctor called all his colleagues present at that time in Presidency Nursing Home to the O.T. to show them one such instance where a mother cries for not giving birth to a girl child. In a country where girl infanticide is a common feature, longing for a girl child is astonishing indeed!

Perhaps I was too romantic, impractical – whatever it is, I learnt a lesson for the first time that everything can not be tailor-made. One can not always get what one desires. I also learnt how to be happy with what God has given me and today I have no regret, I am proud of both of my children.

When my younger son was only five weeks old, we started a new phase of our life in the industrial city of Central India. Keeping the younger one inside the mosquito net and hanging bright soft toys there, I used to bring the elder one from the nearby school. Life became tough and the atmosphere was totally different from that of Bengal. My husband was climbing up the ladder of success and he remained busy with his work and career. In between he was transferred to Burnpur and then again back to the same place. The younger one also started going to school and I started feeling lonely. The intoxication of a newly married life was replaced by a daily routine of performing the household chores, playing the role of a good wife and mother which was more a duty and hard reality than a dream or romance. In order to get rid of the monotony I started doing M.A. in History along with running a coaching class for English at home.

Life took a different turn when in 1993 my husband was transferred to Visakhapatnam. It's a beautiful place where a landscape of a chain of hills and the Bay of Bengal has been mingled along with the abundance of plantain and coconut trees-a vast expanse of green and cool, serene blue -- a visual treat and a solace to the mind. Sitting at home one can see the changing of colours of the hills with the hide and seek of the sunlight on them. Sea here is different from the seas which I have seen at various other places like Andaman, Mumbai, Kanyakumari, Puri, Digha, Pondicherry and Tamil Nadu. Again the hills are not like that of the hill stations of India.

As my husband was busy with his job, I took my children to the best school in the township with a brand name, for admission and met the then Principal, retired Colonel Ratnadeep. He was a jovial man of fifty seven and was very popular not only in the school but also in the whole township. I have even seen the tiny tots of pre-primary classes hanging around his neck and arms and calling him 'Grandpa' very affectionately. Ratnadeep Sir was highly impressed when I communicated with him regarding the admission of my children. He wanted to know about my qualifications and experience and offered me a job as a guest teacher for a temporary period. His encouraging face and confidence in me made me feel confident and overcoming all fear I accepted his offer. I didn't know a born teacher was hidden in me; on the very first day I could win the heart of my students and colleagues. I had to teach English and History at any class between I and XII as and when required, @ Rs. 60.00 per day. I had to help in organizing various cultural programmes also. At the end of the contract after eight months I had to sit back at home but by that time I had experienced the taste of standing on my own feet and creating my own identity.

While I was thinking of approaching Ratnadeep Sir again, like a bolt from the blue came the news, brought by my children that he had left the school, getting a better offer in a school run by the NRIs in Noida where his family was also staying. I had gone back to my old routine of preparing food for my family, helping my children in studies, discussing office related problems with my husband and sparing some time for my hobbies.

One day my elder son came back from school and told me – "Our class teacher wants to meet you. She said she will be coming to our house."

I asked – "Why ?"

He said – "I don't know."

I was wondering why she wanted to meet me, because she was also the Acting Principal at that time. In the afternoon she came and without any introduction, straightway she told me – "We are in need of an English teacher. Colonel Ratnadeep highly recommended your name before leaving. Are you interested to join immediately?"

I thought I was getting the moon in my hand. Here, the Acting Principal of the most prestigious school in the country is sitting on the sofa of my drawing room and offering me a job. Can anything be better and more desirable than this? Without a second thought I said." "It's my pleasure, I'm honoured." She left after having a cup of coffee. I kept on thinking will I ever be able to repay their debt? I don't know where Colonel Ratnadeep is at present but in my mind a place of honour will always be there for him not for providing me with a job but for his confidence in me which resulted in my self-confidence.

I joined as a PRT on 4th October and was given two years time for completing B.Ed. which is compulsory for school teaching.

My school days in Visakhapatnam as a teacher was the most enjoyable period of my life. Life may knock you down several times but the genuine love, affection and respect of the children will always provide you with the strength to get up and face a starry sky above. The colorful world painted by the novice is pure and passionate like the morning dew or the first spell of monsoon shower quenching the thirst of the Earth, a contrast indeed to the contaminated, adulterated artificial inferno fabricated by mature mavins. Their feelings, their understandings, their expression of joy and sorrow, friendship and fighting help you to think in a novel way. A small rose bud presented by a child from his garden is more precious than an expensive bouquet presented by somebody with an artificial smile, expecting some favour in return.

One day, when I was teaching a story in class three, I came across a word 'shy.' As soon as I read out the word, a boy named Anindya stood up and asked – "Ma'am, what is the meaning of 'shy'?"

For a while I stopped to think how to come down to his level to explain the meaning of 'shy'! In the meantime a girl named Ragleena stood up and said – " See Anindya, if some new uncles and aunties come to your house and ask you to sing a song, how do you feel?"

Anindya looked at the floor with a shameful smile. He could not only understand the meaning of 'shy' but felt it too and didn't try to hide his feelings. There is so much to learn from children ! In the primary classes, usually I kept my dupatta on the chair while teaching or writing something on the board. Quite often I used to forget about it and came out of the classroom, leaving it on the chair and every time one or the other of my little students would run after me towards the staff room and feel immense pleasure and pride in handing it over to me with a smile. How can I forget their love?

All of a sudden my calm and quiet life turned out to be a busy one, full of activities. Teaching, organising competitions as a House Warden, working for the school magazine, Wall magazine, House Board, Working as the Chief House Coordinator etc. kept me engaged throughout the day. I tried to realise my real worth, my real value and all doubts regarding my capabilities and efficiency were completely dispelled from my mind. Side by side my preparation for B.Ed. also went on. I learnt one more thing which earlier I never even dreamt of learning i.e., riding a two-wheeler. I had become desperate in learning it and now I burst into laughter to think that one night after dinner when I was practising on the road, my vehicle skidded on some sand and I fell down along with my two wheeler which caused a head injury and for the whole week I was confined to the four walls with a faint hope of learning the riding of a two-wheeler again.

In order to excel in life, the most important thing required is motivation. This, I have realised from my own experience. You praise a child and see how he improves in his studies and in this matter, even an adult is no exception. An adult also craves for praise just like a child. When I got married I was just in the second year of my B.A. Honours. After marriage, gradually I became a graduate, then did my post graduation in English and History, B.Ed., Post Graduation in Journalism and Mass Communication, M.Phil and Ph.D. All these have been possible only because of the encouragement of my husband.

There is one more person who used to praise and motivate me a lot – the Principal at Visakhapatnam, Dr. Augustus Edwin. Going through my Literary work he used to say "You are from the land of Tagore." Although I am no match even to the dust particles under Tagore's feet, I felt great at his compliments and today whatever I am, it is only because of his whole-hearted praise and motivation. Praising my House Display Board he had said – "your House Board is looking like an open encyclopedia." Who doesn't feel like performing even better after this?

The results of B.Ed were out. I started looking for my name in the list for 2nd class qualifiers and was highly disappointed when I could not find my name. My husband encouraged me to check the list for 1st class qualifiers and to my greatest surprise I found my name there! I know under what circumstances I had prepared for B.Ed. Fulfilling my commitments at school, taking care of my children and home hardly I got any time to prepare.

My competition started with myself and work became a passion for me. I didn't even feel the absence of my husband who was again transferred to the place from where we had come. That industrial town of Central India – the very thought was so repulsive. I had to stay back with my two sons in Visakhapatnam because my elder son was in Class XII and it was a very crucial time for him. My four years stay in Visakhapatnam will remain in the treasure trove of my memory as a precious gem forever. My learning of riding a two wheeler came to use as we had to shift to another sector which was far away from the school. Life was not a bed of roses ; nor was it a starry night. It was a challenge and that too in a vicious circle. But all three of us faced life boldly and were successful in crossing the hurdles.

I joined another unit of the same school in the industrial city of Central India as a T.G.T. English on 1st April 1997. I met Veer Parsad the Principal and his wife Ranjita – the 'Rahu' and Ketu' of my life. Before meeting them I didn't know that there can be so much corruption, manipulation, nepotism, backbiting and dirty politics in an educational institution. My trust and faith, my respect and a positive idea about an educational institution which was built up in my mind, day by day, bit by bit, was smashed and broken into pieces like a brittle glass.

I remember the very first day when I attended a general meeting on 31st March, Saturday before the beginning of the new session 1997-'98. Not knowing anything there and the exact time when the meeting will start, I was standing outside the staff room, waiting for the meeting to start. One teacher Lolita Banerjee came out and called me to join them in the staff room. Since then, I had been sitting at the same place, next to her throughout my stay in the school. What surprised me that day was the character assassination of the Principal and his wife by the staff members and the image of the Principal of which I got some hints on the very first day was that of a characterless Casanova who makes his bed warm with the help of innumerable women. Mostly the teachers working on an ad hoc basis were his target as their getting permanent grade was in his hands. His wife knew everything but didn't interfere in his personal affairs as she was interested in something else.

The meeting started at eleven a.m. One Senior Teacher of the English Department who became Senior Mistress later on, sitting next to me whispered in my ears "The drama is being enacted to make the announcement that his wife has been promoted as the Senior Mistress of the Middle Wing." I looked at her; she added –"From T.G.T. Grade IV' to Senior Mistress, ditching all senior teachers. We have been working here from the very first day when the school started."

Till then, my mind was not poisoned with the curse of the civilized society called 'ambition'. I just listened to her quietly without making any comment.

She continued – "Only last year they joined; she used to teach at primary level in the previous school. There also he had managed to uplift her as the Senior Mistress of the Primary School but got a kick from the parents and staff members. Now he has started eating our head here. Does she have any proper background? She continued as a Primary Teacher for fourteen years in a residential school before her husband became the Principal. She hasn't even done B.Ed."

The new teachers were introduced, including me. The name of some teachers were announced who were promoted to the next higher grade. Ranjita's name was announced at the end in a dramatic way as the Senior Mistress of the middle wing.

Veer Parasad said – "It's not my recommendation; she has been selected by the management." Kaveri pinched me with a meaningful gesture.

At the end of the meeting I got the time-table from the time-table in charge. I was given the classteachership of VI B and was asked to teach English and History of various classes from VI – XI. Ranjita used to teach History in classes VI – X. Right from the beginning Ranjita had a hostile attitude towards me. She used to take great pleasure in harassing my younger son who was then in class VIII in order to harass me. This hostile feeling went on increasing as she could sense the soft corner for me in her husband's mind. Initially in various ways Veer Parsad used to show his favouritism towards me. As we had come from Visakhapatnam, where Telugu was compulsory as a third language in classes V – VIII, I got special permission from the Principal to arrange a Telugu teacher from outside for my son in class VIII who will be teaching, preparing question papers for his examinations and Weekly Tests and evaluating his papers. That was something new in the history of the school, so naturally some eyes were rounded up and frowning wrinkled up Ranjita's forehead.

I had left Visakhapatnam before the results of the Annual Examinations were out, hence, could not submit the report card of my son at the time of his admission. After receiving it later on, I went to the Principal's room to submit it along with a copy of my service certificate. Ranjita was sitting there. When I submitted the report card, the Principal smiled at me meaningfully and said – "Report card is not required in your case." I was puzzled; however I left the Report Card on his table and came out of his chamber, thanking him. The incident took place before the eyes of Ranjita. What was her immediate reaction, I couldn't see because I didn't look at her face.

I continued to work but was yet to get the appointment letter which was a matter of great concern to me. I asked Varalakshmi, the P.A. to the Principal about it. She smiled at me and said – "Be rest assured, you will get it."

After fifteen days of my joining, the Principal went on his foreign tour to the U.K. and U.S.A. which he had managed by flattering the then Vice Chairman Naresh Chandra. He came back at the end of the month. Summer vacation started and summer camps were arranged for four days. I had duty with the then H.O.D. English and Activity Incharge Mrs. Sita Raman. After the inaugural function when we all were having our refreshment, I had an instinctive uneasy feeling because of somebody's closeness and warm breath and lifting up my eyes from the plate of sandwich I saw the Principal standing in front of me with his eyes fixed on me. He was practically ogling me. My half-eaten sandwich remained on the plate and that dirty glance remained like a deep sore in my body till I returned home and straightway went to the bathroom to stand under the shower.

It was my first summer vacation in that place of excessive heat and dryness.

For the last two days I was getting a blank call and was mentally disturbed. At about 9.30 in the morning, the telephone started ringing which I attended. There was no response from the other side and the same thing happened thrice. When it rang for the fourth time, losing my patience I gave the caller a piece of my mind and kept the receiver down. Within five minutes came another call and this time I was prepared to be more rude but to my surprise the caller revealed his identity, saying "Hello ! I am Veer Parsad, your Principal. My wife is not at home. I want you to come to my house and give me company. We will enjoy. Shall I send you my car?" I thought of shouting but controlled myself when I remembered that I was yet to get my appointment letter. I pretended not to have understood what he said. He repeatedly said – Look, in reputed public schools only teaching is not enough. You are expected to do many other things to please the Principal and even other members of the management. I am sending the car to your house, you are expected to come within half an hour."

I said – "I'm sorry, I'm not well. It's not possible for me to come. If you give me any amount of school work I'm ready to do but it's not possible for me to meet you for any other reason."

He asked again – "So, you will never come – is it your final decision?" I said very firmly that exactly that was my final decision and it will never change for any reason. He said "O.K." and disconnected the line and from that moment my tension started. I could not enjoy the summer vacation because of constant tension and worries.

Fifteen days after the reopening, I got the appointment letter. While receiving it from the Principal I was trying to observe his expressions but he behaved in a normal way. Days passed on, I became familiar to the new atmosphere. My rapport with my students and colleagues was established. But one thing, which always dominated the discussion among the teachers was the character of the Principal. This is something which I had not experienced at my previous school. I bow my head even today in respect whenever I think of Dr. Augustas Edwin or Colonel Ratnadeep. They had taught me to respect myself and my profession.

I constantly faced problems in trivial matters because of Ranjita's meanness and her attitude towards me and this went on increasing day by day. She could sense that I know more than her which was a threat to her. She started vitiating the mind of the Principal against me. A group of teachers always used to move with Ranjita and they tried to flatter her in order to get her favour. This group of teachers was set against me and with full enthusiasm they started doing justice to their assigned task. They started fabricating stories against my son and me and in every meeting I was publicly humiliated by the Principal for various reasons for which neither my son nor I was responsible. The unfulfilled desire of the Principal and his grudge on me on the one hand and that wicked, jealous woman Ranjita's cunning, manipulative tricks to pull my legs made my life miserable. To add fuel to the fire, Madhushree – the sex bomb joined the English department as an ad hoc teacher, when another English teacher went on maternity leave and at this point started the long saga of the affair between Mr. Veer Parsad and Madhushree.

The Madhushree episode was a long one which was the most spicy items on the platter for everyone at that time. Removing all senior teachers of the English department from their responsibilities, Madhushree was appointed as the Assistant Activity Incharge and the Editor of the magazine apart from taking the classes of the Principal's children. This gave her ample opportunities to meet the Principal every now and then at school and at his residence too; and whenever she went inside that hot chamber, there used to be a long queue of the visitors outside because she never came out before one and a half or two hours and on several occasions the receptionists and typists sitting outside the Principal's room observed her coming out with her dress in a crumpled state or her hair loose which otherwise used to be tied up in a pony. Rumour started spreading at the speed of lightning. She got the permanent grade; her children were given admission. Her glamour started sparkling, rejuvenating the mind and body of the Principal and burning the heart of innumerable competitors and Ranjita too. She started calling Madhushree every now and then and advised her not to wear low-cut blouse or transparent salwar suits at school. The evening and night session at the Principal's office and rest room was shared by Padma and Madhusree every alternative day.

Ranjita had to accept this silently but what she could not tolerate was the Principal's admiration for Madhushree's English. She started writing the speeches for the Principal. In this matter Padma was very clever. Whatever she did, she used to give credit to the foolish woman Ranjita and was thus able to win her heart. She is the only woman who could understand the psychology of Ranjita and because of this understanding till date she has been able to maintain an excellent relationship with her. Padma had started feeling insecure because of Madhushree's entry in Veer Parsad's life and knowing about the pricking of thorn in Ranjita's mind she started pouring poison in her ears about Madhushree. The screaming, shouting, heated arguments which followed at Veer Parsad's house did not allow the crows and the kites to sit on their roof; the servants were highly entertained and with double enthusiasm they started enlightening the less fortunate ones with their first-hand experience.

Veer Parsad's weakness was, ultimately he had to surrender to Ranjita and accept defeat in her hands because she never hesitated to blackmail him in the name of their children.

Madhushree started losing her position and the undivided attention of the Principal, much to the relief of Padma and some other teachers. I remember, whenever any lady receptionist had been recruited, Padma played her role (observing the Principal's intimacy with the lady), hiding important files, writing anonymous letters, criticising the Principal and putting the blame on the poor, innocent ladies. The characterless man, even after knowing the nature of Padma could not do anything because she is his greatest coverture, the witness of his each and every corrupt, unlawful evil act and the clever manipulator to turn any adverse situation in his favour. She also played her role tactfully to remove all barriers from the way of Ranjita to clear her own path also. Whoever had the potential to rise, had to leave the school one after another, particularly the teachers of the English department because Ranjita was cherishing the dream of becoming the H.O.D. English.

Amidst all this, I had a tough time, working very hard with the hope that God will one day turn his face towards me and improve the situation in my favour There was not a single occasion when after a meeting, on my way home I didn't shed tears silently. On several occasions, it so happened that while riding my two wheeler back home, my flowing tears got mingled with the heavy downpour or a light drizzling turning me almost blind on the road. He used to humiliate me in the meetings by bringing false charges and accusations against me. Sometimes he used to say that I have shown partiality and given more marks to the students of my section whenever there was any complaint by the parents against Ranjita's inhumanly strict correction. Sometimes he brought charges against my son saying that he was bullying other students, taking advantage of my position. Once Madhushree had given a Guide book cum Sample paper for English to a student of the same section of class IX in which my son was also studying; some questions in that sample paper were marked important and the boy got the clue and he discussed with his friends about the questions. The same questions came in the half-yearly exam. At the time of result discussion the Principal told me "You have shown the English question paper to your son and through him the paper was leaked. Not only that you have shown the Social Science paper also to him." I tried my best to make him understand that none of the papers were set by me, so there was no question of showing him the paper, but I failed to convince that adamant mule. There, is something called 'Divine Justice' and only because of that my son got the highest marks in English and Social Science from his section in the CBSE class X Board Examination.

Threatened by the sensuality and fine English of Madhushree, Ranjita had started showing a soft corner for me. There was no problem in sharing the classes also as I was shifted to the Senior Secondary Wing to teach English only and she used to teach History and Civics in the middle and secondary classes. There was no interference, no clash. Temporarily there was a peaceful coexistence but alas! That was only a false dawn which I realised very soon.

I had become desperate and wanted to do something remarkable, great to show my ability, efficiency and talent. Right from my childhood whenever I found any obstruction on my way to move onward, I used to become more arrogant and determined, not to accept defeat at the hands of any insolent power. If somebody ignored me, I used to get motivated to prove myself. The opportunity came when State level Essay writing competition was organised by PCRA and the Ministry of Petroleum and Natural Gas and I secured the 1st position in the State of M.P. I was invited for receiving the prize from the then Governor of M.P. but Veer Parsad didn't allow me to go and receive the prize, so the organisers sent it to the school. However there was a slight change in his attitude towards me.

So long I had been kept cornered but now the Principal started giving me some responsibilities. Perhaps my evil phase of life was not yet over – that's why I met with an accident and fell from the staircase of my house. This minor accident affected me dearly as two bones of lumbar vertebrae got fractured and the doctor advised me bed rest for about a month.

It was a horrible phase of my life. I was almost handicapped and had not my husband stood by my side and helped me, I shudder to think what would have happened to me ! At that time when I was confined to bed and could not go to school, I got a telephone call from the Principal enquiring about my health and Ranjita paid a visit to my house along with Padma.

I joined the school after five weeks. All of a sudden I felt a change in the behaviour of the Principal. He seemed to be too soft and polite with me and I fell into his trap.

Now I am able to understand that I was used as a dice in the game of chess.

I was so intoxicated with success that I could not realize the intention of the Principal. Madhushree started cautioning me about the Principal but I thought simply out of jealousy she was trying to instigate me against him. I was given full power to coordinate all functions and events of the school. Within no time I was able to make a place of repute for myself. In the list of staff members my name was on the top. All important work of the school, right from preparing the duty rosters, circulars, signing the bills and cheques as the second cheque signatory, (the first being the Principal himself) and the amount unlimited, preparing speeches for the Principal and other VIPs who came to school as Chief Guests, coordinating all big and small functions, preparing albums after the functions for the VIPs, Editorship of the school magazine, coordinating all departmental work, taking the interview of the teachers and students – the school started shimmering with the radiance of the bonfire i.e. Urja. Without consulting me the Principal never used to take any decision in any matter. All of a sudden I became the most important person, the centrepiece in the school and as I was very close to the Principal, people started flattering me.

In the meantime I won the 1st prize again in the State level Essay Competition on Oil Conservation organized by PCRA. At the National-level of the same competition I got the second position and was invited to Delhi for receiving the prize. At the same time I had to attend a workshop on teaching English at XI and XII organized by EMC in Delhi. I came up to the limelight and Veer Parsad started praising me in front of everybody, even in the Assembly.

A new problem cropped up for Ranjita. The thorn started pricking her mind but she had to endure that temporarily as the episode of Madhushree was still fresh in everybody's mind and removing me immediately would have fetched a lot of criticism. Moreover, there was no one to do all these work and Ranjita had the intention of first learning from me and then snatching.

Veer Parsad started praising me like anything in the Assembly, in the meetings and I forgot his previous behavior and attitude towards me. I conducted the written examinations and oral interviews of the T.G.Ts and P.G.Ts and was asked to join the Principal and the Chief Education Officer over lunch, much to the envy of the other staff members. The Principal's car used to pick and drop me whenever I came for any extra work to school. Daily at least ten times the

Principal used to ring me at home at any time for various reasons. So long I used to be at school, he used to send the peon to call me even from the classes. I was so engrossed in my newly achieved success and the passion for reaching the top that I failed to notice the rumour and comments regarding my relationship with the Principal. That whore Bindiya Bhalla and her group even started spreading baseless rumours, trying to spoil my reputation. She might have remembered her golden days with the Principal even before I joined the school. Staff members say that her son who is about ten years younger than her daughter is not from her legally married husband but his biological father is Mr. Veer Parsad – the all time Casanova.

Madhushree, who was so long the eyesore of people now started receiving their full sympathy. This is the rule of the world. When somebody is in the peak of success, all tongues start bla bla against that person. As soon as he/ she is thrown away from the position, people start showing their sympathy and support towards that person. Sometimes I feel that women are the greatest enemies of women and they are the personification of meanness. One woman's success ignites the hellfire of jealousy in the minds of other women. They don't hesitate to criticise or indulge into character assassination if they find anything suspicious in others but forget their own drawbacks or weaknesses. I have seen the shameless efforts taken by the lady teachers to seduce the Principal for stepping up the ladder. Haven't I noticed the Ph.D. degree holder teacher of the Chemistry department entering the toilet to apply lipstick and compact before meeting the Principal for any official work? (May be personal work on the pretext of official work !!!) Haven't I seen the H.O.D. of Science dressing up in an attractive way whenever she had an appointment with the Principal? But the same lady shared her experience with the ladies of the neighbourhood how she had been trembling with fear when one day she had taken leave due to illness and the Principal came to her house, driving the school car himself while the school was going on. At that time there was no one in the house and she was really scared of the Principal. If that is true then what's the use of wearing a beautiful sari, or applying lipstick or adorning the forehead with a designer bindi while going to the Principal's room? These ladies hold important positions like House Wardens, H.O.Ds, Class Representatives, various Incharges, Senior Mistresses etc. I firmly believe that at least eighty percent of ladies capitalise on their sensuality rather than on their talents or qualities for achieving success in their workplace. Veer Parsads flourish on the Earth only because of such type of women. Quite obviously when these ladies observed Veer Parsad's interest and faith on me, they started feeling jealous and insecure and indulged in spreading rumour about me forgetting the fact that I am the mother of two grown up sons who were at that time in Delhi – the elder one after completing his M.B.A. joined the service and the younger one was doing B.Tech. in Bio-technology.

Ranjita noticed everything very keenly and prepared the ground for playing the game of dice against me. I remained obsessed with work and tactfully avoided the meaningful comments and proposals of Veer Parsad. But the greatest blunder I made was – neglecting my family, my health, my home, I wholeheartedly rendered my service to the school, devoting my entire time and energy, not realising the adverse effect of it in my life. While I was preparing the speeches for the Principal, preparing 'From the Principal's Desk' in the school magazine for him, on the one hand he was relishing the praise of people for his knowledge and style of English with my words and hard work and on the other hand sharpening the knife to stab me from the back. While I was managing the work of ten teachers at the same time, coordinating all functions, all departmental work, he was thinking how long he will allow me to play in the water, releasing the twine and then winding the fishing wheel to pull me on to the ground causing my suffocation. While year after year, I had been working till midnight with the printer after attending school, giving a wonderful shape to the school magazine, he was giving time to his snobbish and foolish wife to learn and snatch away from me to get the credit and applause. While sacrificing my summer vacation and autumn break, I was preparing testimonials for the students and preparing them for debate or any other competition (every time they brought laurels to the school) his useless wife was relaxing at home or enjoying a vacation with her parents or children. Hardly could I understand that they just got everything streamlined by me when things were in a topsy-turvy state and the staff members were reluctant to work.

A rebellion was materialising among the staff members and the situation was worsening day by day. The anonymous letters had made it clear to all that Veer Parsad was responsible for the dispute between the Society in Delhi and local management. He wanted to take everything within his grip. Knowing very well that the members of the local management were too busy with their job, he tried to separate the school from the Society in Delhi and became the lord himself.

Madhushree and about eighteen other teachers gave written complaint against Veer Parsad to the local management and brought the allegation of sexual harassment against him. But those complaint letters were torn into pieces and thrown into the wastepaper basket because Veer Parsad never forgot to send the monthly fat packets to each one of them during these ten years. Moreover they were his companions of the evening sessions with glasses full up to the brim. Turnwise beautiful, sexy teachers from the school made their evenings colourful and as the evenings turned into nights, the cocktail parties transformed into honeycombs. VIPs started spending their evenings in the indoor swimming pool of the school where teachers in swimming costumes served them drinks and after a few pegs the swimming costumes of the teachers and outfits of those members of the so called civilised society remained mute witnesses on the wet floor while they played nude underwater games. I doubt whether the emperors of the Mughal period or the British rulers in India could enjoy so much during their respective reign. Hat's off to Veer Parsad who was born in an illiterate, uncultured, agriculturist family of Haryana but adopted the ways and means to rise up to the highest point. Is he in any way less than the Slumdog Millionaires? Although the guards and night-watchmen were taken care of, a few of them could not remain loyal till the end and nothing remained secret.

Those nineteen teachers who had complained against Veer Parsad were compelled to resign because Veer Parsad, Ranjita and Padma had made their lives miserable, but at the last moment two of them withdrew their resignation. Some of them extended their notice period with the hope that Veer Parsad would be removed before the session ended but were disheartened as no such thing happened and ultimately they left.

In the meantime one more scandalous incident rocked the city. Veer Parsad had the habit of coming to school at odd hours when there used to be no one in the school except the gatekeeper and his driver. One Saturday evening he called a lady to school who had approached him for her daughter's admission. She didn't expect the Principal to be alone and with the assumption that there will be the P.A. and the receptionists in the school, she came in the evening. To her great surprise, she couldn't find anyone in the reception and when she thought of going back, the Principal's door flung open and he himself came out to receive her. What followed that special reception, came in the local daily newspapers with bold headings, describing in details the misbehavior of the dirty Principal towards that lady. FIR was lodged against the Principal on the charge of sexual harassment and his effigy was burnt in front of the school gate by the social activists. But such a big incident was brought under control with the intervention of the then District Collector and the lady was compelled to withdraw the case.

Under the heading "Misbehaviour of the Principal on Pretext of Admission – Investigation Started," in a leading daily newspaper, dated 18th February 2002 came the news that the Principal of XYZ school had been accused of playing with the honour of a lady on the pretext of admission. The victim Mrs. Rajnandini Satpal had lodged a complaint at the local police station regarding the matter. The Principal denied saying that the personal interest of the woman was not fulfilled, that's why she was blaming him. The S.P. and the S.S.P. expressed their ignorance in this matter.

The lady said that she had applied for the admission of her child. On 19th January the written test was conducted, which the child could clear. On the same evening interview was taken. After that there was no response from the school. She got a call from the Principal on 16th February in the morning when he asked her to meet her in the school at 5.30 p.m. The lady also said that at 5.30 p.m. there was absolute silence in the school. When she reached the office of the Principal, he was sitting alone. Except his chauffeur and Gatekeeper outside there was not a single soul in the campus. The Principal took her hand in his own and pulling her towards him tried to kiss her. She made herself free somehow, struggling hard and came out of the Principal's Office and then left the place in her Summo.

Disclosing her own identity the lady said that she had to work in a big business house of the city to support herself and her child as she was a divorcee. Her employer, a renowned wine merchant also spoke to the A.S.P. expressing his annoyance at the misbehavior of the Principal and humiliation of his employee due to availing of ill advantage of the situation by the Principal.

A written report was lodged by the victim in the Police Station. The investigation officer said that the application had been accepted and the investigation was going on.

In the next day's paper came the news that the effigy of the Principal was burnt in front of the gate of the school by the members of a particular political party and they demanded the resignation of the Principal.

Again in the paper of 20th February 2002 came the news that a notice was issued instructing the Principal to go to the Police Station and give his statement. The statement of the driver and gatekeeper of the Principal had also been taken but Padma was yet to be questioned.

After two days of this press report in a dramatic way came the report of the withdrawal of the case by the lady.

The Principal gave an explanation before the staff members at a meeting that the lady had asked for a job which he refused to give because she had not done B.Ed., because of which she brought allegations against him. The staff members had not asked for any explanation from him but out of his guilty conscience when he tried to project himself innocent before the staff, they smiled meaningfully, glancing at each other as the truth was crystal clear to all. Why should a lady who was already earning about forty thousand per month seek for a job of eight thousand per month? Strange ! ! !

The foul smell of the incident was still in the air when another rumour started spreading its odour. One lady was called for an interview which Veer Parsad was taking alone. The lady was asked – "Can you take off your clothes and jump into the swimming pool?" The lady happened to be a friend of the H.O.D. Social Science.

Next was the turn of a young interviewer who was running temperature. Veer Parsad touched her forehead, then cheeks followed by neck and when the hand was further coming down towards her cleavage, she rushed out of the office room uttering abuses.

Complaint after complaint were lodged both at the Society in Delhi and to the local management. The English proverb "Birds of a feather flock together" was perhaps written, keeping in mind people like Veer Parsad and his associates.

It's only when the self interest of an important person is not fulfilled then he takes action, otherwise who bothers for giving justice to others? The same thing happened in 2002 when a termination notice was served to the school because the self interest of the then Chairman Naresh Chandra was at stake due to the greed and atrocity of Veer Parsad. All of a sudden Veer Parsad stopped using some G.K. and Moral Science books published by Har Har Mahadev Publications Ltd. which belonged to Naresh Chandra and which Veer Parsad had been following in various classes earlier in order to please Naresh Chandra to manage his own official foreign trip. Veer Parsad also refused to give admission to the candidates recommended by Mr. Naresh Chandra; also, he refused to give the post of Vice Principal to a more deserving lady who was senior to Ranjita and who at present is not only the Principal of a reputed school under the same brand name but also the Director of three such schools. Why Veer Parsad behaved in a hostile way with Naresh Chandra who had favoured him in various ways in the past? He did it intentionally to vex him to that extent that he was compelled to withdraw the name and logo of the school. If the school is no more under the aegis of the Society in Delhi who would be more benefited than Veer Parsad? Without any problem he would make his wife Ranjita the Vice Principal. For seven years he had kept the post of the Vice Principal vacant. Why? It was preserved with great care for his wife. And exactly this is what he did. In order to justify his action he gave the post of Vice Principal (Upkeep) to Ravi Shastri along with Ranjita as Vice Principal (Academics and Administration). Again here also he was successful in hitting two birds with the same stone. In future the post given to Ravi Shastri will be given to his kept Padma.

Naresh Chandra could have sacked Veer Parsad or transferred him somewhere else but he could not do so because of the faulty contract made between the Society in Delhi and the local management. In order to remove the Principal both the parties had to agree but by bribing huge amount Veer Parsad managed the local management. This huge amount of bribe again, was managed from the donation at the time of admission for which receipts were not given. Those who accept bribes in their workplace, have to do at least some work in favour of the briber but here, simply without doing anything, sitting comfortably at home they were getting very healthy packets. Why shouldn't they support the devil Veer Parsad? Naresh Chandra was furious and in the public notice published in all the leading newspapers he clearly mentioned that the school no more continued to be under the aegis of the Society and Veer Parsad ceased to be the Secretary of the Managing Committee. As the Chairman cum Secretary of the Society which was registered vide Registration No. 21081, under M.P. Society Registration Act 1973, Naresh Chandra issued the public notice for the information of the public at large that in the exercise of the power conferred upon him as per the memorandum of Association he will be exercising the powers conferred upon the Secretary of the Society. Therefore Shri Veer Parsad, Principal of the School has ceased to be the Secretary of the Society and any person dealing with him shall do so solely at his own risk, consequences and peril. The Society shall not be responsible for any liability/consequences whatsoever arising out of the same.

It was further clarified that except Naresh Chandra or any person duly authorized by him none else shall be competent to represent before any government authority, statutory body etc. including making Press statements, issue statements on behalf of the said Society. Veer Parsad highlighted the conditions put forward by the Chairman in every P.T.A. and general meetings but he kept everybody in the darkness and never told the truth that it was him, at whose instigation the then Pro Vice Chairman of the local management body (the person was known as Baa, Baa, black sheep) had already terminated the contract between the Society and the local management. Hence, practically the school was no longer under the famous brand. Black Sheep retired within a short time after this without even thinking about the future of more than four thousand students, particularly those who were to appear for the CBSE Board Examination. Veer Parsad got his work done by paying him more than enough to start a business from his native place. This black money was supplied to him by those parents who paid huge donations for the admission or promotion of their children to the next class in spite of failing. He earned much from the never-ending construction work also. Son of a bitch ! The CBSE affiliation number was also changed overnight. The name and logo were also managed by bringing a stay order from the District Court just at the nick of the time as demanded by the parents.

Before getting the stay order some members of the local management along with a few parents had gone to Delhi to meet the Chairman but he refused to meet them. His only condition was to remove the Principal and dissolve the existing Society formed locally. Veer Parsad was successful in making the local management understand that the school was doing well without any help from the Society. What's the use of giving them a huge share of the profit? Veer Parsad's degree in Law came to his help in many ways. On the one hand it helped him to fight with the Society. On the other hand it helped him to say his points logically in order to convince the local management. In the meetings, first he used to express his opinion and views and then he would ask everybody present there "What is your opinion?" Who had the guts to say anything different to his opinion? Everybody, would say 'yes' to his 'yes' and 'no' to his 'no' and then he would say "O.K., then as per your wish I am taking this decision."

The bitter truth of life is that, when there lies a dead body spreading a foul smell in the atmosphere, the vultures flying high in the sky beyond the vision come to know about it and come down immediately to enjoy their share.

Similarly when we, the staff members along with the students and their parents were worried about our future, those people who were not at all associated with the school, started exploiting the situation. These people obviously, are influential and powerful. Our institution became a permanent source of income to innumerable VVIPs and down the line to their various 'chamchas'. On each and every occasion, one or the other of these people was invited as Chief Guest or Guest of Honour. Great hospitality was shown and gifts were given, not to talk of the monthly or fortnightly alluring white packets, the contents of which were deadly black. Veer Parsad purchased them for his own survival.

The Society lost the case when Veer Parsad managed the stay order. He himself rang me up in the evening and gave the news. At that time we all were in the darkness and whatever Veer Parsad told us, we believed that like the words of Bhagwat Gita or Bible or any other religious book. Next morning it was a joyful scene at school when everybody was discussing about the matter. Sweets were distributed; pool lunch was arranged; only those teachers who had put up their papers remained silent. On 31st March, 2003, they remained absent to avoid the pool lunch and left the school without any farewell.

The new session started. The Society could not digest the defeat and filed a case against the school at the High Court which continued for long, two years. Much water had flowed down the river within these two years. The school had grown from strength to strength. C.B.S.E results of class X and XII were excellent. A large number of students qualified in various competitive examinations and history was created by the school when one student secured the 1st rank in the IIT-JEE examination. The school was progressing in leaps and bounds. But in spite of everything Veer Parsad remained panic stricken and showed his fear and frustration in every possible way. To add fuel to the fire some notorious students started bursting powerful crackers in the toilets of the school at regular intervals. A handful was caught and given T.C. Among them, one was a staff child who was suspended for a week. Later on he took revenge on Veer Parsad by ruthlessly beating his son Amar.

Those who joined the new school left their children at the old school. Poor children ! They became victims of Veer Parsad's frustration and Ranjita's crookedness. How cruelly they were tortured by Veer Parsad and Ranjita ! All teachers were also instructed to harass them. Veer Parsad used to mock at those teachers in every meeting. Those who were in the higher classes were compelled to continue as the new school had opened classes from Nursery to class VII. Those teachers whose children were in lower classes shifted them next year.

Every now and then Veer Parsad used to say that the promoters of the new school and the Chairman wanted to stop our school in order to establish the new school. Without destroying the old school it was not possible for them to set up the new school. Who knows better than me that it's a lie but till date many teachers and parents are under the impression that whatever Veer Parsad said is true.

As the new school under the same brand name advertised for admission test in the month of October, Veer Parsad, breaking the schedule of the school which was being followed from the beginning, decided to conduct the admission test of our school a few days before the admission test of the new school. I was called on a Sunday and asked to prepare the Prospectus on an emergency basis.

At the time of the interview I was called as the subject expert of English for all classes, which was not liked by Ranjita. But she could not do anything at that time because she was junior to me in the Department. By that time I already had ten years experience of teaching English at Senior Secondary level and she had just started taking XI and XII. Moreover Veer Parsad had announced my name on 1st November 2002 as the H.O.D. of English and already I had been working as the same even before that. Ranjita also had a different plan which I could not guess at that time, even in my dreams. In absence of Ranjita things used to go on smoothly but whenever she was present, she spoilt everything and turned my life into a living hell. She had limited knowledge in English but had a wrong, deep-rooted understanding that her English was the best and of such a high standard that it went over the heads of others quite often – Haa, Haa, Haa, height of stupidity in the name of superiority complex ! Once when I was taking interview of some children for admission to school, she was present there as the Vice Principal. I asked a child to correct the sentence "I kindly request you to report at the Reception." The child could not answer, so I told him the correct sentence – "I request you to kindly report at the Reception." Ranjita made a stern, rigid face and at that moment I recalled just few days ago she had sent a notice where it was written "The following teachers are kindly requested to join the school picnic......." Once, at the time of CBSE West Zone Swimming Championship conducted by the school she was making an announcement "The Managers of all teams are kindly requested to get their teams ready." I sensed danger and my premonition was absolutely right. Next day, she called me in her chamber and scolded me for asking that question in the interview. According to her it was a silly question and she also tried to teach me that "kindly request" is grammatically right. Whenever I prepared any script for Drama to be staged on Annual Day or for any competition, she started interfering and replaced the correct words and phrases used by me, with the wrong ones. It was a painful, miserable, horrible experience, which only those who have to work under a stupid, good for nothing boss can understand. Those who were jealous of my success didn't hesitate to make full utilisation of this opportunity. They started adding fuel to the fire by pointing out to Ranjita that I have been favoured by Veer Parsad, I have been showing my superiority to others, I am not allowing others to progress etc., etc., etc. When I prepared the duty rosters for any function, Ranjita intentionally deleted the names of some teachers who used to work in the important areas of the school; later on, she called them separately and pretending to be very innocent engaged them in those important work leaving them with the impression that I didn't want them to get any importance anywhere. On the one hand she turned the teachers against me; on the other hand she instigated them to go to Veer Parsad separately, one at a time and complain against me that I had been rubbing them on the wrong side. I started feeling insecure and knowing my weakness Ranjita started adding poison to my wound.

One day Veer Parsad told me, "My wife doesn't like you. She doesn't want me to give you any responsibilities. I wanted to give you House Wardenship but she remarked "Urja had had her fill." After a few days he told me "Be very firm in dealing with people. Don't try to please everybody." Just two days after this he told me "Be very polite with everybody. You are losing your temperament, you are rude to people and rubbing them on the wrong side." The language seemed to be familiar. That bitch Ranjita must have told him something against me. I was absolutely puzzled – why were they behaving in this way with me? Little did I have the idea that in a planned way they were taking preparation for throwing me out after extracting the maximum from me.

Padma, the veteran player played her role very well. She instructed the typists not to do my work timely so that I get a scolding from Veer Parsad. She shouted at a class IV staff for providing me with a chair when, ignoring the heat of the month of May, I came to school during summer vacation to complete my editing work of the school magazine. Veer Parsad had instructed me to come to his office directly for any official work but this woman Padma – his kept cum Administrative Officer cum bodyguard harassed me by not allowing to meet Veer Parsad. Later on, I always got a tick-off from him for not meeting him. My work also got delayed. It was a really unpleasant and awkward situation. The personal peon of Veer Parsad used to serve tea at the time of meeting. The Principal and the persons holding important position, working closely with him were served in porcelain cups and the rest of the lot in paper cups. Padma instructed him not to serve me a porcelain cup. This, I came to know from that peon and for the first time in my life I felt, to what extent people can be mean if they have jealousy in their mind. I stopped taking tea in school and started carrying my own flask.

Veer Parsad thought it would be better pleasing hundreds of people at my cost and forgetting about what all I had done for him and the school, started supporting those who used to harass me and finding out my faults causing a nervous breakdown in me. I think nincompoops derive pleasure in doing so. By that time he had understood very well that he would never get what he had expected from me. Most probably he had repentance for losing Madhushree also and every now and then started telling me "Madhushree has left the school because of you." Being fined of tasting Madhushree he had thought of changing his diet but was highly disappointed and angry when I refused to satisfy his taste buds. He badly felt the need for Madhushree.

It was the Annual Day of 2003. The Collector's wife had personally requested Veer Parsad to allow a solo dance performance of her daughter who was in class VI. Veer Parsad felt great to oblige her although Ranjita was not happy at all. I was asked to prepare the programme sequence and I kept her dance in between the English skit and the Hindi Drama as a gap filler. It was the fifth item and was supposed to be held at 7.20 p.m. Veer Parsad called me in the morning and told me to change the sequence and place her dance at the beginning as the Collector would leave at 7.05 p.m. due to some other important work. I had to change the sequence although the programme brochure was printed. When the programme was about to start in the evening, Padma came running on to the stage and told me that I have to follow the previous programme sequence as the Collector had changed his schedule and agreed to stay till the end of the programme. As instructed I followed the previous programme but to my utter surprise and disappointment when the English Skit was going on, Veer Parsad send words through some teachers asking me to stop the English Skit and stage the Collector's daughter's dance immediately as he was in a hurry to go. For the first time in my life I refused to obey him because I didn't want to spoil the show and dishearten the young performers of the English Skit. The consequence was not at all pleasant for me. At the end of the programme when I prepared the Press Release and wanted to show him, he kept me waiting in the staff room for more than one hour and ultimately sent words through his P.A. that he would see it on the next day. When I came to school the next morning Veer Parsad was not present in the school. Nobody in the Reception could tell me when he would come. After waiting for an hour I left the Press Release with his P.A. and went home as it was a Sunday and I had invited some guests for lunch. At about 12 noon he called me over the telephone and asked for an explanation in a rude, harsh tone, first of all why I had left the Press Release in the Reception instead of waiting for him and secondly with whose permission I had changed the programme sequence? He refused to listen to my points and didn't believe that Padma had instructed me to do so. He was so rude over the telephone that in front of my guests I could not control myself and broke down spoiling their Sunday as well as mine.

* * * * * * * *

Such type of incidents started happening almost every day and I became a victim of the situation. My sixth sense told me that I will not be able to continue for a long time like this. I decided, if at all, I have to change my job I must do so for a better one. For that I needed more experience and added qualification. I started doing P.G. Diploma Course in Journalism and Mass Communication and after completing that M.Phil in History and did excellently well in both but Veer Parsad was not happy and refused to sanction my leave which was required at the time of examinations and Vivavoce. He asked -- "Do you think by adding degrees to your qualification you will be able to occupy my wife's chair?" I remained quiet but felt like telling him that there are better chairs somewhere else than the one he had kept preserved for his wife. Practically, going against his wishes I did my M.Phil for which time to time I had to go to Chennai and Chidamvaram.

At this juncture I feel like saying a few words about my guide Professor for M.Phil Dr. G. Govindaraju, Head of History Department, Distance Learning, Annamalai University. If Veer Parsad is a Satan, Prof. Govindaraju is God. Such type of selfless, nice persons are rare in this world. While working under him I developed a strong attraction for the ancient temples of the Chola period of South India as that was the topic of my dissertation. At that time when I was passing through a critical phase of my life, this study provided me with a relief. To save myself from the evil, poisonous breath of Veer Parsad and Ranjita, there could not have been a better place than the land of temples.

India is a land of temples, particularly South India is adorned with thousands of temples. Tamilnadu has the maximum number of temples pertaining to Saivism and Vaishnavism. Most of them were constructed by the Imperial Cholas who ruled from 850 A.D. to 1279 A.D.

The Chola queens vied with their respective ruler husband in constructing temples and the women's skill in general made several endowments by these temples and also through the promotion of religions like Saivism and Vaishnavism.

Sembiyan Mahadevi, the dowager queen of Gandaraditya was widowed early in life when her son Uthama Chola was too young to be crowned King. She spent lavishly in renovating old and ruined temples, in building new temples and in making gifts of the images of Gods and Goddesses with valuable gold ornaments set with pearls, rubies and diamonds and made gifts of gold and silver utensils to several temples. Her charities extended throughout the Cholamandalam. Her benefactions not only gave a great impetus to the growth of temple art and architecture but also to religions like Saivism and Vaishnavism. She was greatly venerated during her lifetime and worshipped after her death.

As Veer Parsad refused to sanction my leave, practically without his permission I had to go to Chidamvaram. His grudge and hostility towards me increased but what I got from that visit will remain forever in my treasure trove.

A very ancient temple with four massive gates and Shiva and Vishnu temples on the same courtyard thrilled my husband and me. We felt we had gone back to the 8th century A.D. where time had halted at one point. One king of the Chola period had reconstructed the roofs of the Shiva and Vishnu temples with gold and the doors with silver. The evening 'Aarti' with innumerable oil lamps was a wonderful sight to behold.

My guide Professor Dr. Govindaraju had advised me to do some library work at Institut Francais D'Indologie, a French library in Pondicherry which is another wonderful experience in my life. Not only I got the necessary material for my dissertation but also felt and enjoyed the infinite pristine beauty of nature. The library is situated just in front of the sea. The big French windows facing the sea bring to the vision the foamy waves lashing on the beach and the palm leaves swaying in the cool, sea breeze against the backdrop of the azure sky. How great is the creation of the Almighty and compared to that how mean, how meagre are human desires, seeking for petty power and position, cheap material possession! For a few days at least I could keep myself away from all sorts of malice and meanness.

After coming back I tried to concentrate in my work. In the meantime, I participated in various State and National level competitions and everywhere achieved success. I was absolutely in the limelight, getting the attention and praise of people in the society. Under my guidance the English Department was also doing very well. Ranjita was all set to besmirch my reputation. Although with the help of her followers she tried her best to demoralise me, she could not take the shine out of my work. But definitely she was successful in snatching everything from me gradually.

Face is the index of mind and as the situation plumbed new depths, my face lost all colour because of constant tension, stress and worries. The spark was missing in my eyes and a morose disposition always enveloped my face. This didn't escape the eyes of my motherly colleague Mrs. Geetali Ghosh, a retired lecturer of a college who had been working as a Guest Teacher and used to sit next to me. She used to say "Remember, you are swimming upstream, you will be walking into a minefield. If your face shows your mind, your enemies will be winning half the battle without any effort. Today she is no more among us but down the road her each and every word has been engraved in my mind.

Geetali Ghosh was a wonderful lady who refused to accept defeat at the hands of destiny. When she tied the knots with Ghosh Uncle she was only a Higher Secondary pass out. Within the gap of a few years she became the mother of three lovely children – Anita, Supriti and Anand. The dream of higher education remained suppressed in her mind as she started bringing up her children. Her husband, like many other Indian husbands was least bothered about family affairs or children. His only responsibility was to earn money and nothing else. Each and every demand and requirement of the children were fulfilled by Ghosh Aunty besides giving them moral and emotional support. On the one hand she had to cope with the whims and fancies of her husband who was extremely possessive, fussy about food and many other things and feelingless and on the other hand she had to take care of the education of the children.

Ghosh Aunty's passion was directing and taking part in dramas and plays which was disliked by Uncle. He wanted her to remain confined within the four walls of their house but the strong passion for drama dragged her out, disobeying her husband for which she had to face a lot of torture and humiliation. Uncle showed his grudge on her by beating the children and ultimately he took the extreme decision by separating his bedroom. Although we had a big difference of age, she had confided in me her personal life which apparently happy, could reveal a hidden part unknown to the world. Deprived of the honour which she deserved from her married life, she realised that her marriage was just nine day's wonder. Ghosh uncle kicked up a row with her for anything and everything. He even started suspecting her of infidelity. Her stepping out of the house and going to rehearsal became a bone of contention between them. Her pipedreams fizzled out into the thin air but somehow she picked up the threads of her life once again. Her name and fame had spread far and wide in the steel township and her contribution in the field of drama was literally remarkable. In fact it was she who had started a group for English plays in the township.

When her younger daughter was doing M.A., Ghosh Madam started doing Honours in History and came out with flying colours. She did M.A.in English and her name was in the merit list; not only that, she stood 2nd in the University. Her greatest dream which she had cherished in her youth i.e. lecturership in a college was fulfilled in the middle stage of her life when she joined the Government Girl's College and started teaching the M.A.students. Her daughters got married one after another – the elder one settled in the U.S.A. and the younger one in the capital city of the country. Both of them today are well settled in their life as well as career. Her son also has settled in the U.S.A. and married a Gujarati girl. Geetali Madam's struggle with her life bore ripe, juicy fruits with the success of her son and daughters and after doing all her duties towards her children without any cooperation from her husband, she did Ph.D. in English in her sixties. Her younger daughter presented her with a Maruti 800 and at the age of sixty-two she learnt driving. Isn't it a burning example of feminism? People praise me for the strength of my mind but I think Madam Ghosh was thousand times stronger than me because my conflict and struggle was against the outsiders and I got full support of my husband in all my endeavours but her struggle was against her husband who opposed her at every juncture of life and even refused to sleep with her right from that time when she became the mother of three and was still young. Husband and wife lived like strangers and the children grew up sometimes amidst shattered silence and sometimes amidst a ruction. After the death of Ghosh Aunty, Uncle approached Veer Parsad and wanted to donate a certain amount to introduce a silver medal in the name of Ghosh Madam for the highest scorer in English every year in class X CBSE Board Exam. Veer Parsad insulted him and turned him out of his office room.

Life had taught valuable lessons to Geetali Madam and she could predict my fate in the school. When she observed me overstraining myself doing school work she warned me – "Urja, don't expect anything in return of your hard work. You are just being exploited. Unnecessarily you are wasting your time here. Do something which may be beneficial to you in future. Why don't you register yourself for Ph.D.?"

I asked "Where is the time?"

She said – "If you have time for preparing speeches for the Principal and preparing the school magazine till midnight, I think you will have enough time for your own studies and improvement of qualification."

"Madam, I am head over heels in love with the school magazine; it's my creation."

"But it will soon be snatched from you by the Principal's wife, just wait and see."

I couldn't believe her although I knew the nature of Ranjita very well.

She continued – "Do you know how many times she has asked me to write reports against you that you have not accepted my article for the magazine?" I said – "But I have told you that it was not accepted by the Principal and he had told me not to accept any contribution from the teachers."

"I know the truth but many teachers do not know and they are under the impression that you are sitting on a high horse belittling the effort and talent of others."

"But these allegations are scurrilous." "Can you prove that? Do you think anybody will support you? You don't know how jealous some teachers are and they think that simply by opposing you and following the instructions of Ranjita they will gain her favour and the opportunity to show their talents. It's human nature, everybody craves for importance and if by pulling your legs they can improve their position why shouldn't they try for it? Everybody knows that you are a cut above the rest and in a fair competition nobody will ever be able to outshine you. Their only way is to be the toilet paper of Ranjita whose contribution in the progress of the school is a zilch. They are conspiring to chuck you out so you have to tread your ground carefully."

I didn't know how to tread my ground carefully, I knew only to work without knowing where the road would carry me ! But how true was Madam Ghosh I felt that very soon.

A meeting was called before the Annual Day and Veer Parsad told me at the meeting to write a script for the one Act Play to be staged. Remaining awake for the whole night I prepared the script and submitted him the next morning. The name of the play was Behind the Silver Screen and the characters were (1) Director of a film (2) Asstt. Director (3) Music Director (4) Rich man (5) Beggar (6) Deadman (7) His relatives (3 – 4) (8) Make-up man (9) Cameraman (10) Spot Boy (11) Technician.

Scene I started with the Director and Asstt. Director pacing up and down the stage with thoughtful and worried expressions. Background music is matching with their footsteps. They cross each other twice and then come to the centre of the stage.

Asstt. Director — This is the 5th day we are facing the same problem. Neither the hero nor the heroine has turned up. I think it's high time to cancel the contract.

Director — What reasons are they putting forth?

Asstt. Director — The hero has caught cold and it would take about a fortnight for him to recover.

Director — And what about the heroine?_

Asstt. Director — What will she do without the hero?_

Director — Mr. Robinson! For your kind information, she has to interact with the other characters also. Had she not absented herself, those shots could have been taken._

Asstt. Director — Sir, she said that she finds the studio like an arid desert without the hero.

Director — Disgusting ! This tinsel world seems to have a strong hold on their personal life as well !

Asstt. Director — That's why new faces are required. The popular ones are more demanding and they care a fig for others. One exhibits sincerity till the time one gets established. That's a common trend in this line.

Director — Do you expect me to try new faces in this high – budget film, Mr. Robinson? I can't take such a big risk. Already I have taken a risk by appointing a new music director because of your strong recommendation.

Asstt. Director — I am sorry to say Sir, in that case we have to depend upon the whims and fancies of the veterans and progress at a snail's pace.

Director — Can't help ! By the way, has the music director decided anything about the music?

Asstt. Director — Lyrics are yet to be penned down although the music is ready.

Director — Wonderful ! He is a genius I should say. Let's have an idea of his unique creation. Call him immediately.

Asstt. Director — Sure Sir. (Goes out and comes back again with the music director who is dressed in funny clothes, carrying a guitar and a synthesiser and comes dancing.)

Music Director — Good morning Sir.

Director — Good morning Mr. Jackson. I came to know that you have decided the background music for different scenes although suitable lyrics are yet to be composed.

Music Director — Don't worry at all Sir. My nephew is a promising poet. He will compose the songs which will definitely synchronize with my tune.

Director — Well I don't approve anything without verifying the sample.

Music Director — Shall I ask him to come tomorrow to show his skill Sir?

Director — First let me be familiar with your skill. Would you kindly take the pain of giving a demonstration of your talent?

Music Director — Definitely Sir. Shall I start with the music for the death scene?

Director — I don't think I would be able to take that much strain in the beginning. Please start with the love scene.

(Music Director, with great enthusiasm, plays a cacophonous music.)

Director — Stop ! Stop at once ! Is it a love scene or a war scene?

Music Director — Love scene Sir. In spite of the cacophony the lovers would remain lost in their world.

Director — I am highly impressed by your novelty. But don't you think the spectators would dislike your innovative thought and my picture would be a flop show? Produce something soothing; light, romantic. Now what music have you decided for the death scene?

(Music Director starts playing the National Anthem).

Director — Good Heavens ! What are you doing? How is it going to create pathos?

Music Director — Sir, it's the death scene of a freedom fighter, the father of the heroine's sister-in-law. What else can be more appropriate than the National Anthem?

Director — I am mesmerised by your talent. I don't have the courage to witness the talent of your nephew in case he has been thinking of composing a new National Anthem. The government of India will definitely not accept it although the issue of deleting the word 'Sind' and including 'Kashmir' in the song is troubling the concerned persons a lot. (Looking at the Asstt. Director) show him the way and prepare the set for a shot (Exit Asstt. Director and Music Director).

Scene II

(A scene depicting a rich, kind-hearted person, taking pity on a beggar, invited him to his house for lunch.)

Characters: Make-up man, Spot Boy, Cameraman, Technician, Rich person, beggar, Asstt. Director, Director. Enter all the characters with a background music. Asstt.Director gives instruction to others.)

Director — Sitting on a chair, looking at his watch) How much time will it take to get things ready?

Asstt. Director — Everything is ready Sir (looking at the make-up man) Hurry up.

Make-up man — Yes Sir, just the finishing touches; I have to create wrinkles on his cherubic face.

Asstt. Director — Ready, light, camera, action.

Technician — Rolling "Day After Tomorrow" scene 5 take 1 (clap).

Richman — (to the beggar) Come on you poor fellow, my heart aches at your pitiable condition. How painful is your impoverished stature ! (Showing a table full of food) Help yourself to your heart's content.

Beggar — (Sitting on the chair, looking at the food, giving out a loud burp, presses his belley and looks helplessly).

Richman — What happened? Why are you hesitating? (Picks up food from the table and starts eating).

Director — (frantically) Cut, cut.

Asstt. Director — He is the beggar and he has to hog. You are rich and well-fed and have no fascination for food. You have to bring that expression. Now get ready everybody – light, camera, action.

Technician — Rolling "Day After Tomorrow" Scene 5 take 2 (clap).

(The reluctant beggar is forced by the rich man to come towards the table. He seems to be suffering from indigestion and the rich man very eagerly starts eating without even looking at the beggar.)

Director — Cut, cut ! What on the Earth is going on? Who is the beggar and who is the richman?

Asstt. Director — (to the richman) Now what provokes you to hog like a famine affected starveling?

Richman — Since morning I have not eaten anything. I can't do justice to the role without doing justice to my hunger.

Asstt. Director — (to the beggar) - and what is the problem with you? Do you have any apathy towards food?

Beggar — Not at all! Not at all ! But there is no space left in my stomach. I had had two chicken sandwiches and one plate of vegetable Manchurian in my breakfast.

Director — Pack up, pack up. It's really disgusting.

(Exit all characters except the Director and Asstt. Director).

Asstt. Director — Sir, we can start the next scene.

Directror (mockingly) — Really, can we?

Asstt. Director — Yes Sir. The actors and actresses are ready. It's that death scene. Only a cot is required. We will arrange that soon.

Direcrtor — O.K., O.K., hurry up please (Exit Asstt. Director)

Scene III

(Enter Asstt. Director, make-up man, technician, Spot boy, 4–5 persons with a cot. Asstt. Director instructs one person to lie down on the cot with his eyes closed. Four others stand by the side of the cot. Make-up man applies powder on their faces and when he tries to do so on the face of dead man, gets a scolding from the Asstt. Director.)

Asstt. Director — Ready, light, camera, action.

Technician — Rolling, 'Day after Tomorrow' scene 8 take 1 (clap).

(Three persons start crying hysterically shaking the deadman). Oh father ! Why did you leave us alone? Oh God ! How could you be so cruel to us? What will happen to us?

Deadman (sitting up on the cot) – why are you pushing me so vigorously?

Director — Cut, cut ! Not so loudly; try to make it natural; only sobbing is required. Don't make it a melodrama; (looking at one character) And what makes you so stiff? You are not crying at all !

The rebuked person – They are crying so loudly that I'm not getting a chance.

Director — O.K., O.K., now come on, start again.

Asstt. Director — Light, camera, action.

Technician — Rolling 'Day After Tomorrow' scene 8 take 1 (clap)

(This time the actors and actresses sob but they seem to be cheerful. The deadman slaps his cheek to kill a mosquito.)

Director — Cut, cut, not in this way. You have to express your sorrow but in a natural way. Do it again.

Asstt. Director — Light, camera, action.

Technician — Rolling 'Day After Tomorrow' scene 8 take 3 (clap)

(This time they act perfectly in a natural way).

Director — Wonderful ! I wanted exactly this action. You did very well. I am extremely pleased.

Cameraman — But Sir.....I.....err (starts stammering).

Director — Now what's the problem with you?

Cameraman — Sir, I made a mistake.

Director — Now what mistake did you make when the shot was absolutely O.K.?

Cameraman — Sir, The shot was so perfect that I forgot to click my camera.

Director — Oh God ! Leave me alone, for God's sake, please leave me alone. Pack up pack up I say. Oh God !

(Exit all characters except the Director who sits down on the chair with his hands on his head – in despair; music as the curtain drops.)

Veer Parsad, after reading the script approved it and told me to proceed with the practice. When the rehearsal was going on in full swing, Ranjita, as usual created quagmires. First of all she told Veer Parsad that the script was not up to the mark; there were many other good one-act plays. Next she expressed her dissatisfaction at the selection of characters and tried to change them as per her whims and fancies. Inspite of her best efforts to spoil the play when it was almost ready to be staged, she started calling the students who were participating and gave them wrong and horrible directions. The young actors and actresses were scared of her. They could understand her evil intention but had to obey her out of fear. One day before the programme, when there was full dressed stage rehearsal, Veer Parsad sat in the quadrangle in front of the stage with his wife and the 'spoons' to watch the programme. Because of Ranjita's interference the students were tensed and could not act freely. He criticised them to such an extent that they became more demoralised. I had a tough time, motivating them, encouraging them and bringing back their lost enthusiasm and spirit to perform well and show their best. I knew the weapon which could terminate the atrocities of Veer Parsad and Ranjita. When he called me to his chamber and asked me whether his speech was ready I took the opportunity to ask him – "Sir, how did the Collector's son perform in the play?" He got startled and asked "Is he acting in the play?"

"Yes" I said. He seemed to be thinking for a while and said "I didn't know that." From that moment his attitude towards the play changed. Ranjita also calmed down. Next day when the play was staged, Veer Parsad was all praise for the Collector's son who hardly had a dialogue. He had played the role of one of those three persons in the death scene who were crying. The clappings by the audience made me understand that the play was a grand success and Ranjita was pushed to the wall.

One day after going to the school I found the atmosphere was quite tensed. Lot of whisperings were there but nobody was saying anything openly. Padma seemed to be very busy. She instructed the class IV staff to make seating arrangement in the quadrangle. It seemed to be a preparation for a meeting. Somebody said that the local management members would come to address the staff members. At that time the Annual Exam was over and the teachers were correcting the papers sitting in different class rooms as the staff room is always noisy. I was sitting in my own classroom XII G. Soon Bindiya Bhalla, Rani Samson and one or two teachers of the Science department came there. Bindiya Bhalla said "The school has lost the case at the High Court; now it is no more under the aegis of the Society."

Somebody else chimed – "The affiliation number in my new promotion letter is different from that of my old Appointment letter."

Everybody started talking about the same issue that if the school is not associated with the Society in Delhi and loses its brand name then it would be a mere local school. They also said that nobody ever thought of asking about our opinions, neither the Society nor the local management, nor the Principal. I did a blunder by opening my mouth and saying "Who doesn't want to be associated with the Society? It's a matter of pride and "honour." On that very day it was reported to Veer Parsad. The meeting was cancelled. Everybody went home with a lot of anxiety.

Next day Veer Parsad called me in his chamber and said – "I used to think you were taking my side. I didn't know that you too are inclined towards the Society like others."

I said – "I always give more importance to the interest of the students."

He retorted – "Are we not self-sufficient? What is the contribution of the Society in our achievements or performance?"

I said – "No doubt we are doing well but brand name also matters; otherwise why should people have craze for IIT? They can study engineering at any college in India."

Veer Parsad sternly said –"You forgot so soon that you only had prepared a list of 30 probable names for our school? You forgot so soon that you were just a P.R.T. with 4 years experience when you joined this school ! You are showing your loyalty to the Society ! "

I said – "I am loyal to my service, my profession and to my students. I am not showing my loyalty to anybody else. My personal interests will not be fulfilled whether the school remains under the Society or not."

Veer Parsad then started giving me a long lecture saying the much repeated things which he usually told us quite often in the meetings. I listened with deadly silence and when I came out after three periods, all eyes were on me silently asking what was I doing in the Principal's room for such a long time? One thing I could understand very well that either Bindiya Bhalla or Rani Samson or both must have reported about me to Veer Parsad. The next two months went off uneventfully, although agitated parents sometimes demanded negotiation with the Society.

It was the last day of the session 2004-05. A general meeting was called on 31st March. Just before the meeting started I was called into the Principal's office and to my greatest surprise told by Veer Parsad that the responsibility of Activity In charge will be withdrawn from me and given to somebody else. I couldn't believe my ears ! This man had assured me –

"You work as the H.O.D. English and Activity Incharge and I will give you the administrative post of Senior Mistress in the near future." After working hard for so many years and standing by his side at the time of crisis, now he is withdrawing my responsibilities without giving me any reward ! I remembered Geetali Madam's warning – "Beware ! or you will be led up the garden path;" really I ended up being cheated of false promises. Because of this, day after day I neglected my husband, my children and devoted my whole time for the school? I told Veer Parsad very clearly that I was not happy at the decision which he had taken and came out of the room. I noticed Bindiya Bhalla was also called after a few minutes.

The meeting started as soon as Veer Parsad, Ranjita and their puppet followers Ravi Shastri, Kaveri Thakur and Uma Banerjee occupied the chairs on the dais after keeping others waiting in the M.P. Hall for about an hour in the scorching heat. On the dais of course the air coolers were on. I saw Ranjita sitting with one leg upon the other and shaking it, revealing her dirty, discoloured petti-coat under the sari.

Veer Parsad started with ànalysis of Annual results, whole years review, new session's planning, introduction of the new teachers etc. etc. I was waiting when he would make that crucial announcement. In the meantime Padma went to the stage thrice and whispered something into his ears. Ranjita also tried to draw his attention on something written on a paper. I could understand they were insisting him to make the announcement regarding the withdrawal of the position of Activity Incharge from me. Ignoring their insistence, Veer Parsad concluded the meeting. I thought he had changed his decision; after all he could not be so ungrateful. But I had made a mistake in knowing the swine. He is an expert in extinguishing the light of hope after kindling it himself. Post facto he announced that from that moment I ceased to be the Activity Incharge and that position was given to his one-time woman Bindiya Bhalla who was also a House Warden. Along with that one more announcement was made that one teacher who had been teaching Economics in classes X and XI for three years was shifted to the Primary School for teaching Mathematics. She started crying but I promised I will never cry. I will achieve something better and give him a proper reply. After going home the first thing I did was to call Padma over telephone and thank her for ruining my career. She was also responsible for shifting that teacher of the Senior Wing to the Primary Wing because repeatedly she used to complain against her. She even accused her of using the notebook of her daughter to teach in her coaching classes. How strange ! That teacher taught the students of class XII in the Coaching classes and Padma's daughter was in XI at that time. How is it possible to teach students of class XII with the help of a note book of class XI?

I started losing faith on all and lost interest in my work. Same was the case with that Economics teacher Jyoti Roy. Her daughter is an excellent student and a very talented girl. But Ranjita tried her best to demoralise her in every possible way. Her classmates were instructed not to speak to her and also to give false witness against her that she was involved in a love affair with a boy of the same class and they saw her holding his hand and kissing him. Ranjita managed to get this in writing against the innocent girl by her classmates and started harassing Jyoti and her daughter. The helpless lady wept unconsolably but could not do anything against them. As soon as she got an opportunity she joined the new school under the same brand as a T.G.T. Later on when results of CBSE class X exams were out, her daughter came second in the state scoring more than 95%. The school lost such a good student who took admission in another school of the township.

Veer Parsad and Ranjita had become absolutely shameless. In order to strengthen their position he was nominating himself for various awards and prizes exploiting teachers and nominated his wife for the Best Teacher award which is given to teachers every year on Teachers' Day by the Education Department of the Sponsoring organization. Simultaneously his debauchery and flirtation also was going on as he loved to sow his old oats.

The school decided to file a case at the Supreme Court. In the general meetings he continued to give a brain wash to the teachers. On the one hand he said that the school was doing extremely well without the association of the Society and on the other hand he insisted the teachers to go for PL (Public Litigation) to retain the name and logo. He wanted the school to be completely under him using the name and logo as that would enhance the prestige of the school. He had become desperate – at any cost Ranjita has to be the Principal after his superannuation so that he can carry on with his status and position. Behind the scene he will be doing everything, placing the stupid woman on his chair.

Bindiya soon realised that for namesake she was given the position of Activity Incharge but in fact, what all I used to do was not given to her. It was just a trick played by Ranjita to snatch my power. One thing they had understood that I was gaining popularity through the magazine and different other areas of work and Ranjita's target was to snatch the editorship of the magazine also from me and she did that in no time.

Lolita Banerjee, a House Warden had requested me to take care of her House Function which was scheduled only two days after the incident. I was the in charge of compering and the English play. I was thinking what would happen, how will my assistant manage in my absence? Although I had scripted, directed and the play was absolutely ready for being staged, I had asked one of the gents teachers to collect the props after giving him the list. I had taken the idea of this drama, particularly keeping in mind people like Veer Parsad, Ranjita and Padma and their followers or 'spoons'. The most interesting fact about 'spoon' is that when the crockeries fall on the ground they break into pieces, when utensils fall they also form dents but nothing happens to the spoon; it remains intact.

The name of the drama which I was going to stage was Heaven versus Hell and the characters were the Lord of Heaven, the Lord of Hell, Sorting Clerk, Peon of Heaven, Peon of Hell, Painter, Administrative Officer, Minister, Industrialist, Doctor, Teacher, Principal and Chief Justice of Heaven. The stage direction was like this: Half of the stage is Heaven and the other half is Hell. There is a portion in the middle and on both sides tables, chairs, files, telephone, calling bell, pen stands, register etc. (Table cloth and flower vase in Heaven). The scene opens in the Hell where the Lord of Hell is sitting in a black dress. (The other side is dark). He is looking at a Register and boiling with rage (Rings the calling bell, enters the peon)

Peon — Good morning Sir.

Lord of Hell — Doesn't seem to be good at all. Can you tell me who's responsible for transforming my golden Hell into the second class compartment of a train?

Peon — I'm not getting you Sir!

Lord of Hell — Look at this register. What is the total accommodation capacity of Hell?

Peon — One hundred crore and ten lac.

Lord of Hell — What is written over here?

Peon — Sir, one hundred crore, eighty five lac and twenty five thousand.

Lord of Hell — Why is there more than seventy five lac surplus population?

Peon — All of them are not present here Sir. Some of them have taken birth as monkeys or donkeys.

Lord of Hell -- What's their number?

Peon (thinking) — Say.....about 30 lac.

Lord of Hell — Still 45 lac surplus population which clearly indicates Heaven has been running on deficit.

Peon — Yes Sir, as per Mathematics.

Lord of Hell — Shut up ! Don't teach me Mathematics.

Peon — Sir, actually the sorting department is responsible for this. As per rules it is the sorting department which decides who will go to Heaven and who to Hell.

Lord of Hell — Again you are teaching me rules? After breaking one thousand rules on the Earth, I've become the Lord of Hell. Call the sorting clerk. (Peon goes out and comes back with the sorting clerk.)

Sorting Clerk — Good Morning Sir, did you call me?

Lord of Hell — Yes, I want to know is it the postal department of a democratic country that you are sending letters to wrong places?

Sorting Clerk — "That's why I have been given the post, it's my reward. Tell me Sir, what can I do for you?"

Lord of Hell — Those who are supposed to go to Heaven are coming to Hell.

May I know why?

Sorting Clerk — Sir ! thousands of people are coming everyday and we have only 3 staff members in our department. It's quite natural to make errors.

Lord of Hell — Because of your carelessness there are 45 lac extra people in our Hell. Do you know that? You immediately send 1 lac people to the Heaven.

Sorting Clerk — Sir, that's not possible. Lord of Heaven has gone to Venus with his girl friends. We have to wait till he comes back.

Lord of Hell — I don't want to hear any lame excuse. You have to send them today. Do you want my people to die due to food shortage? Do you think you will be spared?

Sorting Clerk — O.K. Sir, as you say; but only those people have to be sent who have come here by mistake.

Lord of Hell — (looking at the register) I can find here the names of 1 lac painters. It's a noble profession no doubt. Why should they stay here? Go and bring one of them.

Sorting Clerk — (to the peon) – Go and bring one of them. (Peon goes out and comes back with a painter)

Lord of Hell — Hey Mr. ! What did you do on the Earth?

Painter — Sir, at first I used to paint house; then I started painting vegetables as per the instruction of the Agricultural Minister.

Lord of Hell — Vegetables ! What do you mean?

Painter — Sir, stale and dry vegetables look fresh after painting.

Lord of Hell — That's good, giving life to lifeless things. Heaven is the right place for you. Clerk, send all painters to Heaven.

Sorting Clerk — Peon, send all painters to Heaven.

(Exit all, lights off, music, lights on, on the other side).

Scene II

(Lord of Heaven, wearing a white dress, sitting on a chair and looking at a register).

Lord of Heaven — How come the number increased by 1 lac within a day?

Peon of Heaven — Sir, they have been shifted here from Hell. It seems they are supposed to stay here.

Lord of Heaven — I've understood. It's a crafty plot hatched by the Lord of Hell. I have not agreed to the marriage of my handsom son like Pierce Bosnon with his ugly, dark complexioned daughter. That's why he has taken a revenge. Go and call one painter.

(Exits peon and comes back with painter who dances with joy)

Lord of Heaven — You seem to be very happy here !

Painter — Yes Sir, I feel I'm in Switzerland.

Lord of Heaven — You used to paint vegetables and cheat people. Do you know how many people have fallen sick after eating your vegetables?

Painter — Yes Sir, some of them even died. But police used to take bribe and allowed us because we got the support of the minister.

Lord of Heaven — Don't put the blame on them. It's their fundamental right and they are trained for this.

Painter — Don't be annoyed with me Sir, I'll teach you how to paint imitation ornaments to give them a precious look.

Lord of Heaven — Shut up. You are teaching us corruption. Go back all of you to the Earth and take birth as rats.

(Exit all of them – lights off, music)

Scene III

(Enter Lord of Hell and Peon laughing)

Lord of Hell — We have sent one lac painters to the Heaven. I'm thinking whom to send next?

Peon — Sir, there are many doctors, would you like to meet one of them?

Lord of Hell — O Yes, bring one sample (Exit Peon, comes back with a doctor)

Doctor — Good Morning Sir.

Lord of Hell — Good Morning Doctor. I'm surprised to find you here at Hell !

Doctor — But I feel at home here as this place is exactly like the Government Hospital where I used to work.

Lord of Hell — What else did you do there?

Doctor — Operated people without any real cause, you know, just to remove and sell their kidneys and other body parts; sold free and sample medicines at high price etc. Actually we didn't have to study medicine. We qualified due to the quota system of the Government.

Lord of Hell — Then you must go to Heaven. You have done a great job of killing poor people and relieving them of pain and miseries. Peon, all doctors are to be sent to the Heaven.

(Exit all – lights off, music, lights on, on the other side. Enter Lord of Heaven with his peon. Lord of Heaven walks very fast from one end of the stage to the other followed by his peon.)

Peon — Sir, so much tension is not good for your health, please relax.

Lord of Heaven — How can I relax? That wicked Lord of Hell is sending all good for nothing people here and spoiling the atmosphere of Heaven and you are asking me to relax?

Peon — Sir, you can also send some people to Hell.

Lord of Heaven — Right ! It's a good idea. But whom to send?

Peon — There are about one lac administrative officers and I've a strong feeling that Heaven is not the right place for them.

Lord or Heaven — Why? Why do you have such a strong feeling?

Peon — Sir, if you interact with one of them, you will also agree with me.

Lord of Heaven — O.K. bring one of them here.

(Exits peon – Comes back with an Administrative Officer).

Officer — Good Morning Sir.

Lord of Heaven — Good Morning Officer. I want to know what exactly was your duty on the Earth?

Admn. Officer — My duty was to hide the important files of the office in order to make work complicated.

Lord of Heaven — But why?

Admn. Officer — In order to harass others, to please the Boss and take all credit.

Lord of Heaven — I see, you are the most dangerous person.

Admn. Officer — That's true but that's the secret of my success. I was the coverture of my boss also and because of me he was saved several times when he found himself in critical situations.

Lord of Heaven — But I can't allow such dishonest persons to stay in the Heaven and pollute the atmosphere. Peon, send all the administrative officers to Hell.

(Exit – lights off – music, lights on the other side; enter Lord of Hell and his peon).

Scene IV

Lord of Hell — We have sent the painters and doctors and look at their weakedness, they have sent all officers. We have to do something.

Peon — Sir, we have many ministers. I think we can send them to Heaven.

Lord of Hell — O.K. call one minister but handle him with care. (Peon exits and comes back with a minister, yawning).

Minister — What type of a nonsense is this? I was sleeping comfortably, what's the justification in calling me now? Do you know, sleeping in the parliament was an important duty?

Lord of Hell — Very sorry Sir. I just want to know which department was under you?

Minister — Unnecessary and foolish question. My bio-data is there in your register. You can have a look at it.

Lord of Hell — It will take time to search; please answer my question Sir.

Minister — It's not a single department. Do you know the speciality of ministers? They have to be Jack of all trade. Suppose today I'm the Education Minister, after three months I may be Coal Minister and again after six months food minister or transportation minister.

Lord of Hell — How did you become a minister?

Minister — Oh ! that is hereditary. My father, grandfather, his father, all were ministers. My son is also a minister. A hierarchy has to be followed.

Lord of Hell — What is the secret behind this family success?

Minister — That's very easy. A strong banner, a few crores, some anti-social party workers, a little bit of rigging and capturing of a few booths that's all.

Lord of Hell — That's a clean confession. You are so truthful. Heaven is the right place for you. I'm not able to understand why you are here !

Minister — Its' plain and simple. Honest people do always suffer.

Lord of Hell — Would you like to go to Heaven?

Minister — Gladly, but you know, we need A.C. rooms.

Lord of Hell — Don't worry Sir. Heaven is centrally air conditioned. Peon, send all ministers to Heaven.

Peon — Yes Sir.

(Exit all – lights off….music….lights on in Heaven. Lord of Heaven sitting and reading a magazine. Enter peon).

Peon — Sir all ministers have come from Hell.

Lord of Heaven — What? Now this is too much ! All capitalists and industrialists are already here and if they join hands with the ministers then we have to leave Heaven. Call one industrialist.

(Peon exits and comes back with an industrialist).

Lord of Heaven — What's your name?

Industrialist — Which name do you want to know? I have different names for different business.

Lord of Heaven — I want to know the real one.

Industrialist — Let me think. I'm not able to recollect my real name.

Lord of Heaven — O.K., O.K., I've heard that you are a very pious person, you've built seven temples.

Industrialist — Yes, from those seven temples I used to earn 7 lac every month. Religion is the most profitable business.

Lord of Heaven — How dare you? You are polluting the purity of Heaven. Peon, at once send all capitalists and industrialists to Hell.

(Exits peon with industrialist, enters again).

Lord of Heaven — I know there are about 2 lac Principals of various schools and colleges here. I am not very happy with them. I want to speak to one of them.

(Exits peon and comes back with a Principal of a school).

Lord of Heaven — Good Morning Mr.Principal. How do you find this place?

Principal — There is not much difference between this place and the school where I was the Principal. In fact, I am enjoying all facilities and comfort here.

Lord of Heaven — But I have been reported that you and your colleagues used to take huge donations in the name of development of the schools. Not only that, you promoted those students who failed in examinations after taking bribe from the parents. In the meetings you always humiliated good and honest teachers and favoured the wicked ones. Heaven can not be the right place for you. All of your tribe and class must go to Hell. Peon, send them to Hell.

(Exits peon with the Principal; lights off in Heaven. Lights on, on the other side; music – enter Lord of Hell followed by Peon of Hell and two teachers.)

Scene V

Teachers — Excuse us Sir, we have a very big problem.

Lord of Hell — What's your problem?

Teachers — The Principals and their wives or other relatives (Vice Principals) had made our lives Hell on the Earth. In order to avoid them we took shelter in the Hell after death because we came to know that they have gone to Heaven. Now all the Principals have come to Hell and very soon the Vice Principals may come. We don't want to stay with them Sir, they will exploit us here also. Please send us to Heaven.

Lord of Hell — Gladly. You just give me an application that you are willing to leave Hell.

Teachers — Sure Sir (Wrote application and escorted out of Hell by the Peon).

Scene VI

(Lord of Heaven is sitting on his throne, thinking hard. He calls the sorting clerk and asks ....).

Lord of Heaven — Clerk, don't you think the Vice Principals should also be sent to the Hell? After all most of them got that position in unfair ways depriving the right candidates !

Sorting Clerk — What have you started Sir ? You are sending one lac; they are sending one lack. How long will it continue? We have shortage of staff, it's not possible for us to keep account.

Lord of Heaven — We don't need staff at all. Everything has become computerized. I know you all sleep during working hours in A.C. rooms. Just shut up or you will be suspended.

Sorting Clerk — We have our union. We will start hunger strike and you'll be responsible for our death.

(Lord of Hell peeping from his area)

Everybody eats while on hunger strike. Why are you talking of death?

Lord of Heaven — You cunning fellow, you are responsible for everything.

Lord of Hell — Why did you send all good people to Hell?

Lord of Heaven — You are the first to send. You should have discussed with me.

Lord of Hell — Why should I discuss with you? Who are you?

Lord of Heaven — I'm senior to you. I'm the Lord of Heaven.

Lord of Hell — Hell is a bigger place than Heaven. I'm the Lord of Hell; why should I listen to you?

Lord of Heaven — I'm senior.

Lord of Hell — Seniority my foot !

(Lord of Heaven and Lord of Hell start wrestling and shouting.)

Peons — Let's call the Chief Justice, let him take the decision.

(Exit and come back with Chief Justice)

Lord of Heaven and Lord of Hell - (rushing towards him)

My Lord, He is guilty, punish him. No My Lord, he is responsible for everything, punish him, throw him out of Heaven etc.

Chief Justice — Order, order. Both of you are discharged from your duty. We will implement President's Rule in Heaven and Hell from today. Heaven and Hell will be one place from today.

(Peons embrace each other in joy and remove the partition).

Lord of Hell (to Lord of Heaven) – What shall we do now?

Lord of Heaven — I have no problem. I have an account in the World Bank. I will lead a comfortable life.

Lord of Hell — I too have an account there; I will be your neighbour again. (They embrace each other while the peons look at them with surprise, Music – Curtain Drops)).

This was the drama. I recalled the amusing moments when the rehearsal was going on. Children were asked to stay back for practice of various cultural items like dance, song, Hindi and English plays etc. Some of them were participating in more than one item hence always one or two characters were missing and we had to send some of the students present to call those who were missing. So many times, we had to change the characters. Those who were given small parts were not very happy. Lord of Heaven and Lord of Hell were sometimes confused, forgetting their own dialogues and saying the dialogue of the other. On top of everything the whole play was taking more than half an hour. So my assistant teacher of the English department who was helping me and I decided to remove some characters to make the play shorter. The role of Principal and Doctor were removed and the dialogues were written in a different way. The two boys who were playing these two roles were asked to play the roles of the servants of the Lord of Hell and massage his legs. They were highly disappointed as they didn't have any dialogue to say. One boy who was doing the role of the sorting clerk was taking part in the Hindi Drama also. While doing the role of the sorting clerk sometimes he delivered the dialogues of Hindi Drama by mistake. With great difficulty and constant effort ultimately we could prepare them. But unfortunately because of the unpleasant bitter situation created by Veer Parsad and Ranjita, I fell sick and could`not attend the House Function. However, in my absence my assistant managed well. I got Ravi Shastri's phone call when the function was over. He congratulated me for the drama and said it was highly praised by the audience. It was shown through Power Point Presentation also and my name was highlighted on the screen as the writer and director. The Computer teacher Mr.Jhunjhuni Hosain also congratulated me over telephone for the play and said that it was highly appreciated by the audience.

Ravi Shastri gave me some important news. As expected Veer Parsad had asked him, Neelima Pandey and Padma to write report against me. Shastriji confessed that out of compulsion he had to write but as far as possible he tried to express in a neutral way. I could understand the pathetic condition of Ravi Shastri who had to support two families depending upon the salary he got from the school. He had to listen to Veer Parsad. He didn't know what Padma had written but I can very well understand what she had written about me. Neelima Pandey had written four pages report against me and shown to Shastriji. Although he had advised her not to submit the report because later on the case might go to the court, she submitted the report to get the favour of Ranjita. Some more phone calls came and the callers congratulated me for the drama.

After recovering from my illness, I went to school and started my normal routined life. I came to know from my assistant that some more funny incidents had happened during the staging of the play. When the props came, the Lord of Heaven got a gorgeous white dress with a golden crown and other ornaments. The Lord of Hell got only a black dress and two black horns of a buffalo. The horns of his peon were better than those of him, hence he was quite upset. However they all acted very well and the play was highly appreciated. I was expecting a blow from the Devils every moment but in which way or from which corner it will come I had no idea. On the fourth Saturday a general meeting was called after the Parents – Teacher meeting was over. All my responsibilities including Editorship of magazine and H.O.D. English etc. were withdrawn from me. Neelima Pandey was made the House Warden. After all she got the reward for writing four pages report against me. This lady, once upon a time, used to live in a servant's quarter in the township with her family. When a woman of that category becomes a House Warden and get the opportunity of sitting in the front row with the Principal, she gets the full moon in her hand. Another teacher of the English Department who is a pass out from Bengali medium school and college, the greatest gossip monger of the school and who had been angling for my position for a long time was a bit disappointed as her name was not announced as the incharge of anything. But I know, in the near future her wishes will also be fulfilled because taking Ranjita's side she had opposed me in every possible way. There is not much difference between Ranjita's category and the category of these women. Ranjita favours them because they can be kept under subjugation. She prefers mediocrity to excellence for her own benefit.

I consoled myself – "Dear Urja, it is the rule of the world that those who learnt from you, will try to ruin you in order to establish their own supremacy. But remember one thing – hard work never goes unnoticed by worthy people, although it may be ignored and abused by the worthless. So, have confidence in your ability and efficiency and go ahead with the blessings of God. Close a dull, boring chapter and start a new one, - fresh, interesting and glorious. Do you think your enemies do not know your capabilities? They know very well; that's why they are jealous of you and they try to humilitate you in order to ruin your confidence. Because of their foolish ego and jealousy they will constantly try to pull you down. It gives them a lot of sadistic pleasure. The more they try to pull you down, the more confident you should feel. A person who thinks he is just and right, need not give any explanation before the public, using the microphone. If somebody does that he simply exposes his frustration before the public. Why should you care for the opinion of your enemies? Who are they to criticise you? First let them be equal to you, then they can open their mouth to say anything against you. You have been offered important positions not only by one or two persons but by many, even by the Education Management Society. It's because of your personal constraints you could not avail the opportunities but you know your real value. You should feel proud that you are the only one in this school to have the guts to call a spade a spade. You are not like the innumerable, double-faced, double-mouthed women who say something in front of a person and something else at his/her back. Their world is limited. Yours is a broader one. Forget everything and let them lick the leftovers from your rejected plate. Your platter is full, enjoy it ! all the position holders didn't even know how to write an application. They have learnt from you and today they are pretending to be more important than you ! Ha, Ha, Ha ....You stick to your point; you have never compromised with any injustice or wrong thing in your life and will never do so. The cheap women who have written reports against you, chat and laugh at the top of their voice during working hours and stay back after 1 p.m. to correct the notebooks to show how hard working they are ! Any sensible person will be able to understand that. So, don't waste even your precious sputum to spit on the faces of these third class people who have taken your help in one way or other but wrote complaint letters against you to get the favour of Ranjita and Veer Parsad. One person can not pull the legs of all. But unitedly ten persons can pull the legs of one. There is nothing to feel surprised. Make yourself so strong that people get inspiration looking at you. They need not read the books of Shiv Khera or Del Carnegie. Be a living example, make yourself like a live wire. Look ahead, don't look back." In this way I started motivating myself.

Each day brought a new challenge to me. Each day I started learning something new to enrich myself. Some people tried to show their sympathy but I didn't need the sympathy of any one. I know how difficult the situation was. There I was, the closest person to Veer Parsad and everything was going on at my instructions and in the next moment I found myself nowhere.

On the Foundation Day, earlier I used to prepare the duty roster and that year Ranjita did the work snatching from me and my name was missing. The magazine was released on that day; she presented it to the Chief Guest with a shameless smile exposing her yellow canines, capitalizing on my hard work. Her face at that time was looking like a public urinal. Some teachers of the English Department who liked me looked at her with contempt in their eyes.

I decided to leave the institution although I love it from the core of my heart because every moment they would try to demoralise me. My career was doomed but why should I accept defeat? I kept my eyes and ears open in search of a better job. At the same time I started my battle against Veer Parsad and Ranjita with my pen through the Teaching Diary which was submitted to them every month. It was my challenge that within three months I will get the post of Principal or Vice Principal and nothing less than that in a reputed C.B.S.E. school and for these three months I will teach a lesson to the corrupt, wicked couple; of course they are too lowly to understand me. I started expressing myself on the pages of my Teaching Diary. Once I wrote :"The psychopath is trying to pinch my ego but like her, I am neither a hollow bamboo nor an air-filled round balloon which can be depleted. Whatever I have is solid. I am as solid as a diamond. At the right place I will be able to reflect my light. Unfortunately I find myself at a wrong place misused by wrong hands. Whatever I constructed for all these years have been turned into rubbles by inauspicious people. They have ruined my happiness. If they look at the ocean, it will become absolutely dry. If I by chance look at their face in the morning my whole day gets spoilt. A worthless administrator is not able to control anyone but tries to please all in a foolish manner. He tries to justify his actions loudly in the meetings whether people agree with him or not. Whatever I did single handed for five years are now being done by the Vice Principal with the assistance of various teachers. – What does it show? (1) She doesn't have anything else to do (2) She doesn't know anything about administration that's why the Principal has given her my work to keep her engaged in some way. (3) If she does administrative work then the Principal would not get the chance to enjoy a gala time with his lady administrative officer. (4) In order to make his wife the Principal, the Principal has to prove before the Society how hard working, and efficient she is. That's why my work was snatched."

In the month of September I saw an advertisement in the newspaper asking for Principal and Vice Principal in a CBSE affiliated school of the township. I thought what can be a better opportunity than this? Let me try my luck. I applied for both the posts and got a call letter. I went there for interview and was interviewed by the Director of that school and the Director of another reputed school of the City. I did extremely well and both of them were very much impressed by my C.V. and the interview. After a few days I got a call from the Director of the other school offering me the post of Vice Principal in his school. He said "Although you qualified for the post of Principal in that school they will not be able to pay you so much because their salary scale is very low. I know the owner of that school, he is the father-in-law of my nephew." He also told me to meet him at his school for further discussion. I met him at his school after taking an appointment and he introduced me to his brother, the Principal of the school. The final deal was done. I was offered more than what I had been getting. I got the Appointment letter for the post of Vice Principal and H.O.D. of English. While coming back home I was floating on cloud nine. I thought of throwing the Appointment letter right on the face of Veer Parsad and Ranjita. But my husband told me not to lose my sense.

Next day, i.e., on 15th November I met Padma in the reception and told her that I want to meet the Principal. Very reluctantly she allowed me to go inside his room (as if she allowed me to use her undergarments which are absolutely her own). I had carried the invitation card for my son's marriage which I handed over to him and very politely invited him with his whole family. Then in a dramatic way I gave him my resignation letter and told him, "Sir, I want to put up my papers." Most probably he was expecting this. He took it in his hand and read it; I had mentioned there that in pursuit of Ph.D I required more time for my studies, that's why I decided to put up my papers. Veer Parsad looked at me and said– "Do you think I will believe that you will be sitting back at home? You are not that type of a lady. I know where you are going and which post you have got there. There is no harm in telling me." He also said-"I expected you to adjust. You are so much egoistic that you didn't give us the time to do anything for you. We were thinking of giving you the responsibility of House Warden." I felt like laughing aloud. I have already got the post of Vice Principal in a reputed school with more than 6000 students and five branches for Academics and Fine Arts and he was thinking of making me the House Warden which I already was ten years back in my previous school in Visakhapatnam where I was a PRT (Primary Teacher). Then he told me "You have asked for your release on 14th February but as a senior teacher you have some responsibilities. How can you leave before the session comes to an end ?" I said "As a classteacher of XII I will complete my work. I have already completed the syllabus. I will correct their Pre-Board papers, prepare their Report Cards and do all necessary work before going." Still he was not happy and said – "You speak to your new employers and request them to allow you to join from the new session." I came out of his room but made up my mind that I will not approach the Director and the Principal of my new school. I know they will not say 'No' if I request them to give me some more time but why should I lose my seniority even for a day? I am not lucky like Ranjita. I don't have my own people to promote me anywhere. I have to struggle, I have to work hard. Moreover I have to study everything in my new school before the new session starts.

I didn't tell anyone about my success but somehow people came to know. Teachers and students started asking me and ultimately I had to tell them. Count down began. The end of 2006 was quite eventful. My elder son got married with a girl from U.P., born and brought up in Jaipur. It was a negotiated marriage. My father was admitted to the Nursing Home just two days before the marriage as he got a sudden cerebral attack. When I informed at school, all of a sudden Padma became very much concerned and told me not to worry because in that Nursing Home all doctors were known to her and she would tell them to take extra care of my father. Leaving my father at the Nursing Home and my mother under the care of servants and neighbours we left for Delhi and from there we went to Jaipur where the marriage ceremony was held. Everything went off smoothly and we came back to our place with the newly married couple. A grand function was held here and as it was expected Veer Parsad didn't turn up. The excuse given was – interview was being held for the recruitment of teachers. Ha ! In which school interview takes place till 10 o'clock at night? He didn't allow his followers and some of the office staff who were willing to come. Next day we left for Calcutta with the newly wed couple because my nonagenarian father-in-law there was confined to bed and he could not attend the marriage and the Reception function. He was so happy to see Neha – my daughter-in-law. Just one month after this my father-in-law expired. When Veer Parsad came to know this he came to our house with Ranjita, Padma and Ravi Shastri in the evening. With a gloomy face he expressed his great sorrow for the expiry of my nonagenarian father-in-law. Then they all came to the room where my father who had come back from the nursing home was taking rest. My father, of course mistook him to be the Principal of the new school where I was supposed to join. While talking to him, Veer Parsad, at one point said "Without hard work no one can succeed. Your daughter has also worked very hard." Does he know the value of hard work? Had he known, I would have never left the school where I worked for ten years. But this is destiny and whatever happens, that is for good, otherwise I would have remained at the same position where I was.

When I submitted my Teaching Diary in the month of February 2007 for the last time I thanked everybody by writing:

Dear Urja

If somebody throws you away after extracting the maximum from you, don't feel disheartened. You are sure to be picked up with great care, love and honour by better people where your service is required and valued. Hard work never goes unnoticed by worthy people although it may be ignored and abused by the worthless. So, have confidence in your ability and efficiency and go ahead with the blessings of God. After all, you know the difference between Achievement and Manipulation. You have achieved not manipulated but you must thank your manipulators. It is because of them, you tried somewhere else and got this position. They will remain wherever they are and sink into the contaminated, muddy water of the death-well dug by themselves. Congratulate them and see who becomes their next target, whom they can uproot next! Specially thank that double-faced, double mouthed woman who wrote a 4 pages report against you to get the position of House Warden. This woman used to say such dirty things about Veer Parsad and Ranjita pretending to be your friend. Specially thank that Chemistry teacher and the swimming pool In charge who used to peep through the windows of your classroom and give false reports against your class to Ranjita. Specially thank that teacher of the English Department whose face is exactly like that of a piglet and who blamed you for not sending her Essay when she didn't get any prize but you got Antra Rashtriya Sikshak Samman for your essay the fact being that, you not only had sent her essay but also paid the entry fee for her which till date she has not returned. Specially thank that teacher who had called you the 'Chahiti' of Veer Parsad out of jealousy in spite of knowing that you have two grown up sons and who herself is found in Veer Parsad's room every now and then. The list is never ending but thank them all for it is only because of them, today you are the Vice Principal, just one step away from the hot seat. At the same time feel pity for that poor woman who has to imitate you and follow your footsteps in order to impress her husband and draw his attention. Forgive her for she has revealed the penury of her heart.

There is a French adage "To understand everything is to forgive everything." When one can understand the people, their gullibility, their fear, their greed and lust for power, their ignorance and their docility to the man who shouts the loudest, one can forgive. But one can never forget.

I will never forget and the memory will remain forever like a raw wound in my mind. Three months passed away in a jiffy leaving me face to face with the bitter reality on 14th February 2007. My publisher had sent me my newly published books just two days back. In the morning I went to the reception and took an appointment with the Principal. I carried with me two copies each of my books which I presented to him. I told him two copies were for him and two are for the school library as there was heavy demand among the teachers and the students. Then I told him that was our last meeting as I was supposed to get my release order in the afternoon. He told me – "Still there is time; you can review your decision and stay back. I don't want you to go. I know you will not be happy there because it is their family business. You will not be accepted by their family members."

I said, "It's too late and there will be no change in my decision." He said – "I have told my Secretary to arrange for your farewell at 4.30 in the evening. We will meet at the Conference Hall. I think it will be O.K. for you."

I said "There is no need."

He again told me that it is customary and I should come. I came out of the room. What happened at 4.30 p.m. everybody knows. Whatever the other teachers with the same experience had told me reverberated in my ears – "One day you will realise how mean these people are and you have to leave the school on their account." How very true! But I have only one difference with those previous sufferers. They had suffered silently and only whispered into my ears their advice and warning. But I could protest loudly and I have lifted up my pen as a weapon to leave Veer Parsad, Ranjita and Padma naked before the whole world. I believe my pen is mightier than sword. Veer Parsad didn't send my books to the school library out of fear because he could understand that the poem entitled "The Innocent Playboy" is a composition on him and he didn't want anybody to read it. But what will he do when this book will be published and the readers will come to know the truth which is as clear as daylight? What will he do when thousands of people will be aware of his dirty habit and perversion and spit on his face knowing about his lust for women, his sexual relationship with them and his meanness for not even sparing the girl students? When the girls and the ladies practise swimming in the pool of the school, he ogles at their bare body in wet swimsuits. What will Ranjita do when thousands of readers will spit on her face and the face of Veer Parsad? Perhaps nothing! They will break but can't be twisted or bent. They will carry on with their malevolence and profound immoralities.

* * * * * * * *

Within two weeks of joining the new school, I could understand each and every person there. The Director Shri Motilal Trivedi was very frank and took pride in narrating his past. They belonged to a poverty-stricken family of U.P. He was the eldest of five sons and they had no sister. His father could afford only 250 gm. milk and the major portion with whatever little formation of cream was there, was given to him as he was the eldest. The rest was shared by the younger brothers. If his father ever bought a single piece of Gulab-Jamoon, Motilal would eat half of it and the remaining half was divided among his brothers. There was no electricity at home. They used to study in the light of an oil lamp with a chimney. Once the glass chimney got broken but there was no money to replace it for about a fortnight. They had to study in that flickering light producing black soot.

One thing their father had taught them that was to respect the elder son of the family. Had there been one chair in the room, he would sit and others would keep standing. All younger brothers were supposed to touch his feet early in the morning or whenever they met for the first time in the day. They didn't have enough to eat. His father could not pay the school fees every month and they all had to face humiliations. As a teenager he used to think, one day situations will change - they will not remain poor. He decided to take education seriously, with full concentration. After completing his M.Sc. in Mathematics and B.Ed. he understood that until and unless he tried his luck somewhere else he would never become successful. There was his father's exploiter in Gorakhpur and how earnestly he wished the death of this person in his childhood ! When he really died due to road accident how happy that child was ! Leaving Gorakhpur and coming to the steel city was the 1st step taken to construct his own fate. Life at that time was unpredictable. He didn't know where to stay, whom to approach; simply reading an advertisement for the post of a T.G.T. Maths in one of the schools run by the Steel Plant he decided to try his luck. His better half was also with him as in this matter he was weak, he could not stay alone.

When he reached the venue of the interview, it was already late. The clerk was no more entertaining the late comers but due to some unknown reason or the trick played by lady luck, his C.V. was accepted and when his turn came he could satisfy the interviewers. He joined the school as T.G.T. Maths and there started a long journey in the road of education. It was a turning point and he enjoyed this new life in a rented two room flat with his wife. He used to go to his village every month in one of the weekends. His old father used to wait for him anxiously forgetting all ailments whenever his visit was due. The otherwise calm and quiet person even used to hum a tune, elated at his homecoming. Again two days before his scheduled date of returning the old gentleman would become absolutely silent.

This continued for a long time until Motilal decided to bring his parents to his workplace. The wheel of time had rotated fast and smoothly landing him to the peak of success and from T.G.T. Maths he ascended gradually to the post of Principal. His knowledge in his subject, hard work, presence of mind, oratorical skill (presenting falsehood as truth) created a strong and positive image in the mind of people. He gained popularity and became an eminent personality in the town.

Motilal had a vision right from his childhood days. When his brothers used to play with the other boys of the village or enjoyed a ride in bicycle by the riverside he used to dream of doing something great one day. When he earned enough money as the Principal of a company-run school and from private tuition the first thing he did was to purchase 5 acres land. Lands were available at very cheap rate then. His brothers also shifted to the new place with their respective family. In the meantime a very amusing and strange incident had happened. His fourth brother and youngest brother married his two sisters-in law, the younger sisters of his wife, that means three brothers were married to three sisters. Lands were available at throw-away price twenty years earlier. Construction of the school building was not possible immediately. He started a school in his garage with one student and the only teacher was one of his sisters-in-law. Criticism, comments, mockery nothing could stop him and most astonishingly that single student continued to study in that garage – school who was promoted from lower K.G. to upper K.G. They didn't have any car. At night about four to five cows were sheltered in that garage and in the morning after cleaning the cow-dung the garage was made ready for the school with that single child.

The next step was the construction of a school building with eight classrooms and Micky Mouse and Donald Duck painted on the white front outer wall which attracted people from a long distance. Soon people started talking about the new school and as Motilal had a reputation the number of students increased from one to eighty four in the first year. Five-Six teachers were also appointed apart from the family members. In between life had been eventful with the birth of three children, their growing up, education, getting married etc. Motilal's next brother Nageshlal was married to an insane woman but the insanity didn't prevent them from giving birth to two children Chunnu and Ranu. They inherited the eccentricity of their mother to some extent and could not get proper education. Ranu got married with the initiative of the relatives and Chunnu used to take care of a small dairy in the village. Nageshlal himself was a drunkard although he had many qualities. He could not make use of his qualities and talents and ultimately had to live at the mercy of his elder brother. His first wife expired untimely but he didn't take much time to marry again. Now he has two more daughters by his second marriage.

The third brother of Motilal – Yogeshlal was an advocate in Gorakhpur. After practicing for twenty years there he also shifted to the steel township and joined his brother's school as the manager. His three sons have their own business. The fourth brother of Motilal, Adarsh tried to become a doctor but was not successful. He did his graduation with Chemistry but lost one year due to Chicken Pox and his condition was so bad that everybody thought that he would not survive. The ladies of the house had started reading Bhagwat Gita, sitting by the side of his bed. But to the surprise of all he survived. He completed his graduation, post graduation and B.Ed. but joined a company as a junior executive in Aurangabad. He didn't like the job and came to his elder brother's place. While coming by train, on his way through the windows of the train he noticed the advertisement of a coaching class for Physics, Chemistry and Mathematics at one stoppage and for a second the idea of opening one such coaching class flashed in to his mind. He got the job of T.G.T. Chemistry at one of the schools in an iron ore mine area, about two hours journey from the steel township which was run by the steel plant. At 4 a.m. in the morning he used to board the bus for the mines and reach there at 6 o' clock. Again in the afternoon at 2 p.m. he used to board the bus and reach home at 4 p.m. There was a family shop in the township. In the evening he started giving tuition in Chemistry to three students in that shop. Luckily those three students could qualify in I.I.T. Then there was no looking back. That shop was converted to a full fledged Coaching Centre for I.I.T. His elder brother had a long experience as a Principal. Whether it was his influence or by sheer luck, Adarsh was transferred to a school in the township as P.G.T. Chemistry. Now it became more convenient for him to devote his time and energy for the coaching. The younger brother Preetamlal also joined them. He didn't have much education but one thing was common to all, that was business sense. At cheap rate they started purchasing land and flats. The younger brother started a Hindi medium school under the banner of an Education Society of their own. At night they used to fix the banners for the Coaching class. The fourth and the youngest brother used to climb up and fix the banners from both sides and Motilal used to give them instructions standing on the road.

Soon one after another, all of them settled in the locality near Motilal's school. The school had started in 1993 with the primary classes only. Then each year one class was added and very soon it got affiliation for secondary level. Adarsh decided to leave his job at the Steel Plant run school and join his brother's school as the Principal. By that time there were about 1700 students and they could not be accommodated properly. Adarsh took V.R. and joined the school as the Principal in 2000.

After joining, the first thing he did was to take a huge loan of a few crore keeping the school in mortgage. The infrastructure was changed and modified to such an extent that it was beyond recognition. People started feeling attracted towards the modern posh campus with five separate buildings. Besides the two shifts there started an evening college for music and dance. All the five brothers had their separate residential house. Apart from that they purchased land and constructed hostel buildings. Students from all over the State and the nearby States stay in the hostels. Each brother, at present has 4 – 5 hostels. In each hostel there are about thirty students. The annual charge for boarding and lodging is Rs. 30,000.00, all other expenses extra. The coaching classes which had started with 3 students now have more than 300 students in each subject and the charge is Rs. 500/- per subject. According to Hindu mythology Goddess Saraswati and Laxmi can't stay together. But Motilal and his brothers have proved that wrong.

How cleverly and with what vision everything was planned is something to be learnt from this edifice of learning. Motilal's elder son was not so good in studies; he could somehow complete his B.Com. He was given the designation of Chief Administrative Officer and the responsibility of the Accounts section. He doesn't have any sound knowledge of Accountancy but knows very well how to cheat people. Taking money but not giving receipts, taking fine for trivial reasons, depriving staff of their P.F.etc. all these were tackled by him smoothly. There is no need to mention that a major part of this smart income goes into his personal account and he has invested the money very wisely, purchasing his own lands and building up hostels there. Not only that the third school has been started under the same banner in a place which is about 6 hrs. journey from the original school. Ashok and Sarita are the Joint Directors of that school.

Motilal's daughter, Aaradhana who is the eldest of his three children did her B.E. from an engineering college of the State which belonged to their relatives and her uncle Adarsh is a member of the Governing Body of that College. She was married to an ordinary person who failed to get a good job and ultimately had to join his father-in-law's school. Motilal had helped him financially to start a school of his own but within no time he recklessly spent the whole amount and was under the burden of a huge debt. Again Motilal had to pay the debt and brought his son-in-law and daughter to his own house. But there cropped up a new problem. His elder son Ashok's wife, Sarita was always at daggers drawn with her sister-in-law and she ultimately compelled Rajesh and Aaradhana, i.e., Motilal's son-in-law and daughter to take a rented house nearby. Sarita, immediately after her marriage had forced Adarsh and his family also to shift to a separate house. Motilal, in his life got the biggest slap from fate in the shape of his eldest daughter-in-law Sarita. There can not be a more uncivilized, ill mannered savage, foul mouthed woman in the world. But Motilal had no other way but to make her the Vice Principal. He made his daughter also the Vice Principal. Sarita was not happy at this decision. According to her she was senior than her sister-in-law as she had joined earlier. Motilal's younger son was given a lot of publicity as IITian but actually he had done his engineering from B.H.U. with ceramics. Who doesn't know that those who get lowest ranks are given such a branch like ceramics? But in many hoardings in the township people can see his full size photo with the caption Physics and Maths classes of Aneesh Sir IITian – Ha, Ha, Ha. This hero-like son of Motilal did one very interesting thing when he was in college. He fell in love with a girl who was not of his caste. Initially it was not accepted by the family members – they are Brahmins and the girl belonged to the business class – Agrawal. But later on they changed their decision and gave their consent getting the hint of a huge dowry and sensing the business sense of the girl. Sarita felt jealous of her as she herself belonged to a beggar family. She is the eldest daughter of her parents among the five daughters. Her parents and sisters lived at the mercy of Motilal. One after another the sisters got married – the whole expense was borne by Motilal. Sarita's father died of cancer – the entire treatment was done by Motilal. Naturally she became green with jealousy when her in-laws gave their consent in the marriage between Aneesh and Priya – a girl from a stinkingly rich family.

Priya joined the school as a pre-primary teacher. She had a Science background but was not B.Ed. Leaving the students on their own she used to prepare for her B.Ed. sitting in the classroom. Sarita also did her B.Ed. while working. She was made the H.O.D. of the Biology Department.

In the meantime the second brother of Motilal, Nageshlal was removed from the school as he was spoiling the image of the school by drinking openly, asking for loan from various persons and openly declaring that he was the Director of the school. The fourth brother Adarsh had again taken huge bank loan and purchased 15 acres land in the interior of the capital city where a branch of the school was started. There were two more small buildings in the capital where Primary classes were held. Nageshlal was at first sent to that school as a manager but as he started creating nuisance there he was totally separated from the school. He was given some financial help to start his own business there and live with his family. His daughter from his first wife, Ranu teaches Hindi in the Primary section. Chunnu, Ranu's brother one day came to the school from his village with his cows and buffaloes. He started his dairy business inside the school. Adarsh ultimately had to tell him to shift his dairy somewhere else or to dispose off his cattle. He preferred the second option. He was posted at the Library of the school and all of a sudden the other staff of the library including the library incharge started getting cattle like treatment from him. His father's blood was flowing through his veins; he also behaved in the same way considering himself to be superior and could not differentiate between human beings and cattle. His salary was only Rs. 5000/- but his behaviour was like a big boss.

Adarsh's two sons refused to work in the school and wanted to stand on their own feet. The elder one Neeraj married the lean and thin daughter of an education maffia who is the owner of five Engineering Colleges and a couple of temples. Neeraj himself is running one Engineering College in the capital which he got as dowry. The younger one Dheeraj preferred service line and settled in Pune with his working wife and his son. His wife was earlier working in Motilal's school but Sarita didn't allow her to work peacefully. At every instance she used to pick up quarrel with her and ultimately compelled her to leave.

Yogeshlal's elder son married a girl who had done a course in multimedia. She came to great use in preparing coloured prospectus, project files for Kids Academy, cover of note books, calendar etc. She had a limited knowledge, in fact and utilised the typists who had knowledge in this field. But everywhere she publicised her name as if she is a master in this line. Yogeshlal's younger daughter-in-law is also a Hindi teacher in a primary class. Apart from this their relatives, villagers etc. etc. were employed right from the post of nightguard to the top executives.

The younger brother of Motilal, Preetamlal started a Hindi medium school separately and was also appointed as the manager of Motilal's school. His son took charge of a factory which belonged to Adarsh and his daughter got married to a rich businessman. All the family members are associated to the school in some way or the other. All children of the family are the students of the school receiving free education. Every now and then rules change as per the convenience and need of the family members. In such a school, I, an outsider joined as the Vice Principal and H.O.D. English, one fine morning. To me any other school can not be a match to the school where I worked for long fourteen years. Of course the school where I studied from Transition to class XI (XII was not there in those days) is an exception. I still feel proud to say that I am an ex-student of South Point High School, Kolkata. Before joining the new school I had got some feedback from people and also from Veer Parsad about the school management. But I didn't have the idea to what extent they are indisciplined, unsystematic, fickle-minded and insensitive to the feelings of others. On the day when I joined, the Director introduced me to all teachers. I could see the expression of happiness in all faces except that of the senior most teacher of the English Department. Most probably she had expected to be the H.O.D. of the department but my arrival threw cold water on her expectation. When the daughter and the elder daughter-in-law of the Director came, he introduced them to me as Additional Principals. I suppressed my laughter looking at their dress and facial expression. They were looking like sales girls. How lucky are they to be Additional Principals in father's/father-in-law's school ! I anticipated their dislikings of my appointment as the Vice Principal and my anticipation was 100 per cent correct. So long they had been enjoying importance and power. Nobody ever questioned their efficiency or capability. They didn't have any previous experience of teaching or doing any administrative job earlier. Now the joining of an experienced person from a reputed branded school was naturally a matter of concern to them as there was every possibility of being compared to and getting exposed.

On the very first day I noticed that these two ladies actually do all sorts of clerical work right from writing the name of the staff every month in the teacher's Attendance Register. In my previous school there were two time-table incharges and they used to give engagement or substitution classes also in absence of teachers. In my new school the two Additional Principals prepare the time table and they only give engagement to the teachers. The first thing they did to show their power and hostility towards me was to give me engagement classes in absence of teachers everyday. At first I thought may be in Emergency they had asked me to take engagement classes but when it became a regular feature I voiced my protest very politely. They made long faces. In their family school they were managing everything as per their whims and fancies. Either they didn't know that Vice Principals are not given substitution classes in any school or they did it knowingly in order to harass me. I decided right from the beginning I have to be very, very strict and firm and will not allow anyone to exploit me in any way. They had made my seating arrangement in the Administrative Block in a glass cabin where there is no privacy. In my next cabin the Director's elder son used to sit and shout like an Ox. In front of the rooms of the Director and the Principal always a large number of people were found to be waiting and making noise. There was no privacy at all. In the beginning I used to think how will I sit here? All inquisitive eyes were on me. Whenever any teacher used to come to my cabin the divorcee sister of the Director's daughter-in-law would unfailingly come to the next cabin and try to listen to our conversation. For a few days I could not eat my tiffin there because all eyes were practically ogling at me. Then I decided to act smart. Without giving any importance to the inquisitive eyes around me I did all my work normally. Going to the toilet was another great problem. There is only one toilet in the administrative block and that too in the Director's room. The family members use that toilet without any hesitation. But I never felt comfortable although I got the permission. The other toilet was outside which was a common toilet used by teachers as well as class IV staff. The Director used to go to his other school in the Capital after break. Till then I had to wait.

Attending the Assembly was another wonderful experience. The school is supposed to start at 7.00 a.m. but it never happens. Till 7.10 a.m. students and teachers keep on coming. The main gate is closed at 7.00 a.m. but students, mainly the hostellers continue pouring in through the side gate. Some teachers are regular late comers. The Director who conducts the Assembly (most of the days comes in black shirt) comes 10 minutes late. His family members and some other 'chamchas' start touching his feet. That takes another 10 minutes. Then he climbs up the few steps on to the stage and joining his palms in the form of 'namaskar' says "Good morning, boys, girls and teachers......" Then he tells them stories of Mahabharat in wrong English. The teachers start giggling; looking at them the students also try to suppress their laughter. On one side of the stage the Principal Adarsh stands wrinkling up his face as the sunlight falls on his face. Both the brothers look like cartoon characters. On the very first day of my joining, when after telling the students the story of Mahabharat, the Director asked the students to chant "Om" together a dog who had entered unnoticed started crying "U u u u....." which sounded like "Om." There was a roll of laughter.

In the beginning, the Director and the Principal used to enter my glass chamber every now and then to make planning for the betterment of the school. They used to say that the strength of the school was more than 6000; there was no need of quantity but they were interested in quality. They used to take ideas from me regarding enhancing the quality of the school. However, the daughter and the daughter-in-law of the Director were not happy at this. Quantity continued to increase day by day and quality almost vanished. When I started coordinating the English Department, one day the daughter-in-law of the Director Sarita called me and said "You have started working independently immediately after joining our school. First learn from us. Whatever you are instructing the English teachers, should be in our knowledge." I felt like giving her a tight slap, stupid woman ! Without having any proper qualification and experience she is working in her father-in-law's school and I have to learn from her ! I have fourteen years experience of working in a reputed, branded school in a senior position. When the Director and the Principal had appointed me they told me clearly that I would be working directly under the Principal and there would be no interference in my work.

I thought of ignoring her and quietly doing my work in my style. But my fate must have smiled at my effort to solve the problem in such an easy way. Whenever the Director gave me any work she used to oppose it openly and compelled him to take back the work from me and assign her. The ultimate result was zero because she could not do the work herself. Although she was the daughter-in-law of the Director she suffered from insecurity and didn't want me to get any importance. I had to face the same situation which I had faced earlier at my previous school. Sarita and Ranjita belong to the same category. They knew their capacity, their capability, their efficiency, their quality. But insptie of that they always wanted to be in the limelight. When people easily get what they do not deserve, they lose their mental balance. Their greed and expectations shoot up like rocket and in order to fulfil their abnormal ambition they don't hesitate to trample others under their feet.

Like my previous school, here also I prepared the magazine as the Chief Editor but when it was published I was surprised to see the name of Sarita and Aradhana as Chief Editorial Advisors. Practically they had done nothing but the Director satisfied their ego by including their name as Chief Editorial Advisors. Not only that all the suitable and appropriate graphics were removed and family photographs were included in such places. There was no sense in doing so because the photographs of their children and of other family members were not matching with the poems or articles. It was just a shameless effort of publicity of their family members. Another shock I got at the time of admission. Admission is never 'closed' in this school. In the name of admission test they conduct a test of Mathematics only but even the failures get admission. All five Trivedi brothers, their sons and daughters and other family members have hostels and at the time of admission there starts a competition amongst them regarding whose hostel will be filled up first. All parents are asked to assemble in a hall where Motilal and Adarsh give lectures blowing their own trumpets in order to attract the parents. On the very first year of my joining they used me as a dice and repeatedly told the parents that I had left the job of a reputed, branded school in order to join their school. Most of the students are from villages and backward places. Particularly those who join class XI are from Hindi medium schools also. There is no admission criteria; whoever comes, gets admission. For name sake an interview is taken every time. I was also present in the interview. Nothing is usually asked from the subjects, only subjects are allotted as per the choice of the students. Some parents with business class background were asked to give donations for a Cancer patient – a student of the school. I was absolutely shocked because that child, who had been suffering from cancer had left the school long back and died but these people were exploiting his deadly disease and extorting money. The mystery of accumulating so much wealth so fast became crystal clear to me. These people are educationists !

Every year, for at least six months the administrative block remains overcrowded for the purpose of admission. "Admission Closed" is typed in bold letters and pasted at various places but there is always a large number of parents waiting outside the Principal's office with the request of admission. If the Principal says 'no' they approach the Director and manage admission. If the Director is not available they meet the Additional Principals and get their work done. There is no distribution of work. Everybody is looking after everything; hence there is a total chaos. So much difference of opinion is seldom observed in any school. Not only that, the family members, whether appointed as a nightguard or helper in the bus behave as if each one is the Director. The staff members who do not belong to Trivedi family are afraid of them and give them undue respect and importance – thus making them more bold and courageous. Compared to others in the family, the only sensible person is Adarsh, who is sensible to some extent, possessing sound knowledge in his subject, truthful, outspoken and a good administrator. He openly mocks at the two Additional Principals and says that they neither have any experience, nor any capability to manage the school. They know only to spoil the broth. But the Director is absolutely biased and whatever these two ladies say, he accepts that as the preachings of Vedas and Bhagwad Gita.

Sitting in the glass chamber was an aweful experience for me. In my next cabin Motilal's third brother used to sit without any work. Sometimes he used to come to my cabin with the request of writing his personal letters as he could not write in English. Actually that cabin belonged to Motilal's elder son who had a booming voice and always bellowed like an ox. These people lacked corporate civility and always conversed in such a manner as if they were at home. Sometimes they even spoke in Gorakhpuri Hindi. I used to sit there and watch how Motilal's elder son used to catch the 'Ullus' and convinced them that their school was the best in the State and how many Engineers, Doctors, C.A.s etc. completed their schooling from their school; their hostels had all facilities of five star hotels etc. etc. In fact his job was to do publicity for the school and he did that with great enthusiasm and zeal. In 99 per cent cases he was successful and not only that he took a handsome commission in each case. With a typical businessman's brain he invested this extra income in purchasing lands and starting his own hostels. He purchased a few acres of land to start his new school.

In that lounge which was divided into small cabins, just on the wall at my back, below the roof was an air cooler. Whenever it was on, it used to drive away the air of the fan and my cabin became extremely hot and humid. These people are so insensitive and devoid of human feelings that they were least bothered to see that I had to suffer for the whole day sitting in that humid place, sweating profusely. Motilal, Adarsh, Motilal's son, daughter, daughter-in-law and other relatives all used to sit in A.C. rooms. Even the receptionists used to enjoy the air of the cooler. When I joined the school, Adarsh ordered one of the office staff to install a calling bell in my room. As soon as it was installed, Sarita ordered the same type of bell (producing same sound) to be installed in her room. The most amusing thing was her bell was also installed outside my chamber and whenever she rang the bell, the peons or attendants used to come running to my room. After a few days they understood that it was Sarita who was calling them. From the next time when I rang the bell for some reason they rushed towards Sarita's room. Sarita started ringing the bell quite often just to harass me. Because of the constant sound of the bell I suffered from headache. Sarita's sister who used to sit in the reception also ordered a calling bell to be installed in the reception. One more was installed in the Accounts section and when all the bells were in use the attendants became puzzled whom to attend ! One day I overheard Motilal saying to one attendant, "You think it is very urgent to attend the receptionist but not the Director – the owner of the school who is your employer, who is paying you every month !" The attendant Urvashi tried her best to make him understand that she was mistaken and thought the sound of the bell was coming from the reception. Adarsh had given me the responsibility of conducting the written examination of the candidates for interview for the post of teachers. Once, after the candidates completed their written work, the Receptionist collected their papers and was about to give me but all of a sudden Sarita came and snatched all the papers leaving both of us in a state of daze.

Motilal had assigned me the responsibility of being the Judge of all competitions of Kids Academy. Sarita voiced her objection there also and said that I was giving more number of prizes than usual. Where there is mass participation it is difficult to select just one or two children. Some of them were equally good and moreover I wanted to encourage them. In my previous school I had seen that almost all students of Pre-Primary classes are given some prize in order to provide them with moral boost up. But the shrewd and cunning woman with the greed for money could not realise that. She instructed the teachers not to call me as the Judge. I laughed aloud and thought how mean and foolish ! If I am harassed like this nothing will happen to me. I need the experience of Vice Principal for about three years and with that experience I can get the post of Principal at any reputed school. But these people will be the losers. If I am not allowed to work peacefully, I will stop working and enjoy a fat salary without working hard for it. But their school will be deprived from getting something worthy and valuable from my previous experience. Who will be the loser? I understand very well, Sarita was trying to show her authority because she felt threatened like Ranjita. Before my efficiency, quality, qualification and experience she was nothing. Her image was getting suppressed. This is a common problem now in the country. Mediocre people, by the grace of money or source are now in power. They are the big bosses and they get a sadistic pleasure in dominating the thousand times better subordinates. They exploit them for their own benefit – name, fame, importance etc.

Motilal observed everything but could not say a single word against Sarita. One day he called me in his room and said – "Madam, I'm very sorry that you are not being utilised properly in this school. The school has grown enormously but after me I don't find anybody to whom I can entrust with the responsibility of the total administration of the school. I know they don't have the qualities to become Additional Principals or C.A.O. etc. but I had to give them these posts because they are my own people. I know Sarita is not behaving properly with you. It is her nature, her habit, the influence of her parents. At home she wakes up at 8.00 a.m.; my wife, her mother-in-law prepares tea for her and serves her on the bed. Her word is the final at home, otherwise she creates a scene. I'll see how I can utilise you properly. Till then, please try to adjust with her."

I could understand the helpless condition of the old man. I assured him from my side there will not be any problem.

With my initiative one after another the school started achieving in various fields. For a certain period I got back the energy and zeal with which I used to work at my previous school. Adarsh was also highly energetic and I got his full support always, everytime. The other family members were not happy and they made many nasty comments. I wrote to the Principals of all C.B.S.E. Schools in and around the township for attending a meeting in our school with the purpose of opening of Sahodaya Complex. Veer Parsad and the Principal of his rival school also came. I decided which posts to be given to whom. Adarsh had given me that power. After announcing the posts of Secretary, Treasurer etc. I announced the name of Veer Parsad and his rival Principal as the Vice

Presidents of Sahodaya Schools Complex and at the end the name of Adarsh as the President. Veer Parsad's face was worth observing. When the programme was over he presented me with the bouquet which was given to him.

Adarsh had given me full liberty to prepare the Annual Magazine. I devoted my heart and soul and prepared the dummy. After showing it to Adarsh I gave it to Motilal. He highly appreciated it and showed it to the Additional Principals and other portfolio holders of his family. Then they started doing the Post-Mortem. Deleting the beautiful graphics which matched with the articles and poems they included the photographs of their own children in such places. Sarita copied some extracts from the intellectual articles published in 'Cenbosec' and included that in the magazine as 'Message from the Additional Principal.' When the magazines were delivered I was the last person to see. When the first copy was released by the Chief Guest on the Annual Day, whole Trivedi family was on the stage but I was not called. Adarsh in his speech congratulated me and expressed his gratitude for my dedication and devotion in making the 1st issue of the magazine possible. For that he was being criticized by the other family members.

I gradually noticed a change in the attitude of the Director. Whatever he had told me at the time of appointing me and what I found there after joining were absolutely contradictory to each other. He knew the nature of his daughter-in-law but never opposed or even rebuked her for her atrocious behaviour. She was being pampered so much that she started thinking herself to be very valuable. She instigated the English teachers against me and told them not to listen to my instructions. How foolish ! Who will be the loser? It is their school. If with my experience and efficiency I can bring some improvement in the department who will be benefited? But blind ego prevented her from realising this simple fact.

The Director had assigned me the responsibility of judging all the competitions of Nursery to class II. As soon as Sarita came to know that she called the teachers of all these classes and told them not to call me as the Judge. Who wanted to be a Judge? My foot ! The teachers of classes I and II were afraid of her and they stopped calling me for the judgement of their competition. But the teachers of Nursery, K.G.I and K.G.II ignored Sarita and continued to invite me as the Judge. Gradually many teachers started coming to me to take my opinion in matters of English language. I mean, to clear their doubts particularly in Grammar. The English teachers also changed their attitude and gradually became my fan. The desired result could be achieved when we got the CBSE class X and XII Board results. A remarkable improvement was noticed in the performance of the students.

In my previous school a substantial amount was deducted as P.F. subscription and the same amount was subscribed by the school. In this school the first objection raised regarding my P. F. was by the Director's elder son –

famous for cheating people and increasing his bank balance. For about six months I repeatedly requested them to allot me a new P.F. number so that I could transfer my P.F. deposition from the old account. The Director didn't show any interest to start my P.F. account and considering me ignorant tried to give lame excuses. But ultimately they had to start my P.F. Account because of my insistence. I was well aware of my rights but was surprised to see the Graduate and Post Graduate teachers were absolutely unaware and ignorant of their rights. Year after year after year they had been working on adhoc basis. They had no idea about confirmation letter, increment etc. Till my joining nobody got any salary slip. I gave them my salary slip of the previous school and told them to prepare for all in the same way. I also taught them how to prepare Appointment letter. Sarita, as it was expected twisted her lips showing her ignominy without understanding how foolish she looked ! Simply by possessing a lot of money one cannot acquire that status or class which can give a unique distinction and recognition in the society. Money accumulated within a short time adopting unfair means doesn't take much time to perish but notoriety, once gained remains even after death. Instead of being grateful to me for sharing my experience with them and teaching them many things which they didn't know, they became egoistic and tried to show their authority. I think this is the rule of the world. Once the good for nothings acquire wealth and power they try to suppress the efficient and sincere workers keeping them within their fists.

The teachers were very happy to get salary slip, Appointment letter on back date, confirmation letter etc. I prepared their Self Appraisal and CCR forms and based on their performances they were given grades and increments. In me they saw somebody to look up to at their time of crisis or any problem. Aaradhana and Sarita felt the ground shaking under the feet although they had no reason to fear. It is their family school; I am just an outsider. My stay in the school would be temporary. Still they felt threatened.

The reason for shifting me from the Administrative Block to another block in the backside of the school was not absolutely to bring back discipline in that block but also to save the face of Sarita and Aaradhana. When the bridegroom's party comes to a house to see the would be bride for the first time before the marriage is fixed, the better looking young girls are not allowed to come before them in case a comparison is drawn with the ordinary girl whose marriage is being arranged. In order to bring Sarita and Aaradhana to the limelight, it was required that I should be removed and sent behind the curtain.

In each and every matter it started happening like that the management expected me to work behind the curtain and give them full credit of my work. Not only that they started highlighting the fact to the public that I left a branded school in order to join their school. They wanted people to believe that their school was the best compared to any other school. Nobody knew under what circumstances I had to leave my previous school with a bleeding heart and a weeping soul.

The only exception was the Principal Adarsh who is a considerate gentleman and sensitive person. He was like an oasis in a hot arid desert. But his support and attention towards me was mocked at by his family members, who didn't hesitate to make dirty, meaningful comments regarding our relationship. What a nasty, uncultured family !

Shifting of my room to the new block was a great shock to the students as well as the teachers of that block. They lost their freedom all of a sudden. As there was no one to monitor them, the students took the advantage of the situation and misbehaved to the possible extent. The teachers kept their eyes closed ignoring their accountability.

None of the classteachers used to be present in the class at the time of prayer. Here assembly is held in the ground only on Tuesday and Friday; rest of the days it is held in the class. As the classteachers came late, students were not serious about the prayer. They talked loudly, pushed each other, used abusive language, came out of their classrooms and started running in the corridor. When they saw me standing in the corridor in front of the classrooms they got a sudden blow. Entering into the classrooms they stood with folded palms and joined in the prayer. The classteachers came ten minutes after the prayer to take the attendance. Some of classteachers didn't even turn up. I called a meeting exclusively to be attended by the teachers of my block and told them firmly but politely that they have to be punctual and must be present in their class at the time of prayer; attendance should be taken in the beginning of the first period and at the end of the month the attendance register must be shown to me. Until and unless the leave applications were sanctioned by me fine should not be exempted. I also instructed the teachers to tell the students not to come out of the classroom after each and every period. I told them that I expected the cooperation of the teachers to bring discipline in that block.

The Next day I found seventy percent teachers were present in the class during prayer. To some extent discipline was recovered in the block. Those teachers who were not present during assembly came late as usual. I thought of observing them for some more days. When I found no change in them, I called them separately in my room and made it clear that I will not compromise with quality and discipline; they have to come on time and they will be responsible for the discipline of their respective class. Some of them were pet dogs of Sarita. They immediately reported the matter to her. She instigated them not to listen to me. This feedback I got from the receptionist who was present there in Sarita's room at that time. Next day however except two teachers nobody dared to come late. When these two teachers came in their normal, usual time, in front of the students I gave them left and right and told them "As a teacher if you are so indisciplined, what discipline can be expected from the students under your care?" I know which medicine should be applied for which disease and I got the desired result. The Director and Principal were happy at the remarkable improvement in the discipline of the block. but Sarita started burning with jealousy. Aaradhana however remained neutral.

I took it as a challenge. I will prove myself and never shake the confidence of the Director and the Principal on me. I care a fig for bitchy women like Ranjita or Sarita. If I am true to myself and my intention is noble, even a million of Sarita can not do any harm to me. By showing her jealousy towards me she only exposed herself before the whole school. One thing I have understood very well – women like Ranjita or Sarita can never be equal to me. The more they oppose me, the more confidence I will get. They don't have the guts or capability to get a good position facing interview at any school. They can work under the protection of a husband or in their family school getting the support of father or father-in-law.

Children can very well understand who is genuinely concerned for them and who is just working for money. They are just raw clay, whichever shape they get that is not in their hands. So long there was nobody to teach them manners, that's why they were behaving more like animals than like human beings. When I tried to teach them manners and good behaviour, initially they revolted because they had become habituated in behaving in an unrully manner. But when they found that I was insisting them to behave properly and follow the school rules eventually they listened to me and changed their habit. Eight percent of the teachers felt that whatever I was instructing was for their benefit and they started listening to me. Twenty percent pet dogs of Sarita who neither had any ambition in life nor had any commitment towards duty continued with their stupidity of following the instructions of their Guru Sarita. Those teachers were neither liked by their colleagues nor respected by the students. Because of the dirty politics played by Sarita I couldn't get 100 per cent results. But ultimately it was their loss, not mine.

I still cherish the dream of opening my own school, however small it may be. I have the potential, capability, efficiency everything except money. If God grants me three boons I will ask for money to open my own school, wisdom for people like Veer Parsad, Ranjita, Padma and Sarita and politics to be absolutely extracted from the profession of teaching. I dream of a new edifice of learning which will open the closed windows of mind where the divine rays of the morning sun will dispel the darkness of ignorance and prepare human beings in the true sense. My dream will come true one day.................

5

Padmavati–Standing Face to Face

I am born to win. I have come across a long path and seen the ups and downs of life so much so that now I don't like to look back. There is hardly any time for me to reminisce as except hitting the bed at home after the hectic days and performing a few other unavoidable daily chores required for living, most of the time I am with my boss, my master and darling Veer Parsad, whose sweetheart cum P.A. cum Administrative Officer cum Secretary cum Bed Partner I am. If he is the sun, I am his shadow. If he is the sky, I am the cloud, if he is the tree, I am the trunk. I wish, at least once my previous boss should come and see my present position. At his time I was kept cornered and my work was confined to typing letters only, sharing the same table with six other people and working with a typewriter. With the pressure of work my temperament used to soar which was reflected through the speed and sound of the typewriter machine. Now I have my own A.C. chamber with ten other people working under me. Officially my designation is Administrative Officer but unofficially people call-me by many names - 'Head Mistress,' 'Body Guard,' 'Second Wife' etc. of Veer Parsad. I enjoy, I really enjoy every time my name is associated with that of my boss – Veer Parsad – Padmavati Prasad – Veer Parsad - Padmavati Prasad. Actually Prasad is my husband's surname but what a coincidence!

I was born and brought up in Hyderabad, although my father was transferred to a few other places later in his career and we had to move along with him. Ultimately he settled in Hyderabad where my mother is still living alone in the house which my father had got constructed. We are two sisters and one brother. Ours is a lower middle class family. My mother is a simple lady who knows how to read and write but could not progress much beyond that. My father's job was just sufficient to support the family of his wife and four children, to arrange their morsels twice a day. I am grateful to him because in spite of the financial problems he was conscious of our education.

Every family has an heirloom. We also had one – a box full of silver ornaments and other silver paraphernalia. The box with its contents was a perennial source of admiration to us in our childhood. Opening it and observing each and every item was the luxury of the leisure time of my siblings and me. So many memories of the past of my parents were associated with each and every object. While we used to appreciate the artistic beauty of the artifacts, my mother narrated the stories which made them so special. We grew up and to meet the growing demands of the family one after another these silver items had to be disposed of, until one day the box became absolutely empty. My sister's marriage, my brother's going to America, my college fees, whenever required, the silver came to use along with the loan taken by my father. I have seen my mother shedding tears while parting with her precious possession. I promised at the threshold of my youth that I will fill up that box with everything we have lost.

My father has left this world. I will give back my mother her past by filling her box with silver items. For that I don't hesitate to sleep with Veer Parsad whenever he desires so. What's the use of remaining pure and chaste? Neither will I get sexual satisfaction from my husband, nor will I get enough money to enjoy life, nor will I get power and position to boost up my ego. I will just have to struggle to make both the ends meet which my father did throughout his life.

I had requested my previous boss to shift me from reception to teaching field when he was leaving for the Middle East on deputation for two years. But he refused to do as the person who was made the Acting Principal was quite inexperienced. So, very reluctantly I had to carry on with my administrative job of course as a P.A. to the Principal. Today I have no regret. I started this job in 1986, the year I got married and shifted from Delhi where I used to work as a typist earlier. I worked under my ex-boss for long ten years. Our relationship was just professional. He was extremely handsome and his wife was the most unattractive lady but their relationship was unique. On several occasions I had to accompany him to various places as his P.A. We stayed in the same hotel but he neither showed any interest in me nor asked for any immoral favour. I always felt safe and secured and my other colleagues also shared the same opinion. He was a true gentleman and he used to respect ladies; no doubt he made everybody feel important – a shrewd diplomat that he was but at the cost of cutting their purse. The staff never got what they deserved except a sweet smile and a few words of praise. Only one lady was benefited who had joined as an expert in gardening. My ex-boss used to listen to all advices and opinions of that graceful, charming lady of his own religious community. It didn't take much time for her to make an important place for herself in the school administration shifting herself from the beautiful rose garden which was her creation and which contributes to the aura of aestheticism prevailing in the school, spreading the fragrance all around even today. Heaving a sigh I used to watch them and think whether there would be any change, ever, in my dull, monotonous life and job!

My ex-boss left the school in 1995 leaving the charge of the Pre-primary section – the heart of the institution to her. The brain, that is the senior school was left under the care of a Biology teacher who continued for a year as the Acting Principal till Veer Parsad, my present boss joined as the Principal in 1996 and then there was an abrupt change in the scenario.

Somehow, I didn't like Veer Parsad in the beginning. His eyebrows were always wrinkled and his face wore a hostile expression inspite of his tall, slim, sexy figure. His wife Ranjita joined the Social Science Department as a T.G.T. (History) and the first question which troubled everybody was that she was not a B.Ed. trained teacher. Violating the norms of the school, Veer Parsad managed a permanent grade for his wife. They had not even taught any manners to their children. They never used to wish the teachers and whenever there was any cultural or literary function, both Ipsita and Amar used to sit in the front row, clinging to their parents, greedily gulping down the snacks served to the distinguished guests and other important persons.

The first letter which I had drafted for Veer Parsad came back to me with corrections at thirty-five places in green ink and highlighted with an orange colour highlighter. Boiling with rage,I thought of putting up my papers but resisted myself thinking about my mother's antique box which I had promised to fill with silver. My husband Prasad works at a cooperative housing society and his income is meagre. His father is a retired school master whose pension is not enough to support himself and his wife. My brother in-law met with an untimely death due to road accident and his wife stays with us. Moreover my daughter's future was lying in front of me and as a mother I didn't want her to go through all those hardships which I had to face in my life. Veer Parsad wanted me to work with him day and night and a clash was inevitable due to that because I never worked beyond five o' clock in the evening with my ex-boss. Veer Parsad, like a perfect sadist started torturing me. Prasad, my husband told me "Either you have to listen to your boss or leave the job." There was no other alternative. Within a year, Veer Parsad gained a notoriety in the school as well as in the society. People started slinging mud at his character as he indulged in asking for sexual favour from ladies who applied for job as well as from the lady teachers of the school. I had to spend my evenings in the school with Veer Parsad doing all sorts of odd jobs except on those evenings when he used to have an appointment with any lady. My daughter was neglected and the situation worsened to such an extent that I had to write some anonymous letters against Veer Parsad and also E-mailed to the Society members in New Delhi against him. By that time our status had changed as it was progress and upliftment from the typewriter to the computer and I didn't hesitate to make full utilisation of it. Veer Parsad was intelligent enough to understand that it was none other than Padma who was spreading rumour and notoriety against him. I was shifted to the Accounts Section from his Secretariat and became the subject of gossiping for the staff members. I laugh at myself to think that I used to envy Meena, that dark complexioned thin girl with a sweet face, sitting in the reception those days. By that time I had become habituated in staying with Veer Parsad day and night and all of a sudden this rejection seemed to be the greatest insult to me. No doubt, it was a painful period of my life and career because the expression of pity in the eyes of the staff members was unbearable. There was only one way to get rid of this situation – somehow shattering the faith of Veer Parsad on Meena – my professional rival. We knew each others e-mail-id and password and so it was just a child's play. I mailed a complaint letter against Veer Parsad to the Chairman of the EMS in the name of Meena from her e-mail-id and in a tricky way drew the attention of Veer towards it. It was a bolt from the blue to Meena when she was caught by Veer Parsad – the Computer illiterate Principal in this Computer savvy world who is till date unaware of these tricks. It was my crossing the first hurdle in winning the confidence of my boss Veer Parsad. Since then, I never had to turn back.

Meena was sacked and she then started defaming Veer Parsad literally, taking the advantage of being associated with a local daily. When people are blamed with false charges, they in fact start practising those vices which are hurled on them in a groundless manner hurting their sense of loyalty and ego. Meena left, another attractive girl came to the reception but this time I didn't have to rack my brain to turn Veer Parsad against her. She herself decided to leave as Veer's leechy, slimy nature put a pressure on her nerves. In the general meeting however, Veer Parsad managed by saying that she had left as she was not getting enough time to study for M.B.A. which she had been pursuing at that time; utter lie – who knows better than me?

While working with Veer Parsad, the grudge against him in my mind gradually melted like camphor and our chemistry started working. A conflict started in my mind – on the one hand a cool drizzling on the parched ground, blossoming the dry, seer branch which had lost all beauty and colour and on the other hand the sense of morality and ethics tormenting my conscience – will Sai Baba accept my offerings again? In this world two things are difficult to resist – sex and power, because they bring the whole world under your feet. Ultimately Padma Prasad had to surrender before Veer Parsad. I had no physical relationship with my husband ever since the birth of our daughter. Veer Parsad had told me that sex was not the cup of tea of Ranjita – his wife. Their sexual relationship also ended when Ranjita had conceived Amar. Both of us were thirsty and willing and decided to quench the thirst of each other. May be it was the wish of Sai Baba, he brought us together.

Veer Parsad had made one thing very clear right from the beginning that is I had to take Ranjita into confidence in each and every matter. She became my best friend. I was safe; no one could do any harm to me now. With Veer Parsad and Ranjita's backing, I started dominating the staff members, both teaching and non-teaching. No one could meet Veer Parsad before meeting me. My mother's silver box started filling up. My in-laws, husband and daughter started relishing four course lunch and dinner with a different dessert every day. My position not only improved at school but also at home and in the family. My elder sister sent her daughter to me as her husband was transferred to Dubai. It was a boon in disguise as my daughter got a companion and learnt not to miss me anymore.

My brother was in Russia with his wife at that time. Due to some reason their relationship had become strained. I used to counsel both of them over telephone (at the expense of school of course) and during the Diwali – Dusshera break went to Russia to settle their problem. The trip was, not to mention, sponsored by Veer Parsad courtesy school.

Much water has flowed down the river as my life got a new turn with Veer Parsad. The improved financial condition at home kept everybody silent. My mother-in-law even touched the feet of Veer Parsad when he paid a visit to our home. Although my husband works with the Housing Board Society we could have never shifted to our own house had Veer Parsad not showered his benevolence on us. He was successful in attaining the position of God Father in the eyes of my family members.

I started enjoying the importance at my workplace and even after knowing that Veer Parsad is a Casanova who enjoys physical relationship with many women I just ignored the fact. I consoled my mind thinking about Ranjita. If she can tolerate this, being his wife why can't I? Whatever I am achieving is my profit, my gain. Like a fool why should I spoil that ?

The Acting Principal before Veer Parsad's arrival had done one good thing for the old teachers that is giving them P.G.T.Grade. She had upgraded me also. Veer Parsad started criticizing the senior teachers and finding out faults with them. They were kept standing in the meetings and ticked off frequently to which they acquiesced. Veer Parsad wanted to degrade them, morally shattering their confidence. He was paving the way for his wife removing the thorns from her way. Those who were clever and ambitious could predict their dark future in this school and one by one left, getting better opportunities somewhere else. Those who remained, either they had to flatter Ranjita and satisfy Veer Parsad or were treated like slaves.

Veer Parsad's atrocity was not unknown to anyone. Taking blank cheques from the rich parents, sexually harassing ladies, humiliating the teachers, taking undue advantages, manipulating and exploiting efficient staff, availing facilities to which he was not entitled etc., etc., etc........and I was his one and only partner cum witness of all his heinous acts. His success was my success. The new taste of power, importance and prosperity blinded me and covered my mind with a layer of slime. If he used to get a briefcase (full ofcourse) I was not deprived of a medium size packet. If he got a crate of foreign whisky, I could take home atleast a box of sweets for my family. He trusted me with his personal bank accounts, his savings, his office key, almirah key, even the key of his drawer where he used to keep his most confidential documents. Veer Parsad came absolutely in my grip willingly. I came to his use as and when required writing negative, damaging reports against many staff members, ruining their career. Many new teachers joined the school; among them was Urja, the voluptuous beauty and I sensed danger. Each time a beautiful teacher joined the school I had to rearrange my board of chess. After all, who knows Veer Parsad better than me? From day one I could feel Veer Parsad's attraction towards Urja. In her job application she had written at one place "Getting an opportunity to serve the institution, I can show my parts and satisfy both the students and the management with my talents." While sorting out the applications Veer Parsad underlined the sentence in green ink and I understood his intention in trying to find out double meaning. Veer Parsad is desperate and unsophisticated in this matter. He doesn't hesitate to express his dirty desire if he feels attracted to any lady. He doesn't care for me and Ranjita also. Whatever he wants, he gets it by hook or by crook. So far I have kept my mouth shut because I have no other alternative. Something is better than nothing and I should feel happy that Veer Parsad has given me remarkably more than just 'something.' It will be my foolishness if I interfere in his personal life and spoil my position. The previous office-incharge used to call me 'Padma' but now I am 'Madam' even to the senior staff. Whenever I find Veer Parsad's attention has been diverted to any other woman I try to concentrate in the religious books on Sai Baba and forget everything. I know the bird will come back and perch on my branch after tasting the berries of a new tree, which he would find sour very soon.

My ex-boss had started the construction of the new building and left before it was completed. The senior school was shifted to the new building in 1996-97. It was designed as per his taste and instructions. The Principal's office with large French windows is situated in such a place from where one can feel the pulse of the whole school, right from the visitors who come to school and go out to the classrooms and overall functioning of the school. Unfortunately he could not sit in the office even for a single day. It was kept in store for Veer Parsad and he is the lucky person to sit in the Principal's office which was constructed with great care by my ex-boss. This office room is a mute witness of Veer Parsad's corruption and lust.

As per rules, Principals are supposed to take one or two classes. Immediately after joining, Veer Parsad instructed the time-table incharge that he needed some time to be familiar with the atmosphere and work culture of the school; hence he will be able to take classes after some time. In the first year he didn't take any classes at all and in the second year he was given Geography of class XI. There were only a few takers of the subject and the feedback the inquisitive, nosy staff members collected from them was instead of teaching, Veer Parsad used to ask them to read and he himself used to write a few words on the black board choosing from their text books and wrote the rhyming words for those particular words. This continued for a few months and during that period, most of the time I had to come running to the staff room to arrange a substitute teacher for him as he was unable to take the class. There is a proverb in English "Man is the maker of his fortune," which is 100 per cent true in case of Veer Parsad. He has moulded his fate, given it a shape and colour of his own choice.

Within a year of his joining he managed the post of Senior Mistress (Middle Wing) for his wife Ranjita. The old, experienced lady who had been holding the responsibility so long was absolutely ignored and was compelled to resign within a short time. Veer Parsad's next target was the Acting Principal who was given the promotion of Vice Principal and treated with ignominy creating the desire in her mind to quit. He got the opportunity very soon when a new school came nearby and he suggested her name as the Principal of that school to the Society. One thorn from the way of Ranjita was removed with the shifting of the Vice Principal to the new school. Another senior person was made the Vice Principal and then the same tricky game started. At his instructions I also started harassing the new Vice Principal and before the new session started he also left as a Principal of a school under the aegis of the Society. People started whispering "Now he will make his wife the Vice Principal" – to which he reacted in the General Body meeting – "My wife is not Rabri Devi. She has the qualities and qualifications to become the Vice Principal. But she is not becoming the Vice Principal now."

The post of Vice Principal remained vacant for seven long years. One thing I observed which appeared to be strange to me. Veer Parsad's attitude towards Urja had totally changed. I couldn't know the reason but noticed that he was behaving in a hostile manner with Urja. By that time Madhushree had joined and very soon she became the apple of the eyes of Veer Parsad. Mrs. Sita Raman who was associated with the magazine ever since its birth was removed with humiliation and Madhushree was made the Editor of the magazine. She was also given the responsibility of preparing the Press Releases. Veer Parsad started spending maximum time with her on pretext of work. The day she came out of his chamber with open hair, my heart beat stopped for a while. From 5.30 p.m. to 8.30 – 9.00 in the evening Veer Parsad used to keep Madhushree confined in his room for checking the dummy of the magazine.

I started feeling insecure and when Madhushree's husband gave a ring in the reception one evening to enquire about his wife, I played my role and with a dramatic modulation in my voice narrated Madhushree's importance in Veer Parsad's life and work, kindling the fire of jealousy, anger and suspicion in that gentleman's heart. The result was obvious. He spoke directly to Veer Parsad hurling abuses at him. I was successful in drawing the attention of Ranjita towards the dress of Madhushree. Ranjita told her one day not to wear deep neck, low cut blouses and salwar suits. She was clever enough to get the hint. Tension started brewing at Madhushree's house. Her daughters who were also students of our school were neglected and left with the maid servant. Veer Parsad used to drop her home every evening which was noticed by a senior teacher of the school who is now holding the important position of Sr. Mistress of the middle wing. She, infact, instructed her daughters to keep watch and started contributing to the G.K. of her colleagues with the juicy reports given by them. It was the most crispy gossip during the recess among the staff members which I overheard quite many times.

Ranjita, who was hostile towards Urja right from her joining, all of a sudden became sympathetic towards her as she sensed danger on the other side. There was no shortfall to her informers and they started reporting about Madhushree. I know very well when and how to play my role effectively. Have you seen a weak fish in the aquarium? The other fishes of different varieties continuously poke at it till it dies and relish its flesh leaving only the thin layer of skin with the delicate scales. Madhushree was stung by all in the same way, more so, when she came back from Andaman after the summer vacation where Veer Parsad had also gone with his family (co incidence or a planned visit? God knows !) In front of Ranjita Veer Parsad had behaved like a perfect debauche. Wearing a brief and standing in knee deep water of the sea he gestured some of the lady teachers (who also had visited Andaman Islands at the same time) to swim with him. Ranjita was sitting like a stone on the beach and watching Veer Parsad flirting with them. One of them reported me after coming back. I also have my own net work which is very active. Each and every moment of Veer Parsad's colourful days in the Andaman Islands is in my knowledge.

The Annual staff selection committee met after the summer vacation. So far Madhushree had been working on Adhoc and then she applied for T.G.T. post. When she came out after appearing before the interview board, the senior teachers wanted to know from her – which questions were asked? Strange! They were not interested to know about any other candidate except Madhushree. She couldn't tell anyone properly, exactly what questions were asked but out of nervousness came out with the truth that Veer Parsad had assured her that he would present her case before the board of governors in her favour. Neelima Pandey retorted – "Her interview was already taken in the Andamans," followed by a loud guffaw in the staffroom. Most probably she remembered her own special interview taken by Veer in his restroom.

Days rolled on; the school was growing in leaps and bounds; the strength increased with the commencing of each new session. Veer Parsad is a far-sighted person who had fabricated a bright future for himself as well as Ranjita and down the line Amar and Ipsita. I am a part of his each and every plan and programme from the beginning except for the initial few months when Veer Parsad had doubts regarding my loyalty. According to the contract made in 1985 between the company which had sponsored land, building and other infrastructure and the Society in Delhi, the local Society in the name of the school was to function as an autonomous body and the contract was made for an unlimited period. The members of the Governing body in Delhi at that time were real educationists who could not even imagine what a blunder they were going to make. They were not business minded but eminent persons in the Society who were worshippers of education. In the beginning most probably in 1994-95, the new members of the governing body of the Society wanted to renew the contract although as per the original contract there was no such provision and my ex-boss who was the Principal at that time agreed to that. Till date Veer Parsad curses him for this decision but I know him better than Veer Parsad. Neither his wife nor his any relative was associated to the school. He didn't have any self interest and never indulged in nepotism. But Veer Parsad's sole intention was to establish his undeserving wife Ranjita, which was easy for him to do as the school was running as an autonomous body, not under the control of the Society in Delhi.

Naturally, renewal of the contract by the previous Principal after December 2006 was not liked by him. He was afraid of the new terms and conditions which might have shattered his dreams. He wanted to capture everything to his benefit within this period. I told him – in order to do so first he had to crate a misunderstanding between the two parties – the Society in New Delhi and the local body of B.O.Gs. Veer Parsad looked at my face with appreciating eyes and that night I became pregnant for the second time in life after twelve years of the birth of my only daughter. I had to take leave and go outside Bhilai to abort the unborn foetus, the greatest gift I received from Veer Parsad. It would have been my love child but how could I show my face to my husband? I could have kept it a secret to the society but it was not possible for me to convince my husband because we have no physical relationship since the birth of Parna.

Veer Parsad used to show his integrity to the Society in Delhi in the beginning of his tenure particularly when he was sent abroad on official tour. But he started changing his tune and colour after coming back from his official foreign tour. He suppressed the letters which came from the Society and didn't show them to the local management, thus creating a communication gap between the two parties. He also started dreaming of opening a chain of schools in and around the capital of the State under the same banner without the knowledge of the Society. The then Pro Vice Chairman, who retired within two years had a flourishing business, courtesy Mr. Veer Parsad and blindly signed all important papers sent by him without even knowing that he was playing with the future of thousands of students. At that crucial moment both Ranjita and I advised him not to give too much importance to any teacher but to treat all equally. This was the time to patch up with all who were not in his good book because he needed the support of all, not just one or two. Bindiya, who had a gala time with Veer Parsad in the past was ignored by him when Madhushree took the entry in Veer

Parsad's life. She was spreading the rumour – "You know what the Principal has told Madhushree? He will lift her up to that height which no one is able to imagine." Bla, bla, bla was echoing from all corners. Veer Parsad's favourite Examination Incharge cum House Warden left the school as he got the post of the Principal in an upcoming school. Urja all of a sudden won the first prize in a State level Essay writing competition organised by Petroleum Conservation Research Association and became popular overnight due to this achievement. People started praising her. Students have been already her fan. Veer Parsad had to change his mind and involved her in various school activities. Actually Veer Parsad wanted to exploit her talent and quality to his gain and benefit. He could no more keep her cornered as she was getting the attention of all.

Veer Parsad got an opportunity for paper presentation at an international conference in New Delhi on Urdu as a compulsory medium in Primary and Secondary level and asked Urja and Madhushree to prepare the papers for him. By that time Madhushree had come to know about his nature and took the work casually. Urja was given importance for the first time in so many years hence she did the work with full enthusiasm and Veer Parsad was highly satisfied with her work. But even at that time he didn't deviate from his policy of divide and rule. He gave the copy prepared by Madhushree to Urja and asked her to verify whether it was almost the same like the one prepared by her. She came out with the truth and said that both of them had referred to the same books and after discussing they prepared the papers which might have resulted in the similarities. The same question was asked to Madhushree to which she replied in the same way as Urja had replied. Not satisfied with the answers Veer Parsad tried to create enmity between the two in a different way. He used to call Urja and Madhushree separately although they were working on the same project and instigated them against each other in a crafty way.

One day he worked with Madhushree till 12 o' clock at night and while dropping her home told her "I didn't want to involve Urja in any work. She has proved herself and there will be a lot of criticism if I don't involve her. You keep on working, Urja will be removed after some time." However, Madhushree could not trust him anymore and disclosed the fact to Urja. When Veer Parsad failed in creating any enmity between the two he started ignoring Madhushree hurting her ego. He praised Urja in the general meetings, in the morning Assembly and made her very popular. She was assigned the duty of writing all speeches of Veer Parsad. Mrs. Sita Raman resigned as the ignominy she had been facing became unbearable and she decided to settle in Chennai.

A tension was brewing up with the Education Management Society in Delhi as Veer Parsad was not taking their opinion in any matter. They decided to open a new school under their banner and kept Veer Parsad totally ignorant about it. The teachers who were so long facing injustice and humiliation under Veer Parsad and Ranjita, joined hands and decided to stand against Veer Parsad.

About 19 teachers complained against Veer Parsad to the newly appointed E.D. (Works) who was also the Pro Vice Chairman of the school and later on became the Managing Director of the sponsor organisation. Madhushree took a leading role in this agitation. A senior teacher of the Science Deptt. who was very efficient and popular among the students but was ignored and deprived of her due honour as she had refused to give some additional marks to the Principal's son to help him to fetch the Scholar Badge, convinced many teachers to join the new school. About eighty teachers applied at the new school which was quite alarming. The Pre-Primary Incharge, later on promoted to the Primary Wing, who was eligible for the post of Vice Principal, which post had been kept vacant and preserved for the Principal's wife was considered for the post of Principal for the new school. Another efficient in charge of the Primary section who was promoted to the Middle Wing left the school and joined as the Principal of a school started by the Society in Hyderabad.

It became easy for them to frame different charges against Veer Parsad because of his dirty character. He had called a dignified lady of the township on one Saturday evening (February 2001) on the pretext of the admission of her daughter. I was on leave on that day. There was no one in the school at that time except the gatekeeper at the gate which was far away from the Principal's office. Veer Parsad expressed his weakness to the lady and asking for sexual favour pulled her near him and tried to molest and kiss her. She struggled hard to free herself and on doing so immediately came out of his office and left the school. But she took a brave decision in going straightway to the office of a political party and reporting the matter to the party members. Next day the matter was reported in details with the statement of the lady in all local daily newspapers. FIR was lodged by the lady at the local police station. Veer Parsad called me and said it's all bullshit, not authentic. A very senior person was told to write in favour of the Principal and he got the signature of all gents teachers, supporting him. As per Veer Parsad's instructions I called Urja from the staff room and spoke to her in the site engineer's small room attached to the staff room. "Urja, Sir is not like that. Believe me, he can't do any such thing." Urja said "Whether he did it or not you will be knowing better than anyone else because you were also present in the reception." I told her the truth – "No, I was not present." She said – "You are saying he is not like that, I will also say he is not like that but how will you shut the mouth of people? Everybody will say that if he had no evil intention then he should not have called any lady alone in the evening and that too on a holiday." I told her "Ravi Shastri Sir has taken the initiative and got the signature of all gents teachers in favour of Sir. He trusts and likes you so much. You should also do something in his favour. Please write that you have full faith in his character and nature and firmly believe that he can't do such things and get the signature of all lady teachers" Urja wrote one full page on Veer Parsad in an assertive manner but could not get the signature of the teachers. FIR was lodged against Veer Parsad. He utilised his sources. All Govt. officials and political leaders were invited time to time as Chief Guests of various functions held in the school. They were treated with such honour which they never expected in their life and were presented with gifts. On the whole they were pleased with Veer Parsad. One of these eminent personalities acted as a mediator and a compromise was made between Veer Parasd and the lady.

In the evening of the fifteenth day of the incident he dressed up in Churidar Kurta, adorned his forehead with a red 'Tilak' and visited the lady's place – a transit house attached to the office of a leading industrialist where she used to work. In front of the mediator Veer Parsad touched the feet of the lady and apologised. The FIR against him was ultimately withdrawn. This incident was witnessed by some employees of that Industrialist among whom was the brother of one English teacher of the school.

In any small township, society is just like a bog with stagnant water. If a stone is thrown, it will create a small ripple which does not take much time to subside. This incident also became a common topic for gossiping for a few days and then people forgot everything. But this matter was reported to the Society in New Delhi by the group of teachers who wanted the removal of Veer Parsad at any cost. A notice was served to the school regarding termination of the contract which was known by only four persons – Veer Parsad, Ranjita, the then Pro-Vice Chairman and myself. Veer Parsad kept the matter absolutely secret. The agreement made in 1985 for seven years between the two parties was, the school will start functioning with the brand name but the name of the place also attached to it, the administration of which will be carried on by autonomous Board of Governors and its Registration will be done by Society's Registration Act 1960-1973. As per this agreement the school was registered and affiliated to CBSE Board. This agreement was done for seven years under Annexure P-7 on 20th October 1992 and further extended for a period of seven years with effect from 4th October 1999 under Annexure P-8, which was to be continued till 3.11.2006. According to the agreement both the parties were liable to serve a notice before one year to terminate the agreement.

The termination notice was served on 11.3.2002 and was published in the newspaper for public notification. Veer Parsad was able to convince the Pro Vice Chairman that the school had been running without any help from the Society in Delhi very well and will further improve without their interference. The resources and income will be absolutely that of the school and the local body and need not be shared by any other party. His actual intention was to enjoy absolute power because he knew there will be no interference from the local body as people of the corporate world have no time to devote for school or any such set up as they are extremely busy with their own work. Veer Parsad wanted the school to come out of the Society so that he could build up his own empire and start his own family hierarchy. He wanted to open a chain of schools in the State.

Veer Parsad was successful in the first stage of his mission. The Pro Vice Chairman, who was about to retire within a few days, went to Delhi and met the Chairman of the Delhi Society on 01.05.2002 and appealed for the reconsideration of the notice; he also agreed to accept the notice if it was not possible for the Chairman to reconsider the same. After this the school terminated the agreement on 29.05.2002 by serving a notice accepting the termination. Without the knowledge of a single staff member, student or parent, the school was dissociated from the Society. From May to September the matter remained a top secret till a senior teacher who was the Incharge of the Primary section put up her papers during the Diwali – Dussehra break, assured by the Society that she will be appointed as the Principal of the new school. She was a very popular Sr.Mistress and many of her supporters also decided to leave the school.

The school reopened after a short break on 1st November 2002 and a General Body meeting was called by Veer Parsad in the evening. Two teachers who used to criticise Veer Parsad and Ranjita most were appointed as the Senior Mistress of the Middle and Primary Wing respectively. Some firebrand teachers and other neutral teachers were given promotion. H.O.Ds were appointed for all departments. Urja was promoted to P.G.T. and she was made the H.O.D. of English. But Madhushree was not given anything. By-passing the senior teachers of the Science department, a favourite teacher of Ranjita from the Biology department was made the H.O.D. Science. This lady was once the weakness of Veer Parsad and he had visited her house in broad daylight, in absence of her husband, when her daughter was in school and she herself had taken sick leave. The neighbours ofcourse had made full utilisation of their ears and eyes and narrated the incident with great enthusiasm to every second person they met.

After the announcement of the promotion and position Veer Parsad said that he was getting phone calls from various corners inquiring whether the school had become private. He said the school was private right from the beginning and also told the teachers not to pay attention to any rumour. He didn't say a single word regarding the detachment of the school from the Society and also the fact that he was being gheraod (detained) in his office by the agitated parents during the vacation who demanded to know the truth from him. Those who got promotion were so engrossed with their success that they were least bothered to know anything.

Next day Veer Parsad called the teachers in his chamber to handover the promotion letters to them. For one hour he kept on rebuking a senior teacher of the Science department while the other teachers were waiting in the reception. This teacher had a long experience and was the Incharge of NTSE contributing greatly in producing the best results. He did it purposely because he wanted her to quit as he desired all senior teachers with potential, who were in the good book of the Society to leave one after another so that the line remains absolutely clear in front of Ranjita. He had six years more to go at that time and Ranjita was the Senior Mistress of the Secondary Wing. The post of the Vice Principal was kept reserved for her. The school had come out of the Society, hence there was no chance of an outsider, selected by the Society to occupy her cherished chair.

The disappointed teachers formed a group and became rebellious. They started meeting after school and making various plans. They jointly submitted their resignation a few months later and also sent complaint letters to the local management against Veer Parsad. Urja, at that time had helped the school in various ways extending her full support to Veer Parsad. By nature she is sincere and hardworking, her only impractical point being too honest and sincere. Veer Parsad used to appreciate her quality of work and tried to mould her in his way. She got so much importance that Ranjita as well as other teachers became jealous of her. Bindiya Bhalla–ex-darling of Veer Parsad and the mother of his child who was born after many years of the birth of her daughter, commented "Urja has become a 'Chahiti' of the Principal." Within a few days of this comment she was made a House Warden. Veer Parsad was a coward and a characterless both at the same time. He was afraid of his ex-darling.

Ranjita and Veer Parsad changed their strategy and tried to please everybody. As soon as Madhushree submitted her resignation, Veer Parsad called her and started flattering her, assuring her in various ways that she will be given promotion and important responsibilities. But she was adamant. Veer Parsad realised that at that crucial moment if teachers move out, it will be a discredit to him. Ranjita and he both tried to please the teachers to retain them. The parents formed an association and started agitation. They assembled outside the gate of the school and shouted slogans against the corrupt Principal. Madhushree's husband was playing a leading role amongst them.

The situation worsened to such an extent that Veer Parsad's position became absolutely unstable. At one point it seemed that he will have to go as the only condition of the Society was that the Principal should be removed if the local body wants the school to come under the Society again. The parent body decided to meet the Chairman and accompanied the Managing Director and the Pro Vice Chairman who went to Delhi. But he refused to meet them until and unless the existing Society formed by the local body was dissolved.

The session ended in the end of March and the dissatisfied teachers joined the new school which started with a small number of students. These teachers were very much disheartened as they had expected that Veer Parsad would be removed and they would continue in the old school after withdrawing their resignation. Veer Parsad felt amused within himself at their immaturity.

One thing was very interesting – two teachers withdrew their resignation and stayed back because they thought they would not be able to take up the workload of the new school. God knows what was the exact reason behind their changing of decision ! However Veer Parsad refused to give the release order to the outgoing teachers till they gave undertaking that they were leaving the school at their own interest, for their personal growth and not compelled by the Principal or any unpleasant situation whatsoever.

There was one more development by the mean time – a reason serious enough to irk Veer Parsad. On the one hand he was busy in flattering all eminent and distinguished people of the State Ministry, Police Department, members of the Board of Governors etc., on the other hand he was trying his best to please all staff members as per the advice of Ranjita and myself. It was indeed a very troublesome period for all three of us. Very tactfully he had to manage the situation and at the same time exploit it to the maximum benefit of Ranjita, Amar, Ipsita and of course me. Everything was unpredictable, things could have taken a different turn at any moment. Public notice was issued in the newspaper that from the beginning of the new session the school will no more remain under the aegis of the Society and will lose its brand name. The CBSE affiliation number also had to be changed. Pressurised by the parents an appeal was made in the district court for a stay order and just at the nick of time we were successful in achieving it. The Society went to the High Court to contest against the stay.

For the last few years a lunch was arranged on the last working day every year. That year also it was arranged when the group of teachers who had submitted their resignation were about to leave. Ranjita instructed Urja to send a circular as the Activity Incharge informing all staff members about the lunch. She told her to take the signature of all except the teachers who were leaving. Actually in this way she was successful in killing two birds with a single stone; she expressed her malice towards them at the cost of Urja who became unpopular and unfriendly in their eyes. When ambition clouds the mind of undeserving people they don't try to achieve success by working hard for it but apply the tricky and bitchy ways to reach their goal and Ranjita was not an exception. The teachers who left the school developed a misunderstanding about Urja while leaving. However Veer Parsad started depending on Urja for most of the work. A chaotic condition prevailed in the school which was managed very efficiently by her. She used to deal with any work in a systematic, organised way. Veer Parsad used to call her every now and then, after school, in the evening, on all holidays including Sundays for extra work. She always came with a smiling face and never grumbled for any amount of extra work. The most interesting thing was as the departmental Head, Urja used to conduct departmental meetings and chair them and Ranjita the Vice Principal of the school – the wife of the Principal used to sit in front of her with the other teachers listening to her and taking notes in her diary. After the meeting Urja used to write reports every time and submitted to the Principal and every time her reports were copied by Ranjita and signed by her as the co-ordinator or H.O.D. of English which she was not. Urja's reports were torn into pieces by Veer Parsad and thrown into the waste-paper baskets. At her cost Ranjita's future got more secured and the management never came to know the truth. Each time Urja conducted any programme, Ranjita watched it minutely. Urja prepared the duty rosters and programme brochures, Ranjita observed them and learnt. Veer Parsad called her after each function, congratulated her and presented her with a lovely bouquet causing irritation in Ranjita's eyes and mind. She started instigating the good for nothing teachers to report against Urja, sensing their jealousy towards her. These teachers didn't have the caliber to come up to the limelight by showing their efficiency and qualities. Ranjita's 'pallu' was their only saviour and shelter.

Urja had made one mistake right from the beginning. She expected Veer Parsad to take her side being reasonable and just. She didn't know that Veer Parsad would take the side of Ranjita even if she commits a murder. Veer Parsad had to establish Ranjita in order to enjoy his status and position for a longer period. He had the dream of becoming the Director and making his wife the Principal. He had to show that his wife is the best, she could never make any mistake or do anything wrong. He wanted to get rid of his agriculturist background to earn the reputation of an educationist. Ranjita also had shown her loyalty umpteen number of times, each time bleeding within with shame and humility at the shameless debauchery and flirtatious activities of Veer Parsad, but she could never think of getting separated or leaving her home because she knew very well that without Veer Parsad her existence was a mere existence without any power, position, name and wealth. Both were substitutes for each other. Knowing the weakness of both I could exploit the situation and make maximum gain.

I didn't care for the threatenings which I used to get every now and then from outside. Some people even threatened to kill me. At night I started keeping the mobile (presented to me by Veer Parsad) next to me on the bed like my baby. I stopped coming home during lunch hour. Every moment I felt that if I am away from school or Veer Parsad, I will lose both forever. Within a period of fifteen days there were three incidents of bomb blasting in the school – twice in the boys' toilet and once just outside the window of the restroom of Veer Parsad. The third one was defused before it could burst.

The crisis period brought Veer Parsad and me closest to each other. Ranjita had to take care of her children because their lives were also under dark clouds. Anything might have happened at any time. Ranjita stood like a fortress protecting her children and I was providing the required mental support and physical energy to Veer Parsad staying with him like his shadow.

On summer evenings when no one was around except Veer Parsad and I, planning about future, chalking out the strategies, sometimes Norwesters broke out raising a sudden squall smashing the glass panes of carelessly opened windows and closing the doors with a loud bang. We rushed upstairs and along the long corridors trying to close the doors and windows frantically while the storm continued with all its might for quite sometime, ultimately bringing relief in the form of a downpour, washing away all dust and dirt, bringing Veer and me closer to each other in one of the empty classrooms, mingling with the drizzling of our desires, quenching our thirst. Each brick, each pillar, each bench, chair, table, everything remained witness of our love. We could sacrifice our lives but not allow any one to take away the school from us. It's our school, only our – Veer Parsad's and mine and accidentally Ranjita's. Other staff members are just paid employees – they will dance at the movement of our fingers. But we were associated to the school with our heart and soul.

Every evening, during the routine one hour power cut, we felt each other in the darkness, in Veer's chamber, explored the often felt, familiar body parts of each other, lost in our own world which we could create within the boundaries of 14 acres. At home I never took the initiative of preparing food but the small pantry attached to Veer Parsad's office became the most attractive place and preparing tea or coffee for him became my greatest pleasure. I am possessive but somewhere I had to compromise, I had to accept Veer Parsad as he was. There was no choice; had I not accepted his dark sides, his attraction and infatuation towards innumerable ladies, I could have never enjoyed the position which I have been enjoying today. For me there is no fixed timing. I come to school only when Veer Parsad comes. His car picks me from my home and drops me back there at any odd hour. He has given me the honour of Administrative Officer although people call me his 'kept'. I don't care what people say so long things are on my way. I cherish my importance.

I know the crucial moments when to be in Veer's chamber to be with him, to share his feelings, to give him company. When the typist told me about a boy of our school who secured the 1st rank in IIT-JEE, I rushed into the room of Veer Parsad and gave him the news. I was trembling with emotion when I told him the news. He had just then come back from the Assembly and students had already started going back to their classrooms. Actually the typist was sitting in front of the computer and trying to find out the results of IIT-JEE when Veer Parsad was conducting the Assembly. When I disclosed the good news to him he embraced me tightly and expressed his emotion by planting a kiss on my forehead and then on my lips and told me to inform everybody to come back to the Assembly again. I know at that moment I came nearest to his heart. This wonderful result was required as the Society in Delhi had snapped all connections with us and the case was under trial in the Court. This remarkable achievement could bring back the faith of the parents on us.

Veer Parsad arranged a felicitation programme for the 1st rank holder and Urja was given the responsibility to organise the programme. A Silver memento was presented to the boy. His parents were also invited on the Foundation Day of the school and they were felicitated by the Governor.

This news was highlighted in every possible way in favour of the school. We decided that before the final verdict by the Supreme Court regarding the dispute between the school and the Society, we have to construct the staff quarters and the Principal's quarter. I cherished the dream of a transit house where I could spend the nights whenever I was late. The staff quarters were constructed but nobody was interested to shift there as most of the teachers have a second earning through private tuition which would have stopped had they shifted to the quarters in the school campus; moreover they were afraid of giving free coaching to the hostellers in the evening. The most important reason however, was nobody liked to stay in the same premises with Veer Parsad and Ranjita.

Veer Parsad's dream palace was under construction. Veer and I used to go for supervision every day, sometimes in the scorching heat of summer, sometimes in the afternoon of monsoon or in the misty winter evenings. We planned together, we imagined together how it will look after completion but unfortunately we will never be able to stay together under the same roof with the approval of the conservative society. It is Ranjita's house – Padma is only the official Secretary, she can never be the homemaker of Veer Parsad. But the cosy restroom of Veer with the attached toilet and small kitchen cum pantry is my domain. I will not allow Ranjita to rule there. Except six-seven hours at night and two hours in the early morning, rest of the time Veer Parsad is mine, mine only and of nobody else.

Before the inauguration of his dream palace Veer Parsad took me there one evening and we met. We slept in that room which was decided to be the bedroom of Veer and Ranjita. She will never know that her bedroom is not new in her new house; it was already inaugurated by me – Padma Prasad, Veer Parsad's Padma.

I know how much struggle we had to do to save our position. Forgetting our ego Ranjita and I had to practically place ourselves on the feet of the Society members in the capital city seeking for their mercy and kindness. There were two lady members who were very old and gullible. But the gents members were very tough particularly the Ex-Chairman. Veer Parsad was on the verge of being a broke, filling the pockets of the Ex-Chairman to retain the name and logo, otherwise he had to quit. Ranjita also started accepting money for promoting the failures to the next class.

The news of the Chairman's arrival to school was a delightful shock to everybody. The critics started guessing the amount which he had taken in the deal. The general mass was happy, particularly the parents who pay through their nose to avail the education of the best branded school in the country for their children. Chairman's visit to the school removed all doubts of cloud from the mind of people. Behind the curtain what deal took place, ofcourse except a few of us nobody came to know.

Now the ball is in our court atleast temporarily. Till the next contract Veer Parsad will not be removed and before that he will retire. Ranjita's case can not be called a 'sure shot.' She may or may not ascend the throne. But we have enough time to think, plan and manage everything. Without any challenge and obstacle life seems to be boring. The members of the Society also will change by that time. Whatever it is, the person who circulated anonymous letters disclosing the fact to the parents, could shake the throne of Veer Parsad and disturb his sleep for a few months. He had to bow and bend his knees forgetting his ego and this thought is troubling him; he is a defeated man and overnight he has become old. He had to retain his position by licking the boots of the Chairman. I cannot tolerate any humiliation of Veer Parsad. His insult is my insult, his defeat is my defeat.

The school came under the aegis of the Society with the reputed brand. The tag has again been attached to it. Veer Parsad got standing ovation from the teachers in a meeting but it became difficult for him to digest. He got standing ovation from the puppets who don't have any emotion, any feeling and sense. They just know how to please, how to surrender, how to accept everything silently.

Although the school came under the aegis of the Society, a large number of students started leaving the school and joining another school of the township every year after their class X Board Examination. The reason is, that school tied up with Narayana classes, FIITJEE classes etc. and allowed the students to attend such classes instead of the regular CBSE classes. They were given attendance without attending classes. When Veer Parsad complained to CBSE against such unfair practice, they shifted the office of the professional institution from their school premises to another place but continued with the classes.

* * * * * * * *

Within a span of twelve years so many changes took place before my eyes. Old teachers left, new faces appeared, our children grew up and went out of the State for higher studies. The school grew from strength to strength. One thing was in our favour right from the beginning that is the background of the students who took admission in our school. They were either from the township with the parents associated with the sponsor organisation or from rich business class family. The school management always was choosy in the matter of giving admission to students. We always got the cream of the students. The parents are too conscious about their children's education. There was no other diversion or distraction. This is the reason for the excellent results produced by the school so far. The brand name is also highly responsible for creating the craze among the elite class parents for getting admission for their children in our school. In all other schools, for commercial reasons the school authorities are compelled to take students with mediocre or poor background. They do not dare to declare that students who got below 80 per cent in class X Board Examination will not get admission in XI. It is obvious that no other school can ever produce better result than our school. But that incredible incident took place when Urja left our school and joined another reputed CBSE affiliated school in the same township as the Vice Principal and H.O.D. English. That year that school topped in the State. Not only that they were able to beat us in Inter-school Quiz and Hindi Debate competition organised by us and proudly lifted up both the Championship trophies. Veer Parsad became furious and fired the teachers. He received one more shock when he received the Annual school magazine of that school started by Urja. How to transform an ordinary thing into the extraordinary – one should learn from Urja. The history of the school written by her with colour photographs of the infrastructure of the school and various functions right from the beginning of the school till recent times enhanced the status and position of the school to a great extent. At the conclusion of that history of the school Urja had added a few lines which seemed to be mocking at Veer Parsad:

"We believe in work, not in reward

We believe in quality, not in brand

We mould ordinary into excellent

Never choose the best to enrich ourselves

We toil with the learners

Never capitalise on their achievements

We believe in team work

Not in self-interest

We are global in our thoughts

But traditional in our action

We teach students to soar high

But never to forget the ground.

We have our unique identity

In the vast ocean of education

We pay our tribute to our Alma Mater."

Wonderful ! Wonderful ! The school where she worked for fourteen years became an alien to her and within a few months that school became her Alma Mater ! And for whom did she indulge into that big propaganda ! A businessclass family which commercialised education and has been earning in crores !

Veer Parsad got a letter from CBSE to visit the new branch of that school as a member of the inspection committee for the affiliation of Senior Secondary level. He was stunned to see the infrastructure. How could such ordinary, lower middle class family become so stinkingly rich within a span of just ten years? When he verified the staff list he found the number of staff was not sufficient and the payment was also not upto the mark. When he raised question on that issue, the Director of the school said that teachers mostly join their school for experience. After two-years they leave the school and join a better school; so there was no justification in offering them a lucrative pay scale. Veer Parsad was further shocked when he came to know that many teachers were actually from the old school but in an unfair way they were being shown as the staff members of the new school. When he was coming back after the inspection, a gift of a silver mug set worth Rs.10,000/-, nicely wrapped in gift pack was kept on the back seat of his rented car arranged by the school authority at their expense.

Veer Parsad could not forget the humiliation at that school when the initiative was taken by that Principal to form Sahodaya Complex and Veer was invited to be a member. In the meeting Urja nominated him as the Vice President along with the Principal of our rival school with the same brand name and the Principal of the host school as the President. Veer Parsad had never learnt to be no.2; he always wanted to remain on the top. Urja, whom he had pushed from a great height brought him down to no. 2 as soon as she got a chance.

Ever since the school got affiliation for Senior Secondary level, it had always been a centre for CBSE Board Exam. Not only that it became the only Nodal Centre also for evaluation of class X Board papers. But the year Urja left the school and joined another school, for the first time our school in spite of being the biggest school in the State was neither the Examination Centre nor the Nodal Centre. Instead the school where Urja had joined was made the Nodal Centre and Urja was the Incharge of that. The teachers who had gone to that school, after coming back reported about the importance which Urja was cherishing in that school. Veer Parsad took minute details from each teacher. Somehow he could not digest the fact that Urja was happy and was enjoying a thousand times better position in her new school. Just a few days back I overheard the conversation between Veer Parsad and the Principal of that school over the telephone. Anandlal might have expressed his surprise at the withdrawal of the Nodal Centre from our school and the assignment of that responsibility to his school. I heard Veer Parsad saying – "CBSE has given us some relief this year. I personally requested them to exempt our school from being the Examination Centre as well as the Nodal Centre. They asked me to suggest a school who can take the responsibility. I thought who can be better than you? So I suggested your name and school. No doubt your school is next to us." By saying this he could satisfy his ego to some extent. This is Veer Parsad – he will break but never bend. I could imagine the reaction of the person on the other side of the line.

Ranjita now-a-days have started wearing very gorgeous saris – dark coloured, expensive. The person who practises Vastu Shastra has told her to wear dark colour saris. She is spending in lakhs every alternative month on expensive saris and salwar suits. This is another way of showing power. Always look gorgeous whether it suits you or not. Wearing dark red or blue saris when Ranjita dominates the teachers, particularly the new, young teachers tremble with fear. The old ones exchange glances and sarcastic smiles. Ranjita cares a fig for any sarcasm, any mockery, she remains engrossed in her dream of becoming the Principal. She has also started attending the seminars and conferences on behalf of Veer Parsad in order to come into close contact with the influential people.

Sometimes I think Veer Parsad and Ranjita are not human beings of flesh and blood. They have no human emotions and sentiment. No, I am wrong – they have all negative feelings and emotions like greed, lust, jealousy, cruelty, arrogance and single-minded determination to reach the top. Ranjita is least bothered to think about the debauchery and atrocities of her husband. The servants say that they don't even share the same bedroom. It's a fact, otherwise how could Veer Parsad talk to me over the telephone at midnight? Ranjita becomes mad with anger if she finds anybody coming on her way to reach the summit. Now a days qualified and talented teachers are not applying for job in our school in fear of Ranjita. The incident of Urja and some other teachers have created panic in the township. Everybody knows that Ranjita will not allow anyone to work peacefully because she feels threatened. She is well aware of her efficiency and capabilities. A strong sense of inferiority complex haunts her but she wants to show that she is the best. The teachers of the English department are particularly suffering a lot; they don't have the courage to oppose her as she is the Principal's wife. Even after knowing that she gives wrong instructions, they are compelled to follow her and as a result year after year the school is producing the worst results in English in both class X & XII CBSE Board Examinations, ever since Urja left the school.

More number of franchise schools under the aegis of the Society are coming up. Those who once worked under Veer Parsad and Ranjita are now becoming the Principals of such schools. Veer Parsad's dream of opening a chain of schools have shattered into rubbles. I remain with him like a shadow and keep on consoling and encouraging him but I know he has broken from within. It's a crucial time for him. Whether Ranjita will be able to succeed him is still doubtful. Children have grown up but not yet settled. Ipsita is practically not doing anything. She could neither get a job, nor could Veer Parsad arrange her marriage. He was so intoxicated and engrossed with his ambition that he neglected all other sides of life. The taste of success is also bitter to them because of his notoriety and hatred and curse of the people.

At this juncture, the only thing which I expect from almighty is a healthy, beautiful, prosperous and peaceful life for my daughter. She should not step down in her life like me. She should not compromise with her conscience, chastity and honesty. She should not struggle like me or my father.

Sometimes when I am in my pensive mood, I reminisce my childhood days and become nostalgic. My father used to say – "I have three sons." He never made any discriminations between my brother and me or my sister. He wanted us to stand on our feet with our head high. I am standing on my feet, no doubt, but am I standing with my head high? Veer Parsad has given me everything, even my place is in the same line with Ranjita; still something constantly pricks my mind, I become restless, perturbed and a deep dissatisfaction engulfs my mind. Had there been any way of going back to those fanciful, fairy tale days with wonder in eyes and the light of a million stars in mind I would have sprinted back to my mother's bedroom and taken out the box of silver kept under the cot to get lost behind the coverture of love, care, assurance and security. The freshness of childhood moulded by a quilt of innocence and faith pulls me quite often from the moribund life of which I have become habituated. It's a tussle between two strong opponents – on the one side there is power, glamour, wealth, importance and sin; on the other side peace, love, truth, honesty and security. I had to sacrifice the latter in order to achieve the former.

Sometimes I ask myself the question – who is happy ? The characters whom we see everyday around us – are they all happy? The competition among the lady teachers regarding their new designs in ornaments or latest fashionable saris, dresses, bank balance, latest model car, coveted position of husband – are they happy? What happens within the four walls of home and what they show to the world with their false smile are contrary to each other. Sudipa Sarkar is being beaten up by her husband. Komolika is regretting for marrying a man much below the standard of her previous life in her parents' house. Bindiya's husband has impotency. Neera Mehta's relationship with her husband is strained. If I take the name of each teacher, there is something wrong with each one but they are living their lives. Their sorrows, sufferings, deprivations are all mingled under the same roof, in the same campus which is providing them with the strength to live. The future of the Nation is in their hands. Forgetting their personal frustrations they compete for proving themselves to be the best, in the eyes of the students, parents and the management. Secretly they complain against each other to Veer Parsad, to Ranjita and also to me knowing my closeness with the Principal and the Vice Principal. They criticise each other in front of the students also. The school is a strongly built boat which helps them to sail across the vast ocean of life.

Veer Parsad had again started flirting with the new receptionist cum English teacher. Her husband is posted somewhere else. She was staying in the campus alone. Ranjita had gone to Mumbai to meet her parents. Veer Parsad thought that was the right time for 'testing' the new fruit. The lady at first could not understand the evil intention of Veer Parsad and showed him hospitality but as soon as the purpose of the visit was clear to her she straightway directed him towards the door and her loud voice was audible enough to draw the attention of some teachers and their family members living in the campus. They however, thought it was better not to interfere because they were well aware of the habit of Veer Parsad. Even the students staying in the hostel could guess that something unusual had happened.

The lady next day came to school reception and threatened to lodge a complaint against Veer Parsad to Human Rights Commission. I had a tough time convincing her not to do so since her own dignity and prestige will also be at stake. She had brought her resignation letter along with her which she submitted. The school lost one more staff. Within a few days of this incident a peon of the junior school, went to Veer Parsad's office to give him a file and discovered a teacher of the Pre-Primary class sitting on the lap of Veer Parsad in an uncensored position. The peon was at a loss what to do but Veer Parsad winked at him and gestured him to keep the matter secret. It is said that divine judgment comes late but it comes definitely, without fail. I realised that when the XII Board results were out and my daughter could not achieve the desired and expected success because she got very less marks in Economics. I remembered as per Ranjita's instructions I had caused the humiliation of a good Economics teacher of the school who taught at the Senior Secondary level for two years and on the basis of my complaint was shifted to the primary class. Ultimately she left the school and joined the other school with the same brand name. She had wept bitterly before leaving the school. Appu, my daughter could not get a place amongst the first ten rank holders. That year those who got the first three ranks in Commerce Group were not informed to come and receive their certificates from the Chief Guest on the Annual Day. What my daughter could not achieve, I didn't allow anybody to achieve that. The parents later on came to school and showed their dissatisfaction. How does it matter? So long Veer Parsad and Ranjita are on my side I need not worry for anything. But my poor child had to suffer. She could not get admission in any good college. When I managed her admission in a second grade college of Delhi, some senior students who were ex-students of our school, physically and mentally tortured her. I had to bring her back home and when she got admission in a local college she started suffering from inferiority complex. Finally I had to send her to my mother in Hyderabad. In our Roller-Coaster life our children are also a part of the ups and downs and this is my only fear. I have kept my life at stake but I can't take any chance with my only daughter. I have walked a long way; my mother's box is again full of silver but it is not possible to retreat again. The path leads us forward, never backward. Throughout my life, I have to live with the identity of Veer Parsad's kept.

Sometimes I feel jealous of the housewives staying in my neighbourhood. Early in the morning when I rush towards the school riding my two-wheeler, I find some of them relishing a cup of tea and reading the newspaper accompanied by the husband. Some go for a morning walk and storing the fresh unpolluted air in their lungs start their everyday chore. Their home, husband and children are their priority. They anxiously wait for their husband and children to return home. They remain happy at their success and do not have anything to ask from life, for their own. Why couldn't I remain contented like them?

The busy schedule of the school doesn't allow us to indulge in the luxury of any idle thought. As soon as the school came under the aegis of the Society one after another our school had to host various cultural and Sports competitions. There were mixed reactions among the teachers. The talented and hard working teachers were happy to come into contact with so many schools and for gaining familiarity and popularity whereas the lazy ones were as usual dissatisfied for some extra burden of work came to their shoulder.

Veer Parsad has lost his freedom. So long the school was out of the control of the Society, he used to take decisions on his own in each and every matter. He gave promotion to Ranjita and the teachers of his choice, including me. Of course he has given promotion to some teachers in order to get their support. But now things are not in his hands. For each and every matter he has to take the approval of both the parties. He feels handicapped but there is no choice. Now it's a prestige issue. He has to somehow stick to his chair. For that he has to compromise a lot. The future is a big question mark but I have full faith on Veer Parsad. I know he will replace the question mark with a full-stop. He will survive and along with him we – Ranjita and myself will survive. Devils never die. In the fairy tales which we read in our childhood, Whenever one demon was killed, from his each drop of blood millions of demons used to take birth. Like that, the devils know the ways and means to keep themselves alive and safe. We will survive and we will have the last laugh, I'm sure.

We are born to win................................

6

Motilal's Monologue

They will destroy everything; nothing will remain, not even a brick. My family members will not spare anything. If possible they can dispose off even the hair on my scalp. The empire which I have built up was not raised in a single day. I know, starting from a scratch, how much struggle I had to do. Suppressing the pain of leaving my village, home, parents and brothers I had started my journey towards the unknown. I had only 100/- Rupees in my pocket and my better half was also with me. There was no place to put up; food, shelter, the basic requirements of life nothing was prearranged. What a great risk we had taken – my wife and I, nobody can even imagine !

Today my family is eating the fruits of my hard work and sacrifice. I want them to eat; after all for whom did I construct everything? Not for myself of course. I am in the last phase of my life, looking with deep satisfaction in my eyes at my own creation. One after another my brothers, their families – all shifted from the village and joined me. I feel profound peace to think that I could give comfort and tension-free life to my parents who had to struggle hard throughout their lives. Atleast in the concluding part of their life they could experience happy ending.

I wanted my family members to be happy, wealthy and successful. But where did I make the mistake I don't know. Each one is trying to be happy and wealthy in his or her own way; least bothered about the family harmony. That bond, that togetherness, that belongingness is absolutely missing. Greed, selfish attitude, self interest dominate their mind and because of this my creation is being shattered to pieces, turning down to rubbles. There is no feeling of team work among the family members, what to talk about the outsiders? Outsiders are thrilled to see the cold war or hot battle among the family members and they are adding fuel to the fire.

Now we are in a sound financial position but if we are not able to enhance the quality, quantity will gradually reduce and one day we may find that we are running the business at a loss. I have appointed experienced persons with good academic and administrative records from reputed schools so that my daughter and daughter-in-law can learn from them as they would have to manage the school in future. But they are so egoistic, instead of learning they are pulling the legs of such persons and instigating others also to do so. One after another the Vice Principals who were appointed from outside left the school. I don't know how long the present Vice Principals will be able to continue!

At least hundreds of my relatives are earning their livelihood from this school. Practically, in the village they were starving with their children. Now at least they have got free accommodation, free food from the hostel (at the expense of students) and a monthly salary in four figures, not to mention the free education for their children. But look at them ! Each one is behaving as if he is no less than Motilal or Adarsh ! Because of their unruly behaviour other staff members are not able to work in a systematic way. All are giving orders to the staff members and they are in a dilemma whom to follow !

I know my weakness. I am aware of everything but can't go against my family. I am helpless in this matter. I feel like telling them but something restricts my tongue and I keep everything within myself. I give intellectual and spiritual lectures in public, during the staff meetings, in the morning assembly and at various functions conducted at the school but I don't know why I become tongue-tied before my nearest and dearest ones.

I feel embarrassed before the outsiders because of the behaviour of my family members. When I introduced Urja to Sarita and Aaradhana, Sarita remarked "Day by day the number of executives are increasing in the school. Too many cooks will spoil the broth." I noticed the light in the face of Urja extinguished at that moment and I could feel she lost half of her enthusiasm to work in our school.

Sarita has come from a very ordinary and poor family. Practically her family is surviving at our mercy. Her father died last year of cancer. Her mother is still living in our previous house, quite near the present one where we live. One after another, we arranged the marriage of her four sisters. The younger one was divorced after her first marriage. We appointed her as the receptionist but sitting in the reception she started finding out a suitable groom for herself surfing the internet and was ultimately successful. Again we spent a lot for her marriage and Adarsh did the 'Kanya Sampradan.' Today she is the happy wife of a wealthy hotelier who has two children from his previous marriage. But she never bothered to call Adrash, not even once. The day she moved out of Adrash's house after her 'Bidai' she never looked back. Let her be happy – May God bless her.

Sarita has a good-for-nothing younger brother who has been appointed to move around here and there, giving company to Ashok. In order to run a big school it requires strength – I mean our own people who can risk their lives if any problem arises. For that neither knowledge nor intelligence is required; only physical strength to scare people. Nobody will dare say or do anything against us. But they are our liabilities also because they can not be trusted. At the slightest opportunity they don't hesitate to steal money or expensive things from the school, home or hostel. Just the other day Sarita's brother Guddu vanished 1.5 lac in the broad day light when he was asked to bring the bundle from my house which was kept very carefully in the almirah ! We can't even discuss the matter with anyone – it's a matter of prestige of our family. But it really hurts when I find my own relatives making a hole in the same plate from which they are filling their empty stomach.

I failed to teach my family members manners and etiquette. They will always come to the forefront where they are not required. Whenever there is any function, they will occupy the chairs in the front row, not allowing the deserving persons and guests to sit there. During school hours they will come and sit on the sofa in the foyer in front of the reception and talk loudly discussing family matters. Even the children have learnt to feel that they are special. They neither care the teachers nor their peer groups. But I didn't want this. My desire was to see them educated, polished, cultured, enhancing the reputation of the Trivedi family. I wanted them to be enlightened and worthy human beings but my wishes will never be fulfilled. I know that. My relatives will continue to exploit the situation and show their supremacy without any effort to prepare themselves for the honour and respect they demand from others. Children will continue to neglect their studies as they know the teachers would give them more marks in order to make them pass otherwise they will be ticked off.

The most unscrupulous is Sarita. Even after knowing this very well I have to support her because Ashok is not educated enough to carry on with the administration although his designation is Chief Administrative Officer. For the whole day either he is found to be chatting loudly with his subordinates in the Accounts Section or sitting in front of Sarita like her pet dog. I am handicapped in this matter. Blind affection towards my children and daughters-in-law prevent me to say anything against them. I cannot even scold or rebuke them.

Moreover, in my absence they will be the owners of the institutions which are my creation. Of course Adarsh's contribution in the growth of the school is praiseworthy. Since he joined the school, it started growing in leaps and bounds. At present there are more than 5000 students in the old school and about 3000 students in the new school. But mere quantity doesn't indicate the high standard of the school. Quality does matter. Knowing that, two persons from outside have been appointed as Vice Principals. One has a long experience of working in Kendriya Vidyalaya and the other in a reputed branded school of the country. But my family members feel that it is below their dignity to learn anything from these two persons. So they are being ignored and humiliated to the possible extent, although they do the maximum important work. If I show any liking towards them particularly to Urja, my eldest daughter-in-law Sarita becomes furious and throws a tantrum at home. R.N. Mishra – the other Vice Principal flatters Sarita and Aaradhana a lot. He gets up with folded palms whenever they enter the room but Urja never does that. She is very respectful towards Adarsh and me but never leaves her seat when any other family member enters. Why should she? She is thousand times better than Sarita or any other member of my family, even me. But Sarita thinks that as the eldest daughter-in-law of the Director she deserves respect from all – doesn't matter what a high profile that person has or how senior he/she is by age !

Sometimes I feel, I have made a mistake by appointing Urja. I never thought that people would start comparing her with my daughter and daughter-in-law. It's quite natural because quality speaks and Urja never makes any compromise with quality. But those who are lazy, they don't want to work hard like her but always want to be in the limelight. They are jealous of Urja for her success and wants name and fame but are never ready to sacrifice anything for achieving that success. I feel guilty in front of Urja because I had promised her many things when I offered the post of Vice Principal to her otherwise she would have never left her previous school. Of course I got the feedback from my known persons how she had to suffer at the hands of her previous Principal and his wife Mr.Veer Parsad and Ranjita. I didn't waste any time to contact her because that was my opportunity. But Urja is very intelligent to understand everything within a short time. I feel my image of a pious, generous and great personality is being hunched before her eyes. My family members touch my feet in the school, early morning everyday to make me feel great. That image of greatness is instilled among the students, parents and all staff members. It is required in order to keep everybody under control. There has to be a central figure who can maintain the harmony in this large family, at whose direction the rhythm of the family can be maintained. But simply touching feet doesn't mean that they are very respectful towards me. There is no depth in their feelings, everything is hollow. In front of me they pretend to be listening to me but as soon as I turn my back they follow their own whims and fancies. Urja, being very observant is able to understand this.

Putting my blood and sweat together I have made money. I can't express in words how much it hurts when I find my nearest and dearest ones wasting my hard earned money. Those who are with me right from the beginning, are well aware of the hardships. For a single piece of paper teachers used to come to me and now the typists are ordering for reams of papers in order to type the personal letters or any other work of any Tom, Dick or Harry because they carry the stamp of Trivedi family with them and no one dares to say 'No' to them. Ashok and Sarita also have broken my trust several times knowing my weakness for them.

Sarita has been suffering from inferiority complex and behaving strangely. I know the reason. I have made Priya the Principal of the new school because I know her capability. She leaves her children with my wife and does up and down everyday. She can trust her mother-in-law in this matter and doesn't even bother if her children are sick. But I know Sarita will never be able to leave her children with anyone. They need her at every step. I cannot make her Principal because Adarsh is the Principal here. I had suggested that Adarsh should be the Sr.Principal and Sarita can be promoted as Principal. But fearing the consequences Adarsh refused to accept the proposal. Urja's entry in the school caused further jealousy and insecurity in her mind as both Adarsh and myself praised her for the quality of her work. Urja has the inborn leadership quality. Within a few days of her joining she started taking initiatives in various work and guided the teachers. They also started following her which caused a feeling of insecurity in Sarita's mind. She felt her power was being reduced. In order to bring back her lost confidence, I had to declare umpteen number of times in the meeting that according to hierarchy Director is the first person in the school, followed by the Principal, Additional Principals, Vice Principals various Incharges etc. I can feel the mocking smile of the teachers because they have never heard of the post of Additional Principals earlier. Principal and then Vice Principal, the latter either one or two – that is the regular feature in any school. But in my family school I had to create many posts to give importance to my sons, daughter and daughters-in-law. I wanted them to earn the respect of the society although in my heart of hearts I knew that they didn't deserve it.

My third brother spent so much money for opening a B.Ed College but ultimately gave up. I knew this will happen, I was expecting this sooner or later. Chunnu ditched us by grabbing the money which he was supposed to deposit to the school account after collecting from the booksellers. Our books, I mean published under the banner of our school were sent to various places by Chunnu as he was looking after the library and bookshop. Lakhs of rupees just vanished but very soon Chunnu shifted to his own house from the one-room quarter allotted to him at the school premises. Not only that he started his own hostel also.

We had to take a huge loan of several crores for the infrastructures of both the schools and this has to be re-paid. My family members are not able to understand that they are spending lavishly, satisfying their personal needs. The only exception is Panchali – my wife, who was with me at every juncture of life, providing me with encouragement and comfort and never complaining against any adverse situation. She had not only taken care of me but also my brothers, their wives and children, not to mention my old parents. But never in our Forty-five year old married life did she ask for anything. Whatever she had constructed for a long time was shattered into rubbles as soon as Sarita took an entry in our house. Aaradhana with her family had to shift to a rented house first and then to her own house. Adarsh was also compelled to shift to his own house and this was quite painful for all of us. Adarsh's two sons, who call us 'Bade Papa' and 'Badi Ma' cried like anything while leaving the house. Panchali could not eat anything for a week. Adarsh's elder son was fond of eating the thick 'malai' which used to stick to the bowl after the milk was served. He used to say "Badi Ma, don't give the cream to anyone. I don't need milk, just give me the bowl. I'll scrap off the cream." Panchali used to get immense pleasure in serving him milk and the bowl with the cream. Without Adarsh and his family the house seemed to be empty although Ashok and Sarita were there. The younger one was at that time completing his Engineering course in Benaras. Panchali took a long time to recover from this shock.

Sarita entered my room with a serious face. She carried the answer sheets of the interviewees, who were asked to write some paragraphs. It was suggested by Urja that we should take a written test of the candidates in order to know about their handwriting and knowledge of grammar, spelling etc. Anandlal told her to conduct the test and when it was over, the receptionist collected the answer sheets and was about to hand over the papers to Urja; in the meantime Sarita came to know about it and snatched the papers from the receptionist and straight way came to my room. Her complaint was why Urja should be given so much importance? Being the senior she was supposed to conduct the test. I told her "If you want to check the papers you can do so but she is the H.O.D. English and she will be the better person to evaluate the papers." Sarita went out of my room with an unpleasant face.

In the evening, at home Sarita again started complaining against Urja. Urja was assigned the duty of judging all the competitions of pre-primary and primary classes. In order to encourage the students she had given the 1st, 2nd, 3rd positions to many students. Sarita wanted her to award each position to one child only. Earlier Urja had taken my permission to award a large number of students in order to motivate them. She told Sarita but she refused to listen to Urja. Ultimately Urja had to tell her that she would follow only my instructions and not obey anybody else. Her ego was hurt and she wanted me to take action against Urja. That lady has been trying her best to improve the quality of our school and here my daughter in law wants me to take action against her. Why are women so jealous of each other? I have praised Urja in the meeting before the staff members. Sarita didn't like that. People should know that Motilal's family members are very efficient; they are able to manage the school nicely. They don't need the help of any outsider.

Urja wants to do everything in a systematic, disciplined way. I have noticed that the teachers also like her style of working and want to follow her but Sarita and Aaradhana make things complicated purposely in order to keep the teachers under their control. Adarsh is very affectionate towards Aaradhana but he doesn't like Sarita. One comment of Sarita ruined the relationship forever. Her target is Adarsh's chair and one day very impatiently she had remarked – "When will this man die? Until and unless he dies I won't be able to become the Principal." If she can utter such words about her uncle-in-law it's not at all a surprise that she will not be able to tolerate Urja. Because of Urja her image was getting suppressed.

I am helpless; on the one hand I have to do justice to all; on the other hand I have to project my family members and give them a high status in front of the society because after me they have to sit and control the steering. I can't allow them to cause any breakdown of my fast moving vehicle. I saw the smile of sarcasm in Urja's face today. I know what she has been thinking about me. My latest involvement is in compiling quotations and biographies of famous personalities and publishing them in my name. I have also added shlokas from the Mahabharat and Bhagwad Gita. All these books will be made compulsory in my school and students have to buy them. I have not asked Urja to do the proof-reading because it hurts my ego to see the expression of sarcasm in her face. I am just copying from various books and also the internet. It's not my creation, not my innovative thoughts. But in the modern world it is a common trend. Delhi has been declared the book capital but how many books are actually written? Most of them are just copied–plagiarism you know ! At the beginning of the year, the publishers send their representatives with varieties of school books on different subjects. Many of them are similar with the same exercises and examples. Sarita is the in charge of book selection committee. She only gave me this idea – why not start publishing our own books instead of purchasing them from outsiders. There is no need to be creative, just intelligent enough to copy and compile from ten to fifteen different books is enough. Designing will also be done in the school; paper will be purchased and given to the printer and at very low cost we can get the books printed. At least upto class VIII we can include only our own books in the syllabus. As the number is a large one, we can make a huge profit. Moreover the simple innocent public will develop a very high idea about us. We will earn both fame and money. Our world is limited. We do not crave for any National or International recognition. Just a little respect from the people of our own city and surroundings will suffice. But honesty alone can never give you that recognition – your shrewdness definitely counts.

Urja's honesty and sincerity stand as barriers on the path of her progress. Being the H.O.D. English and the Vice Principal of the school, she has ample opportunities to compile extracts from various educational books and publish them in her own name. But she will not do that. She writes her own stories, composes her own poems and doesn't bother whether they are published or not ! Money and recognition both stay away from honest attempts and efforts. If you seek for perfection you will never progress. Don't bother for quality, just keep on doing something and do a lot of canvassing for yourself. The world today is attracted towards the colourful, shining wrappers, not towards the real gift inside. You must also know how to sell your product applying the method of self advertising. During the Annual Week Celebrations both at the old school as well as the new school, exactly that's what I did. Eminent personalities from the State Secretariat and Ministry were invited. At one point of life they were my students when I was either a senior teacher, or the Vice Principal or the Principal. They are obliged to come to my school as the Chief Guest or a special guest and speak in favour of my school praising me and my family. Whenever it is my turn to address the gathering, I start with a Sanskrit shloka. This skill I have acquired right from my childhood. By-hearting Mahabharat and Bhagwad Gita was my hobby which is of great use now. It earns me a lot of respect and enhances my image in the public. Like all other previous years, this year also I stood up on the stage with the mic in hand and addressed the public—

"Respected………………, ………………………………, ………………………………,

……………………,………………………………,…………………………, ……………………,

……………………,………………………………,…………………………, ……………………,

……………………,………………………………,…………………………, ……………………, and my dear students……………………………"

Apart from the Chief Guest, the Guest of Honour, their wives and some other special guests I mentioned the name of my better half, her sisters, my brothers, my daughter, daughters-in-law, sons, son-in-law etc. with a lot of adjectives and in a flowery language and at the end also mentioned about the two Vice Principals among whom Urja was one.

I referred to the stories of Ram and Ravana, Eklavya, Aruni, Shivaji etc. and in a very emotional tone appealed to the parents not to bother about degrees, percentages or marks. Because our country now requires great men, brave soldiers who are ready to sacrifice their lives and become martyrs. "Real human beings are those who respect the moral values and follow them. To them wealth is nothing, position is nothing but what matters most is becoming a human being in the true sense. Among the 2500 students performing on the stage in different groups, are hidden the leaders of tomorrow. Among them are hidden Vivekananda, Gandhiji, Abraham Lincoln, Mother Teresa and many more because our school believes in a holistic system of education and prepares true human beings. We try to keep the spirit and the light of our ancient culture and heritage alive. Have faith on us, trust us and hand over your child to us and see the miracle within a short time. We will transform your ordinary child, who is so special to you and us also into a great personality, a great son of India." The loud applause among the gathering, the sound of clapping among the audience told me how successful I was to touch the mind of people. Outside the hall big hoardings were ready, advertising for the admission in the coming session.

The photos of the scholarship holders of the last three years were included in the hoardings. Like the branded schools I can't include the name and photo of the merit holders in C.B.S.E. class X and XII as there are not many; that's why I utilise the photo of those students who get the scholarship provided by our school. I know manipulation goes on in this matter also. Teachers keep the students under their control and take advantage with the threatening of giving them less marks, depriving them of getting scholarships but there are certain situations where it is better to keep your eyes closed and your mouth shut. We need the respect and admiration of the general mass because among them some are our customers (means parents of our students) and some will spread our fame simply by discussing with others. There is no need to give any importance to the views or opinions of one or two honest and sincere persons. They are not accepted by the public. Why does the majority of people love junk food even after knowing they are harmful for health? Because of the taste, the pleasure, the attraction, whereas a healthy diet prescribed by a doctor or a dietician is ignored by most of the people. To flow with the current is wisdom, to go against it is foolishness, unless you can conquer it.

My brother Adarsh has got many awards ever since Urja joined the school. She is taking the initiative and sending the profile of Adarsh here and there. Within two years he got Best Educationist's Award, Jewel of India Award, Rashtriya Gaurav Award, Kalabhivushan Award, Best Principal Award twice and so on and so forth. Urja had told him after joining the school to send his profile at various places and watch what happens. But when he was not taking any initiative, Urja took that responsibility and prepared his profile and started sending them at various places. Of course he had to spend about 10-20 thousand rupees to become a member of such organisations which conferred him with the awards. But today everybody in the city knows him. Sometimes I feel that his profile is becoming bigger than mine. I love him from the core of my heart but a little tinge of envy touches my mind whenever anybody says that because of him the school has grown in leaps and bounds. This school is my baby. I need the help of my family members for the nourishment and growth of this child of mine but nobody except me can claim to be the father of the dream-child.

I am sixty-seven now although I don't look so aged. The masseur Baldau does the wonder with mustard oil every Sunday for one hour. There is still a glow in my skin and the stamina to climb up the stairs to the top floor at a stretch. The black dye also helps me to look young. If I can remain alive for twenty–twenty five years more I can consolidate the position of Trivedi family in the arena of education. I know, still it is not the right time to leave everything in the hands of my next generation.

Adarsh's sons have no interest in this school. The elder one has been gifted with an engineering college in the capital city by his father-in-law. The younger one is holding a good post at an M.N.C. in Pune and drawing an alluring salary every month. They have proved themselves in their chosen fields and within a short time they will join their own Engineering College. They have started their venture in the arena of film also.

I have entrusted the responsibility of the new school in the capital to my younger son and his wife Priya. The Kids Academy of this school is managed by Mrs. Sharmistha Sen – a very glamorous and energetic lady. But everyday I visit the school which is about one hour journey from my home. I am relieved that Adarsh is there to take care of the old school and under him are two Additional Principals and two Vice Principals. My elder son Ashok is the CAO of the school but only for name sake. He can not be entrusted with any responsibility because he neither has the required qualification nor the efficiency to handle any important work.

My brothers try to be very smart at times but spoil everything. The Steel Plant is not able to manage their schools and hence wanted to dispose them off to private schools. We were very much interested in purchasing one of them. Urja was asked to prepare the applications addressing the Chairman. She prepared the letters but before the final proof was approved my younger brother collected them from the typist and in a hurry went to Delhi to hand over the letter to the Chairman's P.A. Before leaving for Delhi he forgot to give one copy to the M.D. of the Steel Plant. He had also taken two lac for bribing somebody. After a few months it was told that proper procedures were not followed and hence we were not eligible to get the school. God knows whether that two lac had really been given to somebody or had gone to his own pocket ! On another occasion he took three lac Rupees for a similar reason and after coming back told us that he had given 50 thousand and the remaining amount will be given after the completion of the work. He handed over the money to me and without counting I instructed my wife to keep it in the almirah. Next morning Adarsh sent Sarita's brother and one more office staff to my house to collect the money and put it into the bank. When the money was brought to the school and counted before it was sent to the bank there was only one and a half lac. 50 thousand had already been given and there was no trace of one lac ! All are my family members. I can not express any doubt against anyone. My next brother Nageshlal is constantly creating nuisance. A drunkard by nature he comes to the school every now and then and gives his self-identity to the public as the Director of the school. The lady teachers don't like his looks and gestures and want to get rid of him whenever he tries to interact with them. When he was shifted to another branch of the school, there also he earned notoriety within no time.

His son Chunnu can not be trusted with any work. He makes a mess of everything whenever he is given any responsibility. He can never give any account of the money which he spends withdrawing from the school account.

My third brother Yogeshlal is another liability. He doesn't have any specific duty. By profession he is a lawyer but leaving his practice he joined the school ten years back and since then he has been sitting idle and drawing a fat salary every month. My son in law is another good for nothing. I don't know what Aaradhana had seen in him and fallen into love. They all are my liabilities. The school is the only source of earning for all of them. Adarsh, my fourth brother is my right hand. Only he has the sincerity and capability to run the school. I had taken the right decision in appointing him as the Principal.

This year I had to take a very crucial decision of removing one senior lady from the Kids Academy. Long back both of us worked in the same school as Vice Principals. When I started the school she joined as the Principal. When the post of the Principal was given to Adarsh, this lady was shifted to the Kids Academy as the Advisor. Even at the age of seventy-five she was not willing to leave the job. But she had become inactive and practically there was no logic in keeping her anymore. Her parting scene was quite emotional as she was weeping pitiably. But sometimes situation compels us to be rude; there was no justification in wasting money for her anymore.

Ashok and Sarita started their school in Indore. Thrice a week they stay in Indore and for the rest of the time here. Sarita will not leave an inch for any one else but tries to keep everything within her fist. Because of her, we can not utilise the talents of worthy persons.

I never remained satisfied after establishing one school. One after another I started other projects also. I achieved success in some of my ventures, not in all. Now there are four schools under the banner and one college of Music, Dance and Fine Arts. But even after persistent effort I didn't get the permission for a Degree and B.Ed College which was my dream. It doesn't matter at all because the income from all four schools and Music College is more than enough to repay the bank loan of 5 crores, apart from paying the salary of staff and making a huge profit. We had to live from hand to mouth throughout our childhood and youth. After crossing sixty only I started cherishing the taste of success and prosperity. Now at the last lapse I want to relax and enjoy the remaining part of my life. I got two rooms constructed in the school which were absolutely separate from the administrative building where I spend most of the time now. It is so peaceful there, the most appropriate place for meditation.

Visit to Singapore was another wonderful experience. My next destination is Europe. In the month of August we will be going to six different countries of Europe. Adarsh and his wife will also accompany us.

This is the time to relish the fruit of hard work and I am doing that. I believe in Karma. The results of Karma are also before my eyes. But those who are just enjoying the fruit of my hard work without any effort, will they be able to retain everything? Or my dream palace will tumble down and turn into rubbles – who knows? Time will tell us everything but I may not be there to witness. Motilal Trivedi, the founder of the Institution will remain in the minds of students and teachers if the Institution exists. Otherwise just as a bubble rises in water for a moment and bursts or subsides, another history of struggle and success will be buried under the grave of time. I hope my sons and daughter will try in every possible way to help the Institution survive with full reputation and fame. They will not let down the name of Motilal Trivedi. That is my last prayer to God…….

7

Urja's Solo Journey

It was half past ten in the morning. Adarsh had already intimated Urja that the two Principals who were also selected by CBSE as committee members for the recommendation of new Nodal Centres for the spot evaluation of CBSE Board Examination papers would come at 10.30 a.m. and Urja should also attend the meeting. The minutes of the meeting were already decided and kept ready. Only the necessary corrections were to be done and with the signature of the committee members and along with the covering letter it should be immediately posted. Out of the three Principals, Adarsh's name was No.1, so he took the initiative and called the other two Principals to attend the meeting in his office room.

Urja hesitated to attend the meeting because she knew who the other two Principals were. One was the Principal of Kendriya Vidyalaya and the other was none other than Veer Parsad – her ex-boss. Urja thought how to avoid meeting Veer Parsad.

In the morning when Urja came to Adarsh's room to show him the draft of the probable minutes of the meeting, he told her about Veer Parsad's conversation with Mr.Naidu, the Manager of the school who was sent to handover the letter to Veer Parsad. He, at first approached the Reception. The Receptionist told him to go inside and give it directly to Veer Parsad. The first question Veer Parsad asked Naidu was – "At what capacity are you working there?"

Naidu replied – "I am the manager of the school."

Veer Parsad seemed to be surprised – "It's the duty of the peon ! Why have you come to deliver the letter?"

Naidu said – "That is our Principal's decision. Whatever work is assigned to us, we do. That is our work culture."

Veer Parsad was not to be easily knocked down. He said –

"But you are wasting your precious time, your work is getting hampered for this petty assignment."

Naidu wittily remarked – "That is my Principal's look out."

"Veer Parsad killed some more time, talking nonsense and ultimately said, O.K. I will come."

He had no other way but to come. He had taken the initiative two years back to conduct spot evaluation as the only Nodal Centre in the State, but next year his school was debarred from conducting Board Examinations as a Centre and also spot evaluation as a Nodal Centre. That responsibility was given to Urja's present school. It was a great blow to Veer Parsad but he managed the situation by saying:

"We are conducting Board Examination for a long time. CBSE has given us relief this year from all responsibilities. Not only that he told Adarsh "CBSE had given me the first batton of the Relay Race and I have handed it over to you. It was I who suggested your name as my successor." Utter lie ! It was the good rapport of Adarsh with the Regional Officer of CBSE that he was given this responsibility. Moreover it was Urja's constant effort to try hands at different things to enhance the reputation and recognition of the school in the field of education.

Before Urja joined the school, no one from the side of the Management used to take any initiative in shouldering any extra responsibility or assignment which are the features of any reputed school today. Within six months of the joining of Urja, the school got tremendous recognition as she took the initiative and was able to convince the authority to participate in all competitions, send delegates to maximum seminars and workshops and communicate as much as possible with the important people in the State and CBSE. For the first time in fifteen years the school gained name, fame and recognition almost at the same level with that of Urja's previous branded school.

Veer Parsad had got the feed back from his staff members who came for spot evaluation the previous year about the status and position of Urja who was made the Incharge of the Nodal Centre by the Principal Adarsh. In fact she was doing the duty of the Principal.

Veer Parsad wanted to get back his lost position by hook or by crook. When he got the letter from CBSE initially he was unhappy to find his name at the end. But then he thought that this was the only opportunity for him to come back to the track and recover his position. He agreed to attend the meeting at Adarsh's school.

Urja was sitting in her room when she got the call from the Principal at 10.40 a.m. As soon as she pushed the door to go inside, Adarsh welcomed her – "Come Madam, come, we are waiting for you."

Urja understood that he was trying to give importance to Urja before Veer Parsad to make him feel that what he had pushed aside with sheer negligence and ignominy was made a jewel in the crown by Adarsh. While entering the room Urja could see only the back side of Veer Parsad as he was sitting on the chair facing Adarsh who was sitting on his chair i.e. the Principal's chair. It was the most embarrassing moment for Veer Parsad because his staff members always saw him chairing the meetings, not sitting on the other side of the table. His 6 ft tall figure seemed to have been shrunken and somehow he was able to ask Urja– "How are you ?" when she wished him.

Anandlal gestured Urja to take a chair next to him. It was the second shock to Veer Parsad. Had he ever dreamt in his life that a reversed dice will fall on the board? Had he ever dreamt that he will have to take a seat opposite to Adarsh and that too in front of Urja, sharing the same table ?

Urja remembered how she was duped by Veer Parsad and Ranjita when her name was struck off from the report about the Departmental meeting which she presided over and Ranjita's name was included in her place. God's abode is far away but not dark and divine justice comes, it definitely comes sooner or later.

In order to bring himself out of this shameful situation Veer Parsad all of a sudden started discussing about the present political scenario, the cunningness of the people of a particular State which boasted of two ancient Universities – Nalanda and as if he was not able to remember the other name said - "Madam's subject is not only English, but also History. I think she will be able to tell me the name of the other University." Urja was least bothered to remember the name and she very coolly replied – "I don't remember and I think Nalanda was the most famous one." Veer Parsad's intention and effort to perturb her failed. The name Taxilla or Takhshilla remained unuttered on the tip of Urja's tongue.

The Principal of Kendriya Vidyalaya was a newly appointed person, a doctorate in Hindi. He came with the previous Principal. R.N. Mishra, the other Vice Principal of the school also joined the meeting.

Adarsh said – "Now let us start the meeting. As you all have got the letters from C.B.S.E. you are aware of the agenda – that we have to recommend new Nodal Centres for the spot evaluation of Board Exam papers of 2009." At this point Veer Parsad asked – "Did you have any discussion with the Regional Officer?" Adarsh truthfully said – "Yes I had a discussion with him." "When?" - quick came the next question.

Adarsh said – "About twenty, twenty-five days ago."

Veer Parsad said –"I had a discussion with him this morning." All eyes were fixed on him as he continued – "I told him that three Principals' names are mentioned in the letter. But who is the Convenor? He said that there is no Convenor. We three can meet and discuss and send our recommendation.

I again asked - But who will preside over the meeting and send the report? He told me that being the most experienced one I can send the report."

Adarsh said – "Now-a-days nobody looks at experience but how efficiently one works. Everything depends on the quality of work. We will conduct the meeting and immediately send the report. That is Madam's responsibility. You need not worry Sir."

Veer Parsad could not open his mouth before that bouncer.

Adarsh said – "There are two-three options before us. Either we have to send one name or the name of your school and our school or add some more schools." Veer Parsad indicated at the Principal of K.V. and asked – "What about Kendriya Vidyalaya?"

Adarsh said – "I have already discussed with him. In fact I proposed the meeting to be held in his school but he said there is no space in his school, neither for conducting any meeting nor for conducting the spot evaluation of Board papers."

Veer Parsad immediately said – "But you didn't ask me whether I am interested to conduct the meeting?"

Adarsh said – "How does it matter Sir? CBSE has assigned us a duty, we have to obey." When Veer Parsad was still expressing his dissatisfaction, in order to lighten up the atmosphere Adarsh said – "O.K. Sir, let us go to your school now; we will conduct the meeting there." Veer Parsad said – "Come on Sir, let us come to the point. We are not sure whether CBSE wants us to recommend one school or more than one."

At this point Urja said – "I think they have mentioned the words 'Spot–Evaluation Centres' in the subject which clearly indicates more than one school." Veer Parsad as usual continued with his argument for about half an hour regarding the ambiguity in the language of the letter. Next, they discussed which school to be introduced because it was not clear whether they fulfilled the conditions mentioned by CBSE ! Veer Parsad said - "We are least bothered whether they fulfil the conditions or not !"

Adarsh said – "No Sir, we have to be concerned otherwise we will be losing our reputation. We have been entrusted with the responsibility which we have to perform with sincerity."

Another bouncer.

Ultimately it was decided that two more schools will be included.

Adarsh rang up the Principal of one school and asked him whether he was willing to conduct the spot evaluation in his school as a Nodal Centre or not !

That Principal asked – "What is a Nodal Centre?"

When he was able to understand what in fact is a Nodal Centre he promptly expressed his unwillingness to shoulder such a great responsibility. Veer Parsad rang up the Principal of another school, who after initial hesitation gave his consent. Veer Parsad boastfully uttered - "I am not habituated in listening to no."

Urja at this point said – "If they send papers of more than two subjects of both X and XII, then it is not possible to conduct in one school. One more thing should be considered, that is the subjects. If uncommon subject papers are sent, it will be difficult to get teachers for correcting the papers. We can mention the subjects for classes X & XII which will be convenient for us."

Veer Parsad liked the idea and said "We can mention English, Physics, Chemistry, Mathematics and Biology of class XII and the same subjects of class X which were sent in the two previous years, i.e. Mathematics and Social Science." Here R.N. Mishra said, "We will not mention the same subjects for X and XII because sometimes the same teacher teaches in classes IX – XII and so it will be difficult for getting examiners for both the classes. Although CBSE sends a list of Examiners, many teachers refuse to do the duty simply managing medical certificates from Government hospitals."

Veer Parsad said – "O.K., Maths can be removed from class XII then."

Ultimately it was decided that for class X the preferable subjects to be mentioned were Mathematics, Social Science and General Science and that for XII were English, Biology, Physics and Chemistry. Urja's Minutes of the meeting along with the covering letter was almost ready.

All of a sudden Veer Parsad said "We will conduct the spot evaluation for class XII." Adarsh pretended not to be listening and told Urja to get the necessary corrections done in both.

Veer Parsad said – "I'll take your leave Sir. I have called a meeting at 12 o' clock." Adarsh said – "Just two minutes Sir, we need your signature."

Urja handed over the letter along with the Minutes of the meeting to Adarsh which he showed to the other two Principals. The Principal of K.V. didn't say anything. But Veer Parsad again insisted that he should be given class XII.

Adarsh said – "Sir ! we can not decide that; CBSE will decide the matter." Veer Parsad tried to stick to his point. Adarsh instructed Urja to mention that Veer Parsad's school was willing to conduct spot evaluation for only class XII whereas their school was willing to conduct for both classes X and XII.

While the Xerox copies were being made Veer Parsad asked Urja about her children, their job etc.

Then it was time to take leave. Adarsh, all of a sudden took out a letter from the drawer and showed it to Veer Parsad at which he wrinkled his brows. The letter was written in his letter-head-pad without his signature and it was sent to Adarsh requesting him to give permission to the H.O.D. Computer Science Department to attend a Computer Programming Competition at his school. Veer Parsad tried to suppress his annoyance and managed the situation saying – "I delegate certain things to my subordinates. This is related to the Inter-House Competition which the House Wardens will manage." Adarsh said – "I never allow anyone to use my letter-head pad for any reason. Without my signature not a single letter goes out of the school."

Again a bouncer and this time it could perfectly hit Veer Parsad right on his nose.

In order to hide his embarrassment he tried to change the subject and said– "There are four more schools coming up in and around the township under the same brand name."

He completed the sentence looking at Urja. She remained silent and did not show any interest.

Adarsh said – "Yes, I have heard about it. The owner of Chouhan Estate is taking the franchise of one school. Another one will be taken up by a South Indian – I am not able to recall his name at this moment." Veer Parsad got a topic of his liking and for the next ten minutes kept on giving details about the upcoming schools with the same brand name of his school but not under the same Society. The word 'Society' was replaced by 'Pvt. Ltd.', 'Global', 'Trust' etc. Ultimately before leaving he could not help saying – "I am impressed to see the prompt action taken; everything is ready and our report is going to be posted today. It's absolutely ready for delivery !"

Adarsh boasted – "We are always prompt in our action."

Urja thought – "From where have you learnt this prompt action? Where was your institution two years ago?"

Veer Parsad again said – "By the word 'delivery' I remembered a joke. With Madam's permission I would like to share that with you."

Looking at Urja's smiling face he proceeded "Once a lady was delivering a speech in the Assembly". She got stuck up in the middle of her speech and repeatedly said – "I conceived.......I conceived......I conceived......" The Speaker of the Assembly became impatient and said "We could understand that you conceived but when will you deliver?"

More loudly than others Veer Parsad laughed at his own joke which he had learnt just a few days back on the occasion of Inter-School English Debate, when one of the Judges of the competition mentioned the same joke in her speech. Urja got the feed back from the escort teacher who had attended the programme along with the participants.

Ultimately, after spending about two and a half hours in Adarsh's room, Veer Parsad left. Adarsh was happy because his mission was successful along with the satisfaction of his ego. Urja was happy at the completion of an important assignment before proceeding for Diwali holidays which she had planned to enjoy at Kerala and Kanyakumari with her husband and younger son.

* * * * * * * * *

"Urja had read somewhere –

The elements of World –

Earth

Acres of the most pristine stretch

Water

Acres of flowing elixir

Air

Acres of pure oxygen

Sky

Acres of expressive skies

Fire

Acres of pure passion

Acres of phenomenal living space for a

Privileged few."

She had copied the lines in her diary. She felt herself one of those privileged few, standing on the soil of Kerala.

There is nothing as soothing and as rejuvenating in this world as to take a break from the routined life and surrender oneself before the loving embrace of Nature. Mingling with Nature is the greatest booster which revives the spirit and zeal, lost amidst the abominable ways of the society and work places. Urja was elated to observe a week long break at the time of Diwali, mentioned in the school almanac and right from the beginning of the session, planned to utilise the most wanted break in a fruitful manner.

Countdown started when she came back from Delhi after performing her duty as the mother-in-law of a pregnant daughter-in-law and joined the school after Dussehra break. Diwali was just two weeks away and in between there was the supervision of the preparation of results of the first term exams and distribution of report cards. As an executive she does not have to do all these things directly but while supervising she could feel the excited pulse of the teachers as well as the students, eagerly waiting for the break. This excitement instilled a childish longing in Urja's mind too when the Jet Airways flight took off from the city's only airport at 11.30 a.m. to Mumbai where Urja and her husband had to wait for three hours to board the connecting flight to Cochin. Their younger son was supposed to join them at Cochin Airport flying from Delhi. At Mumbai Airport only, they came to know that he had reached Cochin. Urja saw the time, it was 3.30 p.m; that means he had to wait there for four and a half hours.

When the aircraft was about to land at Cochin, there was an announcement that due to bad weather it was not possible to land for another one hour and the plane started circling around in the air. The pilot tried to contact the nearest airports like Coimbatore and Trivandrum. Due to some technical problems Coimbatore could not give permission and ultimately it landed at Trivandrum for an indefinite period. Swapnil instructed Deep who had been waiting at Cochin Airport for more than six hours, to go to the hotel which was already booked and also to have his dinner. It was raining heavily at Trivandrum which continued for half an hour and finally when it stopped, the aircraft took off again for its destination – Cochin.

Reaching the hotel at 12 o'clock night, Urja felt her spirit being dampened to some extent but the next morning was waiting for them with wonderful treasures in her trove.

It was a clear morning with the sun playing hide and seek with the clouds scattered all over the sky. Floating on the back waters by motor launch and periodical halts at various sight-seeing spots included the first half of their pleasure trip. The port, shipyard, synagogue, Dutch Palace, St.Francis Church etc. stood surrounding the vast stretch of water. After lunch, visiting the city of Cochin by hired car was another worth mentioning experience. In the evening while walking along the marine drive and picking up beautiful handicrafts made of rosewood, they witnessed the sunset which was followed by the covering of the sky with a dark veil of dusk against the backdrop of which glimmered the lights of the port, ships, various offices and above all the glowing letters of the signboard of Hotel TAJ. Hot shawarma and steaming tea added an extra layer of happiness and satisfaction.

With a contented mind Urja went to the bed that night while her husband and son kept on browsing the channels of T.V. till they felt it was necessary to take rest.

Early in the morning of the second day they started for Munnar – a beautiful hill station of Kerala. Nature's bounty was abundant in this small place, which they could feel as they went up. Just after monsoon, there was a lot of greenery on both sides of the road, uphill and valleys with the lush green Palm, Coconut, Eucalyptus, Cloves, Cinamon, Cardamom and many other unknown trees. The springs and waterfalls greeted them on the way to the tourist resort and from the terrace of their cottage the moving vehicles on the winding roads looked like toys disappearing at the turning points.

After having a quick lunch of mixed noodles and grilled seafish, they set out for sight seeing. All of them were spellbound to see the dams and the natural lakes. Roadside stalls selling pure honey, home-made chocolates, Marshmellows, Eucalyptus oil, clove oil, various aromatic oils, lemon and Masala Tea, Cardamom packets and items made of Rosewood were an extra attraction to the tourists. Along with the Indian tourists, there were many foreign tourists also. Here and there flashes and clicks of cameras and Video shootings were going on. Urja's son was taking the snapshots and video simultaneously, with full enthusiasm. They relished Masala Tea with hot Onion Pakoras and moved on to the highest point called Top Station. The tea-gardens on both sides of the road, The innumerable shades of blue and green so far their eyes could follow and the clouds floating right above the head made the place God's own land indeed. Who wants to come back from such a place and get surrounded by slimy, dark and crafty creatures? But good things in life are short lived. One has to part with them, however painful it is. Anyway, nature's bounty is endless and when Urja, Swapnil and Deep were coming down the hills the next day with sorrowful hearts, they didn't even imagine how enchanting the back waters of Alleppi would be.

It was a special Diwali for Urja and her family, the most silent one, illuminated by millions of light in their mind. It was a wonderful experience spending one day and night in the house – boat, floating on the lake from Alleppi to Kumarakom and back. They were thrilled to see ferry launches stopping at various places on the water to pick up students and other passengers just as it is done on the land by bus. In small strips of lands, surrounded by water, people live in huts depending on fishing, agriculture and also by selling coconuts which grow in a large number. Urja was thinking what a contrast there was with their routined life. The captain and the crews of the House Boat, which was in no way less than an A.C. double-bed room of a reputed hotel spend most of their lives, floating on water. They don't even have any weekly off. There is a good understanding among them and alternatively, they halt at night near each one's house. They not only can control the boats but also are wonderful cooks. It was the height of luxury, sitting at the dinner-table on the deck and enjoying lip-smacking cuisines prepared by them which included fried sea fish and typical dishes from Kerala while floating on the water, leaving the water, sky and trees behind.

The foreigner tourists waved their hands as their boats passed by. A shoal of fish came near the boat and when Urja was feeding them broken biscuits they jumped and splashed on water. The evening tea was served with biscuits and pakoras. But this time the pakoras were deceptive as they looked like tempting brinjal and besan pakoras; the first bite gave a shock as instead of brinjal, the filling inside was of ripe bananas.

From one of the small islands Swapnil purchased giant size Tiger Prawns which adorned their dinner plates along with other delicious food items at night.

Next morning the hired Innova was ready near the starting point of their boat journey and the destination was Kanyakumari. Bay of Bengal, Arabian Sea and Indian Ocean have met and this harmony is reflected in the chain of waves breaking into surfs on the beach, rocks of Vivekananda Memorial and that of the huge statue of the Tamil poet and saint Thiruvalluvar. The last motor boat was about to start when they reached the ticket counter and after a short journey reached Vivekananda Rock which is said to be India's end point. So many years ago Swami Vivekananda had sat on the rock and meditated. The sound of 'Om' in the meditation hall purifies the mind of the visitors and leaves a lasting impression in their mind. This two lettered word reverberated into the ears of Urja for a long time after she left the place. When the sun set in the Arabian Sea, the twilight painted the sky and water with all shades of red and crimson colours. Against that backdrop the birds formed 'V' shapes and were lost in the horizon, returning home.

Somebody knocked the door at 5.45 a.m. and informed them about the sunrise at 6.05 a.m. which could be seen from their room. The Surya Mantra with which Urja starts her day seemed to be of great significance on that special morning, when with the chanting of Surya Mantra the big, red, round Sun popped up from the water to the Eastern sky. Within ten minutes it was in a position to reflect its rays over the sea water and hit the wall of the bed-room. Such a scene is rare in Delhi where Deep resides, so naturally he was overjoyed. Bathing in the sea, dancing over the waves, allowing the foams to break over their body while the sands moved away under-feet made them forget the time. With a pure, rejuvenated heart and soul they visited the temple of Kanyakumari and offered pooja.

Outside the temple, in a row were sitting the conch-shell sellers. What a variety of shells, each one unique in shape and colour ! Urja bargained with them and was successful in adding a good number to her personal collection. In addition to that she was lucky enough to get two Sea-Horses at a throwaway price. Coming back to the hotel after having a breakfast of hot Uthapams and Idli-Sambar, when she unpacked the treasures of shells and was observing each one of them with passion and unadulterated smile, her husband remarked – "No change at all in thirty years !" Thirty years of their married life he meant.

Out of seven days, only two days were left. Next destination was Trivandrum. After reaching there, they decided to visit the Kovalam beach which was only 13 Kms away. When they reached Kovalam, evening had already tip toed over the Western sky making the foams whiter on the dark water. They located their hotel in the Lighthouse beach where they were supposed to stay the next day and went back to Trivandrum. Urja purchased a Kanchipuram Silk Sari for Neha – her daughter-in-law for the occasion of 'Godh-Bharai' to be celebrated in the month of December.

It took ten minutes to find out a good non-vegetarian restaurant to satisfy their taste-buds that night, as the hotel in which they had put up was a purely vegetarian one.

Urja's son is a voracious meat eater who hates the idea of having veg food. Urja could not take anything more than half a Nan and two spoons of paneer masala. Swapnil is a typical Bengali with his origin in East Bengal – Khulna. He likes only rice and fish curry. Deep experimented with unfamiliar dishes made of pork and chicken. Urja could not prevent him from eating such stuff by reminding him about bird flue and swine flue.

Next morning, after having a complimentary breakfast consisting of pure South Indian and Continental dishes, they started for Kovalam. On their way, they visited Padmanabhaswami temple, Sanmugham beach, Velli Village etc. One thing was noticed everywhere, that is, garbage was not scattered here and there, plastic was in less use and all the places were neat and clean with a lot of greenery all around.

The hotel on the Lighthouse sea beach has its own beach and swimming pool. Time flew away in a jiffy, swimming in the sea at the time of high tide. In the evening they strolled on the beach, watched the sun set and did a lot of window shopping. For the last time they had their fill of sea food at a beach restaurant with grilled lobster, crabs with garlic-lemon sauce and Kalamari (squid).

There was no hurry to get up early in the next morning as there was nothing to do and their flights to Mumbai and Delhi both were rescheduled in the evening. As it always happens, Swapnil could make out time for an official visit of a plant situated in a place between Trivandrum and Kanyakumari. This plant extracts heavy metals from the sands recovered from the sea.

In the evening Urja and Swapnil parted with their son Deep who flew to his workplace Delhi and they took a flight to Mumbai where they met with another part of the Arabian Sea, the same sea which they had left behind in Kerala. Paying a visit to the Radhakrishna Temple run by ISCON, walking along the Juhu beach in the early morning, they were all set to fly back to the Steel City, in their cosy nest. What they brought along with them was more than enough to boost up their pep in the mundane, moribund life of the city. It was like drinking the elixir of life from the brim to the dregs, a lot more than just sipping the bubbles from the top or living in the real sense, not just existing.

With a spring action Urja sat up on the bed, with fully opened eyes at the beep sound of the alarm-clock; 5.00 a.m. sharp; within one and a half hour, she will be back to the school – her familiar world.

Good things in life come in small packages – that's what Urja was thinking while coming back home from school. The first shock of the day she got in the morning Assembly when she saw students of her block in red, blue, green, yellow T-shirts, standing for the morning prayer; again some were in blue trousers/skirts, some in white. It was as if overnight the school transformed into a Comedy Circus. Urja called the Physical Education Teacher and asked him "Who has given instructions to the students to come in six different dresses?"

He replied – "Sarita Madam."

Urja was expecting this. Last year already this issue was discussed in the meeting. The Director, his daughter-in-law, daughter were on one side that is in favour of wearing different types of dress on different days. The Principal Adarsh and Urja were on the other side with the opinion that uniform should be of only one type.

The Director said – "We have already ordered for the T-shirts. It would be our loss if these are not sold and used."

Sarita added – "Students can not be differentiated according to their House if they don't come in four different coloured T-shirts."

Urja said – "What's the use of wearing T-shirts? There can be House Badges of four different colours."

Sarita made a long face.

Adarsh said – "I think Madam Urja is right. Uniform should be of one type. T-shirts can be worn at the time of evening games only, not during regular school hours."

The Director's daughter remained silent but it is known to all that at home she will express her views and get her work done. That is her nature.

Next day in the morning Assembly Adarsh made an announcement that students must come in proper uniform that is white shirt and carbon blue trousers from Monday to Thursday except on Friday when they were supposed to wear full white uniform. This was followed for one and a half year. Urja was really perturbed to see the change again. She noticed carefully and found out that only the students of IX and XI were wearing those fucking type T-shirts but rest of the students were in proper uniform. Urja was intelligent enough to understand that Sarita had purposely, deliberately instructed the students of her block only to come in colour T-shirts; this is nothing but to pull her legs.

After the Assembly, Urja met the Principal and drew his attention towards the matter. Adarsh also expressed his dissatisfaction and said –"These people are typical businessmen. They have purchased the T-shirts from the wholesale market of Kolkata at a cheap price for making profit by selling them at a higher price. That's why they have instructed the students to come in T-shirts on Fridays. They want to clear their stock also."

Urja asked – "Then why only the students of classes IX and XI have been instructed in that way? Why not others? Sir, I think it has been done deliberately because these two classes are there in my block."

Adarsh immediately called one of the Physical Education Instructors and told him –

"You inform the students of IX and XI that they should wear the T-shirts only at the time of evening games not during the school hours."

From the facial expression of that PTI Urja could understand that he was scared to obey even the orders of the Principal because he knew that Sarita would not spare him.

Adarsh said – "Don't worry Madam, I will again make an announcement." Adarsh then asked her in details about her tour and said – "I'll take all details from you later on. I am also thinking of visiting Kerala in winter."

He appreciated the small memento which Urja had brought from Kerala for him. He is the only person in this school who is sensible, cultured, has a good taste, understanding, approachable and is a real gentleman. Except Adarsh, Urja hates each and every member of the businessman cum educationist family. She wonders how without taking a single class, Sarita is the H.O.D. of Biology?

Urja left the Principal's room and came back to her block. She got stuck up in the middle of the staircase as the passage leading to the classrooms and the staircase was still blocked. This is also another regular feature of this indisciplined school. While coming back from the Assembly, after the test periods, after the short recess, while going to the ground in the games period and also at the time of coming back to the classrooms, the students take fifteen to twenty minutes, sometimes even twenty-five minutes. The teachers never tell them anything because they also are relieved of taking the whole period of one hour each. The corridor is always crowded and full of noise. As most of the students come from villages and backward places, they speak loudly in rustic tone in raw, colloquial Hindi which strikes the civilised ears like bullet shot. Urja, with her polished background can't tolerate this.

Urja commanded the students to clear the corridor and enter their classrooms immediately. Within five minutes the place was cleared. She noticed even after that, the teachers came further ten minutes late. Some of the hostellers came half an hour late, that too very casually. Urja heaved a sigh – when will she get a better job and leave this school? Even if she tries to bring discipline, she will fail because neither the Director's daughter nor his daughter-in-law will allow the students to follow her instructions. So long Swapnil is in his present service, Urja cannot leave the place and there is no better option in and around the township.

Before going on leave, Urja had submitted the dummy of the magazine to the Director. He handed it over to one of his relatives – the daughter-in-law of his third brother, who did a multimedia certificate course but writes Designing Head after her name everywhere. She gets all work done by the typists and other Computer Experts and gets the credit on their account. Her worst victim is a teacher of Mathematics who had done advance courses in Computers and Multimedia. She had once burst into tears and narrated her bitter experience to Urja, how her hard work was exploited and passed on as the work of the Designing Head.

After coming back from Diwali break, Urja thought of visiting the Designing section in order to see the progress because the deadline was coming nearer and the magazine was scheduled to be released on the Annual Day.

Urja found Rashi Trivedi, the Designing Head, Parminder Kaur – the worst sufferer under Rashi and one typist Jagpreet, who is more knowledgeable than Rashi, in the room. Parminder was designing the English section of the magazine. Urja felt pity for her because she knew that her toil would run down the drain because the English section ultimately will be in black and white.

Urja sensed the dissent of Rashi as soon as she entered the room. Jagpreet offered her a chair. She asked Rashi – "How far have you proceeded?"

Rashi said – "Madam, I showed you a book the other day, do you remember? That one is missing. It was on this table till yesterday. I thought of taking some designs from that book but ever since I came, I am not able to find it." In a stern voice she asked Parminder – "Have you taken the book?"

Parminder was shocked –"What shall I do with the book?"

Rashi directly accused her –"Only you were in this room since morning. No one else was here !"

Parminder said –"I don't need any book for designing the pages."

Rashi carried on with her jibes "I have told the attendants hundred times not to open the door of my room till I come, but they will not listen; they will always open the door to anybody."

Urja noticed Parminder's face turned red and purple in insult and humiliation. Even Urja felt very bad. After sometimes Jagpreet was called to attend a meeting related to the preparation of question papers for the Half-yearly examination. Rashi also went out of the room. Parminder was showing the design she had made for the English section to Urja but Urja could feel her tension. She said – "Madam, this is the way she behaves with me. I have worked with many reputed designing experts but never faced such type of problems. It's my misfortune that I am compelled to work here. I don't want to leave now because I need experience. I was appointed here as her substitute when she was not able to work. I am not her assistant but she always does the bossing as she is a family member. How dare she accused me of stealing a petty book ! I'm hundred percent sure the book is in this room hidden in a drawer or she has taken it home."

Saying so Parminder started searching for the book, opening all the drawers and ultimately it was found in one of them. Parminder called one attendant, showed her the book and told her – "When Madam comes, show her this book and tell her it was in this drawer and both of us are leaving the room together. We are not carrying anything from here, understood ?"

Within half-an-hour Urja got a phone call in her office room; it was from Rashi –"Madam, Parminder has left the designing work incomplete. She is sitting in the library. I sent Sunita to call her but she refused to come."

Urja said – "My work as the Chief Editor is complete. Now you have to get the designing work done within the stipulated time."

Urja knew that she will be in trouble. Rashi tried to bring Urja to her side- "See how obstinate Parminder is ! Did I tell her anything ? I just asked "Where is the book ?"

Urja said – "She must have felt bad and insulted."

Rashi pleaded – "Madam, you please tell her to complete the work."

Urja said – "She will definitely complete, don't worry."

After two days Rashi again told Urja – "Madam, Parminder has stopped coming to my room. She is not doing the designing work."

Parminder also met Urja and requested her –"Madam, please allow me to sit in Jagpreet Sir's room and do my work. The file for English Section is there in his system because he had done the typing." Urja allowed her to complete the designing work in Jagpreet's room. Due to lack of communication, however she started doing the designing work in an old file, not the latest one where all corrections were done. That means Urja had to get the corrections done again which was a real tedious job. For all these, that bitch Rashi was responsible; because of her non-cooperation and arrogance nobody liked to go to the designing section. Lack of team work spoilt everything.

When Adarsh called Urja for some urgent work, she entered the room with a glum face. Adarsh immediately understood there was something wrong. He wanted to know – "Madam, what's the matter, you are not looking cheerful today?"

Urja said –"Sir, I've become tired and sick of everything. You know how difficult it is for me to control everything, sitting at one remote corner. Once I am coming to Rashi's room, again I'm going to Jagpreet's room but these fools are not able to work to my expectations. On the top of that they have so much ego problem. There is no harmony, no cooperation at all and because of their fault I have to do double work."

Urja then gave a brief summary of the incident which took place between Rashi and Parminder. Adarsh became furious, he called both Rashi and Parminder and told them that the designing room does not belong to any particular person. Anybody at any time can go to the designing room and do their work. He also gave a deadline for completing the designing work. Rashi felt insulted; her image got distorted before her juniors.

In the meantime the Director told his daughter-in-law and daughter to see the magazine in Rashi's Computer. He also called Urja and instructed them that no change will take place in absence of these three persons. If they want to make any change, all the three persons should sit together, discuss and make necessary changes. While looking at the pages of Snapshots, Sarita started making negative remarks –"One whole page on Teachers' Day? Chhee….ee !" – She retorted because her photographs were not taken on Teachers' Day.

Urja noticed while going out of the room (as she had to take a class then) that Sarita and Aradhana almost tumbled over the Computer to see the photographs from a close angle. Urja's mind told her now they will change the photographs of the teachers and include their own photographs forgetting the fact that this is a school magazine, not a family magazine.

Her premonition was true because when she came back after taking the class, she found many significant photographs being pulled out and nonsense photographs of the family members, mostly of Sarita (as if she is somebody g-r-e-a-t) were replaced. The hard work_of long ten months like bearing a child and showing him the light of the world and the intellectual, innovative thought behind the whole process went to the dustbin. Urja promised to herself - next year she will not prepare even a single page for the magazine. She will lose her reputation as the Chief Editor if she is associated with this magazine. The female members of Tiwari family just want name and fame without doing any hard work. They have more than enough money, so now they want establishment in the society. It's better not to involve in such a desperate and a foolish exhibition of power.

Adarsh was out of station on Friday when the next Assembly was held on the Prayer ground. On all other days except on Tuesday and Friday assembly is held in the class. Urja noticed again, in spite of Adarsh's clear cut instructions many students of her block were standing in the prayer lines in red, blue, green, yellow T-shirts. Her blood pressure immediately went up. Are they students or clowns? What is the meaning of uniform if there is no uniformity? She observed carefully that particularly the students of his block were not in uniform. Is it difficult to understand who has ordered them and what is the intention behind this? Urja, as per the instructions of Adarsh immediately issued a notice in which she wrote exactly what Adarsh had said that students should come in proper uniform, not in coloured T-shirts, which should be worn only at the time of evening games. As soon as the notice was circulated to the teachers of class IX and XI, one or two pet dogs of Sarita immediately went to her room and showed her the notice. She didn't take even a moment to flare up. She started throwing tantrums, rang up her father-in-law and spoke to him for about ten minutes and then going to the staff room in a loud dominating voice told the teachers – "You must instruct your students to wear House T-shirts on all Fridays."

Teachers were utterly puzzled – whether they should listen to the Principal or this lady ! As usual Sarita lost her cool and started uttering unparliamentary words, expressing her annoyance and dislikings towards Urja. The teachers enjoyed a free show. There were some teachers among them who were devoted towards Urja. They came and informed her everything. One of them said– "Madam, they have purchased 10,000 T-shirts from the wholesale market of Burrabazaar in Kolkata at a very cheap price. Now they are selling them keeping eighty per cent profit. They just want money. They are least bothered about quality or discipline." Urja heaved a sigh. In what a hell God has sent her ! – She thought.

Next morning Adarsh came to Urja's room and said – "Madam I am always on your side; whenever you send any notice, to be on the safe side take my signature also. Then nobody will be able to oppose you."

Next Friday Urja observed that all students were in proper uniform. A sense of victory touched her mind.

In the evening Urja received a call from Padma. She was thunderstruck to hear Padma's voice. After the initial exchange of greetings Padma expressed her wish to meet Urja. Urja bluntly asked "Why?" as she didn't expect her to come to her house again.

Padma said –"Just like that. I have not met you for a long time."

Urja realised her mistake – "Oh ! you are most welcome to my house. Any time you can come."

Pdama expressed her wish to come on the very next day to which Urja gave her consent. She had been thinking hard what might be the reason? One thing was crystal clear that it was neither a social visit nor a friendly visit, because without any intention or self-interest Padma will not take a single step. For a while she indulged into wild guesses. Is it because she came to know that they were going to dispose off their car as they had booked a Hyundai I10? Or is it Veer Parsad being jealous of Adarsh wanted to uproot her from her new school? If that is the reason, then she will never listen to them. But the curiosity to know what Pdama wanted from her after a gap of long two years troubled her mind throughout the day.

Annual Day was coming nearer or rather it can be termed as Annual week. The practice was going on in the school for Kids Academy function, House function and the main Annual Day function. Zero period was declared from 11.00 a.m. to 12.00 noon. There was no teacher in any classroom and for one full hour every day, the students were absolutely out of control. They misbehaved to their hearts content. Most of the teachers, in the name of organising programme sat at different corners and indulged into gossiping. Adarsh wanted to see the designing of the magazine. He called Urja, Aaradhana and Sarita to accompany him to the designing section. As usual Rashi started playing tricks with the Computer pretending as if the Computer has become slow, files are not opening etc. etc. She knew that Adarsh will lose his patience soon and exactly that happened within fifteen minutes. Hardly ten pages were shown when he said – I'll see tomorrow."

Next day, the Director was also present in the school. He was in a gloomy and morose mood. He lost his expensive digital camera early in the morning. Urja wondered whether it was lost or stolen? She knew the family members very well. It so happened that the Director was carrying the camera from his room to the designing section. On the way one of his cousins said – "Give it to me brother, let me carry it for you."

He said – "No, no, it's not heavy at all; I have no problem in carrying it." When his cousin insisted him to hand it over to him he did so and went to the designing section. After about fifteen-twenty minutes he realised that his brother had not brought back the camera. He sent reminder through one of the attendants who came back and said that the camera was missing.

"Missing ! impossible ! Sailendra took it from me and he was following me only. It can not vanish on the way."

Sailendra was sitting on the sofa in foyer when the Director came back from the designing section. Before the Director asked him anything he was ready with his explanation –

"I was coming to the designing section only. On the way just for two minutes I stopped at the newspaper stand to read the headlines. Unmindfully I left the camera there and next moment it was missing." What a wonderful explanation ! But it is a regular feature in the school as well as in their home. Mobile phones, dresses, silver utensils, money and many other costly items vanish in a mysterious way. Urja is hundred percent sure that the family members only are involved in stealing. Just a few days back when Urja went to the Principal's office, he was sitting with a worried face. Urja sensed something wrong, but her civic sense prevented her from asking him. After discussing the matter for which she had come, when she was coming out of the room, Adarsh told her – "Madam, I am very much upset since morning. There is no trace of 2 lac."

"That is quite a large amount," – Urja was startled.

Adarsh continued – "You know, we applied for getting one of the old school buildings when we saw the public notice regarding it in the newspaper."

Urja remembered she had drafted the application.

"My younger brother who manages land, building etc. told me that our application has been considered and the processing is going on in Delhi. He knows a person who will take 15 lac and will manage to get the approval from the concerned approving authority. Before Diwali vacation he took a large amount from the school account and went to Delhi. However after going there he came to know that the whole process will take some more time. He gave 50,000/- to that person and told him that after the completion of the work, the whole amount will be given. After coming back from Delhi he gave the whole amount to elder brother. He in turn told Bhabi to keep the money in the almirah locker. Nobody bothered to count the money. Next day Adarsh sent the office clerk and Sarita's brother to the Director's house to bring the money for depositing in the bank. The office clerk was waiting downstairs while Sarita's brother went upstairs to bring the money. Then both came back to the school and when the amount was counted they found 2 lac missing.

Adarsh stopped for breath for a while and then could not prevent himself from saying – "I know Madam, one of our family members must have taken the money." The name of Sarita's brother flashed in Urja's mind but she restrained herself diplomatically, although she was sanguine that Sarita's brother had taken the money and Sarita was well aware of that. Sarita and her husband have started purchasing lands and constructing hostels one after another. From where are they getting the money? Stealing, simply by stealing. Sarita's husband – The Director's elder son doesn't give receipt to the students after taking fees or fine. Each and every member of Trivedi family dreams of becoming Motilal or Adarsh.

* * * * * * * *

Chandu came at 5 o' clock to take Urja to the showroom of Hyundai. On the way they picked up Suapnil. The Alpine Blue Hyundai I10 was waiting for them. After the formalities were over, pooja was performed and when they were about to bring it home, it was found that the keys were missing. One of the employees said that the guard had kept the keys in his pocket and gone somewhere. How careless ! But there was no other way but to wait. Padma had expressed her wish to come after a long time.

After waiting for about half an hour finally the guard came and they got the keys. It was no doubt a happy occasion but somehow Urja was feeling a pin-prick in her mind. 1.5 lac had gone from her account – the money which she had been saving with the hope of opening a nursery school in future. Whenever she tried to save with this hope, for some reason or the other the money was spent which could not be recovered again. The first floor of her house, borewell and pump, some furniture, children's higher education and several other instances are there, when, keeping stone on her heart she had to part with her hard-earned money. Her dream of opening a nursery school of her own where she can put her heart and soul together remained a mirrage. Now-a-days she feels that it was destined that with a lot of talents and potential she would have to work under uncultured, tasteless vainglorious, dishonest persons for the rest of her life. These people, simply by the power of money would continue to dominate her and getting their work done by her, take the whole credit. She would see like a dumb witness demoralisation of youth before her eyes but can not create a new world of her own assuring a bright future with new hopes and aspirations for children because she doesn't have the money. During her visit to Kerala she read two books by Chetan Bhagat – 'The 3 mistakes of my life' and 'One night @ the Call Centre.' She desperately wishes some miracle to happen in her life as they happened in the lives of the characters in these two books. How cleverly the author solved the problems of the young generation by bringing even God to the picture. But what is the solution for the problems or the unfulfiled dreams of a woman of fifty who is highly educated but not Computer Savvy like Shyam or Vroom, but whose knowledge in Computer is limited to sending and receiving E-mails and net surfing? If ever she can purchase a plot of 3000 sq.ft. her dream school will definitely be a reality. Not realising the importance of land, her father had sold acres of land at a cheaper price which he had inherited as family property and the money was spent for the treatment of her ailing mother. On the other hand her father-in-law had given his two houses in Kolkata on rent and till date the tenants have not left the houses. There is no hope for the recovery of both the houses. Due to her husband's transferable job, they could not construct a spacious house any where. The price of land has touched the zenith and now it is unimaginable for a middle class family to purchase land for opening a school unless they have blackmoney.

Thinking about a piece of land where she could construct her dream school, when Urja reached home in her new car, driven by her husband with Chandu driving the old one behind them, it was 7.30 p.m.

Mahesh told Urja "Padma Madam had called. She wanted to speak to you." Urja performed her evening pooja, arranged her clothes for the next morning, flipped through the pages of the books which she would teach in the classes on the next day and then sat on the sofa to relax. The phone started ringing. It was Padma on the other side. "Hello ! Good Evening Urja, are you free now?"

Urja had to say – "yes, I am free."

"Shall I come now or on any other day?"

Urja said – "As you wish."

Padma said – "I am coming now."

Within ten minutes she reached Urja's house. Urja was wondering what she would like to say ! After asking each other about their families and children etc. Padma came to the point – "Urja, would you like to earn some extra amount every month?"

Urja asked –"Who would not like to earn extra but how?"

Padma, adopting exactly the style of Veer Parsad said – "You do a lot of net surfing, you must be aware of many latest developments in various fields. You write books, for that you get royalty. You will be a suitable person for marketing job."

Urja failed to understand the link between net surfing or book writing with marketing job.

Padma continued – "I think you have heard the name of Amway."

Urja's curiosity depleted like a squeezed lemon. 'Amway' after all. She had already wasted money after Amway and was not willing to fall into the trap again. She could also understand Veer Parsad's involvement in this.

Padma said – "People from various walks of life have joined and they are earning in lakhs. You can register just paying Rs. 999. If you work you will get good return. If you don't work, you will remain a part of the team. Your team will work for you and you will get money time to time."

Then for the next 45 minutes she continued to explain various terms and conditions, profits at various stages of the business and also showed Urja the catalogues of various products. Urja listened to her with full attention. When Padma came to know about their new car she said – "Now you will need car shampoo. You can try this Amway product." Urja said – "I can't believe that you are doing this !"

She said –"Actually you know, I started in 2006, when for the admission of my daughter I used to go to Delhi frequently. There I attended some seminars where people who are earning a lumpsum shared their experiences and I was really impressed. I thought why can't I ? Let me try and now I have become absolutely involved."

Urja asked – "O.K., you tell me how much you are earning per month?"

To that, of course, she could not give any definite reply. Urja understood that she was desperately trying to include some more members to her team and at the same time to sell the products with the dream of making a big money. She kept the Amway products catalogue with Urja and told her that she would come again. How shameless a person can be – Urja thought, after all that had happened just two years back, how could she approach Urja? Madam Urja, if you want to make money you have to be like her. Forget ego, forget who is your friend and who is your enemy. Just think about business – any person standing in front of you is a client – there is no scope for any personal feelings, emotion, sentiment – nothing. If you sit for a while and start taking an account of the injustice and wrong done to you, if you shed tears for the harsh words hurled at you or the ignominy shown towards you, no one is going to stop and show you any sympathy. The mad race will go on and you will be left behind. It's just a game in which, at one point enemies can not be differentiated from friends. All are just players trying to score a goal or hit a sixer. After all you have to come out of the hell where undeserving persons are playing the role of your boss. They are taking your ideas and passing them to be their own. Would you like yourself to be cheated and exploited like this forever?

Urja's inner mind talked to her but she could not restrain herself from reminiscing Padma's boastful remarks – "I can make or break the career of any teacher." That she could do and had done practically being the brumby mare of Veer Parsad. Urja was sure Padma would not give up so soon; she would approach her again.

At night Urja dreamt of being felicitated by the literary circles as the author of a number of bestsellers. Her books were sold at all leading book stalls and shops in the country and even abroad. There were requests from publishers to write for them. People were pestering her for autographs. In a year she earned thousand times more than her present salary as the Vice Principal. With that money she purchased five acres of land and appointed the best architect of the city to design and construct her dream school which was no more a dream.

The twittering of birds in the branches of the Gulmohar trees outside the bedroom window indicated the appearance of spring and interrupted her sweet dream. With a deep sigh she remembered that she had to get ready for the school, the worst place to go early in the morning. God knows what new plot would be hatched by Sarita, Rashi and some other wicked members of the

Trivedi family. In this school there is only one person who supports and gives protection to Urja – he is Adarsh. But the mean minded, uncultured ladies make meaningful hints at Adarsh's support for Urja because of which he is not able to show his whole-hearted support to Urja. He tries to protect the dignity of Urja and himself. Urja also keeps herself reserved and maintains a distance as she does not want to involve herself into any new problem. She can understand the helpless condition of Adarsh. He is chained in his feet and tied to the post of his family from where he can never get freedom.

Anandlal's wife now-a-days doesn't like to come to school. On the pretext of taking care of her grandson, she spends most of the time at her younger son's house. She doesn't feel like coming to school because of the misbehaviour of Sarita. This bitch wants to get rid of everybody and grab the whole institution into her fist.

Urja cannot understand one thing. What is the reason for giving so much importance to Sarita? Why can't the family members raise their voice against her or at least point out her mistakes?

Urja sometimes thinks that had she been in the place of the Director, she would have slapped Sarita out of her wits and taught her a lesson which neither her parents nor her in-laws have taught her. Her lowly background reflects from the tip of her toe to the parting of her hair. She is jealous of Urja but tries to emulate her in every possible way.

Urja enjoyed the two unexpected holidays bit by bit, relishing each and every moment. As the buses were taken for election duty, holidays were declared on Thursday and Friday. Only classes XI and XII were called on Saturday but which day's time-table had to be followed were not announced. As usual there was a chaos. Without creating a chaos, nothing can be done in the school.

Once it was decided that group photographs of class XII will be taken on a particular day. Urja sent a notice that students must come in white uniform with blazer. But without informing anyone, all of a sudden the Director went out of station and so the photo session had to be postponed. Whenever a date is fixed after consulting everyone, at the last moment for some reason, some inconvenience of anyone of the family members, it has to be postponed or cancelled. Ever since her joining, Urja has been noticing this.

A very funny thing happened early in the morning on Saturday. After waking up when Urja looked at the wall clock she saw it was 5.00 a.m. She quickly left the bed and after brushing her teeth came downstairs. She called Mahesh, her servant and told him to open the main gate as the maid servant would come. As she was sipping tea all of a sudden the alarm clock started ringing. Urja wondered why the alarm rang late ! It was supposed to ring at 4.30 a.m. She went upstairs to put off the alarm and saw the time shown by the clock was 4.30 a.m. She looked at the wall clock – 4.30 a.m. She came down and looked at the drawing room wall clock – that was also showing 4.30 a.m. She understood, by mistake she woke up at 4. o' clock instead of 5. Poor Mahesh, he was not aware of this and could not understand why he was not able to overcome his sleepy state that particular day !

When Urja reached the school she found that she was the first to come. Signing the Attendance Register she went up to her office room. Savitri was cleaning the room. She had opened the large windows on the Northern side. Cool breeze of early winter was coming inside. The green leaves of the huge trees were eventually turning brown. A layer of fog could be seen at the boundary of the Kabir Ashram at the backside of the school. Winter was knocking at the door. There were vapour on the glass panes of the window. Urja lighted the incense sticks before the photos of Sai Baba, Sri Aurobindo and Sree Ma of Pondicherry and another day started.

The pleasant mood of the morning disappeared at noon, when at the request of Adarsh she went to the designing section and found that the Director's son-in-law had added four pages article on travelling, in Hindi in the magazine. Some more family photographs were also included. Urja didn't even know all of them. Parminder had worked hard on the graphics; most of them were removed and again family photographs were used to replace them. Urja felt helpless. There was simply nothing to do. The Director does not have any control over his family members and they will continue to take advantage of the situations and of his weakness. Either Urja has to tolerate everything or she has to quit. But she will not quit, until and unless she finds a better job. She can not change the situation also. From her previous experience she has understood that everybody is moulded by conditions, circumstances, environment, education, acquired habits and definitely of heredity. Urja told herself – "I stood yesterday. I can stand today. I will not permit myself to think about what might happen tomorrow, so cheer up baby, keep on floating – this is just a journey not a destination. Destination is far away, miles to go. Urja can not afford to break down for trivial reasons.

In the evening Padma rang up – "Urja are you coming with me tomorrow to attend the seminar of Amway at the town hall?"

Urja replied –"It is not possible for me because my students will come."

Padma said –"I thought you will be able to make out some time in the morning."

Urja said –"Sorry, my students will come both in the morning and evening."

Padma understood –"O.K., never mind; sometime later we can go."

Urja said "Sure."

"O.K., Bye."

"Bye, Good night."

Urja will never fall into the trap of these people again. They had made her cry a lot. God knows what is her intention ! Urja will not give any scope to them. With a quarter plate of roasted pea-nuts and a glass of Darjeeling tea she sat down to complete the sixth chapter of her novel.

Swapnil was out of station for a week. Urja has learnt to live alone. She is not alone; her dreams are always with her.

Urja was tensed for the last few days. Her daughter-in-law was in the advanced stage of her pregnancy. She was standing at the threshold of stepping into mother-hood which means Urja would join the grandmothers of the world. The tentative date was in March but since the end of January the pain started. Niti's doctor told her that the baby was ready to come out but still it was underweight and it would be a great risk to deliver a pre-matured baby. She gave her steroids to resist the untimely delivery.

Everyday Urja enquired about the latest position over telephone. Her son said that before one month the doctor would not let the baby to come out. Urja had the plan of taking leave as soon as her daughter-in-law is admitted to the hospital because they would require her help after the birth of the child. Moreover Niti's mother came to Delhi in the second week of February.

Swapnil was supposed to go to Delhi on 12th February on official tour. Urja was in the school when she got a call from her son as well as Swapnil informing her that Niti had been admitted to the hospital because of severe labour pain. Urja became restless; last night also her son told her that everything was fine and it would take about a month. Adarsh, the Principal was out of station. Urja tried to contact him over the telephone and ultimately was successful at 10.30 a.m. She explained the situation in brief and asked for leave. Adarsh told her to proceed immediately. Next was the problem of getting a railway or a flight ticket. Swapnil tried for the whole day but it was not available. He went to Delhi in the evening flight with Urja's suitcase too. Urja got the flight ticket next day that is on 13th but not a straight one to Delhi; it was via Kolkata. When she reached Kolkata Airport she got Swapnil's call – "Congratulations ! you have become the grandmom of a cute boy." Urja felt like growing wings and reaching Delhi to see Niti and her baby but just then Jet Airways gave her the most dreadful news that her flight to Delhi is delayed by six hours. Only Urja could feel what she missed. She will never get the chance of being with her daughter-in-law at the most crucial moment of her life. She missed the chance of seeing the face of her first grandson before others. Many people must have seen him by now – Urja thought but there was nothing else to do but to wait.

Ultimately at 6.30 the aircraft took off. After reaching Delhi, there was no space to land. The aircraft started circling around the airport and finally landed at a far off place from the exit. It took ten minutes to reach there by the Jet Airways Bus. When Urja reached Apollo Hospital the visiting hour was over long back. The patients were sleeping. The corridors were being cleaned with detergent powder and water. Much to her surprise she was allowed to go inside. Baby Maharaj was sleeping peacefully wrapped up in a soft blanket. Looking at his face Urja forgot all exhaustions of the day. A tiny, red complexioned cute baby, occasionally opening his mouth in search of milk and falling asleep again – what a wonderful sight, heavenly feelings – Urja felt like sitting with the baby for the whole night but following the rules of the hospital and keeping in mind the generosity of the hospital authority she had to go to her son's house leaving Niti and her baby in the hospital.

Niti's parents wanted to take Niti and her baby along with them after a fortnight. Till then it was the best time of her life for Urja spending the time with the baby – who had appeared on the Earth with a bundle of joy. Urja informed Adarsh and Motilal over the telephone and they congratulated her. Motilal blessed the child and chanted some Sanskrit shlokas also. Adarsh told Urja to attend the 10th National Conference of the Independent Schools' Federation of India which was scheduled on 21st and 22nd of February at Pragati Maidan. Urja could not say 'no' although she didn't feel like attending the Conference, leaving baby Maharaj. Adarsh said – "Madam, this is an important conference as there will be discussions on the report of Sixth Pay Commission and Right to Education Bill. Since you are in Delhi, I am not sending anyone else. You please attend the programme and note down every details."

Urja said – "O.K. Sir, definitely I will attend."

Urja's son and daughter-in-law were unhappy to know this. They said – "You have come only for two weeks and within that short time you have to attend official duty."

Urja told them – "When you are in an important position, you can not avoid certain things. Your duty becomes your first priority whether you like it or not. Today you will not understand but in future you will definitely realise."

Urja had to walk a long distance from gate No. 7 of Pragati Maidan as cars were not allowed to go inside because of some construction work. When she reached the venue she met many Principals of various schools of Delhi and other places whom she had met earlier in the 9th Annual Conference the previous year. Whatever she could understand from the various lectures delivered by the eminent personalities related to education was that the parents had to be taken into confidence before raising the fee structures of the schools in order to implement the pay scale according to the decision of the sixth pay commission.

There was a detailed discussion on the grades and scale of the PRTs, TGTs, PGTs, Office staff, Class IV staff, Executives etc.

During the tea-break, when Urja was conversing with some of her old acquaintances, all of a sudden Veer Parsad appeared before him and extended his hand saying "Hello ! Nice to meet you here." Urja said – "Good morning Sir, how are you ?"

As they were exchanging greetings some more gentlemen joined them.

Urja excused herself and carried on with her known persons. Veer Parsad said "We will catch up later on."

After tea-break the Principals of various schools shared their experience of the reactions of the parents they had to face when they tried to raise the tuition fees.

At lunch time all were moving in a queue. Veer Parsad joined the queue standing behind Urja. Urja informed him about the birth of her grandson. He congratulated her and said "But you are not looking like a grandmother. You are still so pretty."

Urja thought habit and nature can't be changed even at the time of death.

Throughout the lunch, Veer Parsad remained with Urja. He told her how he had been missing her etc. etc. bla bla bla and finally said – "Let's meet somewhere after the conference. I have something to discuss with you."

"How shameless !" – Thought Urja. She left the conference before it was over.

Fifteen days passed away in a jiffy. It was so difficult to part with the baby. Urja never felt such a strong attachment even with her own sons. May be interest is sweeter than the original amount ! Along with Swapnil and her son she stood on the platform of New Delhi station till the Rajdhani Express to Ahmedabad, carrying her grandson, daughter-in-law and her parents went out of sight. Good times are very short in duration and the reminiscence of good times torments the heart along with filling the mind with happiness. Next time when Urja will meet Maharaj, he will grow up a little. Urja's heart pined to hear the call 'Granny' in the soft, pure, innocent voice of Maharaj

Mahesh got married to a Marathi girl. In the Sahu community of that place Inter-caste, religion or state marriages are not accepted. He had to face a lot of problems. Not a single relative attended the marriage function. His parents also didn't accept the daughter-in-law. He was not in a position to take a room on rent basis. He requested Urja to let them stay in the small servant room at the back side of her house, which was so long used as a store room. He said– "Madam, I will do everything, cleaning, cooking etc. but my wife will not do any work. She is more educated than me and she agreed to marry me on that condition." Urja thought what's the problem if Mahesh does all household work. She said "O.K., but if required she will have to work."

When they settled in her servant room, one day she asked Mahesh to show her the last mark sheet of Manju, his wife. Urja suppressed her laughter when she saw it – fail in 4 subjects out of 5 in class X Board Exam and in Hindi, just passed with 33 out of 100.

Urja was trying to wear the socks in the car. The bumpy road and the continuous jerking of the car on the one hand and the irritating sound made by a mosquito near her ear on the other prevented her from doing so for a long time till she could manage it after twenty minutes and the smile of victory appeared on her lips. When she was in school in her childhood the school bus used to stop at a place which was five minutes walk from her home. As her school was in the afternoon and the bus picked her two hours earlier because it had to cover almost half of Calcutta, her mother forced her to eat her lunch at 9.30 a.m. and most of the days she had to run for the bus with socks in her hand which she wore in the bus. One day the stomach was so full, the hook of the skirt came off and she had to manage it only with the belt for the whole day. Next day onwards there started a never ending tussle between the mother and the daughter – one determined to feed her everything she could prepare and the other obstinately refusing to eat anything at all.

Urja heaved a sigh – how quickly just in a jiffy the days passed away bringing her to this juncture of life. The dice has moved from the ruled's side to that of the ruler. As an administrator whenever she counsels or scolds any student, a teen-aged girl peeps at her from the back in whom she finds the reflection of her student life..........

Maths class – the teacher is about to come. One boy is vigilant at the door, ready to make the announcement of the coming of the teacher. Urja and three other friends were busy placing seeds of plum under the four legs of the teacher's chair. By the time the announcement was made, they were successful in their mission. The teacher came, exchange of greetings took place and the next moment he was lying flat on the floor. As soon as he tried to sit on the chair it betrayed as the seeds under its legs played the prank by sliding and rolling and embarrassed the teacher in front of the class. Very angrily he asked "who has done it? Tell me otherwise the whole class will be punished."

The unity of the class could outshine any other bond as nobody opened the mouth, rather all were eagerly waiting for the next incident to take place for which they had prepared the ground early in the morning. The fan just above the teacher's table was off and the blades contained bits of paper which were kept by the students. When the teacher was ultimately in a position to start his teaching, Urja asked – "May I switch on the fan Sir?" "Oh yes ! It's so hot. Why didn't you switch it on earlier?" One of the students said – "Saving electricity Sir."

Urja switched on the fan and came back to her place. As the fan started taking speed there was a shower of paper on the teacher. He jumped and shouted continuously but nobody could understand what he said because there was a roll of laughter which suppressed his voice. The teacher left the class and after sometime came back with the Head Mistress. When she failed to find out the real culprits, the whole class was suspended for a week. What an enjoyable time they had experienced the next day ! Urja can never forget even the class toppers also joined their class picnic but hardly they knew what was awaiting them at home.

The school authority had already informed the parents and taken undertakings from them that in future if the students misbehave they would be rusticated from the school. The parents apologised on behalf of their respective ward and requested the school management to allow the students to attend the school. Hence, the class picnic remained a solitary one without any further extension and the students joined their class from the next day after getting a lot of rebukes from their parents.

There was no end to their childish pranks. Spreading ink on the back of the white kurta of the Hindi teacher Baleswar Jha was one among them. The Bengali teacher Rabin Pal was very popularly known as Ravan Pal. The affair between the English teacher Supriya and the History teacher Subir evoked a romantic feeling among the students. The dhoti-clad Maths teacher with a tall height was nicknamed 'Gupi' after the famous character in Satyajit Ray's 'Gupi Gain Bagha Bain' and as a coincidence there was a lab assistant who resembled Rabi Ghosh who had played the role of Bagha in the same film. School was a place where their childhood sprouted up into teenage and left them on the threshold of youth, ready to face the world. Time has changed, society has changed, the whole world has changed and with that many things have been lost from the world, the most prominent among them being childhood. Urja feels pity for the children who are bent with the burden of studies and are becoming mechanical robots forgetting their innocence and pure joy. Even a student of class II knows about N.T.S.E., K.V.P.Y., I.I.T, A.I.E.E.E. and many other Competitive Examinations. The parents share their dream of making their wards Doctors, Engineers, I.A.S., I.P.S., C.A. etc. with their children. They want their respective children to be all rounders. After school, now-a-days children do not play in the open fields. They either sit glued to the computers or attend music, dance or art classes. In absence of children the open, green fields have shrunken giving space to the multi-storeyed buildings, where in each cage one or two child-robots acquire skills in various fields along with studies but are devoid of heart and mind. Their brain works faster but heart remains rigid. In this materialistic world one can not afford to be emotional or sentimental or indulge oneself into day dreaming.

Urja feels the bond of love and respect between the teachers and the students are missing. Outside the school if a student meets a teacher he/she pretends to be not recognising the teacher. Touching feet is a matter of the past, rarely seen. If at all they greet, they make a shrug and say 'morning'. Who is to blame for this? It is a known fact that teachers are the most exploited class in the society – they are underpaid. They take up a lot of tuitions. Whatever they are supposed to teach in the classroom, are taught in the coaching or tuition classes. The dedication, commitment, love for the profession are no more associated with teaching. But are not the students and the parents also responsible to some extent? The students have become careerists right at a very tender age; they have adopted the give and take policy very well. Parents, sometimes out of jealousy, sometimes for genuine reasons criticise the teachers in front of their children. The image of a teacher in most of the children's mind is now a negative one, not that of a friend, philosopher and guide. Urja feels, this definitely is creating a big impact in the society. As an administrator she tries her best to make the parents understand this point of not criticising the teachers in front of the students. But sometimes, the teachers themselves criticise each other and pave their way to the hell. The whole system, the whole society can't be changed overnight. Moreover jealousy is the other name for failure. The failures will continue to sling mud on others. The respect, the values of the past will continue to diminish.

Urja's thoughts got a break when she reached the school. Sitting on her chair she prepared the checklist of the work to be done. Getting the magazines distributed to the students classwise by the class-IV staff was one among them.

Urja had just started her evening pooja when the mobile phone rang. She let it ring for the first time. When it rang for the second time she received it. "Hello ! May I speak to Mrs.Urja Sen?"

"Yes, speaking."

"Madam, I'm Shamim Parvez; your school magazine has come to my hands. From where did you get the image of Hazrat Muhammad?

"It was taken from the internet."

"Have you ever seen any photo or image of Hazrat Muhammad? We Muslims never use any photo or image of our religious Prophet."

"I have never seen, but the Designing Editor who is also the Chief Designer got the image from the net."

"Madam, you are the Chief Editor. Without your permission how could it be included in the magazine?"

Urja said – "Although I am the Chief Editor, my words are not the last in this matter. You must have noticed that most of the members of the Editorial Board belong to Trivedi family. It's their family school, family magazine. Their decision is the final."

The gentleman asked –"Can you tell me the name of the website where you got the image?"

Urja said –"I don't know anything about it. You please talk to the Designing Editor."

"O.K. Thank you Madam."

Urja was expecting this. When she came back from Delhi she was surprised to see the image of Hazrat Muhammad in one of the separators of the magazine. She had advised to remove the image of Hazrat Muhammad because to her knowledge there is neither any photo nor any image of him. She had also said that it might hurt the religious sentiment of the Muslims. But as usual Rashi – the designer, who is also a daughter-in-law of Trivdei family refused to listen and very confidently said that the image was in the net. She got the support of her family members. Motilal himself praised her saying "What nobody could do earlier, you have done. From this magazine now everybody will come to know how Hazrat Muhammad looked like."

Urja helplessly thought – "The image was so funny; it could not be of Hazrat Muhammad. But she knew it was useless arguing with them. She kept quiet for the moment but some how got the premonition that something serious and grave was going to happen.

Her intuition was correct and now being the Chief Editor of the magazine she will have to face the problem. But why should she? Had she not faced enough problems while preparing the magazine? With a disturbed mind she completed the pooja. Her husband was out of station; anything could happen because she was aware of the fact how fanatic people at times can become on religious issues.

Next day she got the feedback from Parminder that Rashi was sitting in Sarita's room with a dark gloomy face. Urja understood what had happened. She also was sure that these two wicked women would try to put the blame on her.

In the afternoon she got a call from Adarsh. He asked her from where she had got the image of Hazrat Muhammad? She told him that it was not in her knowledge as Rashi had taken the image from the internet and with the approval of Sarita and the Director, included it in the separator. Adarsh told her that the matter had become very serious as the Muslim fundamentalists became furious. A meeting was called at 5 p.m. when the matter will be discussed in the presence of some members of the Parliament and Police department. Urja thought now these people will learn a lesson; they will understand the consequences of interfering in others' work.

Urja came to know about the details of the meeting from Adarsh, the next day. The Muslim fundamentalists shouted and abused in a vulgar way. The MLAs and Police Officers winked at Motilal and Adarsh. They remained silent and then the fundamentalists asked "Where is the Chief Editor? We want to speak to that person." Motilal said –"The Chief Editor is not responsible for this. It was the decision of the Editorial Board."

They said "You have to apologise on behalf of the Editorial Board." They agreed to do so. One of the fundamentalists dictated the draft of the apology letter which was written by the media persons and was signed by the Principal. The fundamentalists also demanded that all the magazines should be taken back from the students and handed over to them. Already about 400 magazines were distributed to outsiders and it was not possible to get back those copies. Adarsh told them that rest of the magazines would be handed over to them. Except Urja nobody was so unhappy to hear this. She shuddered in fear to think about the fate of her creation. What a noble thought was there in her mind when she had suggested that this time each separator of the magazine would be made on each religious Guru like Hinduism, Christianity, Buddhism, Jainism, Sikhism, Islam etc. and at the end the last separator would be on religious harmony showing the equality of all religions, that all paths lead to God. The images of Swami Vivekanand, Jesus Christ, Lord Buddha, Mahavira, Guru Nanak were included and since no image of Hazrat Muhammad is available Urja had suggested to include Akbar. In the meantime when she was not present, Rashi did this blunder of including the image of Hazrat Muhammad which she managed from which website only God knows !

Pre-Board Examination was scheduled on that day but postponing that the students of classes X and XII were asked to bring their magazines from home. All other classes were asked to positively return the magazines on the next day. A few alternatives were there like tearing of the two particular pages, pasting papers on those two pages or painting the images with any dark colour on those two particular pages. Urja had objection in tearing off the pages because on the backside of both the pages there were articles, poems and paintings made by children which she didn't want to get destroyed. Moreover on the page of religious harmony there were images of other religious preachers apart from that of Hazrat Muhammad. Tearing off that page would mean insulting the followers of other religions, if thought deeply. The sequence, page numbers etc. also would be disturbed and would not match with the content. But the school authority did not want to take any risk. They said whatever decision the fundamentalists would take, that would be followed. On this matter there was a difference of opinion between the educated Muslims and the fundamentalists. The educated Muslims said that it was a great idea and with a good intention religious harmony was shown in the magazine but these uneducated, biased, orthodox people will never understand that.

Five thousand four hundred magazines were loaded in a tempo and taken to the fundamentalists. Quite a large number had already gone to various places, some with the images intact, some with paint on the images and some with paper pasted on them. The uneducated, orthodox, heartless ultimately ordered that those two pages should be torn off from all the remaining five thousand four hundred magazines. Can our land still be called Hindustan? Is it really a secular country? How dare the fundamentalists ordered those pages to be taken out from the magazine which they wanted to bury? What right they had to bury the images of Vivekananda, Jesus Christ, Buddha, Mahavir and Guru Nanak? No one dared to say even a single word ! Strange ! Hindus are still considered the majority in this country where the creativity of innocent children was sent to the grave by the so called minorities!!!

Adarsh told Urja to forget everything. He said even the politicians and the police are afraid of the fundamentalists because if there is a riot, unnecessary innocent people will lose their lives.

The magazines were distributed to the students again after postmortem. Everything became normal but Urja will never forget this incident and her hatred towards religious orthodoxy and fanaticism increased ten times. She felt sad for those children whose creativity were murdered for the fault of the grown ups who claim to be always right.

It's so painful to be experienced. Ignorance is a bliss. How desperate one is in childhood but with age the blood cools down because one knows the consequence of certain actions. Until and unless the finger is burnt how can one know that fire has the power to burn everything ? The more Urja is growing old, the more she is becoming conscious of getting hurt. Whenever Chandu drives the car fast she becomes panic stricken sitting at the back. Memories of accidents start haunting her mind. She shudders thinking of a cyclist or a scooterist springing out of the side lanes all of a sudden and coming under the wheels of her car or a head-on collision with any vehicle coming from the front. But once upon a time she was absolutely fearless. She used to do all sorts of desperate things.

There was no railing on the roof of the house where she spent her childhood. It was absolutely open and Urja as a child used to walk along the edges of the roof on all four sides, escaping the eyes of all. One day one of the neighbours noticed her walking like that and complained the matter to her father. The door leading to the roof was locked immediately. Boarding running buses or local trains was another of her adventurous deeds. She had no idea or concept of fear. But with age life seems to be precious and a pain lingers in the mind at the very thought of leaving the world. May be for that reason Urja has become very alert, conscious. Physical injuries or accidents can be resisted to some extent by remaining alert. But what about the mendacious attacks of human beings from the back side whose mephitic effects are difficult to overcome? Now-a-days, of course Urja is able to guess or predict from which side the attack will come. That's why she was prepared to face an unpleasant situation at school after coming back from Kolkata where she had gone to see her ailing mother-in-law.

The results of class XII were out. Urja was eager to know the results. Adarsh's phone call came in the evening of the same day when she came back home. After the initial exchange of greetings Adarsh said – "Madam I came to know that because of poor performance in English, the overall percentage has come down."

Urja said – "Sir tomorrow I will go to school and after looking at the marksheet available from the net, I can tell you something about it."

Adarsh continued – "I am now in Pune. Mr. Mishra told me in the afternoon, after getting the results that only 30 students got distinction in English. The highest score is also very low. Whereas the highest in Mathematics is 100."

Urja said –"Mathematics is a scoring subject which can not be compared to English. We don't have any marks for Practical also like the Science subjects. Moreover I haven't yet seen the results. Sir, tomorrow I will let you know everything."

With a sad and depressed heart Urja went to school, the next day. The first thing she did was to take a copy of the mark-sheet obtained from the Net and straight way going to her room she started verifying and analysing the results. At least ten students got 90 per cent and above. The total number of distinctions was 245 and total number of first division – 583. Maximum students scored within 80 per cent to 89 per cent. Not a single child failed in English and in the range between 33 per cent to 40 per cent there was only one child.

Urja analysed the results of other subjects also. In Mathematics the highest score was 100 but the lowest score was 04. There were 17 failures in Maths and in the range between 33 per cent to 40 per cent there were 34 students. Similar are the cases of other subjects also. Urja knows the standard of English of the students of that school. In class XI they are given admission on the basis of their marks in Maths and Science. Admission test is taken only on Maths. In spite of that the results of English is the best.

Urja immediately called the Principal and informed him everything. He was a little bit surprised. Urja once more became familiar with the meanness and cunningness of the opportunists. In order to hide the fact that there were seventeen failures in Maths and a large number of students scored in single digit only, how cleverly the attention of the Principal was drawn towards English. This man, the other Vice Principal of the school and H.O.D. (Mathematics), although working in the same position, had managed to get three thousand Rupees more than what Urja was getting when salary fixation was done two years back. It became crystal clear to Urja now how he had managed to manipulate. The big, Tilak of sandalwood paste on his forehead seemed to be the most unsacred blotch in the world.

Such type of things happened in her previous school also but somehow Urja wants to have faith on the inherent goodness of human beings. Again and again she is cheated still she doesn't lose hope. After all in the war between good and evil, so far good has always been the victorious.

Urja's Guide Professor informed her that the Viva for Ph.D. had been fixed on 5th June. She also told her about the formalities to be done. She had to purchase expensive gifts for the External Examiners and other members of the department. She had to take care of the boarding, lodging and travelling expenses. On the day of the Viva she had to arrange for the snacks and lunch of all the members of the department including the students. As train tickets were not available Urja had to arrange for flight ticket for the Examiner. The whole expenditure estimated was approximately twenty-thousand Rupees.

Urja thought – what is the value of hard work? How difficult it was for her to manage home, school, family demands and this Ph.D. programme ! So many times she had to meet her Guide Professor after school for her instructions. Sometimes she got stuck up in meeting or any other engagement and could not give time to Urja. Urja's topic was so difficult and challenging that she had to collect data and evidences from various places. Like other Ph.D scholars of that place she didn't try to complete her work, sitting in the library of the University. She went to the National Library Kolkata, the National Archive, Delhi, Central Secretariat Library, Institute of Historical Research, Teenmurti Bhawan Nehru Museum and Library etc. in Delhi so many times. Remaining awake till late night she wrote her thesis and now she had to butter the examiners to achieve the degree ! These people get their remuneration from the respective University. Their boarding, lodging and travelling expenses are borne by the Universities. They get reimbursement, submitting the bills but extract money from the scholars. They are the educationists dispelling the darkness of ignorance and enlightening the raw, innocent minds ! Wonderful ! ! !

It was an open Viva attended by the students and Professors of M.A., M.Phil and Ph.D apart from the Guide Professor and the Externals. The Viva continued for one and a half hour. Urja was thoroughly prepared. She answered all questions with full confidence and to the satisfaction of all. Ultimately they said – "Congratulations Dr. Urja !"

It was one of the rare moments when one feels like floating on cloud nine. Urja asked her Guide Professor when she will get the written order of the University confirming her getting the title of Dr.? She said that it will be sent by post within a week. After inviting them for dinner in a 4 star Hotel when Urja took their leave, her Guide Professor reminded her about writing a paper on I.N.A. which she had to present in a Conference. Urja's palpitation started again when she thought that without submitting this paper to her Guide she could not expect to receive the notification for Ph.D.

Urja completed the write-up on I.N.A. in the name of her Guide Professor and rang her. She said –"The notification is with me. You can come on any day and collect it."

Urja thought why on any day, it's better to go as early as possible. She took a_half-day-leave from Adarsh and straightway came to the University.

Urja couldn't believe her eyes when she got the notification of Ph.D in her hand. Her Guide Professor handed over the letter and congratulated her as Urja handed over the write-up on I.N.A. to her. She was so overwhelmed at the fulfilment of her dream that she forgot to thank her for a moment. She touched her feet when she got back her sense. From that moment she will be known as Dr. Urja. How desperately she pursued for this doctorate !

When Urja got married she was just in the second year of her graduation course. The cloud of uncertainty had engulfed her mind-whether she would be able to carry on further with her studies. Whenever she sat with her books, her Mother-in-law used to come into the room and disturb her by narrating the much-told account of her newly married life, her adjustments with the joint family members etc. After coming back from the college in the evening when she tried to concentrate in her studies, her Mother-in-law expressed her great concern at the anticipated increase in the electricity-bill for switching on the tube light and told her to go to the roof for studying. That was another horrible experience as evening time was the best time for the mosquitoes to quench their thirst for blood and they found Urja's fair and smooth skin very convenient to pierce. The children of the nearby slum also found the place just in front of their house, the most suitable for their evening game. Their enthusiasm, energy, boisterousness were expressed through their shrill voice, heated arguments and quarrels, shattering the effort and concentration of Urja. She could not share her problems with Swapnil as he used to come only on weekends from his workplace and Urja wanted to relish each and every moment of those two evenings and the Sunday.

Sitting on the rooftop at the fading twilight Urja used to think about her future. During her 31 year married life Urja always had to face ups and downs. When she looks back she just wonders how could she overcome certain situations and happenings ! Time has changed; it is a rolling over from one century to another with a new society, new environment and new progenies all around. But the basic nature of human beings has not changed. That same mean-mindedness, jealousy, tendency to unnecessarily hurt a person who doesn't fit into the common mould still exist. And in this matter there is no difference between the outsiders and your own people who are very precious to you.

In this ungrateful world all relationships are based on self-interest and nothing else. Here expectations from any relationship is foolishness. Urja still has miles to go. She will not give up if she doesn't find a single companion on her way. It is her solo journey, half of which she has covered and the remaining portion she will cover herself.

8

Adarsh in his Pensive Mood

Urja is very lucky for us. As soon as she joined our school, one by one we were able to snatch the important responsibilities from Veer Parsad – first formation of Sahodaya Complex and position of the President, next Nodal Centre for evaluation of CBSE class X exam papers followed by Examination centre for AISSE and AISSCE, Centre for IIT Examination, CCE Training for Principals, Cluster and Zonal level Games and Sports etc. One of our students stood first in class XII Board Examination in the State. Veer Parsad could not digest all these. He tried his best to turn my mind against Urja by libeling her to the possible extent. He didn't hesitate to sling mud on the character of Urja. But I am well aware of the character of Veer Parsad, so why should I listen to him? It is because of his dirty habit respectable ladies like Urja and some of her colleagues left the school one after another. It is because of his dirty character, today students of his school dare to hire killers for murdering classmates. Two students even went to the extreme end and murdered one of their classmates, calling him to a remote place and tying his hands and legs. What was his fault? He had threatened them to report to the teachers about their practice of sending dirty SMS to the girls. Poor boy! He was stoned to death and his body was thrown into a pond which was recovered in a rotten condition later on. One of the accuseds was the son of an important position holder in a big organisation. Veer Parsad tried his best to save that boy but failed.

The incident rocked the whole township but Veer Parsad was least bothered. Just within a week another boy of his school was arrested by the police for giving money to a hired killer to kill his classmate. His father's political connection, however, saved him and he is now attending school, hale and hearty. Wonderful ! This is the most reputed, branded school, not only of the State but also of the Nation and Veer Parsad got the Best Principal award. The curse of innumerable victims and their tears could not shake the ground under his feet. With his shameless, poisonous toungue he uttered nonsense against Urja before me with the hope that I would listen to him and stop supporting Urja. I have to see who is useful for the growth of our school. I have observed that sincerity in Urja and within a short time she could prove herself. I can understand Veer Parsad's jealousy at his failure in clipping off the wings of Urja. I can understand his despair for his wounded manhood. Urja slipped off from his hands, so now he wants to trample her under feet.

Because of Veer Parsad only our affiliation of the second school in the State capital got delayed. He was a member of the Inspection Committee and happily took the opportunity to write some adverse remarks against the school. Most probably he had expected something more than the silver mug set worth Rs.10,000 presented to him !

My family members are somewhat convinced by Veer Parsad in forming their opinion about Urja. Elder brother says employees should not have a higher profile than the employers. Urja's high profile is her enemy. Family members have to be projected because they have to take the reins in their hand in future. Urja is an outsider. There is no surety that she will continue in our school forever. If she comes to the limelight that will be of no use to the school. That will only enhance her personal career. Sarita and Aradhana always try to sidetrack her for consolidating their own position. One thing they are not able to understand - that is, a river does not acquire velocity unless there is a resistance. The more Urja is facing opposition, the more she is gaining strength and performing better. Sarita and Aradhana always try to satisfy their ego by showing their seniority and superiority over Urja. They forget that they are holding the position in their own school. It is not their achievement but a gift presented to them by elder brother. Moreover, a person's qualification, talent, efficiency are more important than the position he or she adorns. In that matter Urja is far better than both of them.

Whenever I extend my support to Urja, I face joint opposition from the family. Elder brother also blindly supports them; he doesn't want to go against the family. In order to save Urja from an awkward position sometimes I remain neutral. Knowing very well who is guilty and who is innocent, I still keep quiet because I am afraid to bring any change to the familiar pattern. I shudder in fear to think about the past. I had no shoes to wear to school. Schoolbag, tiffin all these were luxury. Elder brother used to teach us to dream of money and wealth, lying on tattered rags. Poverty could not erase hope from his mind. When he married and left the house for changing his fate we felt orphaned for an indefinite period but after settling down in the new place when he called us to shift there – it was a real turning point in our life. Leaving the village home we came to settle in the steel city.

In the meanwhile my younger brother and I had fallen in love with elder sister-in-law's two younger sisters. It was the romantic period of our life which could hide the dark, ugly faces of poverty under colourful masks. Elder brother wanted me to be a doctor and my younger brother to be an engineer. But our romance and other activities prevented us from fulfilling his desires. Moreover I was down with severe Chicken Pox and there was no hope for life. God had destined something else for me; maybe, because of that, mocking at the chanting of Gita by the elders at home for the peace of the person who was about to leave the world, I survived miraculously. I used to stand at one corner of the room and cry thinking about my absolutely hopeless future.

In school I used to be in the company of students of Biology who all became doctors. But I had to start life again after recovering from my ailments. I got admission in a college for B.Sc. with Chemistry, then did M.Sc. in Chemistry and B.Ed. My younger brother got admission in an Engineering College but could not continue there for more than six months as the College authority refused to retain him on disciplinary ground. He was in the habit of picking up quarrels and fighting with the seniors as well as his batch mates. Elder brother brought him back from the hostel and he also took admission in a local college.

As soon as we got our Master's Degree and got some insignificant jobs our marriages were arranged.

I had to leave home and went to Mumbai to earn my living. My better half stayed with Bhaiya and Bhabi.

Very soon I understood that it was impossible for me to work under somebody. My mentality was just the opposite to that of my boss. I left my job at such a time when my wife had conceived our first child. What not had I done after leaving my job? Right from selling items of daily use from door to door to driving an auto-rickshaw – I tried my hands on everything to somehow earn my leaving and at the same time sending something at home.

Bhaiya called me back home, assuring me that he will arrange for some work for me. One fine morning I started towards home. On my way, through the window of the train, I saw the banner of a famous and popular Coaching Institute. An idea, just like lightning flashed in my mind. After coming back I shared it with Bhaiya. Why not open a Coaching Institute? Bhaiya was also thinking of starting his own school. I don't know from where we got so much courage ! With only two or three students the school started in the garage and the only teacher was my younger brother's wife.

Bhaiya arranged for a job for me in a school in the mines. Getting up at 4 o'clock in the early morning I had to board the bus for the mines. In the evening, after coming back home, I started taking tuitions in our so called coaching class in a shop. In the first year, there were only three students. Luckily, all three of them qualified in IIT Entrance exam.

With repeated effort I managed a transfer in the township where I stayed. Number of students started increasing gradually. Bhaiya's school shifted from the garage to the land which he had purchased. My elder son was born and within three years the younger son also appeared on the Earth with a bundle of joy. Bhaiya forced me to resign from the school where I had been working and join his school as the Principal. This was decided by fate – I was destined to be my own master.

The young generation wants everything ready-made. With least labour they want the result soon. Exactly the same thing, I have been observing among my family members. Particularly elder brother's two sons, daughters-in-law and his only daughter who have got the position of Executives want desperately to get rid of me and elder brother so that they can have the absolute power in their hands. They can't tolerate anybody whc has been appointed from outside. They feel insecured because they know they are in no way equal to the persons who are appointed as Executives from outside. Sarita and Aaradhana applied all their shrewdness to corner Urja. But she is tough. I know she has ambition. She had started working in our school with full enthusiasm. However within a short time she understood that she will never get any recognition here. Everybody will try to exploit her talents. Her previous experiences must have warned her also. She stopped showing any interest or taking any initiative and remained passive most of the time.

Sharmistha Sen, whose husband is an established businessman in the capital of the State, with whose effort the second branch of our school could survive well and who so long was worshipped by our family, is also being ignored recently. The school doesn't need her any longer. It's really strange how soon people could forget her contribution ! What a nasty scene was created in the meeting of Executives of both the schools to discuss about the almanac of the coming session! Sarmistha was humiliated by our next generation important position holders of the school, I mean my nephew and his wife. She cried a lot and was about to go out of the room but elder brother stopped her. She is the weakness of elder brother; maybe for that reason his children, particularly his younger son doesn't like her. Elder brother almost embraced her and holding her hands made her sit on the sofa. His younger son said that he had to take a class in the coaching centre and left the room in great air. I noticed a meaningful smile appeared on the lips of Urja and disappeared very soon. What impression she formed about us, God knows! But who has the time to care for anybody's thoughts or feelings? We have to progress and in that forward journey how many living and non-living things are trampled under feet are not to be cared for.

But the memory of the past sometimes gives me immense pain. When I place myself in the position of people working under us, I really feel pity for them. But I have to keep pace with the current. I have to maintion peace in the family. I can not go against the wishes or decisions of the family. If family decides that we have to take the help of the outsiders but take the whole credit ourselves in order to gain recognition, establishment, fame then I have to agree to that silently at least till my dream project – my own Engineering College is ready.

Aaradhana argued with me yesterday with a raised voice in front of elder brother. She forgot that time when she was almost dying, cruelly tortured by her mother-in-law. Bhaiya, Bhabi had kept quiet knowing everything. She was all in bones and skin. All household chores were forcefully imposed upon her including cleaning utensils, mopping the floor, washing clothes, cooking and serving. I had picked her up from her in-law's place and dropped her at Bhai Sahab's house. We didn't allow her to go back again to her in-law's house. Her husband initially was upset and there was temporary separation as he continued to stay in his own house but gradually he also realised the mistakes of his parents and leaving his home joined with Aaradhana. They started earning and constructed their own house but I became a permanent enemy in the eyes of her in-laws. Perhaps she has forgotten those days. Actually she doesn't like my support and likings for Urja. Sheer jealousy, nothing else. Women feel insecured very soon and without any reason. The reason for her losing temper was also a trivial one. Based on the feedback provided by Urja I decided to shift Shalini from the Examination Deptt. as she was neglecting her teaching and correction duty with the excuse of being too busy which she was not. Aaradhana, somehow, has a good tuning with Shalini, so she protested. Bhaisahab also supported her. He is always blind whenever his sons, daughters in law or daughter are involved. After all, Adarsh is his brother only and brother's place is always after one's own children.

Nobody is happy to accept and follow the new system of Continuous and Comprehensive Evaluation system introduced by CBSE. It is strange that even after 60 years of Independence, the Government of India could not decide upon a stable system of Education. Because of frequent changes the school managements and teachers are also facing problems. A cynic would comment that everything is a farce. But why only a cynic – isn't it true?

The logic behind CCE according to CBSE is that conceptual development is a continuous process of deepening and enriching connections and acquiring new layers of meaning. Alongside is the development of theories that children have about the natural and social worlds, including themselves in relation to others, which provide them with explanations for why things are the way they are, the relationships between causes and effects and the bases for decisions and actions. Attitudes, emotions and values are thus an integral part of cognitive development and are linked to the development of language, mental representations, concepts and reasoning. Continuous and Comprehensive Evaluation refers to a system of school based evaluation of students that covers all aspects of students' development. It is a developmental process of assessment which emphasises on two fold objectives. These objectives are continuity in the evaluation and assessment of broad based learning and behavioural outcomes on the other. In this scheme the term continuous is meant to emphasise that evaluation of identified aspects of students' growth and development is a continuous process rather than an event, built into the total teaching-learning process and spread over the entire span of the academic session. 'Comprehensive' means that the scheme attempts to cover both the scholastic and co-scholastic aspects of students' growth and development.

When I read out from the Teachers' Manual sent by CBSE "The scheme is thus a curricular initiative, attempting to shift emphasis from testing to holistic learning. It aims at creating good citizens possessing sound health, appropriate skills and desirable qualities besides academic excellence. It is hoped that this will equip the learners to meet the challenges of life with confidence and success." – I observed the teachers exchanging meaningful glances.

I started explaining about Scholastic as well as Co-Scholastic aspects of the pupil's growth. Scholastic aspects include curricular or subject specific areas whereas co-scholastic aspects include life-skills, co-curricular, attitudes and values. Assessment in scholastic areas is done informally and formally using multiple techniques of evaluation continually and periodically. Assessment in Co-Scholastic areas is done using multiple techniques on the basis of identified criteria, while assessment in life skills is done on the basis of Indicators of Assessment and Checklists. The further I discussed about Formative Assessment and Summative Assessment including projects, quizzes, Research work, Conversation skills, assignments, oral questions, MCQs, short answer, long answer etc. the more frowns appeared on the foreheads of the teachers. The Co-Scholastic Assessment seemed to be more complicated to the teachers with life skills, thinking skills, social skills, communication skills, interpersonal skills, emotional skills, values, club activities, creative thinking, critical thinking, problem solving, decision making, co-curricular activities, literary activities, aesthetic activities, environment studies etc., etc., etc. CBSE expects the teachers to assess each child on the basis of all these by giving grades and writing remarks for each grade. Moreover exam papers are supposed to be corrected and marks written on a separate sheet and grades mentioned on the answer sheets. The task is mammoth for the teachers but the burden will be less on the students as mostly they have to attempt multiple –choice type papers in which writing part is very less.

When the teachers left my office after the meeting, Urja asked me "Sir, do you think it will be possible for the teachers to assess the children honestly? In all schools the Principals will instruct the teachers to give not less than B Grade. Just like Practical marks are in the hands of the school authority, no one gets less than 28 out of 30, in the same way in class X Board Examination also everybody will pass with good grades but the same students will not be able to perform well in class XI because the course is really tough. All of a sudden they will find it difficult to cope with such a vast and difficult course." Urja is absolutely right but she speaks bluntly. Who will disagree with the fact that class X CBSE Board Examination will have no value as everything will be done by the individual schools right from setting the question papers, conducting the examinations, checking the papers, preparing the results everything! The report cards will be sent to CBSE and with the signature of the concerned authority and the seal of CBSE they will come back again to the respective school. Urja seemed to be really concerned as the standard of education will come down.

I have tested her in various ways. She is short tempered but honest and is not diplomatic. She has been facing a lot of problems in our school or rather in our family. My immediate elder brother's (third in descending order) daughter-in-law who has been working in the designing section and calls herself Chief Designer has started thinking that she is also one of the Executives. With her dirty politics she continuously creates misunderstanding between Urja and other Executives. Bhaiya knows everything but he becomes weak before the family members. In front of the outsiders we have to show our family unity.

Rashi managed to occupy a seat in the front row very cleverly. Whenever asked by Sarita or Aaradhana at the time of any function, sometimes she used to take the name of Bhaisahab, sometimes my name as if we permitted her to sit in the front row along with the other Executives. In the school magazine she included her speech with the heading 'From the Designing Desk' next to the pages of the other Executives. When the Chief Editor Urja questioned about it she said "Babaji (Director Sir) has approved this. When I called her and asked after the magazines came back from the press she replied "The Chief Editor has done it." Everybody knows about her character. She takes advantage of the situation as she knows that to some extent we all depend on her as she can change anything in the computer.

The more the school is making progress, the more there is a competition among the family members to come to the limelight and establish their own identity. The outsiders who are holding responsible positions in our school are facing a lot of problems because of that because ultimately the blames are coming on them for any and every reason. None of the Vice Principals could work here for a long time. I have a doubt whether the present ones will be able to continue further ! Let's see with our fingers crossed.

We are grateful to Bade Bhaisahab for everything he had done for us. In fact without his help we would have remained the same poverty-stricken ordinary people. No one would have known about our family. But with age, his attitude is changing. He is not able to tolerate my success. I know he is jealous. He wanted me to be under his protective wings, to grow as a parasite or remain as a puppet dancing at his indications. When I started my own coaching classes, he had objections. He told me to teach in the coaching classes run by the school. But I was determined to design my own fate. What is the wrong in it? From coaching only I earned 15 to 18 lac per month. The family wheel started running smoothly. For five years I could not see the face of my wife and children in the evening. My wife used to be very much annoyed but I didn't give any importance to that. I wanted to grow like a banyan tree. One day when I surpassed my elder brother, I myself didn't know but a distance started growing rapidly. He started criticizing me in front of people. He didn't like my taking decisions in certain matters independently regarding the school. But I am the Principal and whether he agrees to the matter or not, the school has made remarkable progress because of me. If ever anyone says that he becomes annoyed. On the one hand he talks about values, about selfless service, about working without expecting any results but on the other hand he is not able to make himself free from any attachment or passion. He wants to emerge as a God-like-figure before the eyes of the public. He is absolutely a slave of his super-ego and because of this he has lost his sense of justice. He blindly supports himself, his two sons, his daughter and his two daughters in law. All other relationships are insignificant to him. That's why when my elder son opened an Engineering College, he congratulated him on his face but didn't hesitate to comment before some other family members that he had been gifted the college by his father-in-law. Our second Engineering College is coming up, which I have a plan of giving the responsibility to my younger son. Why shouldn't I? I have not taken a single penny from the school fund to purchase the land for the college. It is absolutely my own money, earned from the coaching classes and hostels. I know brother is not happy but I can't help. I don't believe in previous birth or birth in future. I know there is only one birth and in this only one life I have to achieve the maximum.

R.N. Mishra and Urja reported to me that early in the morning they were being scolded by the Director Sir because he was very much unhappy with the Annual Day Programme. He didn't like the extracts along with captions from the film Iqbal being shown in between my speech and also the entry of the staff members at the end of my speech. Everything was planned by me; neither R.N.Mishra nor Urja had anything to do with the plan but I know why they were blamed and rebuked. Bhaiya, in fact wanted to convey his message to me through these two Vice Principals. He had also told Urja to polish my English and take proper rehearsal before I speak otherwise her effort in preparing the speeches for me would become meaningless. Even without knowing English if I can achieve success and popularity as a Principal, what is his problem? Why should he try to belittle me every time? If he thinks that his English is very good then he is absolutely wrong. Moreover whatever he tries to say is never clear. He gives reference to the past and somehow tries to join the word teacher with that. Audience becomes impatient and starts removing the chairs and gossiping in the middle of his speech. But once he gets the microphone he never leaves it before half an hour. He forgets that each one of us has his or her own identity and individuality; we are all grown up adults and it is his duty to take care of our prestige and honour. But he prefers to behave like a typical elder brother who had once done the duty of a father. I felt so embarrassed one day when in front of Aaradhana, Sarita and Urja he told about me that he used to punish me by stripping me off my clothes and making me stand outside his room for hours together whenever I did anything wrong.

Sometimes I want to forget the present and go back to the past when there was no ego clash between us, when I felt protected under his caring arms, when even after rebukes and beatings from him there was no complaint in my mind against him. My wishes were fulfilled when for a few days we went on Europe tour with our respective spouse. The foreign soil of London, Belgium, Italy, France, Switzerland removed the barrier created between us and brought us very close to each other. We went back to our childhood and enjoyed the fortnight forgetting all tensions. But as soon as we came back from our foreign trip, Bhaiya again became a stranger to me. He again started contradicting and criticizing me and those fifteen days seemed to be a dream, not reality.

In another matter I do not agree with him that is his miserly nature. He tries to save money on petty things and proudly says – "I am the Head of the family. If children asks for Paneer or Kofta not being satisfied with Daal, Roti and Sabji I have to resist them. Every day they should not have Paneer or Kofta; once in a while I can allow that." He became furious when he came to know that snacks packets worth Rs. 14.00 were distributed to the participants during the Annual function. Aaradhana somehow convinced him and managed the situation. He will not say anything if his own people spend money lavishly. Last year his son-in-law spent twenty five lac in preparing posters, banners, etc., for publicity purpose. Everybody knows that it was not only publicity for the school but his self publicity also but Bade Bhaisahab remained silent since his own son-in-law was involved. Earlier also he had taken money from the school fund and misused it. We have second, third and many more sources of living. Because of that we are able to survive comfortably otherwise the fund would have become empty long back.

When I attended the seminar cum workshop on strategic leadership for CBSE Principals organized by Indian Institute of Management, Bangalore, paying the fees of Rs. 25,000, wrinkles appeared on his forehead. After attending the programme I felt empowered and enlightened. After coming back I shared my experience with him.

The Resource persons of the programme put more stress on analysis of the overall performances of the schools through self appraisal, student appraisal, peer appraisal, school appraisal etc. Training of teachers of various subjects is very important. Feedback should be taken from all corners and the weak points should be noted down. Multiple tools can be used such as G.D. Roleplay, Presentation, Feedback, Psycho Test, Desert Survival Strategies etc. Alumni meet should be held once a year. K.G.B. (Kill Good Brain) policy should be stopped in the educational institutions for smooth functioning.

Time management was given pivotal importance in which the following aspects were discussed (i) Priority (ii) Daily planner (iii) Learning from Experience (iv) Delegation (v) Taking 80 per cent of time and giving 20 per cent result and the reverse of this situation which is ideal.

Regarding effective meetings it was said that the agendas should be planned and circulated to the members in advance. Papers should be provided and a brief introduction should be given. Notes are to be taken. The leader should talk less and listen more and over commitment should be avoided.

The seminar threw light on the teachers' role in student assessment. Involvement of the teachers is required to fulfil every need of the students. Communication skill is very important to establish a good relationship between the teachers and students and also among the colleagues and members of the management. Group vision is more effective than individual vision. Everybody should be able to analyse own competencies, skills and capabilities. The teachers should respect each other, help each other and be open to any change.

Wearing different caps at different situations is an important feature of the administration. It means the administrator has to change his behaviour and communication skill as per the situation.

I continued – the National policy on Education gives pre-eminence to people's involvement which means involvement of parents, developmental agencies, employees, professionally competent teachers and representatives of financing bodies to the educational process at all levels. IT is also very important for its operational decisions in educational institutes like attendance analysis, grade information, student records, accounting, payroll, asset information etc. It makes administration very effective. Another important issue which was discussed in the seminar was empowering learners and teachers.

Listening up to this Bhaisahab said "Are we not following all these in our institution? I am not able to understand what is so unique about this seminar? Our system is the best; nobody can say anything against our system. I am really surprised that you have spent 25000 Rupees for attending this seminar!"

He seemed to be very upset. This is the problem with him. He thinks that he knows everything and there is nothing more to learn. Whatever is new and modern is not liked or accepted by him. The frog in the well thinks that the world is so big. It swims round and round the well. By chance if it can take a big leap it comes out of the well and then gets overwhelmed to see the real big world. Listening to the comments of Bhai Sahab and observing his annoyance I thought it would be better to suppress the fact that on the concluding day of the seminar, Amir Khan was invited as a guest lecturer. Bhaiya would have definitely said –"What is there to learn from a film star?" The same Bhai Sahab went to Lucknow to attend a seminar conducted by a famous school there, along with his younger son. Actually he feels insecure whenever he thinks that my image will suppress his image. I never wanted to be his rival. I just wanted to have my separate identity without damaging that of my brother.

So long I had a laptop which was the only one owned by somebody in the school. Recently Bhaiya has purchased one and not only that he has purchased one for Rashi so that she agrees to teach him. He is trying to keep pace with the fast moving time, I really appreciate that. But he does not want me and our other brothers to progress, but to remain under his control forever.

Initially we had only one and a half acre of land for our school campus. We managed to encroach two more acres by paying a lump sum to the land distribution and development authority. The owner of the land lost the case which he had framed against us. He neither got the money nor his land. Had he listened to our request, at least he would have got the price for his land. In front of the school building also, just by the side of the road there is a vacant plot which we are using for parking the vehicles. My eyes are on that vacant plot. We have already approached the owner but he refused to sell his plot. If ghee doesn't come out with the straight finger, then it has to be twisted. In this matter elder brother gives us full liberty. His image should remain clean. He will keep on preaching the messages of Gita, Mahabharat, Ramayana and we, particularly I have to take all notoriety. In order to open and run a school only knowledge is not sufficient. Along with that one must have money, courage, power, physical strength and support of the people. If you are too good, people will think you are too weak. Today's world is a big show business. The more you can show off, the more successful you will be. Without self-publicity no one can come to the limelight. Trivedi family is a familiar name today all over the state. Students come to our school from far away places. They stay in our hostels. They join our coaching classes. Is it because the standard of education is very high here? No, it is because they enjoy here, they enjoy full freedom. They can leave the hostel at any time to go and watch a movie or enjoy a dinner at a restaurant. They dance on the latest Bollywood numbers or hit western music on Annual Day and even the young teachers accompany them. The atmosphere is more like that of a college than a school. For the students of villages or small towns this is the most happening place. Getting admission in an Engineering College is not at all a problem. We have our own Engineering College. We want our students to get ranks below 9000/10000 in AIEEE or other competitive Exams so that instead of going to an ordinary college in some other State or city they would prefer staying at home and study in our college. In IIT also students get certain ranks which do not help them to get admission in any college but it helps us to claim that we have so many IIT qualifiers from our school. We know how to make things positive out of negative. When people see the photographs of those IIT qualifiers on the pages of our school magazine they think what a great school! These IIT qualifiers in the mean time either seek for admission in our Engineering College or wait for one more year to secure a better rank in IIT.

Each time I receive an award I feel guilty. Is it my achievement? What is my credit if a large number of students from our school participate in Science Olympiad? What is my credit when I donate a large amount for the membership of any organisation which gives an award in exchange of that money? My achievements are highlighted every year in the Annual Report read out by the students and shown in Power Point Presentation on the screen amidst a loud round of applause. I notice elder brother's expression at that time. His face looks stern and severe. He finds his God-Father image getting damaged before his younger brother. The next moment he climbs up on the stage and taking the microphone in his hand addresses the audience "My dear parents and students – long ago when God created men, he created role models who came to be known as teachers. These teachers were given the responsibility to shape human lives by preaching the young generation, by sharing their knowledge and values with them. But God's best creation, the teachers forgot God's wishes and became biased. The greatest Guru Dronacharya taught archery only to the children of the royal family. Poor Ekalavya was deprived of his teachings as he belonged to a poor family. When he learnt secretly which was found out by Dronacharya, Ekalavya had to pay the price by cutting his right thumb and offering to Drona. Was Drona an ideal teacher? No, he was the teacher of only the royal children. He was not for the Ekalavyas. In the modern time we find teachers who instead of building the careers of the students are more interested in building their own careers. Instead of wishing for the success of the students they are more interested in getting awards themselves. I appeal to the teachers – Neither be Dronacharya, nor be a self-centred teacher. Neither allow any Ekalavya to cut his thumb and offer you nor capitalise on the credit of the students and get yourself any award. Be a true teacher, give whatever you have and never expect anything in return. If you can teach even one Ekalavya and bring him to the mainstream I will bow my head before you. Thank you." I could not lift up my face in shame. Even a child could understand what he meant and whom he indicated.

How many Ekalavyas has he taught? How mercilessly he had turned down the request of a driver to give an opportunity to his meritorious son to study in the school ! The poor boy worked as a helper in one of our buses and learnt on his own standing outside the classroom. With the help of the teachers of the school that boy could pass class X Board examination and left his home for higher studies. Bhaisahab remained rigid and adamant in this matter till the end. May be he tried to trample down the memories of childhood by being inhuman towards the boy ! At the peak of success rarely one looks down at the foothill. Bhaisahab is trying his best to forget those days when one-fourth litre of milk or one single piece of gulabjamun was shared by five of us and wearing shoes to school was a luxurious dream. The future seemed to be dark, as dark as the black soot which covered the mud walls of our kitchen in our village home.

The present 21st century world is a world of showmanship. If you are internally involved and product centric, if you fail to acknowledge the changing external environment, the tastes and preferences of the customers you are sure to spell doom for your institution. Inward focus is the enemy of growth – one must know how to keep pace with the changing times.

Now a days I find my laptop to be the greatest technology tool. All information regarding my school are on my finger tips like the strength in each section, the number of students in each bus, the progress report of each and every child etc. Not only that, from the internet write ups on any topic are available; quotations on educations are available. These are of great use at the time of delivering a speech. All latest developments in the field of education are available to keep oneself abreast with the latest news. Who cares for originality? Take everything from the internet and sell it in the market in your name. Recently, Bade Bhaisahab also purchased one laptop. He doesn't have much use of it but he wants everybody to know that he is Computer Savvy. He requested Rashi to teach him the basic things and taking advantage of the situation Rashi managed a laptop for herself. Bhaisahab sends e-mail to me everyday with some philosophical quotations although we meet several times every day. Whatever internal clashes or difference of opinion we have, in the eyes of the outsiders we are a very united family where each member is ready to even sacrifice his or her life for the sake of others. Life is nothing but a drama where laughter and weeping are also part of acting.

Amidst all these Bhai Sahab always wants his image to be clean. He expects me to take all notoriety and be the most unscrupulous at the time of need. If somebody from the family does something wrong, he himself will not say anything but he would like me to deal with that person strictly. On 30th night after the Annual Day programmes were over, our nephews (sons of the second and third brothers) in a drunk condition went to a Dhaba at two a.m. and asked for food and drinks. When the Dhaba owner refused to serve at that time of night they started beating him. After sometimes they came back to school from the back gate and asked some more family members, mostly their cousins to join them. Together they purchased petrol, went back to the Dhaba, severely beat the Dhaba owner and burnt down the whole Dhaba into ashes. The Dhaba owner lodged FIR against them and the incident was covered by print media next day. By mistake one of them was reported to be my son. Bade Bhai Sahab, as usual remained quiet and time to time chanted the shlokas of Bhagwad Gita. I could not keep my cool. I know how difficult it is to build up a reputation but how easy it is to defame everything. I thrashed and scolded all of them. My second and third brothers stopped communicating with me as if I have done something wrong. They don't understand how people search for scandals in our family. We are no more ordinary now. We have to be very cautious. There are people like Veer Parsad who would definitely remark with a sarcastic smile – "Look here, they are the educationists. This is their background." Our own people are creating problems for us one after another. Sometimes I spend sleepless night thinking about the future. What will happen once Bade Bhai Sahab and I step down? One day we have to do so; we can't carry on forever! This huge edifice of learning with more than six thousand students, three hundred teachers, state-of-the-art infrastructure, everything will go to the hands of some greedy, power loving incompetent persons in whose vein our blood is flowing. As a cruel joke of time the game of construction and destruction goes on like this throughout eternity.

9

Something is Terribly Wrong Somewhere

Urja started from school for going to the University at 10.30 a.m. When she reached the counter and asked for a form for the convocation, the clerk flatly refused and said –"The last date is over Ma'am. I have got the order not to give any more form."

Urja said –"But I have'nt got any information. You have not sent any letter. Yesterday I rang up my guide and came to know."

The girl tried to stick to her point –"But Ma'am I have to obey orders. I can't give any more form. If you can get the permission of Arvind Shukla Sir then I will give you."

Urja wondered what is the value of Ph.D? For attending the convocation and obtaining the degree certificate a doctorate has to run from the pillar to the post. She searched for Arvind Shukla and met Mahesh, the assistant of her Ph.D. Guide sitting in a cabin. Recently he has been transferred from Social Science Department to Administrative Block. Neither he is happy in his new department nor is Urja's Guide happy to lose him. They had a perfect tuning taking care of each other. Moreover Mahesh was earning something extra there in the form of cash or kind every time there was a Ph.D. Viva or whenever somebody submitted his/her summary or thesis. In the Administrative Block he is new. There are veteran players who knew the field better than him.

Mahesh was happy to see Urja. He guided her to Arvindji. Urja with her Libran charm was able to convince Arvind and became successful in obtaining a form. She quickly filled it up and along with the fees of Rs. 650 submitted it to the counter. Mahesh had accompanied her there. She handed over a 50 Rupees note to Mahesh. Arvind told her –"Madam, you have to come for rehearsal on 16th at 10 a.m. Those who will not come for rehearsal will not be allowed to attend the convocation."

Urja thought again she has to approach Adarsh for half-day-leave.

Arvind continued - "You have to take your gown also for convocation for which you have to deposit Rs. 500 on 16th. You will get back the money at the time of returning it."

Adarsh was in his room, discussing with some family cum staff members regarding a short trip to Kanha forest. When he saw Urja he was delighted and asked – Ma'am are you interested to go to Kanha with us on Saturday?" Urja forgot for what she had come to meet him and said "Yes I will be very happy to join you", but the next moment she remembered that she had to go to the University on Saturday to collect her gown and also for the rehearsal. She said – "Sorry Sir, I have to go to the University because convocation is on 17th and there is a rehearsal on 16th. I can't accompany you."

Adarsh boastfully said – "Madam, why are you thinking about the convocation? You tell me, if you want I can arrange for a special convocation for you. The V.C. is in my pocket. If I ask him, he will give you the award specially in his room." Then his room vibrated with his loud guffaw.

Urja said – "It is a very prestigious function Sir. The Governor, the Chief Minister and other Ministers will come. I don't want to miss the function." "O.K. Madam, as you wish," he said. Urja told him that on Saturday she will attend the school till recess and came out of his room. Her long cherished dream of wearing the red gown of convocation, a sash and a cap with a tussel and receiving the award amidst a large number of spectators was going to materialise very soon.

On Saturday when Urja reached the University she found the distribution of gown had started. She stood in the queue to find out her name in the list. Her number was 43. She deposited the money and asked for the receipt. The clerk told her that it was not required. Her gown was handed over to her. She asked when was the rehearsal. One of the clerks said –"At 2 p.m. you have to come to the auditorium for rehearsal." "2 p.m. !" murmered Urja. What is to be done till then? Three hours were left. At 12 noon she went to the top floor of Kala Bhawan to meet her Guide Professor in her office. Some students were sitting there who told her that she had not yet come to the University. Her library card was also deposited. There was no other way but to sit in the car and wait till 2 p.m.

At 1.45 her driver Chandu told her – "Madam, I saw that Madam whom you used to meet."

"Where?"

"There in the auditorium. Just now she came by a car."

"O.K. let me have my tiffin. Then I will go to the auditorium. I will give you some money. You have a nice lunch from a hotel outside and then come back to this place and wait for me."

Urja knew that except samosa, pakoda etc. nothing is available at the University canteen. Why should the poor driver be deprived of his lunch because of her?

"Good afternoon Ma'am."

"Good Afternoon Urja, so, you have come for the rehearsal !"

"Yes Ma'am. I got my dress at 11 a.m. and since then I have been waiting. I went to your room also."

"Now a days it is difficult for any one to find me in my room. Because of the convocation we are moving around here and there, supervising the work. Come let's go inside. She took Urja inside and introduced her to some of her colleagues. Urja met some other students who also had come to attend the convocation. Urja thought how lucky they were to get the covetous degree at such a young age and how easy it was for them to obtain the degree without visiting any library or archive etc ! She heaved a sigh as she recollected the memories of visiting various places to collect information and data for her thesis. Her life was never a bed of roses.

At the end of the rehearsal Urja asked her Guide whether one person is allowed to enter the convocation hall to watch the programme. Her Guide said – "Invitation cards were distributed from the library. Yesterday I asked my colleagues there. They said not a single card is left."

Urja said – "In that case my husband will have to wait outside till the function is over."

"No, he can sit in the library and watch the live programme in the screen. Urja didn't feel like continuing the conversation further. The only person, who, like her shadow had helped her at every step while she was pursuing Ph.D., who accompanied her to different libraries at different places taking notes, getting that typed, encouraging Urja in every possible way will sit in the library watching Urja receiving the degree in a screen ! Why? Because the invitation cards were distributed to the Guests of Raj Bhawan, to the Principals of various colleges, to the freedom fighters, media persons, relatives of the employees of the University but not to the scholars who would be receiving the degree. Wonderful !!!

Next day at 12 noon she got a call from her Guide who instructed her to reach the University earlier and collect her (Guide's) card. She also told her to bring a sticker with the name and designation of her husband and stick it over her name in the card. Within half an hour Urja and her husband got ready and left for the University.

The convocation programme started exactly at 3 p.m. The procession comprising the V.C., the Registrar, the H.O.Ds of various departments, the Governor, the Chief Minister, the school Education Minister, the Higher Education Minister, the Leader of the Opposition party and an eminent Scientist who was to receive the Honorary D.Lit. award marched straight to the dais while all the recipients of degrees clad in Convocation gown remained standing in their honour. The tune of the National Anthem was played after which everybody took their place. The degree holders were administered oath before they were given their award certificates. Extending their right hands forward they had to take the pledge that throughout their lives they would follow the path of honesty, truthfulness, respect the country and worship parents as Gods and exhibit exemplary behaviour and conduct.

After the award ceremony one by one the V.C. and the honourable Guests spoke on the present Education system and the various reforms which can be implemented. The Vice Chancellor said that after a steady journey over a long period of 46 years the University has succeeded in achieving a grand stature in the realm of higher education and relentlessly benefiting the youths of not only this state but also the neighbouring sates. The university has also gone up in the stature that naturally comes through the alumni working on the high positions in India and abroad. He congratulated all the students who received their degrees at the convocation. He concluded his address with the hope that the students and scholars will use their knowledge and education in the service of the Nation and humanity through their resolute efforts, trurthfulness and honesty. They will be the new architects in the process of transformation, of developing India into one of the most developed and the mightiest nations of the world.

The great Scientist and a fellow of the Royal Society said – "We need to integrate education in the fields of Science, Engineering, Humanities and Social Science. Only then we would be able to educate adequate numbers of students to tackle enormous problems facing the nation and the world, e.g., environmental degradation, new sources of energy, food shortage, shelter, optimum utilisation of water resources, bio-terrorism etc. As highlighted by a task force of World Bank and UNESCO sometimes ago "without more and better education, developing countries will find it increasingly difficult to benefit from the global knowledge-based economy." We need a revolution in our educational system in order to meet the basic needs of food, healthcare, shelter and economic prosperity of our urban as well as rural population."

Quoting from Tolstoy, the Higher Education Minister said that people should feel proud of his workplace and his place of work also should feel proud of him. Until and unless we respect ourselves we will never get any respect from others. Self respect comes when we are totally devoted and dedicated towards our service. Educational institutes are the workshops for character building and dedication towards duty. Simply getting a degree or a gold medal is not sufficient. Students must remember that in their practical life also they have to deal with all problems and challenges with the same excellency.

The Chief Minister is a very good orator. He said – "At the end of anything there is a new beginning. The real and bigger challenge starts after getting the degree. Education is a continuous process and time to time it teaches us how ignorant we are and there is still so much to learn. Success is achieved by them who know how to keep pace with time. At the same time it is very much essential to follow the culture, tradition and values of India."

The Hon'ble Governor said – "Convocation provides an opportunity for self – introspection to an individual and also to an institution. It is an occasion to review the past and design your future. Unfortunately our education system, instead of becoming the driver for creating the new social and economic order, has remained outside the expanding social and economic systems. Our emerging society is fast moving towards a society of organisations where most of the administrators and organisers would need broader horizon of knowledge and vision with quest for rationality and search for human happiness. The question which needs to be asked is whether our existing rigid curriculum and lack of relevance of large number of degree courses being offered, would meet the needs of the students.

Teachers play a vital role in the process of quality assurance of higher education. University should provide congenial environment for the teachers to carry out research in their domain of interest that is relevant for the overall benefit of our society. Teachers are the managers of knowledge and knowledge comes from research. The research – enabled teachers are the best managers of knowledge. However, teachers alone cannot accomplish everything. Students are the fulcrums of our society. They have to be honest with their attitude, goal and orient themselves in such a way that teachers themselves will get motivated to acquire the latest and updated knowledge.

As a Nation, therefore, we should not just be producing qualified individuals who have little or no concern for the society and those who would pursue their personal gains as mercenaries without regard to others. Rather, we should provide a more holistic education, develop a more rounded personality with commitment to higher values, inculcate sensitivity for societal issues and develop their capabilities to address these issues. It is a collective responsibility of all of us as parents, educators and administrators."

The cultural programme was cancelled as the organising committee got the news of the demise of Shri Jyoti Basu, the former Chief Minister of West Bengal. The recipients of degrees and medals could not suppress their dissatisfaction at the announcement but were delighted at the next announcement of joining over tea and snacks which were arranged for all.

Urja came out of the auditorium with her husband and following the crowd came to the enclosure where tea was arranged. Some volunteers told them that only the guests of Raj Bhawan and Ministers will be served tea there. Others have to go to the Bio-Technology Deptt. Again following the crowd they landed up to a building which Urja could recognise within a short time. She had collected her gown from that building the previous day. She found many students were returning their gown. Urja thought of returning her gown before going for snacks and tea. In her attempt to do so she had a horrible experience.

The place was a living inferno with Ph.D. scholars and gold medalists pushing each other, shouting at the top of their voice. Urja could not understand where was the beginning or the end of the queue. All were standing in a scattered way and trying to reach the table where two clerks were taking back the gowns and returning Rs. 500 which they had taken as security money. After standing behind some scholars for about half an hour and being pushed hard by those standing behind her ultimately Urja reached the table. It was so difficult to stand there because of the constant pressure. One of the receiving clerks asked her "Madam which number was given to you?" Urja said – "At the time of taking the gown I got the number 43. But in the hall I got seat number 58. The clerk said – "You find out your number in this list." Urja saw both the numbers were given to some other persons. She tried to find out her name several times but couldn't. Her name was missing in the list. While she was searching for her name, the students and scholars standing behind her didn't show the courtesy to wait. They continued to push her, extending their hands holding their convocation gowns, impatient to return at the earliest grabbing Rs. 500/-. How many elbows hurt her, how many shoes trampled her feet, she could not understand and felt sick. She asked the clerk- "What shall I do? My name is not in the list. Yesterday I got the number 43 and today my seat number was 58. But in this list both the numbers have been given to some other persons." The clerk was too busy to listen to her. Urja found that 5/6 more persons faced the same problem. Their name were also not included in the list. It was totally a chaotic situation. Urja repeatedly requested the clerks to accept her gown but they refused. She asked whether she should take the gown home to which one of them replied "It's your wish" and the other said –"You go out of the room and let others return their gowns." Instead of helping her, those who were waiting behind, pushed her out.

Urja was sweating profusely and was totally exhausted when she came out of the room. Swapnil asked her what was the matter but she was too tired to explain. She told him to drive home. He asked – "Won't you have tea?" Urja replied – "Forget it."

While coming home Urja was thinking what was the wrong with the education system that provoked the Ph.D. scholars and gold medalists to behave like animals? How soon they forgot the oath they had taken in the convocation hall ! How soon they forgot the intellectual lectures delivered by the eminent personalities ! How soon they forgot they were educated and exposed their nails and teeth in a shameless way !!! After coming back home when she switched on the T.V. the news reader was narrating the horrible incident of the murder of two more Indian students in Australia. With this the number increased to twenty.

Urja took out the card of the photographer of the University from her purse and saw the address written was that of her own township. She called the photographer and asked him whether he would be available at home in the evening. She wanted to order for the photographs taken at the convocation hall. The photographer told her that he will be available at home in the evening. Urja went to his house with her husband to select and order for the photographs.

The photographer welcomed them and introduced them with his wife and daughter. Urja came to know that she is a student of her previous school. Her father very proudly said – "She remains within top ten rank holders and is scoring 95% and above."

Urja congratulated her and told her to keep it up. She came to know that her class teacher was Tulika who had once tried to instigate her to complain against Veer Parsad and Ranjita to Human Rights Commission.

The photographer Mr. Sunil Yadav said "Ranjita Ma'am is also doing Ph.D. Veer Parsad Sir will be retiring this year. She wants to be the Principal, so she is trying to complete her thesis very soon. R.D.C. is already over and six month's report also has been submitted. I carry everything to the University for her and also for Padma Ma'am. She is also doing Ph.D."

Urja wondered how without visiting the University and sending everything through this photographer both of them will manage Ph.D ! But there is nothing to be astonished. Veer Parsad, Ranjita and Padma – this trio could manage everything smoothly so far and this degree is just a child's play to them. After selecting the photographs when they were returning home, Swapnil asked Urja –"Have you understood why the photographer's daughter scores 95 per ent and above and remain within top 10 position holders? Her position is secured till your Ex Boss's wife gets the Ph.D.degree." Urja heaved a sigh. This degree will act as powerful weapons for both Ranjita and Padma to grab the position of Principal and Vice Principal respectively. How cleverly Veer Parsad had arranged the dice on the Chess Board. First of all keeping the position of the Vice Principal vacant for five years, instructing his wife to get the Masters Degree in English so that she could teach the subject in classes XI and XII, helping her to obtain the B.Ed. degree also, promoting her to the post of Vice Principal at that time when the school was not under the E.M.S., compelling the senior English teachers one after another to leave the school so that Ranjita could become the H.O.D. English and now this highest degree of Ph.D. sitting at home. Her seven year's experience as Vice Principal, five year's experience as H.O.D. English, Ph.D. degree all these will go in her favour to succeed Veer Parsad as the Principal. It will be difficult for the Education Management Society to appoint any other person who would be better than her in qualification and experience. People never come to know what happens behind the stage.

The one time typist Padma who is now the Administrative Officer will also step into the shoes of the Vice Principal in the same way. As now there are more than 150 schools under the Society, they have appointed Zonal Heads. The Zonal Head under whom Veer Parsad is working is in very good terms with him. Veer Parsad knows with whom to maintain cordial relationship and when. Just one signature of this Zonal Head will enable Ranjita to shift to Veer Parsad's office room and Padma to occupy the chair of Ranjita. The tears, curse, sighs of innumerable staff who were deprived of justice could not do any harm to them. The more the sound of suppressed cries and gagged protests will whirl around their edifice of learning, the more these three evil trio will cherish their success. There are two ways of achieving success which can be explained with the help of two lines. One line grows inch by inch steadily which is a symbol of success. Another line parallel to it can grow on its own without touching the first line. But it can grow also by wiping off the first line. Veer Parsad and his associates prefer the last option. Darwin's theory of the survival for the fittest may be applied in their case to some extent.

Motilal entered the Principal's room all of a sudden. As usual Adarsh, R.N.Mishra and Aaradhana stood up with spring action and rushed forward to touch his feet. Urja feels awkward in such situations. She said "Good Morning Sir" with full respect and when Motilal folded his palms she also folded her palms and said "Namaskar." Somehow, she doesn't like to touch anybody's feet in the workplace. Motilal asked Adarsh – "Have you explained the matter to Madam?"

Adarsh said –"Just now we were discussing that."

Motilal turned towards Urja and as if not being able to trust his brother repeated the same thing to Urja which Adarsh had already told her. "You have to take charge of the publishing house which we are going to set up. From each department at least one Sample Paper should be prepared by the teachers which will be given to the students at a low price. We are not going to make any profit but the expenditure has to be recovered. You will coordinate with the teachers of your department as well as the teachers of other departments also so that we can get at least two books from each department before Half-Yearly Examination in the coming session."

Urja said – "Yes Sir, I will be glad to take charge of the Publishing House." Next day she called a meeting of the English teachers. "Let me start with my department" she told herself. "Good Morning teachers, please take your chair."

The teachers with anxiety written all over their face were eager to know why she had called them. Urja said – "You will be happy to know that the school is going to set up a Publishing House in the coming session. From each department teachers have to prepare atleast two Sample Papers. There are five to six teachers taking a particular class. You have to distribute among yourselves the lessons, drama, poetry etc. which are taught in each class and prepare a number of questions both solved as well as unsolved. You have to prepare questions from Reading, Writing and Grammar sections as well."

Like the change in the formation of clouds in the sky, Urja observed the change of expression in the face of the teachers. From anxiety the expressions changed into utter dissatisfaction and irritation. They said – "Madam, we are over-burdened with correction work. Bundles of papers we have to check and after that again invigilation duty, correction of Annual Exam papers, preparation of mark sheets, report cards etc. We are not free even for a minute."

Urja said – "That is a part of our duty. But we have to accept any challenge and prove ourselves in every new field."

One of them asked – "Madam what is the Management going to do with the Sample Papers?"

Urja said – "They will be given to the students at nominal price. Instead of buying the guide books from outside they will read the answers prepared by us. They will practise the papers which we are going to prepare."

They discussed for some time and Urja was able to convince them. She distributed the chapters and told them to prepare at least two sets of questions each from the Reading, Writing and Grammar sections – one solved and one unsolved. When they understood that the burden would not be too heavy on them and their H.O.D. will also prepare questions they switched over to a lighter mood.

One Bengali teacher whose son is studying in Urja's previous school said – Madam, just imagine there are about 60 – 65 students in each section and in each class there are 12 – 13 sections. These books will be sold not only to the students of this school but to other branches also. When a large number of books are printed, the printing charge is very less. Even after paying the employees of the Publishing House they will make huge profit, however nominal the cost of the books are." This thought had come to Urja's mind also but the joy of creation always dominates her mind and she was not bothered at all how much profit the Management was going to make, exploiting the talent and energy of the teachers.

She told the teacher – "You need not think or discuss all such things. Think how much our students will be benefited. That will be our reward. Moreover, you will love to see your name in print on the cover of the books."

At last smile appeared on all the faces.

"I am giving you two weeks time. By fifteenth you have to submit the complete grammar portion of classes IX, X, XI and XII."

"O.K. Ma'am," they said in unison and left the room.

Urja started thinking – people are no more fools. They have understood that one class of people are working hard and another class of people are simply making money, capitalising on their hard work. That's why day by day people are losing interest in work. A teacher's job is no more confined to class room teaching and correction of copies. The authority expects many things which the teachers of the 20th century could not even dream of. As the big industries and business houses are going for diversification, in the same way the private schools are also going for diversification. Tuition fee is not the only source of income; there are various other sources also.

When a fresher first joins a school, initially he or she works very hard in order to become permanent. As soon as the person becomes permanent for the first time he or she expresses her views against the system. PRTs start thinking that they deserve TGT posts. TGTs think they are victim of injustice because they are in no way less than the PGTs. The PGTs think they deserve administrative posts. The administrators think they also have the capability to open a school and be the employers instead of the employees. Among the employers also there is a competition regarding who is more efficient as a boss. Bottom to top no one is happy and the famous quote "Work is Worship" sounds more like a joke than anything else.

Recently one more thing can be observed in the society. The neo-rich class are opening schools in order to come to the limelight. Simply money can not fetch them name, fame and prestige in the society. But overnight they can gain power and honour both if they somehow get connected to the field of education and the best way is to open a school or a college. Urja remembers the previous CM of the State had given green signal to 200 illegal colleges and when more than one lakh students paid huge admission fee through their nose, one fine morning by the order of the High Court those colleges were closed. The owners of such colleges vanished in the thin air with the money, permanently dooming the future of a large number of students. The Ex CM's secret account however overflowed with money.

Urja was surprised to see one of her Ex colleagues from her previous school in her drawing room when she came down from the first floor. She had given time to Prasansha, her student to come and clear her doubts before her Pre-Board Exam. Jolly, her ex-colleague started sobbing as soon as she came to the room. Urja understood that something must have been terribly wrong with her daughter and tried to console her.

Jolly managed to say while sobbing – "Madam, I'm no more able to tolerate. I've lost all my patience. I have been spending sleepless nights at home. I want to take rest in your home for some time."

Urja said – "You are most welcome. You take rest and please be cool. Let me first attend my student then I will listen to you."

After guiding Prasansha how to attempt her Board papers and explaining the important passages and lines from the lessons and poems, ultimately when Urja became free she told Jolly – "Now tell me what is your problem? But before that I must tell you one thing – never show your weakness in any matter before the students. They will lose faith in you and moreover they will discuss the matter with their parents or peer group and ruin your image. I can guess why you are worried so much and if we discuss the matter we will be able to find out some solutions."

Jolly said – "Rupali, my daughter is becoming arrogant day by day. Because of her obstinacy and rude behaviour my husband is falling sick. Last week he was admitted to the hospital."

"But Rupali is a very good girl. She came second in the whole state in class X Board Exam. So far I know she doesn't have any diversion also," Urja said in her favour.

"Madam, if you see her now, you'll find that she has absolutely changed. She spoilt her XII Board Exam joining FIITJEE classes. In competitive exams also she could not do well. In fact she had lost all interest in studies. She got a chance in BITs Pillani Deogharh branch. We spent so much money for her admission but after six months she came back. She wants to try again in IIT and AIEEE but simply she is sitting at home and chatting with her friends either through net or over phone. If we say something she reacts in such a way as if we are her enemies."

Urja said – "Don't worry. That phase comes to almost every student more or less. It's a matter of time only. She has her own worries and on top of that if you make her feel that you are worried for her she will react more. Just for a few months stop giving her any advice and let her do whatever she thinks best for herself."

Jolly said – "She has developed this idea that I discuss about her with everybody and degrade her in the eyes of people. Urja said "something must have happened which she is not able to share with anyone. Since you are scolding her she is not able to have confidence in you. If you behave with her in a friendly way she will trust you and share her problems with you."

All of a sudden the bell rang. When Urja opened the door she saw Rupali standing outside. As if nothing has happened, in a very normal tone Urja called her inside and asked her to sit. She was looking suspiciously at her mother. Urja winked at Jolly and she also behaved normally with Rupali.

Urja said – "Deogharh is a boring place and you have taken the right decision to sit for the competitive exams again. May be you were tensed last time and became nervous. But this time surely you will get a good rank."

Rupali said – "Let's see."

Urja diverted her attention towards the latest films she had seen and the latest books she had read. Luckily Rupali's favourite chocolate cake was there at home. Rupali relished her own piece and took a big bite from Jolly's piece of cake too. Children are children after all, thought Urja; the complications of the adult world make them confused and they turn hostile towards everybody.

Rupali left before Jolly in her own two-wheeler. She told Jolly to come home soon as she wanted to go somewhere. Jolly stopped near the gate and told Urja – "See, she had come to spy on me, she wanted to know whether I was telling you anything about her."

Urja said "Inspite of everything you have to keep your cool."

Jolly continued "Madam you don't know how argumentative she has become. If we tell her anything she starts gulping down all sorts of medicines available at home."

Urja said "It's just a temporary phase and she will again go back to normalcy as soon as she gets admission in a good college."

When Jolly left, Urja thought counselling is required not only for the students but also for the parents. Both the mother and the daughter have lost their mental peace. They are so much traumatised and if one looks back, it all started with the wicked acts of Ranjita, who, in order to harass Jolly, had accused her daughter of being involved in a love affair with one of her classmates. It was a sheer lie but some of her classmates and even the teachers were compelled to write reports against Rupali. The poor girl had to face a lot of humiliations and after producing an outstanding result in class X Board Exam she preferred to change the school. That incident, however left a deep impact in her mind. She became arrogant, obstinate and lost interest in studies. The more her parents became concerned about her the more she became rebellious. That bitch Ranjita is responsible for this change in the girl.

In order to show her power and for terrorising people to establish her authority she has ruined the career of many teachers and students. Suddenly the face of Ranjita flashed before the eyes of Urja – the typical face of a vampire with sharp canines and blood dripping from the cruel lips, smiling cunningly, rocking in the chair in which Veer Parsad has been sitting and ruling for fourteen years. Like a cancerous growth in the body this unscrupulous couple is growing in the society, poisoning it with their venomous spite. Cancer is uncurable. If it is removed from one part of the body it occurs again at some other part. Veer

Parsad and Ranjita will remain, dominate and spread poison like cancer. Urja felt there was no light at the end of the tunnel as it was a blind one.

* * * * * * * * *

Students of class XI came to Urja's room with a big, hand-made invitation card. They wanted to arrange a fare-well party for class XII. Urja asked about the programme. The Vice Head Boy said Madam, the programme will start at 4 '0 clock in the evening. Urja said – "The programme should be as short as possible."

Vivek said – "We have kept two speeches – one of the Director Sir and the other of the Principal Sir. Then there will be two dances, a few group songs, one or two games and we will ask the students of class XII to speak something if they wish. Principal Sir has told us to continue with the programme till 7 p.m. After that there will be high tea."

Urja has become accustomed to the culture of the new school. She thought – "however hard I try I will never be able to change the culture because the school authority is in favour of it."

The farewell party was fixed on 30th January. In the evening when Urja came to school she couldn't find any teacher. Only the organising students were present. Urja came to the Principal's room where the other Vice Principal R.N. Mishra was also present. Adarsh was lying on the sofa, covering himself with his coat. They had ordered Dosa which was served on the centre-table. Urja hesitated to enter the room. Adarsh in his booming voice called her – "Madam, please come and have your seat. Actually we didn't go home for lunch today as we were busy preparing the documents for the inspection of the Newtown school which is due on 1st February."

They finished their Dosa while Urja was sitting there. One by one the other family members started coming. The son-in-law of the Director had ordered for 25000 saplings to be planted overnight to create some greenery in the new school compound. The Head Accountant who is also the one and only brother-in-law of Adarsh refused to pass the bill for the saplings. He said – "You better get it sanctioned by your father-in-law. I will be scolded later on if I pass the bill." Urja wondered whether really 25000 saplings were supplied or not!

At quarter-to-five Adarsh asked if the other staff members had come or not? They all came out of the room. Very few staff members were present. Students were still pouring in. The boys were dressed in Jeans and fashionable jackets; the girls were clad in transparent saris and sleeve-less deep cut blouse, revealing their naval area and almost half of their breasts. When they were bending down to touch the feet of the Director and the Principal except the tits the full breasts were exposed. From the back side the hips were exposed till the parting line which were adorned with sleek chains and lockets. The Director said – "These girls are either unaware of the fact that they are revealing their body or they are doing it intentionally. In the hostel also sometimes I feel uneasy when they come near me, not properly dressed. May be I am backdated and traditional."

Everybody kept quiet as he continued again – "We only told them that the dress code should be Sari so that they can come in a decent way. But it's really shocking how they are presenting themselves."

Urja said – "I'm surprised to see that they are wearing sari. Now-a-days girls don't wear sari. From where did they manage the saris and the blouses so soon?"

Adarsh said – "That was not a problem at all. They purchased the saris from our own boutique and we got the blouses stitched by our own tailors.

Urja remembered Adarsh's eldest daughter-in-law owns a boutique. So, they managed to do some business from the farewell party also!

At five p.m. Urja became impatient and told some of the students of class XI – "You must go to the hall and tell the organizers to start the programme and they should come and call the Director Sir and the Principal Sir."

After ten minutes the Vice Head Boy and the Vice Head Girl came to call the Executives. Urja noticed still students were coming in large numbers.

When they entered the hall there was utter pandemonium. The announcer was trying his best to make some announcements but his voice could not be heard because of the cacophony and pulling of chairs. The Director asked for a microphone and instructed the students to keep quiet but nobody bothered to listen to him. Aaradhana went back to control the students but she came back unsuccessful. The announcer invited the Director to speak a few words of wisdom and give his blessings. He went up on the stage and for about half an hour spoke on values, giving instances from Ramayana and Mahabharata. The more he spoke about values the more the students shouted and whistled loudly. When he came back to his seat he was sweating profusely.

Next was the Principal's turn. When he went to the podium and addressed the gathering, students started shifting their chairs, making room for the late comers. The Director told Urja – "I am not able to understand why the students are behaving in this derogatory manner today! What message will go outside? Is it my mistake to allow them to arrange such things? I wanted them to be free from stage fear and be smart."

Urja thought "they have become over-smart; they can buy you in one market and sell you in another. You have dug the pit for yourself."

The Director said – "There is no place for values at all."

To this Urja agreed – "Yes Sir, those who try to follow the values are being mocked by others. They are considered fools."

Adarsh was standing on the dais for about ten minutes. Ultimately when the students stopped making sound with the chairs he started:

"Dear students, it's a very emotional moment. We have the pain of parting with you but at the same time we are happy that very soon you will be facing a more challenging world and deal with it without our help. Director Sir spoke to you about values; try to remember his words. I would now like to narrate a story, may be you have read it somewhere. A man had deep faith in God. He believed that nothing harmful can ever happen to him because God is there to save him. Once there was a flood in his village. When the water level started rising, a jeep was sent from the nearby city to pick up the stranded people. But he refused to go. Then after sometimes a truck came there to save people but the man said that God will help him and refused to go. The water level started increasing farther. A boat appeared and the man was asked to go but he again refused thinking God will save his life. As the water level started increasing very fast he climbed upto the roof of his house and there came a helicopter. The pilot told the man to board the helicopter but this time also he refused to do so. Ultimately his house drowned under water and he died. After his death when he went to heaven he was very angry with God. He asked him – "Why didn't you save my life, God?"

God said – "I tried to save your life four times but you refused to take my help. Who do you think had sent the jeep, the truck, the boat and the helicopter?" So my dear students we have also taken tests throughout the year. We have taken pre-model and model tests in which many of you have failed. So you know where you stand. Don't say later on that we have not helped you. We have helped you and warned you several times but it is up to you how much you could take from us. I bless you from my heart, all the best."

Saying this he came down from the stage. Again a lot of whistling sound came from the audience and this time a new type of sound – "Lakka laka, laka, laka – Huu, haa, huu, haa" was repeated thrice. Urja remembered the students of class XII used to cheer up the basketball players at the time of CBSE Cluster XI Basketball tournament, in the same way.

Students were waiting for the speeches to get over. A big cake was brought and kept at the centre of the stage which was cut by the Director in presence of the Executives and teachers. That took another ten minutes. Then started the much awaited cultural programme with Western Dances, Remix Dances and songs. When the class XII students were asked to speak about their experience in the school only very few of them spoke reminiscing the school days.

The next item was giving some conditions and whosoever could fulfil that condition became eligible for a prize. Then titles were called out and students were asked to guess who was the owner of the respective title. That person was also called on the stage and was given a badge by the hands of teachers. Some of the titles given were Mr. and Ms. Attitude, Mr. and Ms. Book Worm, Mr. and

Ms. Best Smile, Mr. and Ms. Notorious, Mr. and Ms. Sportsperson, Mr. and Ms. Eve, the Best Group, the Best Student etc. After giving the badge to the Best students (as per the decision of class XI) the Principal went to the podium and from there he said "I can not control myself from saying "Lakka, laka, laka, laka." Prompt came the reply "Huu, Haa, Huu, Haa."

Urja was requested to honour a student with a badge and after that she was asked to share her feelings. Urja took the microphone in her hand and said – "My dear students, I don't want to deliver a long lecture because I believe action speaks louder than words. I bless you whole heartedly for your Board Examination as well as for all your future endeavours. Today for the last time you have assembled here. You are enjoying the evening. We are happy to see your smiling faces. But one thing we all have forgotten that is today is 30th January– the Martyrs Day. In 1948, on this day the Father of our Nation Mahatma Gandhi was assassinated. Let us all stand up to pay our homage to him and maintain silence for just one minute." Everybody stood up and there was pin-drop silence in the auditorium. After one minute Urja said "Thank you" and came back to her seat. She left the function at 7 p.m. without waiting for tea and snacks.

There was tension in the air and everybody seemed to be busy. The inspection for the new school date was fixed on 1st February and a lot of false documents were to be prepared like Teacher's pay list, service book, papers of the land, papers of the Registration of Society, audit papers, balance – sheet etc. The school so long was running as a Hindi medium State Board school which was going to be converted to CBSE English medium school. The land was a disputed one. The construction was illegal. The school was not registered under the Educational Society. Not a single document was ready. The Principal asked R.N. Mishra to use the documents of the main school, including staff list etc. Some staff members were sent there for a temporary period.

The two persons who were coming for inspection were the Principals of Navodaya School and D.A. V. School of Orissa. Among them one reached the school three days earlier. His boarding and lodging arrangement was done in the rest room of the Director but most probably the big portraits of the divine figures from Ramayana and Mahabharat made him feel uneasy and he refused to stay there. He said that he was a chain smoker and a non-vegetarian, so, it would not be possible for him to stay in the school premises. He would prefer staying at the hotel. Adarsh told R.N. Mishra to arrange for his stay in a 4 – star hotel nearby.

On the first day when R.N. Mishra met the gentleman in his hotel room and discussed about the inspection which was fixed on 1st, he asked the latter to keep ready a lot of document papers. When Adarsh came to know this he gestured at R.N. Mishra to hint the person that he will be paid his due for which he need not bother at all. The other person came on the day of inspection.

They were taken to the venue from the hotel. They were astonished to see the infrastructure and the staff (nothing belonged to that school of course) in a school with only 225 students on roll. The students got their first lesson of telling lies as they pretented to be the students of that school. The inspection committee members were highly satisfied with the hospitality of the school management. The deal was done; the crispy notes added warmth to their pockets in the chilly, winter morning. They enjoyed a sumptuous lunch and when they were asked whether dinner should be packed for them each one of them asked to pack dinner not only for themselves but for their family also and took the bills to produce them in their respective school for reimbursement without paying a single penny. It will be an exaggeration to say that the school got affiliation for classes upto IX even before a single child got admission in the school.

The school management was quite hopeful that in the first year they will be getting atleast 600 students. Staff members were sent regularly to give an impression to the parents that already a large number of students have taken admission. Pamphlets were distributed in the township and nearby places. Personal letter assuring people of quality education and bright future of their children were sent to every house. However nobody could know what happened to those 25000 saplings which were supposed to enhance the beauty of the vicinity, adding greenery to the environment.

Adarsh asked Urja one morning "Madam, are you interested to meet the Chairman of CBSE? Urja promptly said "Yes" without knowing when, where and how! Adarsh cleared her doubts, saying "He is coming to a school as the Chief Guest of their Annual function. This school is about 100 kms. from here. Let us start now so that we can attend the conference where he will be answering to all the querries of the Principals." Urja thought whether to go home first and change her dress but there was no time. She handed over the house-key to her driver and was prepared for the day. R.N. Mishra and Sarita also accompanied them. When they reached the school, they found Director's younger son had already reached there.

When Adarsh entered the conference room with a big bouquet and a battalion behind him twenty pairs of eyes looked at them while the Chairman continued with his answer to some querries of the Principals already present there. Urja noticed the big, rounded up eyes of Veer Parsad glaring at her while the extra chairs were placed for them.

The Chairman seemed to be a very simple person, thin and puny but very confident as he answered all the questions asked by the Principals regarding the new Grading system to be followed in classes IX and X. When the session was over, the Chairman was taken to the school library where the students wanted to interview him. Before he left the room Adarsh presented him with the bouquet and introduced his team members to the Chairman. Veer Parsad was asked to propose the Vote of Thanks.

When the Chairman left the room, others remained there interacting with each other. Adarsh asked the owner of the school "How do you manage to bring people of high profile to your school ? It's a new school only, started hardly three years ago but already filmstars, cricket players, educationists have visited !"

He smiled mysteriously and said "guess"!

Veer Parsad and Adarsh glanced at each other. This man, one Mr. Arora is a businessman, who manufactures tubewells, handpumps etc. His education is limited to school only as he could not enter the premises of any college, being pressurised by his father to join the family business. But that didn't prevent him to open a number of schools in the village areas, appointing qualified teachers, paying them huge remunerations. But in spite of everything, out of 10 students from his school in the first batch of AISSE, only 3 passed. Being a practical man he said "Result depends upon the quality and background of the students to a great extent. Here, I am providing the students with excellent infrastructure and qualified teachers but mostly they come from agriculturist families. Their family background is a big barrier in their path of being educated." Veer Parsad with a stern face (most probably he remembered his background) said – "I don't agree with you. Now a days good teachers are rarely available. Even after paying a covetous salary, you can't get good teachers." In order to lighten the situation Adarsh said – "I am training the teachers and Mr. Veer Parsad is alluring them with a fat pay – packet and snatching them from me, Ha, ha, ha…" Veer Parsad had a quick glance at Urja but remained silent with a smiling face.

When the interview of the Chairman by the students was over, everybody was called to join the Chairman for the inauguration of a new building and plantation followed by lunch. Urja suppressed her laughter with great difficulty when she noticed there was a competition between Adarsh and Veer Parsad to stay nearest to the Chairman. When they sat for the lunch, Veer Parsad managed the seat next to that of the Chairman.

After lunch the Chairman was taken to the stage for prize distribution. Veer Parsad followed him there and whispering something into his ears left the place in a hurry. After half an hour when Adarsh took leave of the Chairman and the owner of the school, Urja was happy as she had a lot of things to do including packing of bags and suitcases for visiting Calcutta and Delhi to attend the 5th birthday of the adopted daughter of her brother-in-law and the first birthday of her grandson Maharaj.

10

Lessons Life Taught Urja

What a wonderful book is The "White Tiger" written by Arvind Adiga ! It's absolutely true what the author has written about the creatures of darkness, about their exploitations and strong desire to take revenge on their exploiters. But isn't it true in case of the educated middle class also, who remain slave to their employers and bosses throughout their life in spite of their education, talent and potential?

Now-a-days, whenever I read a book, I keep on thinking about it and try to relate myself to the characters and situations of the story. Somehow I find a link between me and all exploited, rebellious characters who are different. Urja Sen is also a white tigress who quite often thinks of smashing the head of Ranjita and other vulturous women who are barriers on the way to her progress but can not do that because she is not a creature of darkness. She is an educated lady of the enlightened world where it is wiser to hide feelings. I keep on assuring myself with the moral of the triumph of good over evil – "Urja, never lose hope. That day will come when your exploiters will live at your mercy," although in my heart of hearts I know that will never be possible. If at all I come to the top, these people, by that time will be completing their tenure and basking on the success they had achieved, live a peaceful relaxed life, or I may be far away from them. Happy endings happen only in Fairy-Tales.

Sometimes I think who are the real enemies of mankind, of the world and the society? The people who are making money, sucking the blood of the poor or the rebels like the Maoists, Naxals, terrorists who are ruthlessly killing innocent people and damaging National property in order to terrorise, God knows whom? Because I think their target is wrong; their method is wrong and they are also puppets in the hands of the dirty industrialists and politicians. They are neither able to kill the corrupt rich who are sinking under blackmoney, nor able to change the life of the poor who live below the poverty line. Poor people suffer from both sides – on the one hand by their rich and dishonest exploiters, on the other hand by the terrorists, losing their lives due to their destructive actions. The backward people have been taught how to prepare bombs, how to blow up railway tracks, how to cause explosions but they were not taught how to read and write, how to start small scale industries and be self-independent. All the 'isms' are a failure. Everything is going terribly wrong but everything is still going on, the world has not come to an end because of the existence of God. But why is God there for everybody even for a criminal? The red vermilion mark on the forehead of Veer Parsad every Tuesday, the chanting of prayers in the school temple of Motilal, the performing of pooja every now and then in the school premises of both my previous and present school and sitting of Ranjita there and ladies of the Trivedi family here covering their head with the pallu of their sari – all these seem to be farce to me because I know to what extent each one of them is dishonest. But God is not blind, he can see everything, then why does he accept the pooja of these dishonest people? Or is it true that God helps only those who help themselves?

Veer Parsad's greatest competitor, the Principal of the other school under the same Educational Society arranged a gala party at the only water resort of the township to celebrate the wedding ceremony of her son. Almost all staff members of both the schools were present there. When my husband and I were about to climb up the stage to congratulate and bless the newly married couple I saw Veer Parsad and Ranjita standing just by our side. After the exchange of formal greetings when I tried to avoid them and moved away from the place, Veer Parsad started following me everywhere and tried to keep the conversation alive by asking silly questions. Ranjita's face was worth seeing – it was just like the dark clouds of July. My colleagues later on said "Veer Parsad is still dying for you." Let him die, how does it matter to me?

As soon as the new session started, there was a notice from the Collector's office to close down the schools due to excessive heat and shortage of water. Children shouted in joy when they came to know about this unexpected holidays but teachers made a long face as they were supposed to come. For Executives there is no summer vacation. Last year I requested the Principal to grant at least ten days vacation leave to the Executives to which he agreed but reduced the E.L. from ten to five. This year when I applied for the vacation-leave (V.L.) he said "You keep your application with me; later on I will decide but don't worry. I will do something."

Next day when I was about to sign in the Attendance Register, I saw somebody has marked L (Leave) for fifteen days against my name. Immediately I reported the matter to the Principal. He smiled and said – "It has been done at my instructions. I was puzzled but remained silent because among all members of Trivedi family, if at all I trust any one, he is the Principal Adarsh.

After two days the Principal told me "Madam, I will give you a very important work. You have to go to the CBSE Office in Delhi and follow up the case of affiliation of our new school."

I said "O.K. Sir, I am going to Delhi to stay with my children and grandchild. That's why I have taken leave for fifteen days. I will go to CBSE Office and do the work."

He said – "If you can bring the affiliation order then I will show 'On Duty (O.D.) in place of L in the Attendance Register. Moreover you will get to and fro railway fare for A.C. 2nd Class, 15 days T.A., D.A. and other expenses. But you have to get the work done." Some more family members of the Trivedis were present in the room. The sarcastic expression in their face told me that they had no faith in my ability and efficiency or atleast they tried to ignore me inspite of knowing my capability.

It was a real challenge to me. I said –"So far I know the affiliation order is not given by hand."

Anandlal said –"Even if they assure you and a positive reply comes in my mailbox then also I will keep my promise." I said "I'll try my best Sir."

Going to Delhi is always a matter of immense joy to me. After a gap of two and a half months I will see Maharaj – my grandson. There is nothing precious to me in this world like the smile of Maharaj showing his four tiny teeth. Incidentally it was Mothers' Day when we reached Delhi. My elder son received us at the station and I was given a special welcome by Niti, my elder daughter-in-law. Their gift of a small purse and a small cake for me to cut touched my mind. Now-a-days atleast 80 per cent of the parents are self independent. They do not expect financial support from their children. Just a gesture of love and care is all they need. But somehow I feel there is something wrong in the modern education system which teaches children to be selfish and self centred. They are always so engrossed with their own life, future and career, they have neither any time nor any concern for the parents. Respect is a word of the past century. Children now a days do not know the importance of relationship.

Preet Vihar is not very far from my son's house. When I reached there the driver could easily locate the CBSE office. I told him to wait and went inside. When I approached the Receptionist and said that I wanted to go to the Affiliation section, I was told to wait as a gate-pass was to be prepared. After waiting for about one and a half hour, I got the gate pass and went to the first floor to meet the Director-Affiliation. When I gave him the reference number and told him that inspection of the school was done in the month of February but after that we haven't got any information regarding affiliation, he opened the internet and took out the print out of a letter mentioning about some deficiencies on the basis of the report given by the Inspection team. The deficiencies were:

1. The school is required to complete the construction work first within a stipulated period and the completion certificate of construction work should be submitted to CBSE Office.

2. As per the report of the Inspection Committee the school has 10 sections against 8 classrooms. Therefore, the school is required to submit the clarification for the same and further more classrooms should be increased.

3. Teachers should have adequate qualifications with main and elective subjects specially T.G.T.

4. As per details of enrollment of students of the school, optimum limit is not maintained in all classes. Hence section-wise enrollment of students may be restricted with optimum number of 40 students per section.

5. The school is required to pay salary, DA and other admissible allowances to staff at par with the corresponding categories of employees working in the State Government schools. Also salary to be disbursed through a bank against single cheque issued in favour of the Bank.

The Director (Affiliation) told me that definite compliance of removal of deficiencies should be sent immediately otherwise the application cannot be processed further.

In the letter it was also mentioned "It is further informed that school should not start classes under CBSE pattern (IX/X) without grant of affiliation by the Board otherwise the Board will not be responsible for consequences arising out of it." I tried to impress him by saying that the school was originally a Hindi medium State Board School where students of very poor families, whose parents are not educated, study. We want to impart quality education with subsidised fees to these children. Without affiliation the parents are not able to trust the school authority. After requesting him to consider our case and thanking him for giving me so much time when I came out of the office it was 1.30 p.m. I immediately called Adarsh and informed him everything and told him that I will be sending him the letter through fax at that moment. After sending it I confirmed whether he has got it or not. He got the letter and told me to SMS the address of my son. He would send the reply through Speed Post.

On my way home the car stopped at an odd place due to some technical problems. The driver said that it will not move and told me to go by an auto. For half an hour I had to wait on the road under the scorching summer sun and ultimately when I boarded an auto my tongue was dried from the tip to the end in thirst and I felt as if somebody had placed a sand-paper in my mouth. The water in the bottle which I carried became hot and tasteless and could not help much. When I reached my son's flat on the top floor of a four–storeyed building in Vasundhara Enclave, not a single drop of energy was left in me. When Neha opened the door and Maharaj with a scream of joy rushed towards me with his stumbling feet, I forgot all physical discomfort and exhaustion.

It took three days for the letter to reach my son's letter box. In between I spoke to the Principal twice. He had gone through the letter and used abusive words against the Inspection team members – "Those sister-fuckers had been given 2 lac as a bribe. They were well fed in a five star hotel and given VIP treatment, still they have given negative report."

He further told me – "Madam, don't hesitate to offer money to the officers in the Affiliation department. I am ready to give them any amount." Now this was really difficult for me because I didn't know how to approach people to offer bribe. After getting the reply letter I rang him up again. At one point I had a doubt. While showing the details of enrollment of students section-wise, they have mentioned about 32 students in class IX also, whereas it is clearly written in the letter of CBSE that without affiliation no school can start class IX. When I discussed this matter with the Principal he said – "No problem, it's a well-known fact that every school starts class IX before getting affiliation."

The results of AISSCE of Ajmer, Chennai and Panchkula region were out next day. I could understand that people will be awefully busy there in CBSE office. So leaving that day, next day again I went to the affiliation section along with the compliance letter. This time the Director was very busy in a meeting so I was asked to meet the Asstt. Affiliation Officer. He is a nice gentleman who read the letter but as I had feared he pointed out the number of students in class IX and asked me – "At present till which class are you running the school?"

I said "Upto class VIII."

"Then why is it mentioned here that there are 32 students in class IX?" he asked.

I was ready with my reply.

I said – "They are the old students of the Hindi medium school who passed class VIII. They want to continue in this new English medium school with the hope of getting better education. They have enrolled but we have not yet started class IX. So they are waiting for admission as soon as affiliation is received." He said – "Then you please write here the same thing and put your signature."

I did the same thing. He further asked – "Who is the Principal of this school?"

I took the name of Mr. R.N. Mishra which is another lie. In fact there is no Principal of that school till date. I congratulated myself for telling lies. After all I have learnt something from Trivedi family. All of a sudden I remembered the Principal had told me to offer bribe. Adding ten kilos of sugar in my smile, very politely with a very innocent face I asked him "Is there anything else Sir, which we can do for you? Our Principal Sir said he will be obliged to do anything for you. You can tell me Sir if there is any other requirement."

With a red, smiling face he said – "No Ma'am, nothing else is required. I am forwarding the letter to the Director and the CBSE Chairman. Very soon you will get the affiliation."

I said – "Sir my Principal has told me to collect the affiliation order. I request you to give it to me personally."

He said – "We never give affiliation by hand. But I am assuring you within 3 weeks you will get the affiliation."

I thanked him repeatedly and came out. Sitting in the hired car I rang up the Principal and informed him everything including the mistake of mentioning about number of students in class IX and my reply to that. He was very much pleased and said – "Well done ! you have done a good job. I am going out of station and will be coming back on the third of the next month."

When I came back, within a week the affiliation order from CBSE came to the net. I got the call of the Principal –"Congratulations Madam, we have got the affiliation."

I could not believe – such a difficult job was done so easily. We had not paid a single penny to anybody in CBSE. That means there are still good people on the Earth. I thanked Sir; he seemed to be in a very happy mood.

Next day was my day at school. Everybody congratulated me. Adarsh said "Whatever I had promised, you'll get."

We went to his room and wher we were discussing the matter in details Adarsh said "Madam, you have done a wonderful job. Without spending a single paise we got the affiliation, really credit goes to you." Aaradhana, the Director's daughter, with a pale face remarked – "Those officers in the Affiliation department must have liked you very much because of your fair complexion." The atmosphere became vitiated at once. One by one everybody left. Adarsh signalled me to wait and told me to bring the Attendance Register. When I gave it to him, he called the Receptionist and in her presence changed all L marked against my name to O.D. and put his signature there. The Receptionist went out with the Register with an astonished face. He asked for the T.A.Bill which I handed over to him. The tickets of the trains, taxi bill etc. were attached to it. He observed it minutely and then said –"I will deduct Two Thousand Rupees from the total amount otherwise my family members will be annoyed." I was expecting this. I know how mean-minded the members of this family are ! I thought O.K., let me donate Two Thousand Rupees to these neo-rich family whose members are nothing else but beggars mentally. I pretended to be very happy and thanked him insincerely with a false smile. I have saved lacs of Rupees, managing the affiliation without paying any bribe and here he deducted Rs. two thousand from the bill in order to please his family members ! Earlier, whenever anyone of his family members went to CBSE Office with any work, that person took 1.5 lac to two lac from the school fund in the name of paying bribe. Whether the money was really given as a bribe or went to his own pocket nobody knows!

One thing I noticed after coming back from Delhi that although the results were out nobody was discussing about it. I had received the result of the school in my e-mail box sending request to CBSE. Sitting in my room I started doing the analysis. As expected there were innumerable failures in Physics, Maths, Chemistry and except in English, Computer Science and Home Science there were failures in all subjects. There were hardly one or two students who got 90 per cent in the aggregate. I did the result analysis and submitted one copy to the Principal. He said "I know, there are many distinctions in English. We have seen the result." I know nobody bothers to do the result analysis in this school as they are afraid to face the bitter truth. I said –"I've done the detailed result analysis, please have a look at it whenever you find time."

He took the sheet from my hand and kept it under some books and magazines on his table. I am hundred percent sure he will neither study it properly nor show it to anybody else. Who would like to wash his dirty linens in front of others? If at all he studies the analysis report he would prefer to keep it within himself. On next day's local newspapers I read the news about the performance of the students of our School in AISSCE and AISSE. It has been reported that in class X the result is 100 per cent with more than 150 students scoring 90 per cent and above and in class XII the result is 99.9 per cent with 55 students scoring 90 per cent and above. This statement is absolutely wrong and against the Right to Information Act. But who is there to verify? There are thousands of people living in the nearby places who dream of providing quality education to their children. Everybody can not get a chance in branded schools so the rush is maximum in this school as parents are attracted by false reports and colourful advertisements blowing the trumpet of the school. If they do not get admission in a straight way they do not hesitate to give donations. Adarsh calls it admission through Management quota. The amount of course is not fixed. It is flexible, starting from five thousand to a few lacs. Starting from the month of January the admission tests are never ending till the end of August. Any time is admission time during those eight months. Classrooms fall short due to the strength. Adarsh becomes nostalgic time to time and says "At one point of life there was nothing to eat at home."

I can understand, still they have the fear of losing everything. That's why they try to earn as much as possible from innumerable sources. They try to save for the rainy day also by depriving the staff of whatever they deserve. At the time of passing any bill, Adarsh deducts certain amount from it. But whatever he does, is crystal clear to everyone; he never tries to hide anything. The elder brother is a hypocrite who pretends to be very pious, very religious but in fact is very shrewd and cunning. His attraction towards Sarmistha Sen, the Director of the Kids

Academy in the branch of the school at the capital of the state is a common topic of gossiping among his family members as well as the staff. This lady, being humiliated by the Director's son and daughter-in-law had promised to leave the school. The Director practically fell on her feet and somehow stopped her from leaving. Actually the top boss gets added attention from the society if he moves around with a beautiful lady by his side. That gives him strength, courage and confidence also. After that incident she had stopped coming to our school. But when the workshop on Effective Teaching and learning was conducted, on the third day she came at the special request of the Director and throughout the programme sat next to him, forgetting her real position and status and pretending to be very important. Actually this became possible because of the Director's weakness for her. She knows how to manipulate this weakness. Today her son is studying MBA in U.K., half of the expenses being borne by T.C.S. company because of her coquetry with the Director of the school. Had the school authority not helped the boy to clear his twenty-two papers in different years of Engineering in which he failed, by their personal influence with the University and had they not appointed somebody else to appear in his place for the written examination at TCS, he would have been nowhere today.

Beauty and coquetry can sometimes be very powerful capitals.

Summer vacation is coming to an end although there is no indication of monsoon. The temperature is soaring upto 47 degrees in the afternoon. Showing his thumb to the State Administration, Adarsh has called the students of class XII through SMS and even before the summer vacation ended, they are attending classes from seven to twelve. The ceiling fans are of no use as they are throwing hot air turning the classrooms into furnaces. Both the teachers and the students are sweating profusely and the smell of sweat and body odour is making things worse. There is no water in the toilet as the never ending construction work is going on and the labourers are using the water to their hearts' content not allowing anybody to fill up the overhead tanks. The stinking smell of the toilets on the ground floor and the first floor makes me sick. I am compelled to keep the windows of my room shut. The cooler is on but it is making the room more humid. A.C. has been installed in the rooms of the family members of the Trivedis. R.N. Mishra and myself are outsiders, so we have to be satisfied with coolers. Most of the time R.N. Mishra is found to be either in the Principal's room or in the room of Aaradhana. So, his problem is not so serious. But my room on the top floor, without AC is really horrible. The members of Trivedi family are so heartless that they never think how I spend the summer months in this room ! Being an Executive I don't have summer vacation. I am deprived of that and along with that I am deprived of many other things which the Vice Principal of a big school deserves.

I had to get the signature of the Principal on some papers. When I entered his room, his family members were present there. They were discussing about the accident of Jyaneshwari Express in West Bengal. A boy of class IV of our school had expired along with his parents. One of the family members said "In a way it is a publicity for our school."

Adarsh added – "Yes, whenever four persons sit and discuss about anything, even accident or death, if they mention the name of our school, it is a publicity for us." I felt like throwing up at this discussion. Just one day earlier there was a condolence meeting when everybody present in the room prayed for the peaceful rest of the soul of the boy and his parents who died in the accident. How ugly are the faces behind the masks ! Behind each and every kind word there is some self interest. Behind each and every deed of charity there is some self interest. Everything is calculated. This reminded me of the charity done by the Birlas. Forty years back they had taken my father-in-law's house on rent to set up a charitable dispensary there. All sorts of illegal abortions used to take place there in the name of treating the poor people. Our repeated request to vacate the house as we needed it badly, were in vain. They are still running that charitable dispensary in our house although we don't have any place to stay whenever we go to Kolkata. Forty years back the rent of the house was Rs. 225.00 and now it is Rs. 700.00 In metro cities even a small garage is not available at that much rent? Who is doing the charity? If the Birlas want to do some charity why are they doing it at our cost? Don't they have any house of their own in Kolkata? My husband inherited that house after the death of my father-in-law. We decided to construct the first floor of the house so that atleast we can get a shelter. The plan of the house could not be sanctioned over a period of one and a half year under the left front government and Trinamool. Ultimately we had to dispose off that house. The Maoists and Naxals are provoked and guided by the wicked politicians. Sometimes I feel like guiding them to the right path to get rid of the corrupt rich, benevolent charitable parasites who suck our blood to show their benevolence. The characteristics of these people are same everywhere – whether it is the big industrialists in big cities or people like Veer Parsad or the Trivedis. With age, I am able to recognise them better. Like a caged bird I beat my wings on the iron bars of the cage and hurt myself. My wings are stained in blood and the pain becomes more intense each time. Still I don't give up and struggle hard to make myself free from the cage. Like the hypocrites I can not smile or laugh at the cruel jokes and sadistic remarks of my employers. I can not praise them in flowery language. My jaws become stiff and lips tight each time I observe something in them which I don't like. I have still not learnt the lessons of life. I have dreams which can not be fulfilled in an honest way following a straight path. I have to take twists and turns and jump into the muddy puddles and bogs. Being afraid of stains will not land me anywhere. If I can't do that I will be defeated at the hands of Ranjita, Sarita and many others. But if I am able to do that, then I have no right to even think of taking revenge on them.

"What are you thinking Madam? You seem to be in the room physically but mentally you are somewhere else?" – Adarsh asked me. Prompt came the answer in my mind – "I'm thinking about my younger son who has gone to Singapore on official tour."

"Has he gone alone ?" – he asked next.

"He has gone with his boss."

"See, life has become so tough now. The companies are paying well but extracting more from the youngsters. I don't know how long will they have the stamina to work. Moreover their family life is very badly affected."

I said – "It is not a problem for the children of your family. Any time they can join the school or the college as these are your own institutions. But think about us, we have no other options. We used to work hard with the hope that our children will live comfortable lives but now they are also struggling hard. Only difference now is that their purchasing capacity has increased."

All of a sudden he asked – "Have you made any plan about what you'll do after the retirement of your husband?"

I didn't tell him that already I have started applying in different schools of Delhi. I said – "My husband told me to request you to appoint him in your college."

He said – "I'll be happy to get a person like him with such a long experience in projects. I know he is very sincere and honest in his work."

"He will be an asset for your college, this much I can assure you."

Then he took out a blue print of the proposed college building which can compete with the best college buildings of abroad.

I heaved a sigh; each brick of this building would be constructed by some amount deducted from the earning of the staff shedding their sweat.

"From the next year it will be difficult for me to sit on the Principal's chair for the whole time. I have to visit all the schools and the college also." Adarsh said.

"Then who will be the Principal?" I asked.

"Bade Bhaisahab has to decide that. Between the two Additional Principals one will be the Principal here." I shudder in fear to think about that day. I have to escape before that otherwise they will make my life a hell !.

Adarsh seemed to be thinking something very deeply. Then he wanted to know exactly when Veer Parsad was going to retire.

"When is your Ex-boss going to retire, Madam?"

I remembered the date very well.

"On 15th September Sir."

"Who will be the next Principal there?"

"I don't know, but he is trying his best for his wife."

"Will she be able to run the school like her husband?"

"She will just sit on that chair. Her husband will be doing everything from the back stage.

You know, he wanted to join our school. I have told him to leave his school first or after his retirement we will appoint him in our school."

"Really ! Did he approach you?"

I asked although I know very well Veer Parsad will never approach him. However hard the Trivedi family blow their own trumpet, Veer Parsad will never compromise with his ego and approach them. If at all he had shown his interest to join the school of the Trivedis, that must have been a mockery or sarcasm, nothing else. But everybody wants to know what will happen after a few months when Veer Parsad's tenure will be over. His pet dogs and bitches would request the Society in Delhi to promote Ranjita to that post. After all, he had given them promotion out of the way. He had sent them to America, U.K. and some other places on educational tour. Had they ever in their dream thought of achieving so much? How does it matter to them if Ranjita occupies the chair of Veer Parsad?

The conversation was interrupted as the youngest grand-daughter of Adarsh flung the door open and came inside. Adarsh planted a kiss on her forehead and made her sit on his chair. She smiled broadly and asked "Am I the Principal?"

Children can make the atmosphere lighter within no time. But what is stored for the future, God knows ! These children will grow up and become the heir to such a big property. If they stay together they will be able to retain everything otherwise this empire will tumble down like one made of playing-cards.

"Dadu, give me a chalk," the little girl requested Adarsh.

"Why, what will you do with a chalk?" Adarsh asked her.

"I'll write A.B, C, 1,2,3….." She replied.

"No you'll spoil the doors" Adarsh refused and turning towards me he said "Madam, you know, she has spoilt each and every door of our house by using them as black boards. She writes alphabets and numbers on them and teaches the imaginary students." I smiled and told him – I used to do that forty-five years back but instead of spoiling all doors I used to spoil only one at the end of the staircase leading to the roof. The different steps of the staircase were the benches where my imaginary students used to sit so many years ago to receive the first lessons of life." Hardly had that tiny teacher imagined to what juncture her life would bring her and make her stand face to face with the bitter realities which are poles apart from the rosy dreams of childhood ! That world, forty-five years ago was different. The air was not so polluted. We were satisfied with animal shaped biscuits and colourful round toffees. Grandmothers and mothers loved making pickles, cooking traditional food and telling stories.

Anandlal's grand-daughter insisted him to give her a piece of chalk. When she failed to convince him, she made a long face and left the room. Adarsh smiled and said – "She will forget her anger by the time I reach home. She will come running towards me listening to the horn of the car,."

I said – "She seems to be the apple of your eyes."

He said- "You are right. Although I love all three of my grand children still I have a special place in my mind for this girl. I have kept aside 50 lac for each of them for their higher studies." I jokingly said "I wish I were your grand-daughter."

A loud guffaw reverberated in the room which startled the people sitting in the next room. Aaradhana and R.N. Mishra opened the door and peeped inside with rounded up eyes and question mark in their face.

Niti's phone came at 4.30 p.m. She sounded very excited – "Ma, India T.V. came to take my interview."

"For what?" I asked.

"They will be discussing on the issue of Dhoni's weight gain by 14 kg. They required a dietician's opinion and approached me for that. They took my interview for about half an hour which will be telecast in the evening at 7.00 p.m. You must see and tell me how you liked it please."

"O.K. definitely we will see and give you a ring."

I told Swapnil when he woke up from his afternoon siesta. At quarter to seven we switched on the India T.V. channel. The programme started sharp at 7. It was a long discussion on the weight gain of the Indian Cricket Team Captain Mahinder Singh Dhoni who himself had confessed that his weight was 88 kg. which was about 14 kg. extra. Then the anchor of the programme said 'Let's see what the doctor says."

Niti appeared on the screne and said –"A person with 5 ft 11 inches height should be around 72 to 74 kg not more than that." Her half an hour interview was cut short to a few seconds by the Editor's scissors. We waited for some more time to see if she comes again but no! There started a comparison between Dhoni and Yuvraj who was also over-weight and the comments of one more dietician was taken. I rang up Niti and congratulated her saying, "It is a great publicity for you in one of the National channels." She was happy to hear this. Taking the advantage of the excitement of his parents, Maharaj did some mischieves like pouring water on the bedsheet and opening the glass door of the T.V. stand and increasing the volume of the music system.

Wishing good night to them and switching off the red button of the mobile I started thinking there are so many things in life which go waste. Half an hour interview is just an example. In our workplaces, so many plannings go waste; half completed or full completed work, sometimes have no value; creativity of people remain in the darkness for which there are innumerable instances. Just as the left over food is thrown into the dust bin to be gulped down by the street dogs or beggars, human potentials and talents also are ignored and rejected ruthlessly. Life's lesson can be taught by life itself, not by any other edifice of learning. Each year the ideas expressed by the staff on paper regarding the progress and improvement of the school are taken out of the suggestion box and examined by the Executives. But only those are accepted and implemented which satisfy their self-interest and need. Appreciation is not given to any individual but to a group and the major portion of the credit for any task is taken by the person sitting at the top. High profile can be maintained by the top boss but subordinates must keep their profile low and feel happy at the success of the boss and the institution or atleast they must pretend to be happy otherwise there is every possibility of losing even the yearly increment.

At this point I laughed at myself. A small incident like Niti's interview in Live India T.V. compelled me to think all these.

At night there was a squall. The branches of the Gulmohar trees swayed with full might and thrashed against the walls and window panes disturbing our sleep. Dust swirled in the wind and as it was expected there was a power cut. I remained awake throughout the night and kept on thinking about future. What will happen after ten years from now? Where shall we settle? For the first time I regretted for not settling in a big city right from the beginning. In that case our children would have stayed with us. They had to go to Delhi leaving our home for higher studies and job as there was no opportunity in a small city like ours. Among all species on the Earth, it is human being only who need education and money to survive. Separation from children has not only made us lonely but also complicated their lives where they are constantly struggling to build up their career and future. We all are living like separate isolated islands. What will Maharaj gain from us? He will grow up into one more self-centered person indifferent to everything around him. Will he ever realise the value of relationship?

People who are less educated, who have no hope for future, who struggle hard to make both ends meet and live in a hand to mouth situation are happy as they have a strong feeling for their family members. They will not miss the opportunity to attend the marriage or any other celebration within the family. At the end of the day they may be licking their fingers after eating coarse or broken rice with starch sprinkling a pinch of salt but have the satisfaction of eating together. They may be sleeping on rags, huddling together but experience the pleasure of sharing their fate and dreams instead of spending sleepless nights on comfortable beds in isolation where deep sighs yearn for the company of nearest and dearest ones within the four walls. Old parents either die in Old-Age Homes or lie in a pool of blood, murdered by antisocial elements while children are busy taking part in the meaningless rat races. This is the outcome of education in the modern age.

The long night came to an end. I got up from the bed and went to the roof. The bright red colour was slowly appearing out of clouds in the sky. Leaves and dry twigs were lying scattered all over the roof. Chanting the Surya prayer and pleading for the welfare of all my family members I came downstairs to start another day. While sitting in the car and proceeding towards the school, I forgot whatever I thought the previous night and started thinking about the preparation for the presentation which Adarsh will be giving in the seminar he was going to attend in London.

The Director didn't want Adarsh to go alone. He wanted his younger son also to accompany him. But Adarsh wanted to take the credit of attending a seminar in London alone. One of his followers said that the news should come in the local papers both at the time of going and after coming back. He applied for Visa which he got. He gave me the brochure where all information was given about the seminar and told me "Madam, you keep it in your room. I don't want anybody else to get any information. I'll go first and then in future I may send somebody else but not now." He was afraid of the height, voice and personality of his nephew. He would not get any importance there if his nephew also accompanied him. How poor are these people in their heart ! Ambitious people at all ages and times are same, their main characteristic being jealousy. Consciously or unconsciously they reveal the penury of their heart before others.

One day before the reopening of the school after the summer vacation, teachers were informed that there will be a general meeting in the Natraj Hall. The teachers assembled there at 9.30 a.m. The Director and other Executives following him, including me reached there at 10.00 a.m. Without any introduction the Director started reading out a result analysis of class X and XII prepared by the greatest manipulator Mr. R.N. Mishra, hiding the drawbacks of their own subjects particularly Mathematics and highlighting the negative sides of English, Hindi and Sanskrit. With his wrong English he attacked the Language teachers particularly those who teach English and said I consider the Incharges are responsible for this. Do they allow the Incharges to work independently? Whatever I instruct my teachers are always contradicted by his daughter and daughter-in-law. They instruct the teachers of the English Department as per their whims and fancies. Then how are the Incharges responsible?

When the meeting was over, the teachers of my department told me "Madam, how cleverly he suppressed the fact of the number of failures in their own subjects ! He didn't mention that there are 55 failures in his daughter's subject that is Physics. He didn't mention there are 25 failures in Mathematics and more than ten in Chemistry !"

I said – "Let us not bother about the number of failures in their subjects. Let us think how to bring improvement in our own subject."

One of them said – "Actually time for Annual increment is coming. All family members are from Science and Maths department. They will be given more increment whereas we, the language teachers will be getting less. It happens every year. He just made the line clear as a justification to his injustice towards us."

May be they are right. But, somehow, slowly I have been losing all interest and fighting spirit. Now-a-days, every moment I feel that I have been wasting my time and energy in this third-class school. It's high time I should start something of my own-may be a crèche or a play school and devote my life for it. But first of all I have to decide where to settle ! Children have settled in Delhi, they don't want to come back to this steel city. There is a special attraction for Kolkata also that being our native place. Wherever I go, I have to wait for atleast one more year, till the retirement of Swapnil because at this age I don't want to leave him alone here again. This time we have to think hard in order to take the final decision for our settlement for the rest of our life. However painful it is I have to carry on like this for some more time. I don't know exactly how long !

For the first time in 17 years, Inter-School Quiz Competition was held in our school. Motilal, the Director was very much excited and told me instead of Inter-School I should mention State-level Quiz Competition in the letters and entry forms to be sent to different schools of the township before the competition. I tried to convince him with great difficulty that it was not State level but only among ten to fifteen schools of the township. The last date for sending the entry forms was 5th July. On 3rd July he asked me "Are you doing the following up work?"

I could not get him at first. He carried on "Have you asked them over telephone how many schools will be coming?"

I said – "The last date given is 5th August. Till now I have got ten entries. I think by 5th I'll be getting some more. Then I'll ask the remaining schools whether they will participate or not." He became very much impatient and annoyed and loudly expressed his annoyance "You don't know how to work. Immediately after sending the letters you should start asking the schools whether they will participate or not. If required request them to send their entries. Don't you know that people sleep over the papers?"

I thought it's better to keep quiet. I felt that minimum time should be given to the schools to decide whether they would participate and if so whom to select for the participation. I have the experience of conducting such type of competitions in my previous schools. But who will make them realise that? They think that they know everything If they know everything then why couldn't they organize any competition within seventeen years? Why couldn't they publish any school magazine before my joining? I know these questions will remain in my mind forever. I won't be able to ask anyone ever.

The Quiz Competition was organized very well. Everybody praised me except the Director. He called all teachers to thank them and in front of them praised his daughter saying "Aaradhana is very good in organising any programme. I had told her that for any problem, anywhere I will not spare her."

The puppets kept quiet in his presence. Later on some of them came to my room and said – "Madam you did everything. Without your guidance and instructions we could not have managed anything so nicely but he didn't take your name even once. He praised his daughter and gave her the whole credit."

A deep sigh came out from the core of my heart as I told them –"Never mind, I have done my duty and everybody knows who has done what. I cursed Veer Parsad once more; today because of him I am not in my familiar and most beloved reputed school. Leaving behind my most favourite school I find myself as a part of a family comedy circus, amidst some businessmen who consider themselves smart but do not know how comic they are !

Veer Parsad's school secured the third position in Inter-School Quiz whereas the other school with the same brand name stood second and our school became the winner with maximum points. The Rolling Trophy was given to the second position holders as the host school was not supposed to take it.

Within a few days Veer Parsad also conducted the Inter-School Quiz Competition and did not allow the participants from our school to qualify even in the written round. He was afraid that if they qualify in the written round then they will definitely defeat his school in the final round on the stage. At his instructions the organising committee of his school selected the weakest of the schools along with their own school in the final round and killed two birds at a time. On the one hand they had no fear or doubt regarding their win in the final Quiz; on the other hand they wanted to show how weak our team was, that they could not qualify even in the written round. Naturally doubt came in the minds about the previous win of the participants in our own school. Veer Parsad and Ranjita know such type of mean tricks. Our participants were very much disheartened as the written round was quite easy and they were sure to qualify. When the teacher escort along with the boys came to meet Adarsh after the competition was over, he told them not to feel bad. "It's not your fault that you could not win. Your only fault is that you represented our school. So, forget everything and concentrate in your studies."

At that moment I decided not to send any student to Veer Parsad's school for any competition at least not for Quiz Competition where there is 100 per cent chance of manipulation.

The Investiture ceremony was pending for a long time. As soon as I got the green signal from the Principal, I arranged it within two days in the Morning Assembly. As I announced the names there was much excitement among the students. They came to the stage and took their position. They were presented with badges and were administered oath.

Later on some students who were not selected met me and asked why they were not selected. In our student life we could never even think of challenging the decision of the school management. But now-a-days the students are fearless and they don't hesitate to approach the authority if any decision is not in their favour.

The practice for the Zonal level Debate on the issue of Population Stabilization organised jointly by Jansankhya Sthirtha Kosh and DPS Society New Delhi was going on in my room. The participants both for and against the motion were speaking one by one while along with two teachers of my department I was listening to them and doing the necessary corrections here and there. All of a sudden the prayer for the afternoon shift started. Eight different tunes in chorus started coming from eight different sections. It was impossible to continue with the debate, so we were compelled to stop till the prayer ended. Then as soon as one of the speakers started there was a loud commotion accompanied by the sound of the heating of duster on the wall. I saw students of the classroom just in front of my room were coming out and standing in the corridor. "What happened? Why did they get punishment even before the period started? Savitri just go and find out what is the matter !" - I asked my attendant. She said –"No Madam, they have not got punishment. It is the order of Sarita Madam that the rooms have to be broomed at 12 noon. That's why the students have been asked to come out". "It will take atleast 10 minutes to sweep each room; and in that case the whole of the first period can not be utilised for teaching purpose because turnwise this sweeping work will be done by one or two class IV staff in all the classrooms and turnwise children will come out of their respective classroom and make noise."

Savitri said "Students of the day shift occupy the classrooms as soon as the morning shift students leave. There is no gap between the shifts when the rooms can be cleaned. That's why from now onwards it will be done in the first period. Not only that Sarita Madam has ordered that sweeping should be done at 3 p.m. after the recess."

The two teachers present in my room and the students could not suppress their laughter as simultaneously my face wore two expressions – one – I have to tolerate this nonsense everyday in the first period of the day shift and the other – thank God, I will not be present at 3 p.m.

In the meantime Savitri had called the boy who was heating the duster on the wall. I forgot why he was called and asked him "Yes, what do you want?"

He said "Madam I don't want anything. This aunty told me that you are calling me."

I said – "Don't heat the duster on the wall. Clean it using some other method but not by heating it and damaging the wall."

He made a face as if I was telling him something absurd as he had already been assigned with this responsibility by his class teacher. However nodding his head assertively he left the room.

After this temporary disturbance the debaters spoke again. The boy speaking against the motion was very confident and spoke very nicely. I am sure he was not touching his books and copies but was totally involved in the debate. The girl speaking for the motion stammered and halted at two places. I told her – "You have to practise more. In spite of that if you forget any point, skip that portion and carry on without any hesitation because the audience will not know what is there in your speech. You have to win. Do you know what is the prize money at the final round in Delhi? It is thirty thousand Rupees."

She said – "Ma'am Delhi is far away. I'm not sure whether I will qualify in the Zonal round." I told her – "Delhi is not far away, it is just in the mind." At that moment I saw the reflection of determination in the eyes of the boy who was supposed to speak against the motion. This twinkle will take him very far I'm sure.

Madhushree surprised everybody by putting up her papers. Not only Madhushree but many other teachers of that school with a brand name started leaving one after another when the school authority failed to give them salary as per the sixth pay commission. Madhushree had approached Adarsh but he could not give her any assurance. Ironically enough, the school authority sanctioned salary as per the sixth pay commission just within two months of the leaving of the teachers. Now their ego prevented them from going back to the same school where they had to join as juniors. Rumours started spreading about Madhushree.

Somebody said –"She is going to join Veer Parsad's school again." Some said – "She is going to be the Head Mistress of a new school to be opened shortly in the township with the same brand name." Again some said "She will start her own coaching class in the township." Her husband said "She will study M.Phil, that's why she has left the job."

In one marriage party I observed her talking to Veer Parsad and Ranjita. I know Veer Parsad is eager to get back his lost love. Now-a-days all ladies have become alert. Veer Parsad's notoriety is not unknown to anyone. His condition is like a thirsty dove; quite obviously he would try his best to bring back Madhushree. I came to know that she shifted to the township, near her old school leaving her house where she had shifted after leaving the old school.

There is one more rumour in the township that Veer Parsad has got extension for two more years. I was expecting this. Everything was absolutely in his favour and this is even better than his wife becoming the Principal because husband and wife both will be drawing fat salary and enjoy all other facilities for two more years. After two years chances for his wife to become the Principal will be the ripest, as her experience as Vice Principal will be about ten years by then and she would also be able to complete her Ph.D. Knowing that there will be enough fruits in the tree, who would not like to pick up the maximum from the ground at present? Moreover, if one knows the right steps and accurate calculations, nothing can stop him from reaching his goal. By giving promotion and position to some dishonest and undeserving persons and sending them abroad on educational tours, he has paved his way strong which will be even protected by these followers. Everybody thinks that simply by magic he is achieving everything in life but no one is able to imagine the functioning of his brain, how fast and excellent the working of his brain takes place. Even it was beyond the imagination of his thumb – impressionist parents who left this world with the knowledge of only half of his success. Those who are sitting far away, are aware of only the positive sides of Veer Parsad, that is his strong administration, his credit in producing excellent results year after year in AISSE and AISSCE, his credit in producing a large number of IIT-JEE qualifiers etc. They are least bothered to know about the negative sides of Veer. How does it matter if he sexually abuses the lady teachers or uplifts his wife in an unfair manner? Why should they bother to read the complaint letters against Veer? They are concerned only about the name and reputation of the school which Veer is able to retain. If there is anything called previous birth, then Veer Parsad and Ranjita must have done a lot of virtues, the fruits of which they are getting now. I will not be surprised if Madhushree joins her old school and shows her loyalty to Veer Parsad. Truth is sometimes stranger than fiction. Justice was denied to innumerable women by granting extension to Veer Parsad for two more years. Their curses, tears, deep sighs could do nothing. Madhushree, perhaps thought it would be better to forget everything and join hands with her old boss; who knows whether she will be able to visit Europe or America next year, escorting the children on an Educational tour? What's the use of missing such an opportunity, foolishly trying to protect one's ego?

Human mind is the most unpredictable. Which direction it is going to follow, even the person himself does not know. A feeling of dissatisfaction is always chasing everybody and the other bank of the river always seems to be fertile. Some of the teachers who left that school and joined our school with the assurance of the Director that they will be getting 6th Pay Commission are now repenting but are helpless. They have to carry on here half heartedly as there is very little scope in this small township. Madhushree was also interested to join our school and had submitted her application but was not called for interview. But she didn't wait for any call from our school; before that she had put up her papers in her school which shows that she had already decided to leave that school.

But why am I thinking so much about her? Veer Parsad had accused me for her leaving his school. Now who is responsible? I am sure Veer Prasad had sent many adverse reports against me to the Education Management Society in Delhi as reasons for my leaving his school and so that I could not apply in any of the schools under the Society in future. I know his nature very well. He likes to nip all buds which have the potential to bloom, so that his track remains hazard free and no one can ever surpass him. But Veer Parsad is not the only person. I have seen his reflection in his wife and also in all members of Trivedi family particularly their head Mr. Motilal Trivedi – the emperor of the vast kingdom he has constructed squeezing the blood and sweat of innumerable persons. The Roman emperor Nero used to play flute while Rome was burning and people were screaming. This modern emperor chants shlokas of Sanskrit to show his sanctity of life while ruining and exploiting thousands of lives.

Veer Prasad celebrated the Silver Jubilee Foundation Day of his school in a grand style with the Governor of the State as the Chief Guest and all members of the Board of Governors of the school, both from the capital as well as local as the Guests of Honour. All the local daily newspapers carried his photograph with the Governor and other dignitaries, bringing him to the limelight once again. But one thing was really puzzling; Ranjita's name was nowhere mentioned in the press report. Her photograph was also not there in any of the newspapers. Was it the prediction of a tempest in disguise? Hibernating herself before occupying the hot seat ! May be, but that is not possible for two more years because Veer has already got extension.

Veer's son in the meantime recovered from his severe head injury due to rash riding of his byke in Bangalore. He was going to meet his girlfriend Pooja who was once his counterpart in school. He was the Head Boy and that girl was the head Girl. They were always found together and this relationship continued after a short break when Veer's son got admission in an Engineering College of the State and the girl went to Bangalore. After one year Veer sent him to Bangalore managing a seat on Management Quota. The old relationship revived with double vigour as a result of which he failed in the first year of his college and had to wash his hands off with the NTSE scholarship which he had managed, copying all answers from his friend and Veer's personal influence in the final interview. Veer Parsad got a slap of fate in the matter of his children. He was so busy building up his own career that he totally neglected this side of his life. Now, as his career is coming to an end, he is able to feel that. He is cent percent successful in his career but absolutely a failure as a father. His corrupt actions have come back to him as a boomerang hitting his two dearest assets. Motilal, Adarsh and the other Principals of the city are jealous of Veer Parsad but if they come to know about this side of Veer's life they would feel pity for him.

Motilal and Adarsh told me to include all activities in the Annual Almanac this year, which are followed in my previous school. Motilal said – "you have a long experience of organising various events. I expect you to organise Inter-School Competitions and other Activities in the same way." It was a real challenge thrown to me because I know him and his family members. If they find that things are going on very smoothly, they will definitely interfere and spoil everything. Exactly it happened one after another. When Inter-School Quiz was held in an excellent manner, Motilal praised his daughter whole-heartedly, completely ignoring me as if the whole credit was her. At the time of Inter-School Drawing and Painting Competition he called the teachers of Music and Dance and told them to organise national level Music and Dance Competition. The teachers, whom I had allotted duty for Painting Competition were engaged in the other competition which went on simultaneously, creating confusion and chaos in both the places. On top of that Parents – Teachers meeting was also scheduled on the same day. For the Music and Dance Competition, one thousand rupees entry fees was charged at his instruction. The prize money was one thousand for the first position, eight hundred for the second position and five hundred for the third position. Along with that some sponsored medals and certificates were given. The teams which came from far away places were very much displeased as they had spent one thousand as entry fee and more than that for reservation of railway tickets. They expected better prizes. I was told that the same medals should be used as prizes for the painting competition also and one extra shield was there which could be used as the Rolling Shield. The Art teachers had to remove the stickers from the medals and paste new stickers with 'Inter-School Drawing and Painting Competition' written on them. Everybody in and outside the school started discussing about the miserly nature of the members of the Trivedi family while a few lacs were added to the school account on account of the National level Music and Dance competition.

Next was the T-shirt issue. One fine morning there was unmanageable noise and commotion in all the classrooms when disturbing the classroom teaching, the students were called in groups for distributing House-T-shirts to them. They had already paid the money at the beginning of the session and were too excited to get the T-shirts after six months. The teachers were standing impuissant, helplessly as this distribution procedure continued for two-three periods. The same thing was repeated in the day shift also.

Now I am no more surprised. I know it is a regular feature in this school cum industry where money is carved through various sources.

I prepared two students for zonal level Debate competition organised by National Population Control Board. The boy who was speaking against the motion prepared the speech as per my instructions and won the first prize. The girl disagreed with two points which I had written for her and purposely skipped those points. She couldn't get anything but as the total marks of the two speakers were more than the other teams she was also allowed to go to Delhi for the national level along with the boy. Two speakers from another branch of our school were also selected. Total four students and two teachers were to go to Delhi for the final debate. As I had feared, Motilal took the speech of the girl for whom I had written as she was in his hostel and said that it was not up to the mark and it has to be improved by two other teachers who were his favourite. I know his tricks; he wanted to disturb me on the one hand, because I never used to flatter him which he expected; on the other hand he wanted to give my points to his niece who was also one of the participants from the other branch of the school. The girl told me "Madam, Sir has told me that your speech will be improved by Preeti and Neha Ma'am". I said – "You better give me back my speech and ask them to write for you again." Instead of feeling ashamed she left my room and met those two teachers and approached them to write for her. But when they refused she again came back and said "Those two teachers are very busy. They have no time to write. Chairman Sir said that I can use your speech."

I said "First you change your attitude and then come to my room."

When she was going back from my room, her two hostelmates were with her and my attendant Savitri overheard them saying – "Why should we give her so much importance? Our Chairman Sir will help us. What does she think of herself? We do not care for anybody else but Babuji."

As the family members (next generation) call Motilal 'Babuji', the students of his hostel also call him 'Babuji'. In order to gain popularity and business both, he is giving this training to the students, teaching them to ignore other teachers who are outsiders, who are paid employees of his school. I thought enough is enough. I am not going to write a single word for anybody in this school ever. In my long teaching career, whenever I wrote for anybody – whether it is debate or elocution or essay that student secured 1st or 2nd position without fail. Earlier, when Ranjita had noticed that teachers and students were trusting me in this matter and I was gaining popularity she did her best to disturb me by interfering unnecessarily. The same thing I observed here again. My employers wanted me to work for them but didn't like me to gain popularity. When undeserving people come into power, they know their capability as well as their weaknesses and are always afraid of losing everything. They try to clip the wings of those who soar high, to keep their path clear.

I didn't feel like preparing the boy also who won the first prize at the zonal level and half-heartedly listened to his debate. The escort teacher who went with the students was a Sports teacher. He was aware of the incident which happened before going. When none of the participants could secure any position, he rang up the Chairman and the Principal and told them that they could not win because the content of their speech was not good. Motilal felt elated and took it as his victory and at that moment the Sports teacher became his favourite. This is how people look for opportunity and simply without doing anything gain the favour of boss.

If I want to march forward I have to forget these incidents as the most insignificant and trivial ones, but I don't know why I can't forget anything. I take everything to heart and this is my greatest drawback.

Veer Parsad, Ranjita, Motilal and such types never brood over spoilt milk. The other day when Adarsh was introducing the Chief Guest who is the Vice Chancellor of a Technical University who had come to grace the National level Music and Dance competition, he said that the Chief Guest was an alumni of IIT Khairagarh instead of saying IIT Kharagpur. The audience in the jam-packed auditorium nudged each other trying to suppress their laughter. Later on when I told him about this he himself with a loud guffaw said "I don't care what people think about me when I say something publicly. I am not a professional speaker. I can make mistakes." Such is the confidence !

The Municipal Corporation decided to felicitate some teachers from every school on Teachers' Day by the Chief Minister of the State in order to gain their favour as the election for the Municipal Corporation was coming nearer. They sent some forms to be filled up by the teachers. After filling up the forms when I submitted it to the Principal, he said, "Madam, I am forwarding it but the final selection will be done by the Chairman Sir." I smiled and said "If fair selection is done, then definitely I will be selected."

I had a doubt whether fair selection will be done or not because I was sanguine that Chairman Sir will never lose the opportunity to give this honour to his daughter, daughter-in-law and son-in-law. My doubt was hundred percent correct when all three were selected but along with five other teachers my name was also there in the list. I understood that my comment was conveyed at the right place by the Principal.

Just a few days before the Teachers Day Veer Parsad again came to the limelight through both electronic as well as the print media for physically and mentally abusing the staff nurse of the primary school. As she belonged to the minority community, the matter became serious. That community, after exhibiting their agitation in front of the school reported the matter to Human Rights Commission. Veer Parsad became the talk of the town for a few days. Adarsh asked me "Madam, have you heard about your Ex-Boss?" I said "Yes, but it is nothing new to me."

Veer Parsad must have been laughing at his chamber. When his veils were protecting him by giving statements in his favour, there was no need for him to worry at all. Moreover, astonishing everybody, his photo with the news of receiving the National Award from the President of the country was published in all the daily newspapers of the city.

"Madam two drivers have left the job without any information," Chandu informed me while waiting for the railway gate to open. "How did you know?" I asked him. "I sit at Babulal's office for the whole day and come to know everything," he replied with confidence.

"Then you must be knowing why they left !" I wanted to know.

"Payment is very less here. They used to work in double shifts but hardly got three thousand. They have joined another school with a better salary."

I thought, if the teachers can change their job frequently with the hope of a better prospect then why can't these poor drivers?

Chandu again started –"Here Babulal is the Lord. Everybody has to obey him. He has been given a room with a table and a telephone. He is the main-person for the selection of drivers and conductors. If somebody presents him with a 'bottle' he will select that person. If somebody is not able to please him he will engage that person in carrying heavy load or digging the earth etc. Simply by pleasing him the drivers and conductors are managing their attendance also."

I was astonished to know that bossing is not confined only to the educated class. Even illiterate person can be the boss if he knows the art of manipulation. A few days back he was standing with an innocent face in Anandlal's office when two drivers were found to be involved in illegal affair with girl students. One of them fled with a girl and was caught by the police after a month. The other one could not go to that extent as he was removed from his job by Adarsh and the girl's parents were informed.

Chandu said–"Babulal knew everything but didn't inform the management as he was enjoying his share from both the drivers."

The Trivedi family members trust Babulal more than any other person and he is aware of that. Right from inception, this person has been working in the school. He was a bus-driver earlier and now he is the Manager of the drivers and conductors.

Two goods train and Amarkantak Express passed one after another from both sides. The railway gate opened and our discussion came to an abrupt end as Chandu concentrated in crossing the track along with all other impatient drivers who were waiting there for the past fifteen minutes.

While going home I was thinking about the girl students of the hostels run by Trivedi family. As I was sitting in Adarsh's room a lady wanted to meet him. I was about to come out but Adarsh told me to wait. When the lady came inside, Adarsh, without any introduction said – "Madam, your daughter is in the hostel; you please go and meet her."

She said – "I'm her grandmother. Her parents are in Kolkata. I have informed them to come. You please allow her to stay in the hostel for two more days." I was not able to understand anything.

Adarsh further said - "I have not told anyone. Her room-mates were told that she had gone to her local guardian's house with the permission of the hostel warden. We have taken every care to protect her dignity. But we can't allow her to stay in the hostel any more. You, better, ask her parents to take her to Kolkata; at the time of exam she can come and write her papers. But now let her study at home."

The lady expressed her gratitude for taking care of the girl. Adarsh called a class IV staff and told her to escort the lady to the hostel.

When she left, Adarsh told me –"You know, Madam, this girl Sikha Singh escaped from the hostel last night and spent the night somewhere else. We asked her local guardian also but she was not in their house."

I had already got the information that girls were going out of the hostel without informing anyone. I kept quiet as the question came to my mind how could they escape, particularly at night? Isn't there any one in the hostel to take care of them? If the vigilation is strict then I am hundred percent sure even a fly can't escape the eyes of the warden.

When I came back to my room I was surprised to know that everybody in the school knew about the incident. Some teachers who came to my room to submit their Teaching Diary enlightened me with further information – "Madam, in each hostel there are atleast ten to fifteen girls who had undergone abortion more than once. They come from poor families in remote villages. Their family members can not meet up their growing demand which is the curse of city life and which they can't avoid because they feel they are in no way less deserving than the girls of the city. Lending their body is a business to them which can give them comfort and luxury. Covering their face with dupatta or scarf, they go to their places of business, trying to hide their identity."

Everything became crystal clear to me. Now a days girls are found on the road covering their face while riding their two-wheelers or as pillion riders. I used to think that they try to protect their complexion from the heat of the sun. But why should they cover their face at early dawn or in the evening? It's only to hide their identity.

When the teachers left, Savitri told me – "Whatever they said is absolutely right Madam. Rohini takes them to Hospital for abortion."

Rohini is the warden of the Girls Hostel. That means the school authority is aware of everything. Strict action is not taken because in that case the seats of the hostels will not be filled up. This school is very attractive to the students because they can do anything here; there is nobody to control them. They can enjoy life to the fullest extent. The day they will feel that the Management is very strict, the number of students will come down to half from 6000. Abortion was a horrifying word to utter even in our teenage. But now without the knowledge of the parents innumerable girls are experiencing that without any fear or shame. This is shocking to me because I am backdated. But as a teacher what am I doing to prevent this pestilence in the society? As educationists what steps are we taking to give back a healthy, happy life to the young generation removing all complications which are engulfing them day by day? Human beings are so alone. I feel like standing by their side. Human beings are always crying. I feel like standing by their side with love in my mind. But I can't. The cobweb spun around me doesn't let me cross my limit.

With a sad heart I reached home. I could not relish my lunch that afternoon. I felt each and every penny I earn, comes from the helpless parents who pay the school fees through their nose with the hope that one day their son or daughter would make them proud. When they find their dreams shattered, their deep sigh coming out from the core of their heart, their silent tears eloquently curse the teaching community. How will I save myself from that curse?

One needs the guts of Veer Parsad or Ranjita or the members of the Trivedi family to bask at their success which they achieve at the cost of students – the innocent students – the future of the civilization. That's why they get CBSE award or National award for being great educationists. But why do I think all these? Why can't I relax closing my ears and eyes? Because I shudder in fear to think about the future of my nearest and dearest ones. I shudder in fear to think about the future of my grandson Maharaj. Which society are we going to leave for them?

At the same time it is also true that if one or two sentimental fools like me try to counsel the young generation they will turn a deaf ear to us. One can feel the burning sensation only when one is burnt.

In the evening I got a call from my Ex-colleague Jolly Roy – "Urja Madam, I am going to submit my resignation."

"Why what's the matter?"

"Madam, these people are so mean, they have deducted fifteen days salary because I was on leave due to my accident." I tried to pacify her – "Jolly, don't be emotional or impulsive. Nowhere you will find the working atmosphere absolutely satisfactory. Until and unless you get a better opportunity, you should not leave."

"I am not able to tolerate any more. I have done so much for the school but the management has no consideration for me. There are a few persons who are Madam's favourite and she listens only to them. Whatever they report, she blindly believes in that," she said.

I know whatever she said is true. But leaving the job means escaping. So once again I tried to make her understand. She could understand the validity and logic of my opinion and decided to continue.

She informed me –"You know Madam, the Zonal Head is very much annoyed with Madam and gave her a piece of his mind." I said – "I was expecting this, because that person is very close to our Ex-boss Mr. Veer Parsad. Quite obviously he will make Madam's life a hell as she is the greatest competitor of Veer Parsad."

Veer Parsad is a champion chess player. He knows how to move his dice very carefully and cautiously. Throughout his career he played the game of power-sex but no one could touch him. He could save his skin always and even at the end of his innings he could hit sixers by grabbing extension and National award both. I know his target is to achieve Padmasree. Seven-eight years ago he had taken the name of a lady Principal of the school with the same brand name in Delhi and said "If she can get Padmasree why can't I?" I will not be surprised, if he really gets Padmasree. In order to get awards talent is not required, ability is not required, only the art of flattering the influential people and supplying them with crispy notes is required. So, very clearly I can see the near future when Veer Parsad will be receiving Padmasree with a broad smile stretching his gutter-like big mouth from one ear to another.The only thing he had to do is to please the person who will forward his name for the honour.

The newspapers next day brought the blood cuddling news of the spot death of two students in road accident at night and the serious injury of four other students. I was shocked to know they were from my previous and present school. Three girls and three boys enjoyed a party till midnight and were returning to their respective hostel. One of them was driving the car. All of them were under the influence of alcohol and drugs. The vehicle was running at full speed when it dashed with the road divider and a tree and turned turtle. The boy who was at the steering wheel and the girl sitting next to him died on the spot. Four other students who were sitting in the back were hospitalised and their condition was serious. Police once more got the opportunity to earn some extra income by harassing the school authorities. People of the city got a topic to discuss for a few days. Then everybody forgot the issue. Out of the seriously injured one died in the hospital, one lost his left arm and right leg and two were released with a horrifying memory for the life time. Three parents lost their children for ever but everything went on at a normal pace and there was no change in the daily routine of the schools and lives of the people of the city. Nobody bothered to ask the school authorities, how could the children come out of their hostels at night? Why nobody could find out that some students were missing? Actually people like to live within the narrow limit of their individual, personal lives. Getting up in the morning, having breakfast, going to office, coming back to home in the evening, going to the market or neighbour's house or helping the children with homework, having dinner and going to sleep – this is the daily routine. The house-wives have one more thing to do, that is gossiping with a cup of tea and snacks. Anything beyond this is risky and different. The other day one student of my previous school was driving a new Honda City of his father towards the school. On the way he knocked down a person who was riding a Moped and a rickshawpuller. He left the car at the spot, took lift from a school bus and coming to school sat in his place in a relaxed manner. Nobody came to know about this for the whole day. When the car was taken to the police station, for a week there was no claimant. Ultimately the owner was traced from the R.T.O. office and then he settled the matter by paying certain portion of his black money. What an easy solution! The family members of each of the dead persons got one lac compensation amount. The killer, a student of the most reputed, branded school is attending his classes without any tension. He is yet to have a valid licence. But how does it matter? If he wishes to drive a car, he will be gladly allowed to do so.

Adarsh and some other Principals of the city were invited by the leading daily newspaper 'Dainik Surya' to discuss about the passage of the Right to Education Bill, the guidelines of which are like this:

- Compulsory Education for children between 6 – 14 years.
- Rs. 10,000.00 fine if any child is prevented from going to school.
- No selection and screening process to choose preference over candidates.
- No physical punishments.
- States need to plan techniques to monitor advancements in the programme.
- Roping in private schools to keep 25 per cent seats reserved at entry level.
- Banning capitation fees.

It is a commitment which could not be implemented properly for a remarkably long period. Various organisations and schemes have been fighting this problem. In 2003, the Magsaysay Award was given to Shantha Sinha in recognition of her work to end child labour, a major reason for illiteracy. The Sarva Siksha Abhiyan launched in 2001 was to ensure that all children in the age group 6-14 years attend school and complete eight years of schooling by 2010. District Primary Education Programme launched in 1994 has so far started more than 160,000 new schools, including almost 84,000 alternative schools. The National Literacy Mission, launched in 1988 aimed at attaining a literacy rate of 75 per cent by 2007.

Now in 2010 also the problem still exists. We know most of the Govt. Primary Schools do not run properly. There is neither proper infrastructure, nor educated faculty members. Children often fall sick after consuming the mid-day meal prepared and served by these schools. Now the State Government wants the private schools to take the responsibility of providing free education to 25 per cent BPL students. Quite obviously it is a big blow to the owners of the private schools.

Adarsh attended the meeting called by 'Danik Surya' to express his opinion. He said, as it was expected that it is the duty of the Govt. to take care of the unfortunate children and provide them with free education. But on humanitarian ground the private schools can adopt a limited number of children every year.

Earlier, once CBSE had suggested that free education should be provided to single girl child but the schools had refused to bear the burden. Where education is a big business, it is foolishness to expect the owners and administrators of the schools to be benevolent. Moreover if the children belonging to the BPL go to school and receive education of the enlightened world who will do domestic work at low payment? Who will pull the carts, carry burden, work at restaurants, tea-stalls, construction sites at low wages and bring some relief to their parents as well as to the civilised society? Next morning Adarsh called all of us in his office to show us his interview and photograph in the newspapers. The inclusive education system is a sort of publicity of some so called educationists whose dream is to achieve fame, awards, identity in the Society.

The Chairman Motilal, now-a-days every now and then says – "I am the Chairman. Whatever I say is final." He has ordered us to send him e-mail daily reporting about our day to day work. On the first day after reading our mails he asked "What is the creativity in these daily work?"

It became difficult for us to make him understand that there cannot be creativity in each and every work daily. He became very angry and ordered us to work one hour extra daily. He changed our timing also which was not at all convenient for us. I told Adarsh later on that if I am to follow this new timing it will not be possible for me to continue in this school. He said – "Madam, don't worry, like all other things this also will not be followed for a long time. He will forget very soon. But for a few days we have to obey him in order to satisfy his ego."

Then he asked –"What is the progress regarding my paper presentation in IIT Mumbai?"

I said – "I have asked two teachers to collect some points on the new role of the Principals from the net. They will show me tomorrow. I will also add some points and then the compiling work will be done."

He said "O.K. Madam, but time is short. We have to send the abstract within one or two days." "It will be done Sir" I assured him.

But in my heart of hearts I felt – no, no more; I have done enough for others. I will not write anything for any one any more. From now onwards I will write only for my own pleasure my own satisfaction, just for myself.

After coming back to my room, I sent Savitri to call the teachers of my block to discuss with them about the increasing indiscipline in the school. Whenever they are called at a particular time, they can never be punctual. They come separately at separate time and I have to repeat the same thing again and again. This time I decided to make them disciplined first. I told them – "I want all teachers of this block together. One of you please go and call those teachers who have not yet turned up." Within five minutes everybody came into the room.

I started "You must have noticed day by day the students are becoming indisciplined. They are not wearing proper uniform, using abusive language, shouting, whistling, fighting, coming out of the classroom after each and every period, even breaking the furniture and switch boards. During the assembly they are not standing properly in the line according to their class and section. Class IX students are standing with the students of Xth standard. They are simply going out of control. Don't you think as class teachers you have some responsibilities?" One of them said "Madam, now-a-days we are not able to say anything to the students. If we say, they complain to the Executives belonging to the Trivedi family and we are called and insulted."

I said "I am not asking you to punish the students. But you can't avoid your responsibilities. If they do not stand properly in the prayer ground, who is responsible for that? Are you not supposed to come to your respective classroom and take them to the prayer ground? I have seen in my previous school as soon as the first bell rings the classteachers go to their classroom, take the attendance and then along with the students come to the prayer ground." One teacher said– "Madam, if we take the attendance before the prayer starts, then half of the students will be marked absent because majority of the hostellers come late. More than five hundred students stand outside the gate everyday at the time of prayer."

This is of course true which can't be denied.

The Games Teacher continued –"We can't take any action against the late comers because they stay in the hostels of Trivedi family."

Another teacher said "I took some students to the Principal but instead of taking any action on them, he asked me in front of the students why there is indiscipline only in my class, not in any other class!" They all said – "Madam, even the students know that we can't give them any punishment. They talk among themselves that in this school students can do anything; nothing will happen." The classteacher of IX J said – "I told one mischievous boy of my class that I want to meet his parents. The next day he came with a boy of class XII in civil dress and said "He is my father."

"We have tried our best to counsel them but it is of no use. They turn deaf ears to our counselling." I told them "O.K. you give me a list of indisciplined students. I will speak to the Principal."

After getting the list I went to Anandlal's room and told him what the teachers had said.

He said – "Their parents should be called. I want to meet the parents. The letters were drafted and given to the classteachers.

In my daily report to the Chairman I mentioned this. Prompt came his reply – "I don't like that parents should be called. The teachers should go and meet the parents."

What an impractical and illogical thought ! After managing the classes of more than sixty students in each class, correcting large bundles of test papers, calculating the percentage of test marks, preparing innumerable lists, taking substitution classes, preparing students for co-curricular activities where is the time to visit the parents and that too not one or two but many? But a person who doesn't have any work and who thinks that as the owner of the school, he knows everything better than others, will never understand the problem of others. His idea is that the teachers just sit in the staff room and gossip.

Sometimes I feel like writing to CBSE and media about the plight of the teachers. Now a days everybody talks about the psychology of children, how they are mentally and physically tortured by the teachers etc. But such cases are one or two in a million. But who cares for the psychology of the teachers? On the one hand they have to maintain discipline in large classrooms and on the other hand they can't be strict with the students. Both ways they will be reprimanded and humiliated by the authority. They have to suppress their personal problems and sorrows in their heart as if keeping them in air-tight containers and carry on with their work. On top of everything, the teachers are the most poorly paid class. Has anyone ever thought of improving the lives of the teachers who are the Nation builders? If they are not happy, how will they prepare the future citizens? If we think deeply on this matter we will get the answer why the students are becoming indisciplined day by day.

A cool war has started among the members of the Trivedi family. As usual the Chairman with his daughter and daughter-in-law is on one side and Adarsh with his wife is on the other side. The worthless son-in-law of the Chairman is rolling like a tennis ball on both the Courts trying to instigate both the parties. Frequent order has started coming from both sides and teachers have become bugged by frequent meetings which are just one man show. Either the Chairman or the Principal address the gathering and in their horribly wrong English keep on saying all sorts of impractical rubbish. Leaving their huge bundles of correction work the teachers are compelled to listen to them. I don't know why God gives money and power to wrong persons?

Adarsh showed me an e-mail of the Chairman which he received that very day. The Chairman had expressed his wish that in the next session the Additional Principals will be designated as Principal Scholastics and Principal Co-scholastics, the Vice Principals will be designated Additional Principals and some senior teachers will be promoted to the post of Vice Principal. Adarsh himself would be the Managing Director. Classes VI – XII will be there in both the shifts. In reply to this mail, Adarsh wrote that before taking such type of decisions, meetings should be held.

I understood a great change was coming but before these two ladies come into power, I made up my mind to quit. The Chairman has used a lucrative bait to get Adarsh's consent. Of course, if he does not give his consent, nothing will matter much. The Chaiman's decision is final. In the meeting he declared that there will be total seven functions during the Annual Week.

A meeting was called without any agenda known to the other Executives apart from the Chairman or may be the family members were well aware of the fact; only the outsiders like me were in total darkness.

In the beginning the Chairman told me to write the minutes of the meeting and get it typed and to circulate it among the teachers as if I am his P.A. In this bloody school of these business-class family there is no P.A., no Private Secretary, nothing. The front desk Executives can't write a single line in correct English. If they are asked to draft a letter, they come running to my room with the request of helping them.

After giving a long lecture on improving the quality of teaching and to make the target of zero-failure taking remedial classes, he came to the issue of Annual Day. He said that there will be total seven Annual functions, four separate House Functions, one function for Kids Academy including classes from Nursery to Class II, one function of Classes III to V, and one main Annual Day function of Classes VI to XII. People would not have been more shocked had there been an explosion in the hall. I understood that he was taking revenge on his brother Adarsh for scolding his daughter-in-law Sarita, the other day when she suggested that the Grandparents' Day can be celebrated by Classes III – V separately, not with Kids Academy where the Director is Adarsh's wife and the Sr. Mistress is Adarsh's dream lady who every now and then reveals the attractive parts of her body bending down on the table of Adarsh.

Conclusion

Sweety could not believe her eyes! Again and again she pinched herself to make sure she was not dreaming. She had opened the built-in cupboard of her hostel room which she shares with three other room mates Medha, Rohini and Bipasha. She wanted to take back the Physics Guide Book which she had lent to Rohini. Something fell down when she was taking out the book from Rohini's shelf in the cupboard. When she bent down to pick it up, she became absolutely still and stiff; as if she had no feelings, no sensation at all. She picked up the shining bracelet and observed it minutely; there is no doubt it is the same bracelet which she had seen in Rhishav's wrist and which he had been frantically searching for, just three day's back, when they all were celebrating Pappu's birthday at the 'Orchid'. Medha, Rohini and Bipasha – all three of them were present along with their friends. The thirty-five gram gold bracelet was a gift to Rishav from his uncle in California. Sweety remembered Rohini was the first to mention about going back to the hostel at about nine-thirty although earlier they had enjoyed many late night parties. So, this was the reason! Because of this she had a bad headache.

Rohini and Medha are chain-smokers. They try drugs also and even take injections for ecstasy. Bipasha and Sweety failed to make them understand that they have chosen a wrong path and are spoiling their future. Both of them hail from stinkingly-rich families where no question is asked if they ask for a few thousand every now and then.

Sweety sometimes feels lonely as her family background is absolutely different from that of her room-mates. Bipasha also belongs to a modern family with a sound financial background. Her father is the Deputy Director of a multi-national company and her mother is a very popular model cum T.V. serial artist. Bipasha's monthly pocket money is more than what Sweety gets in the whole year. Bipasha wears revealing transparent dresses and goes out with boyfriends. Quite often she comes late at night and hits the bed without even changing her dress. She is a regular customer of Bharat Medical Shop in the vicinity, openly purchasing I-pills. Only once it was too late and she had to take the help of the Hostel Warden to go to the hospital which is included in the panel of hospitals tied up with the school to get her aborted. Sweety's mind becomes heavier to think how her room-mates flutter around like butterflies without any burden on their mind and soul!

Sweety waited for Rohini to come back with the bracelet in her hand. As soon as she came filling the room with the odour of burning tobacco, Sweety charged her "Can you recognise this bracelet?"

As if nothing had happened, Rohini gestured coolly - "It was Rishav's bracelet. Now it's mine. Within a couple of days it will go to the hands of a jeweller to fetch me enough to arrange a booze party. You'll not understand all these." – saying this she pressed the chin of Sweety. Sweety was not in a mood to stop. She continued – "But don't you get enough from your parents? What's the use of stealing?"

"Aare, there lies the fun. Rishu always shows off. How many times he said that his Uncle from California presented him the bracelet. I wanted to teach him a lesson. Who doesn't know that his father is a black marketeer?" Sweety was about to say something when Medha and Bipasha entered the room and said in unison – "Have you seen today's local channel? Again Veer Parsad has done something scandalous. This time a young class IV staff."

For the next fifteen minutes the girls had a nice, enjoyable time discussing about Veer Parsad and his latest girlfriend cum sex partner Chandrima who sweeps the administrative block and cleans his toilet. The issue of bracelet got suppressed in front of a spicy issue of illegal physical relationship which never becomes old although it is there from the beginning of creation.

At the dining hall Surbhi was missing. Sweety looked for her at all the tables but no, she was nowhere. She told herself Surbhi is either not well or she must have gone to her local guardian's house, but after dinner she could not prevent herself from peeping into Surbhi's room.

In this hostel, if at all Sweety has any real friend, she is Surbhi. Her parents had separated when she was only three years old. Fate had played a cruel joke with her as her mother didn't get her custody although she appealed with a crying heart but had to part, leaving little Surbhi with her husband and mother-in-law. Surbhi does not know the reason behind the divorce between her parents but she can never forget her mother. She knows that her mother can never be wrong.

Sweety saw Surbhi was lying on the bed with her face downwards on the pillow. She went near her and touched her softly. Surbhi was sobbing silently. The caring touch made her more emotional. Sweety tried to console her first without asking any question. When Surbhi wiped off her tears and sat up on her bed Sweety asked her – "Why are you so upset?"

Tears filled her eyes again as she replied – "My father is in love with a married woman."

Sweety was dumb-struck. All she could do was taking the hands of Surbhi into her own, she sat with her and silently shared her sorrow.

After midnight when Sweety tried to sleep on her cot she felt one of her roommates was stealthily going out of the room. Without even looking at her she could feel it was Bipasha going out in her night adventure with one of her boyfriends.

The morning was like any other day. Walking towards the school in a group, standing in the Assembly and listening to the nonsense of the Chairman and the Principal, then proceeding towards the classroom. But just before the recess something happened which was not expected even in somebody's dream. The sound of bursting of powerful bombs shook the school building. The class IV staff ran towards the second floor toilet from where billowing smoke was coming out along with the heart-breaking, blood cuddling screaming of two boys. Before half an hour it became clear to all students and staff that two students of class XII Saurabh and Aman were taken to the hospital. One of them Saurabh died on the way while Aman became blind for ever. There was no authentic proof but some of the students knew who was the culprit and what was the reason behind it !

Nobody was allowed to come out of the classroom during the recess. Police jeep came to the school blowing siren and picked up the most notorious students Vicky and Byom from class XII G. The Principal had nothing else to do but to inform the parents and cooperate with the Police. Both the students were suspended from their previous school and got admission in their present school only after their respective parents paid donation which was huge enough to construct a hall and purchase four more buses. The parents, owners of Cinema halls and rice mills are close associates of the members of the ruling party of the state. Vicky and Byom, so far have got political protection but this time they crossed all limits of notoriety by killing and severely injuring their classmates. The reason was that they were in love with the girls on whom the murderers had fixed their eyes. So they thought of removing the thorns permanently from their path of temporarily enjoying with the girls. Bipasha and Shruti, in fact became stiff like stones. The intensity of their shock was so severe that they even forgot to cry. Among the staff there was not a single person who opened his mouth. Teachers who were always the first to react for any social cause have died long back, leaving no ghosts behind them. The new generation of teachers know how to save themselves from any unwanted problem. They always play safe games.

Sweety's world, which was well protected by the love and affection of her parents, grandparents and siblings, turned out to be an absolutely different one just within one year of her hostel life. How desperately she longed to go back to her village house far away from all pollutions and corruptions of the modern, city life. Every night she silently wets her pillow shedding tears which her room-mates are not aware of. She is not able to share her experience with her family members lest they become tensed and take her back to their village. She has to fulfil her dreams and those of her parents which is not possible if she stays in her village. She is determined to endure all hardships and shocks in order to become the first Engineer in her family. She is getting the lessons of life along with enhancing knowledge in various subjects. Somehow she has to stay here for one more year.

Sweety has understood one thing, that is basically her friends are not bad; they are just vindictive. In their attempt to take revenge on their parents, teachers and the whole society, they are punishing themselves and losing track of a healthy life. The spikes, tattoos, ridiculous dresses, cigarettes, alcohol, intoxicating drugs, abusive language, disrespectful behaviour, unrestricted sex, late-night parties are different tools to fight against their previous generation. But in this fight their victory is more harmful to them than anyone else.

In a special programme conducted by Derek O'Brien today, their Chairman was giving instance of Winston Churchill who had failed in class VIII more than once. Derek himself also said that in order to be successful in life failure is very much essential. One needs to get tremendous shock in order to come to the right track. But Sweety doesn't want to fail. She knows her father has been paying her school fees through his nose. She will never let him down. She knows how to extract only the precious jems leaving aside all trash. She knows how to light lamps in total darkness. Neither the debauchery of people like Veer Parsad, nor the greed and hypocrisy of Trivedi brothers, nor the meanness of the opportunists, nor the destructive attitude of the peer group could shake the trust, faith and confidence of Sweety and her types.

The motivational speech by Prof. Swaminathan from Mumbai gave her a moral boost up. It was just like a piece of log which helps a drowning person to float in the turbulent ocean. Once more she felt she is not alone. There is someone above her who has been filling her with positive energy. She came to know from the lecture of Prof. Swaminathan that just as energy flows from higher potential to the lower potential, God's positive energy and power flow down to his best creation human beings. Urja Madam helps her a lot. Whenever she is not able to understand any poem or chapter in English she approaches her in her free time. She explains everything wirh patiencc and gives her sample papers which ohe gets from the publishers as complimentary copies. Madam knows about her family conditions and encourages her a lot. In Sweety's mind she has a special place.

Sweety doesn't even have a mobile phone. Her friends can contact their parents or relatives whenever they wish but Sweety has to wait eagerly for the whole month to see her parents. She can not send E-mail because there is no Computer at their village home. Her father could purchase a black and white T.V. after a prolonged and continuous request from her mother and grandmother. Urja Madam said "This need will make you big one day. If you get everything in the beginning of your life you will never realise the value of things and moreover you will lose interest in life."

Sweety thinks that she is absolutely right. Her own classmates and roommates are the greatest examples. At this age they have got everything – all new and modern products launched in the market, more than enough cash, bykes, even four-wheelers but they neither love themselves nor the society. The disease of dissatisfaction and frustration has brought them under its cruel clutch from where freedom is a distant dream. Sweety and her types live with hope, with a vision, with the desire of a bright future. They dream of a better world, a different world where there will be no generation gap, where everybody will be able to respect the value of relationship.

Urja tells her students about that world, which only they can build. She reminds them about the teachings of Prof. Swaminathan – "Believe in yourself and respect the God within you. You all are equal. Try to see Ali in Diwali and Ram in Ramjan. Respect and love your mother and mother Earth. In this world the most powerful thing is the blessings of mother. She has brought you on the Earth and mother Earth sustains you. You are indebted to both. Try to repay your debt by making your mother proud and by planting a sapling on your birthday."

Urja observed the change of expression in the innocent faces. This change she could never find in the face of Veer Parsad, Ranjita, Padma, Sarita and many. Children are raw clay after all; they can be given any desired shape but the artist must love the clay also not only the mould and colour. Adults are hardened pots which will break if any attempt is taken to change their shape.

Urja feels that her world is becoming limited whirling around the known faces and characters. She has to spread her wings and cross the boundaries of this limited world. Limitation makes one mean minded and poor. The very thought of taking revenge on her exploiters is preventing her from creating a new world with the young innocent.

As Urja was thinking seriously to leave the place and going somewhere else, may be to Delhi where her children have settled, she heard a knock at the door. Urja was able to keep her cool even when the tenth student came to her room with the request of half-day leave. This is something she was able to stop after a sincere effort of four years as the Vice Principal in this school. Students, with the excuse of ill health or an appointment with doctor used to take half-day leave and instead of going back to their hostel or home roam about in the streets or went to see noon-show picture. When Urja tried to stop this in the beginning, she became a victim of mockery of the Trivedi family members. Students also came to know that if Urja Madam refused to sanction half-day leave then some other person of the Trivedi family will do so. So it continued like that; students were in their usual practice of getting their half-day leave granted by either of the two Additional Principals or any other member of the Trivedi family until one day some residents of the nearby locality came to the Principal's office to complain about the nuisance some of the students, both boys and girls were creating in the nearby park. They were found in objectionable condition sitting in the park and it was a matter of concern for the residents as they had grown up children in their family.

Adarsh immediately ordered that half-day leave should be stopped until and unless the parents come with the request. Considering it to be Urja's victory the Trivedi family members twisted their lips. The students reacted by breaking the switch-boards of the classrooms. Urja remained silent but in her heart of hearts she felt that she was right. She also felt that although slow, a change was coming. After the incident of bomb bursting in the toilet when the two culprits were taken to police custody, the Students Council members met Urja. They all had gone to the cremation ground with her to bid goodbye for the last time to Saurabh and stand by the side of the bereaved parents. Urja consoled Saurabh's parents by saying "You have lost one child, but all his friends who are present here are your children. They will always respond to your call. In them, you will always find Saurabh. He is immortal."

As Motilal had refused to bear the expenditure of the treatment of Aman who had lost his eyesight due to the bomb blast, Urja told the students "It is your moral duty to help the poor parents who can't afford to carry on with the treatment. Each one of you will contribute something from your pocket money for Aman's treatment. You will get the help of all teachers including me."

It was, a very touching scene as Saurabh's body left the world lying on the funeral pyre. The members of the Students Council took a resolution that they will never allow such things to happen in the school again. Urja told them – "Never, ever think of taking revenge against any negative action by doing something negative. It will never benefit the society in any way. Do something good each time you face any injustice. This will be your protest against anything wrong. The evil intention of the wrong-doer will be frustrated by your good action. Don't think of punishing the wicked. They will be punished by God. Ignoring the wicked, you keep on doing good and change everything around you. The evil will be defeated on their own as your combined good deeds will push them to the wall. Urja felt relieved after opening up her heart before the students.

Those green and salad days of late 70s and early 80s were the most romantic and modern period of Urja's life with dreams in her eyes, ideals in her heart and the determination to accept everything which is new and to rebel against everything which seemed to be old and backdated. In this new millennium also the younger generation discards everything that is old fashioned and accepts the new but their style of adopting modernism is different. It is more vulgar, naked and painful. Recently she started feeling that she is not fit for this modern times. She has lost that mind of her youth. She hesitates to get drenched in the monsoon shower. She hates picking up a puppy or a kitten from the road which she loved doing in the past. She thinks twice before gulping down a panipuri now which was her favourite item in her school or college days. The very thought of the dirty hands of the panipuri seller troubles her more than the mouth-watering taste. Is it because of her age? Urja knows that basically the younger generation is not bad; the only thing they need is proper guidance to trail through the right path. Speaking to the students, Urja felt that she had gone back to her teens. After a long, long time she picked up Dabang, a puppy brought by her servant Mahesh from the road who was sitting in her garage, and gave it a saucer full of milk. At this unexpected VIP treatment, Dabang took three speedy somersaults and licked Urja's feet.

Forgetting about the dirty hands of the panipuriwallas, Urja relished both papri chaat and panipuri in the evening. She felt young and free like the white clouds floating in the sky. The tune of a forgotten favourite song of her youth came back to her mind again and again and she started humming the tune.

This is her last week in the steel town. As the date was coming nearer she was feeling how difficult it is to snap all bonds. May be for the first time in her life she wished that Sunday should not come at all. As a school student Urja always felt that Sundays take a long time to come. In the mid autumn of her life Sundays appear very quickly making her older each week. Now, it being the last week in this small city Urja wanted to feel each moment, each trivial matter with her heart and soul. All of a sudden Veer Parsad, Ranjita, Padma, Sarita, Motilal– they all seemed to be close to her heart. She could not feel any anger or hatred towards them. It would hardly matter if Ranjita becomes the Principal and Veer Parsad becomes the Director of the school where they ruled for more than a decade. How does it matter if Sarita becomes the Principal in her father-in-law's school? How does it matter if Trivedi family earns crores of rupees by cheating people? Urja has no grudge against anybody.

Urja thought of taking leave of each one of them in the last week. She thought of starting with Adarsh. This person had taken her side on several occasions earlier. Although the typical mean-mindedness of the Trivedi family is very much present in him also, still he is better than other members of his family.

Adarsh was sitting with a thoughtful face. At first he could not feel Urja's presence in the room. When she came near his table he woke up from his absent-minded state and offered Urja a seat.

"Are you thinking something Sir?" Urja asked.

"Madam I am so tensed, I am not able to sleep at night." – Adarsh seemed to be really tensed.

"Why, what's the matter Sir? Is there anything wrong?" Urja wanted to know.

"Madam, you know how adventurous my sons are ! You will be shocked to know about their latest venture !" Urja could no more hold her patience "Why what have they done?"

Adarsh, with the expression of a worried father said "They are producing and directing a film." Like a veteran actress Urja was able to hide her real feelings "Really? It's unbelievable ! But why are you worried Sir? They will definitely be successful." Adarsh continued in a tensed voice – "Our hard-earned money; if they are not successful, we will be ruined." Urja thought – if they at all waste the money, it will be your elder son's father-in-law's money. Retaining the smile in her face she said assuringly – "Your children are jewels. They will never let you down. Rather they will enhance the name and reputation of the family."

Adarsh smiled with difficulty as he could not be so sure about the success in this venture and said "Let's hope so; I have kept my fingers crossed." Urja then came to the point. "Sir, I don't know how to tell you, but I have made up my mind, I'll be leaving this place very soon. I want to put up my papers." As if a thunder had struck the Principal, he sat with a gaping face for a few seconds. When he came back to sense he asked "Is there anything wrong Madam? Are you not happy here?"

Urja said – "I am very happy here but I have decided to settle in Delhi with my children. I miss them every moment Sir." For half an hour Adarsh tried to convince Urja in many ways to prevent her from submitting her resignation but failed to do so. Urja will not change her decision. At the last phase of her life she would like to be with her nearest and dearest ones. Not only that she wants to do something independently for the student community. Too much of red-tapism and dominating attitude of the seniors are standing like walls between Urja and the students. If she can prepare even ten ideal students that would be her achievement and real contribution in the field of education and nation building. Urja is all set to cross her known boundaries and proceed towards an unknown. If she is not able to change the world, she would mould at least a few children to create future leaders. She will not let her dreams fizzle into the thin air.

News spread faster than air. For the next few days Urja became tired of answering the question of the students and the teachers – Why? Where? When? etc. Her colleagues did not believe that she would not join any other institution. They guessed that she was going to Delhi to join any institution as the Principal. Urja is not bound to tell them anything. She will start a completely new life at the age of fifty-two which will have no connection with the past.

Urja believes still there is time and hope to establish a new edifice of learning where innocent, pure, young students will receive the first lessons of life. Urja will again start from the scratch. She goes back to a time forty years ago to her house in Kolkata where she started her first class in each step of the staircase with imaginary students and a door leading to the roof as her blackboard. Those imaginary students will come alive again at the twilight of her life in a new place with new hopes and visions making her dreams true.

At the penaltimate stage of life's drama, Urja's deep realisation is that vindictiveness can never give mental peace. Nothing can be achieved by taking revenge. At the same time it is true that revenge is taken by life, by nature at the right time without any provocation. Today Veer Parsad got extension for two years; may be his wife Ranjita will succeed her but one day will come when this success will be meaningless. However, proud and powerful Motilal is today, things may not be the same tomorrow. His successors may demolish everything in a single blow when he will lose his power and physical strength. Already they have started misusing the money by investing in film or other things. But it is utter foolishness to wait for nemesis, spoiling one's own opportunities and future. The word success is also relative. To some people success means possessing extreme power to rule others; to some success means to possess wealth, money, name and fame. To Urja the meaning of success is absolutely different. Success depends on the acceptability of the general mass. In that sense the Yoga Guru Baba Ramdev is the most successful person in this world who doesn't have anything except the dhoti which he wears. In the dirty society created by the Education mafias if Urja can create a handful of real human beings, she will consider herself successful and that would be her tightest slap on the faces of her exploiters. It sounds very dramatic and bookish but it will happen one day when a handful of educated human beings will again transform the society and innumerable corrupt people will perish like virus killed by antibiotics.

Urja's work will not remain confined to only one place. There are thousands of Veer Parsads, Ranjitas, Padma, Motilals, Saritas etc. etc. etc. Urja is not an escapist; she is ready to face more challenges in life. Her too clam, too much uneventful life with the hope of divine justice is extremely dull and unbearable. She will wait no more.

Urja slept peacefully on the last night in her familiar place. For the whole week she could hardly sleep as she had to attend farewell parties and returned late at night. Swapnil accompanied her in some places and in some places she attended alone. Eleven months were still left for Swapnil's retirement. After that he will also leave this small city and join Urja.

While packing her suitcase, Urja switched on the television. The newsreader was reading the Hindi news in a grave solemn voice. The video slides attracted Urja's attention as she saw her old school. She sat, back with full attention.........it's unbelievable. Veer Parsad, handcuffed, with two police constables on his both sides was being guided towards the police jeep. The news reader was explaining the reason – due to income tax raid in his official quarter within the school premises where crores of property in cash and kind was found he was taken to policy custody and a case was filed against him. The new Income-tax Commissioner, an ex-student of his school only, was not convinced by his explanation and was quite adamant to put him behind the bars.

Urja closed her eyes and thanked God for preparing at least one human being who received education from that edifice of learning where Urja had rendered her dedicated service for long years. But she could not keep her eyes closed for a long time as the next news item almost stopped her heartbeat – Sarita's husband Ashok was beaten up on the previous night by an angry mob for his misbehaviour with an unmarried, young girl and for assaulting her sexually. Among the mob were students from his hostel. As a result of the beating his right hand and right leg were fractured at several places and the injury at the right heel was beyond repair. The most reputed doctors of the biggest hospitals of the city have told there was no chance of recovery. He was immediately taken to Mumbai but chances are very less. What is this? Divine Justice or Nemesis! These are not just terms used in drama. The daily newspapers confirmed the news. Urja switched off her mobile. She knew hundreds of people will now waste her time discussing about the two crispy news. She is least bothered to know anything about the persons in news.

As the train left the platform, Urja's 'goodbye' to her well-wishers remained unuttered; her students and colleagues waved their hands from the platform and remained there till their faces became blurred in Urja's vision but framed in her mind forever.